What readers are saying about Walks with the Wind

"I would highly recommend *Walks with the Wind* for readers who enjoy literary, quality writing, and powerful life-changing, emotional themes."

KC Finn,
Readers' Favorite

"Steve Physioc plays the emotions of the characters well. He gives them the right nudge, builds up the atmosphere, and then begins the action to make the most of it. Everything combines to bring something very special for readers to enjoy."

Rabia Tanveer,
Readers' Favorite

"Steve Physioc is a great storyteller who writes believable characters, with conflict against a historical backdrop that has been widely written about, yet he creates unique scenes and a plot that is original."

Romuald Dzemo,
Readers' Favorite

"I am very grateful Steve chose me to read his book. He was very respectful of our Ute culture and truly understands that our spiritual beliefs and songs are what kept us going. When you find your inner spirit, you will find your peace."

Hanley Frost,
former Sun Dance Chief and Southern Ute
Cultural Education Coordinator

"*Walks with the Wind* is so well crafted it draws you in, evokes visceral feelings for the characters and incredibly immerses you into the environment."

Lieutenant Colonel (Retired)
Scott K. Fehnel, P.E., U.S. Army

"I think anyone will enjoy this read. Phiz did a really nice job of painting great pictures with words as it relates to this special young man, his family, and his incredible abilities."

Jeff Montgomery,
Kansas City Royals Hall of Fame pitcher

A NOVEL

STEVE PHYSIOC

Walks with the Wind
Steve Physioc

Copyright © 2021 by Steve Physioc

All rights reserved. No part of this book may be reproduced or transmitted in any form or by any means without written permission from the author, except in the case of brief quotations embedded in reviews and certain other non-commercial uses permitted under copyright law.

ISBN: 978-1-7360804-0-5
eISBN: 978-1-7360804-1-2
Library of Congress Control Number: 2021901539

Edited by Nicole Ayers
Cover design by Cathe Physioc

CHAPTER ONE

Pargin Mountain, Colorado

December 2004

The snowball blasted off the right buttock of the white-tailed deer, scattering ice crystals into the frigid Colorado winter morning. The surprised buck kicked its legs in the air and bolted into the pines and oaks until it finally disappeared. Sam Cloud-Carson winked at his father and opened his hand.

"How'd ya know that was the buck who knocked over your mom's bird feeder?" Daniel Carson asked as he reached into his pocket and pulled out a wrinkled dollar bill.

Sam took the dollar and then pointed to the track in the fresh snow. "Big bucks walk flat-footed, and their stride is wider than a doe's."

"But that could have been any buck." His father grinned, unable to conceal the pride he had for his only son. The boy was a natural tracker, incredibly sensitive to the mysteries of the wilderness that seemed to reveal itself easily to him. Daniel wanted to say something, anything, to let his son know how much he loved him. Before he could, Sam knelt down and pushed away the top layer of snow to reveal the true print.

"Check out the indentation of his dew claw, Dad. Left front has a tiny fracture that's shaped like a backward C. I saw the same track all around Mom's bird feeder."

"It's the same buck, all right. Big track too. Not as big as Old Mel's, but he's only a ghost until we see him for real."

They both smiled at the thought of finally seeing the big buck they had been tracking for years. Old Mel had by far the largest track they had ever come across. Probably a three-hundred-pound mule deer and, by the wear of his track, over ten years old. He was a wily buck too, who seemed to track man, sensing his presence, knowing his habits, and then silently moving into brome grass the same color as his hide.

"I'd give anything to just get a glimpse at that old boy," Sam said.

Daniel reached down, grabbed some snow off the ground, patted it into the size of a baseball, and handed it to his son. "Another dollar says you can't hit the knot in that old pine."

Sam winked as he took the snowball, eyeballed the knot that was some fifty feet away, came set as if he were pitching in his high school game, brought his left leg slowly up into a balance position, separated his hands in a style that would have made All-Star Greg Maddux proud, and delivered a perfect strike into the middle of the knot.

His father laughed as he reached into his pocket and pulled out another dollar.

"Most boys your age would be happy to be good at one thing," he said as he slapped the bill into his son's hand. "You're the best seventeen-year-old I've ever seen at two things—pitching and tracking."

The Carsons came from a long line of Ute trackers. Daniel's grandfather was one of the first men hired to survey the Rocky Mountains after President Woodrow Wilson signed a bill in 1915, making a large portion of north-central Colorado a national park. The family worked as guides for outfitting companies in northern Colorado until Daniel decided to go out on his own. He headed south, past Arapaho, White River, and Umcompahgre National Forests, and didn't stop until he came to the southern edge of the San Juan Mountains in southwest Colorado. That's where he found a job as a guide for a wilderness company on the Southern Ute Indian reservation, and where he met a girl.

Susan Cloud was the camp-and-school manager for SJ Outfitters when Daniel first walked through the door. He could tell immediately who ran the show. Susan was three-quarters Ute and was no stranger to packing, tracking, and sometimes sacking an employee who didn't do their job well. It took only two weeks for Daniel to ask her out and two more months before they were engaged. Sam was born nine and a half months after the wedding, and their daughter, Jenny, arrived five years later.

"We'd better start back," Daniel said as he checked his phone. No service. "Mom had to take your sister to the doc again, so we oughta hustle back and finish our chores before they get home."

Sam sensed worry in his father's voice as he followed him back down the trail. "Everything's okay isn't it, Dad?"

"I'm sure it is," Daniel said, but then he quickly changed the subject. "You had a nice basketball game against Bayfield last night. Seventeen points and seven assists is pretty good for a junior."

"We would have won by twenty if the ref was any good."

Daniel froze and slowly turned to face his son. "You think kicking the ball after he called a foul on you was a good idea?"

Sam's smile slipped. "It was a clean steal, Dad."

"It doesn't matter. The ref called a foul. He was doing his job. You made it worse by kicking the ball and getting a technical. It could have cost your team."

"But it didn't." Sam hesitated. "We won."

"At what cost? Did you see the way your teammates looked at you? They were like, here he goes again, blowing up about one silly foul." Daniel made sure his son looked him directly in the eyes. "I know you're very competitive, Sam, but if you ever want to lead a team, you're going to have to learn how to control your emotions."

He put his arm around Sam and led him down the hill. "It's a little like tracking. The best way to find the right path when you're lost in the wild is to slow down, breathe, and open your awareness to more than the five senses. It's about trusting more than yourself, trusting the knowledge that's already inside you, and then letting it guide you to make the right choice."

* * *

For the next few minutes they walked in silence, Sam, embarrassed by what he had done the previous night but confused about how to handle it, still holding onto his father's scolding. It was about winning, wasn't it? Winning. Any way possible.

His father seemed to know how he was feeling and gave him a playful shove to snap him out of his daydream. "It's time to come back to the right here, right now, young tracker. Do you notice anything?"

Sam closed his eyes and calmed his breathing. The morning wind was in their faces, so there was little chance that a deer or coyote had their scent. It wasn't sound but sudden silence that made him pause. A creek gurgled off to their right, but the usual chatter of birds was now an unnatural quiet. He opened his eyes and slowly panned his vision from right to left, before stopping to stare down the trail. He spotted movement, maybe four hundred yards ahead. The speck became a man, and Sam recognized the gait.

"That's John. He rarely hikes out this far. He must be looking for us."

John was their closest neighbor, a retiree in his seventies who lived about a mile from the Carson cabin. Daniel knew John was a bird-watcher, so he let out a loud warble of a mountain bluebird. John stopped to locate the whereabouts of the sound, saw the Carsons in the distance, and waved for them to join him.

* * *

"Doc Goodman's been calling you but said it went straight to voicemail," John said when they arrived. "So he called my house and asked if I'd seen you."

Daniel straightened up to his full six-foot-four height. "Is it about Jenny?"

John shrugged tentatively. "Doc didn't say. Only told me he needs you and Sam at the hospital."

CHAPTER TWO

Ignacio, Colorado

December 2004

Sam ran his hand over the bandage on the inside of his left elbow where the needle had entered to take his blood. The nurse who had administered the procedure had said nothing about why his blood needed to be tested. Now, as he sat in the waiting room, he leaned toward the office door, trying to make out the conversation that was coming from beyond. His father had been in conference with Dr. Goodman for more than ten minutes, and even though he couldn't make out the words, he could tell the tone was serious.

For more than a year, Sam had watched his sister's declining health, yet whenever he asked his parents about what was wrong, they only said that she was continuing to get tests. But Sam had coached his sister's soccer team and had always wondered why the other players were browned by the sun while Jenny remained a pale gray. Her stamina had also been withering in recent months; there were no more long hikes into the San Juans or rafting adventures down the Los Pinos River. Only constant treks to doctors and specialists throughout southwest Colorado, none of whom could diagnose what was wrong with the Carson girl.

The outside door suddenly opened, and a flash of light streamed in. Sam turned to see two men enter, both dressed in business attire. One boasted an arrogance that immediately told anyone nearby who was in charge. That man kept his mirrored sunglasses on, as if to deflect any probing eyes to his intent.

"You're the Carson boy?" he asked.

Sam nodded but remained quiet.

"Your father teach you to track?"

"Yes," Sam said. His voice seemed to choke on the heaviness in the room.

The man came around to face him and sat down in a chair. "Is your old man in with the doc?"

Another nod from Sam, but no words. His father had always told him, if he was ever in a confrontational situation, to spare his words. The less a man talked, the more restless the other person would become, and eventually he would share useful information. Sam raised his vision to meet the man's eyes but remained quiet.

Within thirty seconds, the man shifted uncomfortably in his chair and offered his hand. "I should have introduced myself. Drake Dixon, DiamondBar Security." He nodded to the man seated next to him. "This is my lawyer, Barry King. I thought your father would have told you about me after he led my staff on a hunting expedition last month."

Sam shook both men's hand but still said nothing.

Again, there was an awkward moment before Dixon said, "He mentioned you were a pretty good ballplayer. Led Ignacio to the state playoffs in both basketball and baseball."

"We have good coaches," Sam said.

The man smiled as he leaned back in his chair and clasped his hands behind his head. "I've heard that you're a better tracker than your old man. Is that true?"

"No."

Dixon looked over at his lawyer and winked. "Pretty talkative family, aren't they? Maybe they're just not used to indoor conversation. Why, I wish my wife was a little more like—"

The door to the doctor's office opened and out came Sam's father and Dr Goodman.

Daniel Carson stood frozen for a second, as though unable to believe his eyes. "What are you doing here?"

Dixon stood up and reached out to shake his hand. His father didn't accept it.

"I heard your family had health issues and wanted to help," Dixon said.

Daniel turned back to the doctor. "I thought there were laws that kept a family's medical history private."

Dr. Goodman looked genuinely surprised. "I have no idea how this information got out."

"It's common knowledge your daughter's been ill." Dixon feigned a look of concern. "And you without very good insurance—I think we can help each other out."

Daniel's jaws clenched tightly, but he remained quiet. He motioned for his son and Dr. Goodman to give him some privacy. As soon as the door closed behind them, Daniel turned back to face Dixon.

"Leave my family alone," he said in a low threatening tone.

Dixon held up both hands as if to calm the big man. "Just hear me out, Dan."

"I'm done talking." Carson pointed to the door. "Get out."

* * *

Susan Carson was alone on a couch, her eyes swollen from crying.

Sam hurried to her side. "Mom, where's Jenny?"

She hugged her son and then looked up at Dr. Goodman.

"Your sister has acute renal failure," the doctor explained. "It's a very serious kidney disease that's more common in our Native American community than in other cultures."

For a moment Sam looked confused, too stunned to speak. And then, very slowly, he turned to his father. "She can have one of my kidneys."

"You and your parents are not a match," Dr. Goodman said. "That's why we took your blood. I wanted to see if your kidneys were healthy and if you could be a potential match after you turn eighteen. You're not." He took a deep breath. "But Jenny has end-stage renal disease. Only about ten percent of her kidneys are working. She's going to need a transplant as soon as possible."

* * *

It took three days for the doctors and nurses to control the infection and stabilize Jenny's ailing kidneys. Sam was going from the hospital to school, to basketball practice, and then back to his sister's bedside. His mother and father were taking turns sleeping at the hospital but found a few minutes on Friday night to slip over and watch their son lead Ignacio High to a seven-point win over Durango. Sam took a quick shower and came straight to the hospital to give his parents a chance to sleep at home. Both returned the next morning to find their son curled up on a cot next to his sister. Sam felt their presence and quietly raised up and tiptoed out of the room.

"You need a shower, boy," his mother whispered as she lifted his arm and took a whiff underneath. "I can't believe your stink didn't wake up Jenny."

"I showered after the game."

"Did you use soap?" She pinched her nose. "Why don't you and Dad take the day off?"

"We have a noon practice."

"It's optional," his father cut in. "I called Coach, and he agrees with your mom."

"Go on up to the hills." She put her hand to her ear. "I hear the wild calling."

Sam chuckled. "What's it sayin', Mom?"

"It's saying, 'Carson family hungry. Mom no wanna cook. Men get food.'" And then she playfully shoved her son and husband toward the exit.

* * *

Sam slipped his bow over his shoulder and led his father across a field of scrub oak and native grass up into the foothills of Pargin Mountain, an 8,400-foot summit northeast of Ignacio and the Carson home. Silence was their conversation as they listened to two crows cawing and a ruddy duck's ticking noise as it courted its mate. Father and son communicated through eye contact and nods. Words meant little now as they moved quietly through the meadow in search of track.

As they passed through a stand of pinyon pine and juniper, Sam suddenly raised his hand and went to one knee to study a track. Mule-deer buck. Approximately two hundred pounds. Studying its print, Sam determined its direction, and moved up the hill to find a second track and then a third before coming to a giant stretch of granite that might hide the buck's trail. He inhaled deeply as he studied the stone and then let instinct guide him across until he found a scratch that showed something had startled the buck. It had taken off up the mountain. It could have been a coyote, mountain lion, or hunter that frightened the deer into changing its course so dramatically.

He followed the track up the mountain another quarter mile until he discovered the disturbance. Hunters. The freshness of the prints told him they had passed by within a couple of hours. And their boot prints showed that they had walked right by the deer. Sam reclaimed the buck's trail only fifteen feet from the hunter's path and tracked it another half mile before spotting him feeding near a large Gambel oak stand.

As he watched the buck from behind a granite boulder, he calmed his breathing and drew an arrow from his quiver. He always said a prayer before a kill, thanking the animal spirits for making this deer available for his family's nourishment. His parents had taught him to be grateful to the Earth and all her creatures, and that he could honor the deer by killing it in a respectful fashion. Most hunters would aim for the heart or lungs because it was a larger target, but Sam knew that also meant there would be a greater chance for the deer to suffer longer. The Carson men chose the brain or spine for a quick kill.

Sam notched his arrow, drew the bowstring back, and then stepped from behind the rocks. His movement was smooth and calm, as though it had been done a thousand times before, and he waited for the buck to raise his head to look his way. Sam's target would be two and a half inches above the eyes. Not many could hit it. But a perfect shot to the brain would instantly incapacitate the animal, and death would follow in only a few seconds. He gave a soft clicking sound, the buck raised his head, and Sam let fly his arrow. It pierced the animal's skull, the arrow forcing its way deep into its brain. The deer wobbled for a moment on unsteady legs and then collapsed onto the cold ground.

His father nodded approval as they walked over, knelt down, and placed their hands near the deer's heart. They gave thanks to the animal for its gift and blessed its soul as it rose to the great beyond. Sam had grown up with stories about the ancients from his tribe: that the world was a great mystery, and that the sun, moon, sky, and earth were all part of the Great Spirit with no end. His father's mother had been part Cherokee and told the story of Awi Usdi, the Little Deer, to Sam and his sister.

Back when the world was young, animals and humans could talk to each other and lived in peace. But when humans discovered the bow and arrow, they began to hunt for more than food and skins. So the animals met in council and asked Awi Usdi to talk with the humans. He went at night and whispered into the ears of the hunters, telling them to respect the deer and ask permission before a kill, and then to show respect for its spirit when it was done. Some humans listened; others did not.

Sam and his father immediately went to work making a travois to haul the deer back to their truck, for every piece of this buck would be honored. The hide would be made into clothing, the bones and antlers into tools, the tendons turned into thread, and the intestines into bow strings. It was a tradition Susan Carson asked they continue, a way to honor both the deer and the Great Spirit's bountiful gifts to their family.

Sam found a branch that had fallen from an oak tree and cut it into three pieces. He pulled the netting from his father's backpack and lashed it to two poles in the shape of a triangle. He then added the third shorter pole to the underside to stabilize the frame. His father pulled the deer onto the netting, lifted both poles, and began the three-mile trek back to their truck. It was only then that Sam finally spoke what had been on his mind.

"Why did the Great Spirit bless me with good health yet make Jenny's life so hard?"

Daniel slowed his walk. "You can't ask those questions, son, for there are no answers."

"We're told that God is the All-Providing One, and we pay reverence for His providing the needs to everyone. Yet He's given Jenny only hardship."

"You're seeing with only the body's eyes, Sam. Look deeper."

"All I see is me being able to go on this hunt with you while my sister lies in another hospital bed."

"You see what you want to see," his father said as he dragged the deer carcass back across the rock that marked where it had once been spooked. "Empty your mind, son. Let the answers be given to you."

It was just like his father to give him some vague message that forced him to think beyond what his eyes actually saw. But he was tired of seeing his sister suffer.

"I know I'm a gifted tracker and athlete, but what's Jenny's gift?"

His father gave him a crinkled smile. "You don't see it?"

He shook his head.

"Have you listened to her pray?"

"Yes."

"What does she pray for?"

Sam paused for a long moment. "She prays for peace."

"Jenny never prays for anything specific or even for her pain to go away. She only prays for peace."

It was true, Sam thought. He remembered his sister's words on the day she entered the hospital. She had them all hold hands around her bed as she asked God to bring peace to her mind, peace to her body, and peace to the world. Pretty darn insightful for a twelve-year-old.

"Your sister is the most forgiving little person I know," his father went on. "She never compares, and she never complains. It's as if she has this direct link to the Great Spirit to see past her troubles." His father stopped by the pinyon pine and juniper stand where they had first discovered the deer tracks and handed the travois poles to Sam. "Jenny's so proud of your success. She's the greatest cheerleader you'll ever have."

"But I want her—"

Daniel held up his hand to quiet his son. "Just be *her* cheerleader, Sam. Try and see the gifts she was given."

* * *

His father was quiet on the drive home, as if there was more on his mind than what they'd just witnessed. It wasn't until they arrived back at their cabin and skinned the deer that Daniel spoke. "I have to do something that I don't want to, son."

Sam gave him a puzzled look.

"The hospital bills are piling up, and the insurance plan I bought years ago isn't enough. If Jenny is going to get the dialysis and transplant she needs, then I have to take that job with the private security company."

Sam stared at his skinning knife for a long moment. "It's that Drake Dixon guy, isn't it? He wants you to teach soldiers to track?"

"No"—Daniel paused—"he wants *me* to track."

"What? You're going away?" Sam drove his skinning knife a full two inches into the cutting board.

His father nodded and then gently placed his hand on top of Sam's. "I'm sorry, son. We need the insurance . . . for Jenny."

CHAPTER THREE

Ignacio, Colorado

March 2005

A late winter wind swept off the flatlands, north of the Ignacio High School baseball field, forcing Jose Lopez to grab the bill of his cap before it flew off into the chain-link backstop again. He sat down on the dugout bench next to his best friend and exhaled loudly. "Geez, Sam, how do you throw strikes in this tornado? Dove Creek batters have to battle the wind and cold and then face your filthy stuff."

"The quicker I get 'em out, the quicker Teresa can warm you up." Sam winked and nodded to Jose's girlfriend, sitting in the stands, as he pulled on his parka to keep his right arm warm.

Jose gave his friend a playful shove and then searched the stands for Sam's family. "Where's your press agent? You said Jenny was out of the hospital, so I figured there was no way she'd miss her top client's game."

Sam stared out at the field where the opposing pitcher was getting ready to pitch to the Ignacio left fielder. It had been three months since Jenny had been diagnosed with kidney disease. She was now home, but on expensive dialysis, fully covered by DiamondBar insurance, and waiting for the transplant that owner Drake Dixon had promised the family.

Sam had gone through a myriad of emotions about his sister's illness and his father leaving: sadness, anger, worry, and finally depression. He had moped around the house for two weeks, helping his mom with chores, learning how to administer the hemodialysis to his sister, and even replacing his father by guiding a hunting expedition for some men from Albuquerque.

It was his twelve-year-old sister who had finally cut through his gloom.

"Why are *you* so unhappy? I'm the one who's sick," Jenny teased him.

He forced a smile. It was true. His sister had to spend three days a week at the dialysis center and then come home to receive nocturnal care while she was sleeping.

Her gray skin seemed to brighten as she poked him in the side and grinned. "I know what will make you happy. The Bear Dance."

Sam couldn't help himself and laughed out loud. The Bear Dance was a Ute tribal custom they participated in every May. It was a time of rejuvenation, when Mother Earth began a new cycle, and the bear awakened after a long winter's sleep to welcome in spring.

"I think that's an excellent idea!" their mother called out from the kitchen. "Jenny, why don't you and Grandpa sing so your brother can dance?"

Jenny clapped her hands and winked at Grandpa Douglas Cloud, who was sitting in his favorite chair.

"Let's go, Sammy! You have to do like Grandpa and bless the ground to have a good year and then stand up and be strong."

"I'm not gonna do that. It's stupid."

"Yes! You have to. Right, Grandpa?"

Douglas sat up straight and nodded at Sam. "The bear is one of the powers the Great Spirit gave to the Ute people, Samuel. Perhaps now is a good time for you to be the bear."

Sam rolled his eyes at his sister. "You're both crazy."

Their mother walked over to the closet and pulled out a feathered vest she had worn to last year's Bear Dance.

"These plumes represent the worries and tensions built up over a long, hard winter," Susan Carson had said when she helped Sam on with the vest. "The dance, of course, will help you release those troubles."

He remembered thinking the entire escapade was foolish, but had followed along because his sister had asked him. And, for her happiness, he had been thankful.

* * *

A hearty pat on the back woke him from his daydream.

"One more inning!" Jose tossed him his glove. "Make it quick, dude. I'm freezing!"

Sam nodded solemnly and headed to the mound. Besides his family, he found that the baseball diamond had become his island in the middle of his ocean of sorrow. He worried about his father, and his sister's daily pain made his heart heavy. Yet, when he took the mound, he had discovered that all his troubles seemed to vanish in the two or three hours on the field. He had the unique skill to block everything out and focus on the present. It was as if he were alone in the forest, just Sam and the trail, calming his body with cool, even breaths and tuning in to the track or the target. Today, the target was his catcher's glove.

Jose Lopez dropped one finger for a fastball low and away to a Dove Creek right-handed hitter. Sam nodded, came set, took a deep breath, and with a full windup, set sail a heater that popped the center of his best friend's glove.

"Steee-rike!" roared the umpire, and the inning was underway.

CHAPTER FOUR

Washington DC

March 2005

Drake Dixon rose up out of his leather executive chair and looked out of his window at the largest office building in the world. He had set up a new DiamondBar Security bureau across from the Pentagon to make it easier for their leaders to stop by and discuss what it would take to keep America safe. Most of the generals and politicians Dixon had met with had already done their research. They knew that Drake came from an affluent background and that his father, Dean, had started a company in the midseventies that produced the chemicals used in hydraulic fracturing.

While Dixon Industries made hundreds of millions, first son Drake was drawn to the military and the easy money one could make by selling equipment and services to the US government. He debuted DiamondBar Security in 1999, set up a state-of-the-art training compound in southern Virginia, and now was attempting to expand his empire in Washington.

His tenth-floor suite wasn't that big, but it could have easily doubled for some rich senator's on Capitol Hill. The walnut desk reeked of power, and there were pictures covering the walls of Dixon with every imaginable celebrity. There was Dixon with the president, Dixon with the CIA director, Dixon with the governor of Maryland, and Dixon with the general manager of the new baseball team in town, the Washington Nationals.

A polished oak bar was next to the window that provided a spectacular view of the Pentagon. It was highlighted by Dixon's favorite scotch, a Highland Park eighteen-year-old single malt, front and center, as if it were an invitation for the power brokers to come in and join him.

This was a day Dixon thought he deserved an early gift, so he broke the seal of a new bottle and poured two glasses of the Highland Park. He motioned for his lawyer, Barry King, to join him.

"Not a bad first expedition," Dixon said as he handed King a scotch and nodded at a map of Afghanistan hanging on the wall. "Our man tracked the enemy all the way to the border, where he found them holed up in one of their 'impossible to find' caves."

"Impossible for a satellite," agreed King.

"But not for a man like Dan Carson." Dixon took a sip of his drink and held the smooth liquid on his palate before slowly letting it drift down his throat.

"How did he get the enemy location back to headquarters?" King asked.

"He carries a satellite phone but doesn't use it until he's sure about the target. Says the technology only inhibits his intuition."

King gave a look of doubt. "You're trusting this Indian's gut over twenty-first-century computers?"

Dixon glared at his lawyer. This was a time he needed to do something bold to get Senator Ed Richardson, the Vice Chairman of the Senate Appropriations Committee, to continue to choose DiamondBar over other private security companies. Richardson's committee held jurisdiction over all discretionary spending in the Senate and approved of defense spending to contractors like Dixon. But Ed was also an old family friend who had been CEO of Dixon Industries after Drake's father had passed away in 1992. Richardson retired from the company in '98 with a package worth $21 million, and he still received deferred compensation. The important politician owed his family and had proven it by giving DiamondBar preferential treatment with a no-bid, three-year contract in Afghanistan. If he could make an ally like Richardson look good with a daring strategy in protecting American interests, well, perhaps that could lead to his ultimate goal of obtaining mineral rights to a mountain in the Nuristan Province.

Ten years earlier, Dixon Industries had sent a team of geologists to the province, where they discovered a huge vein of mineral wealth, east of the Parun River, before being run off by a band of insurgents. But now, with the war reigning chaos throughout the country, Dixon thought it might be the perfect time to return and strike a deal with some corrupt Afghan politician. The amount of rubies, emeralds, lithium, iron, and uranium rumored to be in this mountain could be worth billions.

Unfortunately, the mountain was in a remote region of the Hindu Kush and ruled by a warlord, Abdul Hazrat, who wanted no part of dealing with outsiders. So first things first . . . Dixon would have to prove DiamondBar's excellence in protecting diplomats, uncovering Taliban trouble, and providing security for the Provincial Reconstruction Teams, or PRTs, before chasing after his mountain.

The only thing Dixon thought his elite security company lacked was instinct. Someone who didn't need to rely on the sophisticated technology of the twenty-first century to track down the terrorists who were making life miserable for military outposts and construction projects in the mountains of Afghanistan. The Taliban were now sending small bands in for quick strike attacks and then retreating into the mountains. Their times were so random that it made it impossible for satellites to track them. That's why Dixon needed a man like Daniel Carson.

He quickly sold Senator Richardson on the low-cost idea and trained Carson at DiamondBar's Virginia compound for a few months before sending him to Afghanistan. Carson's job was to simply track trouble and report the coordinates. The military would send in Special Forces or a drone to take the insurgents out. If it worked, Dixon would receive accolades for coming up with the idea, and if it failed, well, the security company had a very good history of covering up their mistakes.

"What did Senator Ed have to say?"

King's question broke Dixon out of his trance, and he paused to take a sip of his scotch before responding. "He loved it. Said he mentioned me in his report to the president."

"You're on your way, big boy. DiamondBar will soon be America's top guardian."

Dixon smiled proudly as he thought about his lawyer's statement. It was indeed a boost to his ego, but going around the Secretary of Defense, General Bill Clifford, could get him into hot water. In Dixon's opinion, old man Clifford, an executive who took forever to read Drake's research and then dutifully report to the politicians in Washington, moved with the speed of a box turtle. Dixon did all the work, but his plans rarely got to the DC power brokers, which pissed him off.

Knowing it could take weeks for Clifford to make a decision, he and Richardson had bypassed him and sent Daniel Carson overseas without the secretary's knowledge. The Department of Defense was big on chain of command, so he was taking a serious career chance by talking directly to Senator Richardson without General Clifford being involved.

"Have you done anything about Carson's kid?" King asked.

The question took Dixon by surprise. He didn't speak for several moments as he thought about the boy he had met in the doctor's office. He remembered Sam Carson as being stoic, almost impossible to read, and he remembered the discomfort he felt as the boy seemed to study him. But the detail from DiamondBar that Dixon had sent to masquerade as a "hunting party from Albuquerque" had reported back that Sam Carson was the most natural tracker they'd ever met. One of the men in the hunting party was a psychologist who diagnosed another trait of Sam's that drew Dixon's interest. The Carson kid had a photographic memory and was fluent in three languages, English, Spanish, and his tribal tongue. It was then he had decided he would recruit the boy the same way he had manipulated his father. He would use his family as leverage.

"The boy is right where we want him," Dixon said with a serious tone. "He'll graduate from high school next year, and we'll recruit him like we did his old man."

King cocked his head to the side. "I meant the Carson's daughter? You remember—the one who needs the kidney transplant."

His lawyer's words seemed to rattle Dixon, and he took another sip of scotch. "They're now covered under our insurance plan, so it shouldn't be a problem."

"But you told Carson that you'd get his kid a transplant."

Dixon sighed heavily. He had lied to Carson about knowing people at the National Kidney Foundation, but at least he was having his secretary, Marsha Nettles, work with DiamondBar's insurance company to speed things up. They'd get it done. Everything in life was about making deals: you scratch my back, I scratch yours. You track for my security company, and I'll get your child a kidney.

"We're still working on it," Dixon finally said, "but our focus right now has to be on protecting America."

CHAPTER FIVE

Durango, Colorado

May 2006

Jenny Carson celebrated her fourteenth birthday the same day Ignacio High won the regional baseball championship game. Even though a year had passed since she had started her kidney dialysis, and her health had continued to decline, she had managed to attend every one of Sam's home games. She'd seen him no-hit Dove Creek and Pagosa Springs, and strikeout fifteen of the twenty-one batters he faced in a complete game win over Durango. Today, it was a 5–1 win over Sargent to nail down the Bobcats' first regional championship in fifteen years.

When Sam fired the final strike by the opposing batter, Jenny gave a war whoop so loud that it echoed off the back wall of the snack shack and startled a fan's pet dachshund so much it ran for cover under the wooden bleachers. Her cry finally broke Sam's poker face, and he smiled her way just before he was lost in the sea of Bobcats celebrating on top of the pitcher's mound.

* * *

"On to State!" Jenny cried out when her brother stepped off the team bus in front of the Ignacio High gym later that night. The Bobcat band started into the school fight song as the boys were greeted by their fans, parents, and girlfriends. Jenny watched as a cute cheerleader hugged Sam and whispered something in his ear. He gave her an innocent smile and then left to find his mom and sister.

"Well, aren't you Mr. Romeo," Jenny teased when he arrived. "All the girly girls are sweet on the baseball star."

Sam's ears turned bright red. "Shut up, AJ." AJ, short for Agent Jenny, was Sam's pet name for his little sister.

"C'mon, Sammy, you won regionals," she continued to needle him. "Kaylee's pretty. Why don't you ask her out?"

"When do I . . . uh . . ." He glanced from his sister to his mom, who was covering her face to keep from laughing, and then back to Jenny. "When do I have time to go out on a date?"

"Why not tonight?" Jenny gave a Cheshire grin. "Mom and I can survive without you."

"I've got homework, playoffs are coming up, then summer league—"

"You always have an excuse."

"We have a prairie-dog hunt, fly-fishing trips to prepare for, and Mom needs me to fix the horse stalls and paint the barn."

"Blah, blah, blah, you're just chicken."

"I am not."

"Are too." She made a face at him. "Your problem is you want to be alone."

"That's not true."

"Yes, it is. You love being alone. Alone on the mound. Alone in the mountains. Alone. Alone. Alone. No one to bother you. Completely in control. All I need is me." She placed one hand on her heart and leveled the other above her eyes as if she was staring out at the horizon. "Sam Cloud-Carson. Solitary man. Don't need no date."

He heard his mom break up in laughter and jerked around to face her. "Why are you siding with AJ? Somebody has to do what Dad used to."

He felt rather than saw his mother stiffen. His father had been home only once from Afghanistan since his deployment. For a week over

Christmas. It had been like old times. Seven wonderful days of dinners and hunting and laughter and family. His father had raised his voice just one time. At a basketball game when Sam got another technical foul for snapping at a referee near the end of Ignacio's fifteen-point win over Ridgway. He was having a great game too. Twenty-five points, eleven rebounds. In the zone, hitting threes, stealing passes, creating havoc on defense. But he had lost it on one play, a clean block on the Ridgway forward. The whistle blew, and he spun back to the ref, shouting, "No fucking way!"

Despite a crowd of over five hundred inside the gym, he heard his dad's voice over everyone else— "Samuel!"—just before the ref T'd him up. Again. It always unsettled him the moment after it happened, knowing he had completely lost control of his mind and actions. Even after the victory, the drive home was a quiet one until Jenny cracked one of her stupid jokes, and then they were back to being a family again. But the memory of his anger and disappointing his father had stayed with him for much longer.

"We got another letter from Daddy!" Jenny blurted out, as if intentionally trying to change the subject.

There was a long silence before Sam responded, "What—what did he say?"

Their mom's face brightened. "He said he's doing well and thanks you both for your updates on the team."

"I'll write him tonight to let him know we made State." Sam paused to steady his voice. "It's not fair that he won't be able to see us next week in Pueblo."

"I'll take video of you striking everybody out." Jenny mimicked her brother's windup and let loose an invisible fastball.

He gave her a playful shove. "This won't be Sargent or Centauri we'll be facing, AJ. It will be the big schools from Denver and Colorado Springs."

Jenny tossed another imaginary pitch. "Those city boys haven't seen the Carson Express exploding fastball!"

"Express exploding what?" Sam raised an eyebrow in amusement. "Where do you come up with this stuff?"

"That's what they called Nolan Ryan. The Express. Hitters said his fastball exploded when it came to the plate!"

"Nolan Ryan?" Sam said with a skeptical look. "He's a little before your time, princess."

"I YouTubed him. He's the best. Most strikeouts, hundred-mile-an-hour heat, and yellow-hammer curve."

Sam laughed out loud as he tousled his sister's hair and then opened the car door for her. "Get in, munchkin. Time for dinner. I can't let my PR agent go hungry."

*   *   *

They grilled venison and vegetables for dinner. Afterward, Susan left her children alone outside, but she cracked the kitchen window so she could hear Jenny's request to her brother.

As Sam cleared off twigs and leaves from the back patio, he looked up at Pargin Mountain. He never tired of the view of the ten-mile-wide sierra that ranged from brown cuestas to tan mesas, to forest green bluffs. He'd hunted and tracked the entire range and had memorized the flat, narrow stream bottoms and rolling hills that led to the family's hunting grounds. The setting sun's rays were now barely touching the highest peak, and for a moment, the mountain looked cold and dangerous. *Ah, the death of another day,* thought Sam as he grabbed a baseball from atop the picnic table and tossed it to Jenny. She caught it with both hands and turned the ball to find the seams and grip it the same way her brother did. She stared at the ball for a long moment and then said, "I want to be part of this year's Sun Dance."

Sam chuckled softly. "Yeah, right."

Jenny sat up straight and waited for her brother's eyes to come back to hers. "I'm serious. I want to be part of the ceremony."

He looked at her as if she had lost her mind. "You can't."

"Why not?"

"You . . ." The words caught in his throat, but he had to say them. He had to let her know. "You could . . . die."

Jenny cocked her head to the side and gave him a crinkle-eyed grin. "I'm already dying. That's why I want to do the Sun Dance before—"

"Don't say that! We'll get the transplant and you'll be fine again. Why do you think Papa took the job with DiamondBar? To get insurance for the healthy kidney you'll be getting soon."

"This is important to me, Sam. I want *you* to be part of my Sun Dance."

"You can't—and I won't. It's only for men, and there's four days of fasting. No water. No food. You can't do that."

Jenny's entire body softened, as if to help her older brother understand the depth of what she was asking. "I watch you every week on the basketball court or the baseball field, surrounded by people trying to beat you. And you never give in. You find a way—any way—to win. The Sun Dance is *my game*, brother."

"The Sun Dance isn't a game, Jenny."

She sighed. "I know, but I had a dream. And in the dream I was called to be in the ceremony."

The mere mention of the dream made Sam pause, for this was a message he respected, one he was told came directly from the Great Spirit to the recipient. The Sun Dance was a quest for spiritual strength, a purification, or communion, with some higher power that he didn't truly understand. He respected Ute tradition and wanted to follow the ways of ancient stories, but at the same time, he didn't know how to apply them to his own life. Why couldn't this higher power heal his sister? Why would it take a father away from his family? And why did his mother have to work so hard to keep SJ Outfitters going?

His father had told him, *You can't ask those questions, son, for there are no answers.* Yet there they were, flying through his mind like an oak leaf chasing the wind. Where was the Great Spirit in his questions? He didn't know . . . but he believed his sister did. It was as if her physical suffering led her past human doubts and fears, to a certainty beyond. Still, he was afraid, and a look of worry gripped his face until he heard the kitchen door open. It was their mother.

"I talked with our tribal leaders about Jenny having a role in the ceremony," Susan said in an encouraging tone. "She won't go in the Sun Dance lodge with the men, but she will be allowed her own tipi on the periphery. Her fasting, of course, will be limited. That's where Jenny wants you to help her."

He turned away and again stared out at Pargin Mountain. Even though the sun had set, transforming the mountain into a jagged edge of darkness, it no longer looked cold and dangerous. Perhaps there was freedom in what Jenny sought from the Sun Dance. He turned back to find his sister grinning up at him as if she already knew that he would cave in.

"Put your moccasins on, Sammy! I need to teach you the steps to our dance!"

CHAPTER SIX

Pueblo, Colorado

May 2006

Sam let fly a two-seam fastball that at first looked like it would hit the Limon High School batter until at the last instant it took a right turn and snapped across the inside corner.

"Steee-rike three!" roared the umpire.

The Limon coach growled, "No way, Blue! That pitch was way inside."

Jenny leaped to her feet and mimicked the ump, punching the air and practically knocking over her mother's water bottle as she exclaimed, "Fifteen in a row, Sammy! Keep mowin' 'em down!"

Ignacio was holding a slim 2–0 lead in the sixth inning of the semifinals of the 2A State Playoffs. Sam had given up a double to Limon's first batter of the game and then retired fifteen straight: nine strikeouts, six groundouts. Scouts from both pro and college were now drifting over from other fields to watch the right-hander from southwest Colorado who displayed both impeccable control and a fastball that was touching eighty-eight miles per hour on their radar guns.

Two more Carson sinkers sliced down Limon batters as they weakly grounded out to end the inning.

"Atta boy, Sammy!" Jenny squealed. "Keep that Limon line movin'! Back to the dugout!"

An embarrassed Susan Carson's eyes went wide as she swept her index finger to her lips to quiet her daughter, but even the Kansas City Royals scout in the row in front of them had to chuckle as he listened to the little girl's chatter.

Jenny leaned over the veteran scout's shoulder. "What was the velo on that last two-seamer?"

"Eighty-four," the scout said with a grin.

Jenny's face puckered up as if she'd bitten into a sour lemon. "You must be using a slow gun. The Rockies scout had him at eighty-six."

The scout's grin creased into a broad smile as he turned around and extended his hand to Jenny. "Roberto Francisco. Kansas City Royals. You must be this pitcher's agent?"

"I know who you are." Jenny shook the man's hand firmly. "It says so on the name tag of your briefcase. But you better get your gun readings right if you're thinking about drafting my brother. I mean, look who else is here. The Brewers, the Rockies, and four different colleges, three in-state and one from the Big-12."

The scout bit his lip to soften his grin. "Have the Yankees shown up yet, Ms. . . . ?"

"Jenny. I emailed all thirty teams video, so I'm sure they know all about Sam Carson."

Francisco moved up a row on the wooden bleachers, introduced himself to Susan, and then turned back to Jenny. "So tell me all you can about your client, Ms. Carson."

"Four-seam, two-seam, curve, change," Jenny rattled off. "His change is a good ten miles an hour less than his fastball and has late fade. All of his pitches come out of the same arm slot and release point, so he's tough for a hitter to read."

The Royals scout raised an eyebrow at Jenny's mom. "She's good."

Susan smiled back. "She does her homework."

They quietly watched the home half of the sixth—three up, three down—and then Francisco nudged Jenny with an elbow. "What kind of student is your brother?"

"Top five in his class. He'll graduate, age eighteen, with a four point two five GPA," Jenny said. "He'll probably double major in Environmental Science and Wildlife Management, so it will take a big bonus if he's gonna bypass college."

Francisco again had to bite his lip to keep from laughing. Sam was back on the mound, finishing his warm-up tosses, as the first Limon batter of what could be the final inning stepped to the plate. Francisco raised his radar gun and looked down at Jenny. "Seven innings for high school games, so let's see if your brother lets it rip."

Sam dotted the outside corner with a four-seam fastball. The ump raised his right arm to indicate strike one, and Francisco showed Jenny the gun reading. "Eighty-six, Ms. Jenny. Bonus babies need to throw a little harder than that."

"Velocity, velocity, velocity," Jenny said with a shake of her head. " All you scouts care about is velocity. It's so sad. Greg Maddux said location first, movement second, and velocity *third*!"

Sam got a swing and a miss on a changeup and then got the Limon batter on a soft come-backer to the mound on a sinker for the first out. Jenny gave Francisco her most dramatic scowl. "Now, that's pitching. Sam sped his bat up with off-speed, then fooled him with the two-seamer."

"Maddux indeed would have been proud, Ms. Jenny, but my boss wants a little more *velo* in my report if your brother's gonna get picked in the top five rounds."

Jenny frowned until her brother struck out the Limon cleanup hitter on three pitches for the second out. "That's it, Sammy! Hum baby it in there!"

Francisco showed her the radar reading of eighty-seven miles per hour. Jenny shook her head, stood up, and cupped her hands over her mouth. "Rock 'n' fire, Sammy. Let's get it over with right here!"

Sam Carson's final pitch was a seventy-eight-mile-per-hour changeup that completely fooled the Limon batter, who futilely lunged for the ball as it dipped out of the strike zone and tapped a soft grounder to first for the final out. Jenny shrieked with joy as the Ignacio team piled on top of her brother, who led her beloved Bobcats to their first ever state title game. She spun around to the Royals scout and waved a finger in his face. "That's what you should be looking at for your first rounder! A pitcher who knows how to win!"

    *   *   *

Washington, DC

  Drake Dixon winked at the pretty blonde female reporter from ABC as he hurried up the steps of the historic Willard Intercontinental Hotel in Washington, DC. He could tell by her inquisitive look that she was trying to figure out who he was: an obviously influential stranger, attending the most important Defense Department party, just two blocks from the White House.
  He laughed to himself, knowing there would be a time when everyone in the Capitol would know his name.
  The Crystal Room was already crowded when he stepped through the door. Senator Ed Richardson spotted Dixon and immediately waved him over. He inhaled a deep breath to gather his strength. He was weary after the all-night military flight from Afghanistan, where he had gone to check on his celebrated creation.
  Daniel Carson had not disappointed. Both his security officers and Army Special Forces had raved about the tracker's brilliance in the field and how Taliban attacks on the Provincial Reconstruction Teams had diminished since Carson arrived.
  "Congratulations to us," Richardson said as he handed Dixon a glass of his favorite scotch. "There was talk on the hill today of enemy strikes being down in the Afghan mountains, and I, of course, intimated that my boy, Drake Dixon, had a little something to do with it."
  Dixon was surprised. Secrecy was of the utmost importance if his program was to work. If the history of their covert operation got back to the Taliban, Carson's identity would be compromised. Still, the senator's compliment felt good, and he smiled as he clinked his glass to Richardson's. "Thanks, Ed, but discretion is important for continued success."

"Of course. But we have to give the committee and the media something to chew on, or we don't get the credit." Richardson motioned him to a far corner of the room. "If we pull this off and America brings peace and democracy to Afghanistan, both of us have a chance to make a fortune from the natural resources in those hills."

Dixon looked over his shoulder to make sure no one was listening to their conversation. "I still need to get a deal with the Ministry of Mining and Petroleum. We don't want some oversight committee or international watchdog looking over our shoulders."

"As long as you do everything legally, Drake, you shouldn't have a problem. You get approval, and our old company will provide all the equipment to build their roads and extract their minerals."

Dixon forced a smile but remained quiet. Senator Ed obviously didn't know Afghanistan, where just about every decision their leaders made bordered on the illegitimate. One had to be able to read the ever-changing political landscape of a country that had been torn apart by three decades of war. But chaos always provided opportunity. And opportunity meant money.

"How was your trip?" Richardson asked.

"Good. Carson was scouting trouble spots for one of our PRTs when he came across tracks that led to a hideout near the border. It happened to be a cave where a Taliban warlord, Rashid Jafari, was hanging out. Carson gave Special Forces the coordinates, and they sent a drone in to take him out." Dixon raised his glass of scotch. "That victory rather dramatically reduced enemy attacks on the PRT this month. To zero. Nada."

The senator grinned from ear to ear and again clinked his glass to Dixon's. "That's exactly how we ascend Capitol Hill. It's called following through on your promises. I told the Appropriations Committee of a new security plan that would cost very little, and they couldn't have been happier to support us." Richardson drained the rest of his glass and said, "But the entire key is continued victories, Drake. Americans don't mind us killing terrorists; they just don't like reading about us slaughtering innocent citizens."

"It's not that easy figuring out who's a terrorist and who's a civilian, Ed."

"That's why I gave DiamondBar a no-bid contract." Richardson winked. "Because my friend, Drake Dixon, will make sure we don't make those mistakes."

*   *   *

Jenny woke up with a temperature of 101 on the morning of the Colorado 2A State Championship game. Ignacio versus powerhouse Burlington. College coaches from Colorado State, Mesa State, Regis University, and Oklahoma State had all visited with Sam after his brilliant 2–0 shutout of Limon in the semifinals. But the stress of both travel and games had taken a toll on his sister, and Jenny now lay in a cool bath as her mother tried to get her temperature down.

"I can't leave," Sam said from outside the hotel-bathroom door.

"There's nothing you can do," his mother replied as she swept a cool facecloth across Jenny's forehead. "We shouldn't have stayed out so late celebrating your semifinal win."

Sam inhaled a deep breath, conflicted about what to do. His team needed him on the field in their attempt to do something no Ignacio team had done before—win a Colorado State Baseball Championship. But his sister's health was more important. He knew Jenny's kidneys were working overtime in an effort to push fluids through her body and regulate her temperature.

A knock on the hotel-room door snapped him back to the present.

"Time to go, stud!" his best friend called out. "Time to take State!"

Sam didn't answer as he considered what to do. He felt awful. He would die for his sister, but she had had so many flare-ups in recent weeks, he wasn't sure whether this one was a false alarm or not.

"Sam! You in there?" Jose pounded on the door.

"Just a second," Sam answered and then rested his head against the bathroom door.

"Please go." It was his sister's voice, coming in short, breathy gasps. "I promise . . . I'll feel better . . . if you go."

His jaws clenched upon hearing her voice.

"Mom?"

"Go."

He hesitated. "Will you at least call that Drake Dixon guy and ask him when he's gonna set up that meeting he promised with the kidney specialist?"

"Yes," she said softly.

"Okay…I love you guys." Then he gathered his gear and started for the door.

"Sammy–" Jenny groaned, and Sam jerked back to the bathroom door.

"I'm still here."

"Don't forget"–she coughed–"the Burlington starter . . . will only throw his curve . . . when he's ahead in the count."

Sam snorted back a laugh and tossed his equipment bag over his shoulder. "Thanks, AJ. I'll keep that in mind."

*   *   *

The sun peeked through a hole in the clouds as Sam made his way to home plate in the fifth inning of the Colorado 2A State Championship game. Burlington led 2-0 on a walk and back-to-back doubles in the first inning off Ignacio's nervous number-two starter, Willie Tucson, who finally had calmed down to throw scoreless ball the next three frames. After Sam's complete game shutout of Limon in the semifinal, Colorado prep rules would only allow him to pitch two innings of the title game. Coach Flores told him he'd start at shortstop the first five, and if they had the lead, he'd close out the game.

"Grip it and rip it, Samson! Let's go!" Jose barked from the on-deck circle as Sam swung a weighted bat over his head.

Sam grabbed a handful of dirt from outside the batter's box and rubbed his hands together. Two on, one out. The Burlington pitcher had to throw to him this time. With first base open in the first inning, Burlington had intentionally walked Sam to pitch to Jose, and had induced the Ignacio catcher to ground into an inning-ending double play.

Sam glanced over his shoulder to the stands where his mom and sister usually sat, but of course, they were back at the hotel, trying to get Jenny's temperature down. Instead, in their row were scouts from several Midwest colleges and one pro scout he recognized, Roberto Francisco of the Kansas City Royals. Sam had seen him at every game of the tournament.

"Concentrate," he whispered to himself and then looked at Coach Flores for a sign. Swing away. As the number-three hitter, he knew he wouldn't be asked to bunt, but Coach would want him to at least take one shot at right field. Stay out of a twin-killing.

Sam stepped into the batter's box and dug his right foot against the back line. Feet set apart, knees flexed, body bent slightly at the waist, he took a couple of practice swings, brought the bat up to his right shoulder, and stared at the mound.

Todd Spencer, right-hander, above-average fastball, good curve, but no confidence in his change. No way he'd throw off-speed in this situation. But he knew his real opponent wasn't Spencer. It was the baseball. That's what he was going to be hitting.

First pitch, fastball away, but the ump yelled out, "Stee—rike!"

That's okay. Sam nodded and dug back in. If the ump called that last pitch a strike, Spencer may go back there.

The pitcher did, but Sam swung a bit late, a line-drive foul down the right-field line. Strike two.

Okay. That was my one shot to right field. Now, protect the plate. As Sam brought the bat up to his shoulder, his sister's scouting report suddenly came to him.

"The Burlington starter will only throw his curve when he's ahead in the count."

A slight smile creased his face as he took a practice swing and then set up for Todd Spencer's pitch. *Keep your head down. Breathe. Focus. Curveball. Yes. Swing.*

Aluminum bat against baseball. *Ping!* The outfielders didn't even move as the ball shot to the sky, a tiny speck lost in the puffy white clouds high above the Pueblo plains . . . and gone. As Sam circled the bases, he couldn't stop grinning. "Agent Jenny, you're the bomb."

*   *   *

"Yessss!" Two voices shrieked from inside Room 103 of the Motel 6 near downtown Pueblo, Colorado. A dog barked from an adjacent room as Jenny leaned across the bed to turn up the radio.

"Sam Carson's three-run homer gives Ignacio their first lead of the 2A State Championship!"

Jenny pumped her hands in the air. "Sam-my, Sam-my, Sam-my," she chanted and then dropped her sweat-drenched head back onto her pillow. "Just three more outs and we'll be state champs."

"It's only the fifth inning," her mother said with a raised brow.

"Sammy will be on the hill in the sixth, Mom. Game over." Jenny beamed.

*   *   *

Tucson did get those three outs needed and handed the one-run lead to the most talked about player in the 2A playoffs. As scouts reached for notebooks and radar guns, Sam made his way to the mound with his catcher by his side.

"Let's finish the job, brother," Jose said as he slammed the ball into his friend's glove.

"First pitch, curveball, to give 'em something to think about," Sam whispered, his lips barely moving. "Then two-seamers away."

Jose nodded and jogged back behind home plate. "Good luck with the gas, dude," Lopez said to the Burlington cleanup hitter as he dropped into a crouch, pulled his mask over his face, and gave two fingers for the curve.

Sam nodded, went into a full windup, and flipped the curve toward the plate. The hitter's knees buckled as he took the pitch down the middle.

"Stee-rike one!" barked the ump.

Jose fired the ball back to Sam. "Atta boy, Sam, hum baby it in there!"

It took Carson only eleven pitches to strike out the side. 3–2, Ignacio going to the final inning.

*　　*　　*

"Our Bobcats need another run," Susan said after Ignacio was shutout in the top of the seventh. "I'd breathe a little easier if we were up by at least two."

Jenny lifted the cool, wet washcloth away from her sweat-drenched forehead and scowled at her mother. "Oh, ye of little faith. Sammy's on the mound. It's in the bag, Mom." Then she turned up the radio even louder.

"This will be a challenge for Burlington, having to comeback against one of the best pitchers in all of Colorado."

*　　*　　*

Sam slowed his breath to a smooth, even cadence. All sounds and images seemed to blur into nothingness as his body and mind came together for one singular purpose. To execute the next pitch. He heard no baiting from the opposition, nor cheers of encouragement from his own side. There was only the complete awareness that he was born to be on this mound, at this very moment. His windup was easy, his balance perfect. The ball left his fingertips like an arrow seeking its target.

"Stee—rike three!" barked the umpire, and the Ignacio faithful screamed in delight.

No emotion from Sam as he accepted the throw from his catcher and placed his fingers along the seams. Sinker. No reason to throw anything except his best pitch. Deep inhale. Slow exhale. Windup and delivery. Strike one.

Deep inhale. Slow exhale. Windup and delivery. Strike two.

Deep inhale. Slow exhale. Windup and delivery. Strike three. Two outs. It was simply an elevated game of catch between him and Jose. One out to go.

Sam peeked up at the stands. No sign of his mom or Jenny. This final out would be for them. Pinch hitter. Left-handed batter. He remembered the kid's picture from the program but didn't know his name. Strike one. The Burlington batter seemed nervous as he gave a choppy, abbreviated practice swing. No problem. Strike two.

The Ignacio faithful on the third-base side of the stands rose up from their aluminum benches and began to chant, "Bob-Cats." *Clap, clap, clap.* "Bob-Cats." *Clap, clap, clap.*

Sam placed his index and middle fingers along the red stitching. He would throw at the batter's right hip and let the natural movement of his sinker run back over the inside corner of the plate to end the game.

Deep inhale. Slow exhale. Windup and delivery. The pitch was perfect. It came off his fingers relaxed and smooth, beautifully moving left to right . . . but instead of backing away, the hitter leaned in, and the baseball creased the tip of his right kneecap.

"That got him! Take your base!" shouted the ump.

The relieved Burlington hitter started down the line.

"No way!" barked Sam. "He leaned into the zone!"

"Back off, kid. You hit him."

"That was fucking strike three, Blue!"

"Watch your mouth, boy."

Jose sprinted from behind home plate and grabbed his friend. "Chill, dude. Let it go." He put his arm around Sam and led him back up the mound. "This is your game. Get back in that way cool zone."

Sam's entire body finally relaxed, and he glanced up at the scoreboard, which still read Ignacio 3, Burlington 2.

Back on the mound, Sam studied the next hitter. *First baseman. Big guy. Left-handed. Slow bat. 0 for 3. Fastballs in, changeups away. Get it over with.*

Jose put down one finger next to his right thigh.

All right. He's on the same page. Inhale. Exhale. Let 'er fly.

"Stee-rike one!"

The Ignacio crowd roared.

Jose put down two fingers for a curve. Sam shook his head. Jose wiggled four. Sam nodded. The Colorado State Championship was right now. Inhale. Slow, even exhale. Windup and pitch.

The location was perfect. Off the plate, low and away, but somehow, the big Burlington slugger got to it, diving out over the plate to get the bat head on the ball that was four inches outside the zone.

The white orb took off on an arc, starting down the left field line, but instead of twisting foul, at the last second, it clanged off the yellow foul pole. Home run. Game over. Sam stared as if frozen in time as the Burlington Cougars poured from their dugout and dog-piled on the big, slow first baseman who won the Colorado 2A State Championship.

*   *   *

Jenny snapped the radio off, pulled a pillow over her face, and let go a primal scream. It couldn't have happened. Impossible. No one beat her brother. And Sam deserved it. Hell, *she* deserved it. It was the only thing she really wanted.

She felt her mother's presence next to her, but no movement, no understanding pat on her shoulder, or sweet saccharine words of sympathy. No, her mother was suffering just as much as she was. And yet her mother wasn't at the ballgame. She couldn't be there to console her only son because—because of her daughter's illness. Jenny bit hard into the pillow and screamed again.

CHAPTER SEVEN

Washington, DC

May 2006

"It will all blow over," Dixon said to his lawyer as they walked up the steps of the Pentagon. "It's not as if we're talking about Americans dying. They're just Afghans. Collateral damage of war."

Barry King shook his head. "But pictures of dead children could cut into our support."

"Forget about it. The damn liberals will always find something to bitch about."

Just before they went through security, King leaned close to Dixon. "I think we should just listen today. Don't comment unless you're asked a direct question."

* * *

As Secretary of Defense, General Bill Clifford's office was less impressive than Dixon expected. There were no displays of awards or achievements, nor pictures of political or athletic stars with Clifford adorning the walls. No polished oak liquor bar like Dixon had in his own Washington office. It was a bland office with three blank manila folders laid out perfectly on a simple metal desk one might find at Office Depot or Walmart.

Clifford stood up from his chair when Dixon and King entered, shook their hands, and motioned for them to sit in the chairs across from his desk. "Good work on the reconnaissance in the Kunar Province. Your man showed good judgment to alert our Special Forces that the enemy was on the move."

Dixon nodded proudly.

Clifford opened the first folder. At the very top was the same picture of dead Afghan children that the Senate Armed Services Committee had seen the day before. "Unfortunately, your team was overly aggressive in authorizing the attack of this village near the border."

Dixon wanted to respond but remembered King's advice and said nothing. His team, led by Daniel Carson, actually had warned the Army that they hadn't completed all the intel on the tiny mud-walled compound near the Pakistan border. But something went wrong in the communication, and two unmanned Predator drones launched Hellfire missiles and killed two families. Four of the dead were under ten years old. Dixon would have to take one for the team. He stayed quiet.

"We chose DiamondBar because we were told you were the best at dealing with international terrorism, that you were the best at training government agencies in antiterrorism techniques," Clifford said.

"We are." Drake couldn't help himself. He had to say something. "I hire only the best people. Former Rangers and Special Forces—"

Clifford cut him off with a flip of his hand and opened the second manila folder. "It says here: Carson said, 'No go,' but one of your goons gave the go-ahead anyway."

Dixon winced at the word goons and bit the side of his mouth to remain quiet. He had hired over three hundred new security men in the last calendar year, and there were bound to be a few wild hares in the bunch. Hell, most were former soldiers who had experienced the worst of humanity: living through car bombs, being shot at from rooftops and mountain hideouts, and watching their best friends die from a sniper's bullet or roadside bomb. These were men who had a learned hatred of the enemy, and some, Dixon knew, went a bit too far. Those were the men

Director Clifford was likely speaking of now. But they were Dixon's men, men he had hired for private security in Africa, Iraq, and Afghanistan, and he had witnessed firsthand their ferocity in battle. The US government had given them a job to do, and they did it. So what if they made a few mistakes along the way and a few innocent ragheads died—that was the price of war.

The general scanned the sheet and shook his head. "The decision to attack was made by Billy Cutthredge and Rob Marcus?"

Dixon swallowed hard. Cutthredge was a retired soldier he had personally recruited when DiamondBar opened in 1999. Billy was brash, immature, and erratic, but absolutely fearless in combat. And he had information on Dixon that could be damaging.

"Sergeant Billy Cutthredge was accused of shooting an Iraqi soldier in the back of the head during Operation Desert Sabre in '91," Clifford said.

Dixon squirmed in his chair. "He was never found guilty."

"I read the report. He was turned in by one of his own men. A man I completely trust, who now works at the department."

King gave a brief shake of his head to Dixon. The message was clear. Keep your mouth shut.

"Unfortunately, war brings out the worst in some men." Clifford opened the third folder and began reading from a stapled multipage report. "1993: Billy was asked to leave the military after assaulting a female team member at Fort Hood. '94: he joined a security company contracted by Angola State Oil . . . fired in '97 for selling heroin to some of his teammates." He paused to turn a page. "1999: Billy's recruited by DiamondBar Security, teaming him with old Army buddy Rob Marcus to protect US interests in Sierra Leone. One year later both Billy and Rob are accused of raping two underage strippers. Your company gets them off under the agreement that they'll participate in drug counseling."

"Both are clean now," Dixon said, perhaps too quickly.

Clifford slowly raised his vision, his eyes locking onto Dixon's. "I was with Special Forces, Drake. They're highly trained, disciplined, loyal, fierce warriors who understand their duty and responsibility. But also, soldiers who served with *honor*." He dropped the folder he was holding back onto his desk. "Billy Cutthredge and Rob Marcus are cold-blooded animals—and you hired them to work for DiamondBar?"

Dixon shifted uncomfortably in his chair and was trying to think of a defense when his lawyer leaned forward. "I'll make sure both of them are on the next plane out of Afghanistan, General." King then got up from his chair and put his hand on Dixon's shoulder. "Time to go, Drake."

Dixon sat frozen for a moment and fought back the urge to say something. He needed Cutthredge and Marcus. They knew too much. They had snooped around and discovered that he was involved in insider trading with a Saudi Bank and that he had overcharged the US government by millions for several security projects. He'd have to get them out of Afghanistan and give them another assignment. One where he could keep his eye on them. Finally, he stood up, nodded to General Clifford, and then followed his lawyer out of the room.

CHAPTER EIGHT

Pargin Mountain, Colorado

July 2006

A cloud of steam hissed from the sweat-lodge entrance in the foothills of Pargin Mountain. The sound made Jenny raise up to watch their Ute leader enter the wooden-and-buffalo-robe structure and gently close the door behind him. She wanted to follow inside and be part of the Sun Dance ceremony, but her illness and tribal rules would not allow it. It was also never part of her vision, the dream that showed her outside with her family, dancing with her brother, experiencing the tradition of *tagu-wini*, or standing thirsty, one of the most important ceremonies of Ute culture.

She also felt her brother needed to be part of the Sun Dance. Sam had yet to surrender the disappointment of Ignacio's loss in the Colorado State Baseball Championship. She saw the torment so heavy on his face when he sat alone on the front porch, as he likely replayed over and over his final, fateful pitch. More than any person she'd ever met, her brother held onto the past: mistakes, unjust treatment, and good pitches that had bad results.

Thank goodness work, college recruiters, and preparing for the Sun Dance had provided some distraction, or he may stayed in his depression for months. Less than a week after the title-game loss, Sam had accepted a scholarship to Mesa State College. While MSC had a very good baseball program and was strong in her brother's desired major of Environmental Science, she knew he had made the decision because it was only a four-hour drive from family, and closer to the people he thought he could protect.

*   *   *

"Water?" Sam tapped his sister on the shoulder with a canteen as she continued to stare at the door to the Sun Dance lodge.

"No, thank you," she said softly and placed the canteen by her tipi. She went back to work on cross-stitching her personal tribal flag. It was artwork of a peace pipe, a leaf branch, and a red willow. The pipe represented her desire to have harmony with others, the leaf branch represented peace, and the red willow represented respect and spiritual protection.

"You haven't had anything to eat or drink in a day and a half." Sam moved the water closer to her side. "I don't want you to have another setback and wind up in the hospital."

She turned and gave him a look that would have frozen steam. "Would you please respect why we're here? The Sun Dance is not just for me. It's for our family and our people—that means *you*."

He flinched in embarrassment, then sat down next to her, picked up a stick, and began to stir their campfire.

She placed her hand on top of his. "Please get quiet, Sam. Close your eyes, and see me healing right now."

Her request of *see me healing right now* was like a knife to his heart. He was being selfish. In trying to protect Jenny, he was getting in the way of her vision, her spiritual quest.

She squeezed his hand. "Let it go, brother. If you are trusting in your own strength, you have every reason to be afraid. Give it all to the Great Spirit. He is our safety in every experience."

He honored her appeal and closed his eyes, but his mind continued to churn with doubts and fears for his sister. What did she know that he did not? He remembered his father's words when they were hunting on Pargin

Mountain about Jenny's spiritual connection. *It's as if she has this direct link to the Great Spirit to see past her troubles.*

He inhaled a deep breath and settled back against a fallen oak log.

The foothills were alive with the music of the Sun Dance. The rhythmic chanting and pounding of drums began to stir his soul as he released a long, slow exhale.

"Let it go, brother. If you are trusting in your own strength, you have every reason to be afraid. Let it go."

His breathing became light and calm, his face serene as the vibrations transported his mind to another world. Words came to him that were not his own.

Honor the Creator. Remember our traditions that were taken away. Your power will be released the moment you have faith. Preserve only what is good, only what heals, comforts, and blesses. Give back to Mother Earth.

Sam was gone, lost in his breathing, witnessing visions of the past: of cold, clear rivers rushing down mountain passes and endless green prairies filled with buffalo and coyote and elk. There was laughter and song from an ancient Ute tribe around a campfire, a recognition that everything on Earth was one. There was no separation between man and the natural world.

It was the most beautiful experience he had ever had, and as soon as that thought came to him, it was gone. His eyes fluttered halfway open to see an otherworldly, out-of-focus image of his mother and sister and grandfather dancing to the Sun Dance drums. There seemed to be a light glowing from Jenny as she looked his way and smiled. He smiled back and then drifted back into his dream.

* * *

"You look like you went somewhere special," Sam heard someone say.

He shook his head to clear his mind. Jenny grinned from ear to ear as she stood over him. His mouth opened, but no words came out. He was absolutely drained. He tried to swallow but could not, and just sat there staring dumbly at the lodge where family members continued to dance in support of loved ones inside. It was dark now, and he began to wonder how long he'd been gone, how long he'd been dreaming.

"Now you know where I go." Jenny sat down next to him.

He finally swallowed successfully and cleared his throat. "What . . . time is it?"

"Eleven."

His mouth fell open.

"You've been gone three hours. Mom even had a conversation with you. You didn't make much sense. You were talking about flowers and buffalo and the Great Spirit, and then started singing some song we couldn't understand."

Sam gave a look of great skepticism. "No way."

"Yes way. You were in the spirit world—one you know quite well."

He raised a quizzical brow.

"Think of something you trust that you can't see or feel, Sammy."

"What are you talking about?"

The right side of her mouth curled into a lopsided grin. "When I was healthy and we went on hikes, I was amazed at how easily you found our way back home, through bramble and forest, following some invisible trail. You didn't rely on your eyes or ears to show you where to go—you just trusted." She paused and looked over at their grandfather, who gave an agreeable nod. "You do the same thing when you pitch. Your conscious doesn't throw strikes; your subconscious does. It's beautiful. You just trust your body to send the ball where it's supposed to go."

Sam's mind traveled back to that fateful day in Pueblo. "My subconscious didn't help us win the State Championship."

"We don't always get the results we want, even when we throw the perfect pitch."

Sam gave a bewildered look to his mom and grandfather, and then back to Jenny. "How old are you? Geez, you talk like you're one of the elders."

Their mom laughed quietly. "She does spend a lot of time with Grandpa and the elders."

"Or has her head buried in some book," Sam added.

"I've been studying Ute, Lakota, and Navajo vision quests, and reading about Buddha and Jesus and A Course in Miracles," Jenny said matter-of-factly.

Sam blinked, entirely taken aback. "You've got to be the weirdest fourteen-year-old in the world."

"And a tired fourteen-year-old." She picked up her blanket and headed for their tipi. "I'm going to bed."

He reached for her. "The doctor said you have to eat something after forty hours."

"I already ate." Jenny then spun around and snatched an imaginary microphone from the sky and brought it to her mouth. "Mom fed meeee . . . while you were singinnnng . . . about the lovely elk and red willows and fields of golden dandeliiiiiiions."

Sam turned a bright red and put his head in his hands as his sister, mother, and grandfather sang even louder and danced into their tipi.

CHAPTER NINE

Durango, Colorado

July 2006

Dixon covered his eyes from the glare of the sun as he watched the Learjet touch down at Durango-La Plata County Airport. He wanted to be there when those two degenerates got off the plane. He had flown all the way from Washington, DC, to make sure Billy Cutthredge and Rob Marcus didn't screw up another mission. Everything was falling into place. DiamondBar had a $500 million deal with the US government, and one of the top senators on Capitol Hill was singing his praises to the president and Congress.

The Learjet cruised to a stop, the side door opened, and there stood a bear of a man, his long hair pulled back in a ponytail and a beard that fell all the way to his chest.

"America! Home sweet home!" the man roared as he stepped off the plane. "Land of the free! Home of the fuckin' brave!"

"Hello, Billy," Dixon said as he shook the man's hand. He then shook Marcus's hand, who had now joined them.

"Thanks for getting us out of that Taliban shithole and giving us a sweet vacation in Guam." Marcus wiped a filthy sleeve across his mouth and winked at Dixon.

Both obviously had been drinking. A lot. Their breath reeked of vodka, and Cutthredge wouldn't let go of Drake's hand as he pulled his old friend in for a hug.

"Look at you," Billy snorted. "All GQ with yer silk shirt and tailored suit." He snatched Drake's sunglasses off his face and stared at the inscription inside the frame. "Stefano Ricci. Damn, these cost a fuckin' grand!"

Dixon gently but firmly reclaimed his sunglasses and motioned for his security men to follow him to a waiting limo.

"Ridin' in style, Robbie!" Billy playfully shoved his buddy toward the open door.

Dixon waited until they were all inside and he had closed the door before speaking. "What happened in the Kunar Province?"

The question seemed to immediately sober up Cutthredge, who leaned back on the soft leather couch and shook his head. "That's over with, Drake."

"Children were killed, Billy."

"Kids die in wars all the time."

"But Carson said to wait."

"That guy's a damn pussy. Always wanted to wait, see what was on the other side of a tree or some damn rock crag. Shit, we missed so many kills because he was slow to fire."

"That's his job"—Dixon moved his glare from Cutthredge to Marcus—"to track, study, investigate, and make the best possible decision before communicating his findings to DiamondBar or Special Forces."

"Dude slowed us down." Marcus opened the limo's cooler and frowned, disappointed to find no alcohol inside.

"This isn't about notches on your belt, Rob. It's about success. We had a one hundred percent success rate with Carson until you two went against his advice —"

"Screw Carson," Cutthredge cut him off. "We heard Abdul Hazrat might be inside the compound, so we went for it."

"Hazrat?" Dixon's brows came together in greater interest. "What made you think he was in the area?"

"Your intel. DiamondBar's crack staff."

"Hazrat wasn't in the report."

"Of course he wasn't. We told them not to put Hazrat in to protect you. Figured you wouldn't want to make it look like it was personal."

But it was personal. Abdul Hazrat had refused every offer from Dixon over the last three years in his quest to obtain the mineral rights of a mountain the warlord controlled. Eliminating him would make it so much easier, and then he could begin negotiations with whoever took over. The State Department wouldn't waste time investigating Hazrat's death if Dixon could prove he was, or even accuse him of being, a Taliban leader. Yet the time wasn't quite right to hunt down Hazrat. Not until he secured a mineral-rights deal with the Afghan government, and not without Dan Carson on the inside, quietly uncovering where the secretive Hazrat was hiding out.

Dixon eased back into his seat and turned to Cutthredge. "Who gave you the intel that Hazrat was in the compound?"

"Charlie."

Charlie Whitson, thought Dixon. Yeah, he was belligerent like Cutthredge and Marcus, but Whitson had served with US Army COIST, the Company Intelligence Support Team, during Desert Storm, and his attention to detail was excellent. More than likely he had recruited sources in the Kunar and Nuristan Provinces that tipped them off on Hazrat.

"Only Charlie's eight-man team knows about our plans," Dixon said. "But how long can he keep Carson in the dark?"

Cutthredge shrugged. "Probably forever. He spends most of his time at the Special Forces compound. Colonel Tomlinson likes hearing his intel."

Dixon let go a frustrated exhale. He didn't mind sharing information with Special Forces, but he didn't want them getting credit for what was his idea. He wanted DiamondBar's brand front and center of the American media any time they had success overseas. It was he who had discovered Carson on a random hunting expedition in southwest Colorado in 2004. He had recruited and trained him at DiamondBar's exclusive academy in Virginia, and now someone else was going to reap the benefit of his project? No way.

"You got us holed up in a trailer park?" Marcus brought Dixon back to the present as the limo turned into Summerset Mobile Home Park, south of Durango.

"I don't want to hear any complaints. This will be just like Guam. A paid vacation. All I ask is that you stay out of trouble, check out every outfitter in Colorado, and watch the boy. Have him take you on a few hunts and see if he's worth my investment."

CHAPTER TEN

Grand Junction, Colorado

November 2006

Sam flipped his glove up to catch Jose's throw from inside Mesa State's Brownson Arena. The building was designed for basketball, volleyball, and wrestling, but those respective coaches didn't mind if another Maverick athlete wanted to work out when the weather was bad. In this case, it was terrible, with seventy-mile-per-hour winds howling down from the Rocky Mountains, snapping off branches from the aspen and cottonwood trees, which grew along the Colorado River and around Grand Junction.

"You ready for finals?" Sam asked as he gripped the baseball across the seams and let it fly. Jose didn't even move as the ball zipped in perfectly to the center of his catcher's mitt. He ignored his friend's question and nodded toward the girls' volleyball team practicing only twenty yards away.

"You ready to say yes to Tammy's invite to the winter formal?"

Sam felt himself flushing. He glanced over at the pretty freshman setter he had met in his Ecosystem Management class. Tammy was a friend, but he didn't feel comfortable going to a crowded college dance. He didn't know why. Life was just so much simpler being alone. He had responsibilities too. After talking on the phone with his father, who was at Bagram Air Base, two days earlier, he felt his focus needed to be on baseball and the family business, SJ Outfitters. Sam was now their top guide.

He accepted Jose's return throw and changed the subject. "Dude, I asked you a question. Are you ready for finals?"

Jose shrugged and gave Sam a low outside target. "I have Thanksgiving break to get ready."

"C'mon, man, you got a *C* on your English midterm. You better bring that up if you're gonna be eligible next semester."

"School ain't that easy for me, Sam Bam. You entered Mesa as a sophomore after flying through high school in all those advanced classes. Hell, I busted my ass to pass Phys-Ed."

Sam bit his lip to keep from laughing. "I said I'd help you if you minored in ALP."

"I'm not taking the Adventure Leadership Program." Jose groaned as he fired the ball back as hard as he could. "I'm not gonna kill myself doing Avalanche Assessment—that's crazy. Any course that has a class called Winter Leadership Intensive has to be miserable. No thanks."

"The wild wax currant we found on our hikes is delicious."

"Gross. I'm not gonna eat leaves off a bush."

"It's not bad. My mom makes a jam with the berries."

"Yeah, well cow-pie stew would probably taste good to a backwoods turd like you."

Sam finally did laugh. "Geez, if you wanna be a cop, you're gonna have to go through some tough times."

Their conversation ended when a blast of wind whipped through an open door. It was their baseball coach.

"Carson!" Frank Elba shouted across the hardwood floor. "There's a call for you in my office. It's your mom."

* * *

"How's Jenny?" Sam asked breathlessly when he reached the phone.

"She's fine," his mom said. "She's in her room, reading a book about Ute stone circles."

He gave a relieved sigh. "You called me out of practice to talk about rocks?"

"No." She laughed. "I wanted to know what time you'll be home?"

"Jose and I are almost finished with our workout. Then we'll shower and head home. I'm guessing the weather scared everybody off for tomorrow's final day of deer season?"

"All but one. The party that requested *you* as their guide."

"They must have read your endorsement of me in our SJ Outfitters pamphlet."

She laughed again. "That's why I'm calling. I tried to cancel, but they insisted on going."

"Then we'll go."

"These winds are gonna be with us for several days."

"Dad and I have been out in worse."

"These hunters will be disappointed when they come home with nothing, Sam. Deer can predict weather better than NASA. The strong winds will mess with their senses, so they'll hunker down away from trouble."

"I know."

"You still think you can find them?"

"Sure."

There was a long pause on the line. He sensed worry.

"C'mon, Mom. I'll be fine. These guys will probably be so worn down by the San Juan winds that they'll quit before sundown."

"All right. I better let you go so you can finish up and hit the road. Your party will be at our house at five tomorrow morning."

"Sounds good. Oh, Mom, what's the hunter's name?"

"Hang on." He heard her turning the pages of her scheduling book. "It's William . . . William Cutthredge."

* * *

Bitter cold wind and sleet stung Sam's face as he grabbed his backpack from the cab of his 1992 Nissan Truck STD and headed up the steps to his parents' house. It was already dark, but he could still see the silhouette of heavy, low-slung clouds in the northwest that forebode nastier weather was on the way. Tomorrow certainly would not be a good day to go hunting.

His mother was on the front porch, shawl pulled tight around her shoulders, bright smile lighting her face as she waited to hug her son.

He did, lifting her off the ground in a bear hug and then setting her down gently.

"Where's AJ? She's usually the first to greet me when I come home."

"She's in her room with Teresa, finishing up dialysis."

"So that's where Teresa is?" Sam put his arm around his mom and led her back inside the house. "Jose was bummed when I dropped him off and she wasn't swooning on the front steps, waiting for her man."

"She gets college credit for helping Jenny with her home dialysis."

He hung up his coat, walked down the hall, and knocked on Jenny's bedroom door. "AJ, you in there?"

A squeal of delight came from inside. "Sammy!"

He opened the door and forced a smile, a bit stunned by his sister's gray color and loss of weight. Still, he felt compelled to encourage her. "Hey, peanut! What's up in the book world? Harry Potter? Major League Baseball Prospectus? A Course in whatever it is you've been emailing me about?"

"Have you read it?"

"Not yet." He leaned over her to avoid getting tangled with all the wires and hoses from her dialysis machine and kissed her forehead. "I've been studying for finals."

He looked around the room that was littered with baseball and spiritual books. There was a book of quotations by Black Elk next to Ted Williams's *The Science of Hitting*, the Holy Bible was next to *Nolan Ryan's Pitcher's Bible*, and there was a *History of the Ute Tribe* resting against a Major League address book.

He winked at Teresa. "Has AJ been demanding you bring her every scouting report of pitchers from the twentieth century?"

Teresa laughed. "No, but she did send me to the post office to mail videos of you to every Major League team."

Sam rolled his eyes and looked back at his sister. "Would you please let me play just one game of college baseball?"

"You're going to dominate—" Jenny coughed, and then put her hand on her chest to catch her breath. "The Rocky Mountain Conference . . . has never seen . . . a pitcher like you."

"Sergio Romo was pretty good for Mesa last year, winning fourteen games, AJ."

"He doesn't have your command or focus."

Sam dropped his shoulders in complete surrender. "Geez, you're impossible."

Both girls laughed, and then Jenny reached down and disengaged her empty bag of dialysate. She had learned to do it herself, putting a bag of dialysate into her peritoneal cavity through a catheter so she could go to school and go about other daily activities. She fumbled with the exchange, but Teresa was quickly there to set it correctly.

"Andiamo!" Jenny clapped her hands and reached for her brother.

"Andi—what?" he gave a puzzled look and helped his sister out of bed.

"It's Italian for 'Let's go.' I'm taking an online Italian class."

"Of course you are. That's where I'm taking you as soon as we get that new kidney."

Teresa tapped him on the shoulder and brought her index finger up to her lips as if suggesting he not go there.

"Wait—" Jenny put her hand on her brother's shoulder to steady herself. "A little dizzy—I just got up too fast."

* * *

Susan scraped cherry tomatoes off her cutting board into the mixed green salad and leaned toward her son. "I call every day," she whispered and then glanced to the dining room where Jenny and Teresa sat waiting for dinner. "I've had no response from Dixon other than his secretary telling me he's been in contact with the Kidney Foundation."

"Give me the number," Sam whispered back, his jaws clenched in anger. "I want to remind him that he owes our family."

She didn't respond.

"Dad called me on Wednesday. He's mad at Dixon too. They had a deal. Track for DiamondBar in exchange for a transplant."

A numbing grayness seemed to paralyze Susan as she stood listening to her son continue to vent.

"Dad has emailed him several times, but he said that Dixon's replies are like worthless form letters, filled with promises and prayers, but no answers."

"That's enough, Samuel."

But Sam couldn't stop himself. "I googled Drake Dixon, Mom. The guy's a gazillionaire. He was born rich and then started a private military company that does security in Africa and Afghanistan. Believe me, Dixon has the power to move Jenny's case forward."

"Hey! We're hungry in here!" Jenny shouted from the dining room.

Startled, Susan whirled around and handed her son the salad bowl. "Please calm down," she said in a voice only Sam could hear. "Please—for Jenny's sake."

He gave an irritated nod, then forced the most convincing smile he could muster. "On the way, AJ!" he called out as he walked over and placed the entire salad bowl in front of his sister.

"Your Majesty," he said with a royal flair, then bowed dramatically before taking a seat next to her.

"You don't fool me. I know what you and Mom were talking about. Kidneys and transplants and promises and . . . dumb stuff." She scowled.

"It's not dumb stuff."

"It's my body. Maybe I don't want a damn transplant!"

"Jenny!" her mom scolded her. "We don't talk like that. Now, say grace and eat your dinner."

"Bless this food, amen," Jenny grumbled, and then turned back to Sam. "I've given this a lot of thought. I don't want to die when Western medicine says it's time for me to die. I want to go when the Great Spirit calls me home."

Sam's mouth fell open in shock.

"What do you think I discovered at the Sun Dance? I was hoping to find new strength, both spiritually and physically."

His eyes narrowed in confusion.

"I was depressed after the ceremony, Sammy. I—I thought my health would improve. But it didn't. It wasn't until I visited Teresa at Mercy Medical that I began to understand."

He didn't respond, only gave his sister a nod to explain.

"Teresa was busy, so I walked around the hospital until I came to the pediatric center. A nurse invited me into a room where she was comforting a baby boy who had been given up for adoption, and was waiting to be placed with his new parents. He was crying so much his whole face was swollen. The nurse placed him in my arms, and he immediately stopped crying. She later told me that it was the first time in days the boy seemed at peace."

Jenny paused, as if to collect her thoughts. "That night a bear came to me in my dreams. He told me that the Great Spirit created everything to serve. The sun serves life by giving warmth and light. The trees and plants give us food and oxygen. Storms serve us with rain to quench our thirst, and the buffalo, deer, and elk serve us with their meat for food and their bones to make tools. The bear told me I would help myself if I served others."

Tears came to Sam's eyes as he studied his sister. He knew she was right, but he was afraid. Afraid she was letting go, giving up, accepting her fate. Afraid that no kidney would be donated in time to save her life, a life that would keep their family whole.

"Jenny started a help-line at Mercy," their mother said. "She talks to children who are suffering from kidney disease and encourages them."

"She's really good," Teresa chimed in. "I overheard her talking with kids about not letting their bodies limit their minds, that there's a reality beyond what their body feels and their eyes see."

Sam sat there, mouth open in awe, trying to make sense of his little sister. Fourteen years old going on eighty. Was she indeed a medicine woman the elders spoke of, someone whose dreams were to be respected and trusted? He didn't realize he had been holding his breath until he let it out. "You're . . . amazing."

Jenny giggled, and then began to spoon the salad onto her plate. "I'm only slightly amazing. We shamans still have to eat."

Sam looked uncertainly from his sister to his mom, his mouth still open as if trying to figure it all out until a faint noise from outside snapped his eyes to the front window. Despite the howling of the wind and tree branches slapping against the roof, his keen sense of hearing caught tires on gravel coming up the drive.

"Who would be out on a night like this?" he said, then stood up and walked to the door.

Just as he stepped outside a black Ford F-150 came speeding up the drive, windshield wipers on high, swishing sleet away as the truck roared toward him, coming to a stop just inches from the front porch. A gust of wind crashed off the truck's hood, sending a spray of frozen pellets across Sam's face. As he wiped the ice from his cheek, the doors of the truck opened and out stepped two huge men.

"Shitty night to go hunting," the driver shouted through his thick beard. He hurried up the front steps.

Sam's face was carefully blank as he shook the man's hand. "My mom said you were going to be here at five tomorrow morning."

"But there's only one more day to legally hunt." The man chuckled. "We wanna get after Bambi ASAP. We got all-weather gear and plenty of ammo, so we figured, let's get after it."

"Mr. Cutthredge?"

"At yer service."

Sam looked the men over, taking in every detail of their appearance. Both were outdoorsmen, that he could tell: ruddy, weathered skin, reddened by the cold, and likely no strangers to a fight. He noticed a scar on Cutthredge, from jawbone to chin, while the other man's nose had obviously been broken several times.

"This is not good weather to track deer," Sam said in a voice that was more than a suggestion. "Their senses will be compromised, so they'll stay under cover."

Cutthredge snorted. "We heard you were the best tracker in these parts. Now, we arrive and find out a little rough weather scares you?"

Sam swallowed hard, but he didn't answer as his mom came through the door and glared at the two men.

"What are you doing here?" she said defiantly. "We agreed on a five a.m. departure."

"You must be Mrs. Carson!" Cutthredge extended his hand. "The lady who was singin' this boy's praises. We was just excited to get after it."

She shook his hand, but her eyes were anything but courteous. "And I said five a.m."

Cutthredge released her hand, reached into his coat pocket, and pulled out a roll of cash. He peeled off five one-hundred-dollar bills, stuffed them into Sam's shirt pocket, and winked back at Susan. "Is five hundred extra enough?"

"Please leave," she demanded and was about to say more until Sam grabbed her hand and nodded at Cutthredge.

"May I have a moment with my mom, sir?"

"Sure thing, dude," he peeled off another hundred-dollar bill and slid it into the pocket of Sam's shirt. "Nothin' I respect more than a boy takin' care of his family."

*　　*　　*

Sam pulled his mother inside and closed the door.

"Are you crazy, Mom? We're talking six-hundred-dollar bonus."

"I don't care. I don't like those men."

"I don't like all my teammates, either, but I get along with them."

"Your teammates aren't dangerous."

Sam inhaled deeply and placed his hands on his mom's shoulders. "I promise I'll be careful, but this is my job. This is what you and Dad trained me to do. And sometimes we take out hunters we wouldn't want to spend ten minutes with outside the workplace." He gave her shoulders an affectionate squeeze. "Plus, it's six hundred dollars."

Susan took a deep breath, glanced out at the two men on her porch, and then back at Sam. She sighed. "All right, but call me immediately if there's any trouble."

"I'll have you on speed-dial express, Mama." He then opened the door and waved for Cutthredge and Marcus to come inside. "Why don't you gentlemen warm up while I fetch my gear." Then Sam was gone, out the door, headed to the SJ Outfitters shed by the side of their house.

* * *

"What's that awesome smell?" Billy Cutthredge asked as soon as he closed the door.

"Butternut squash soup," said Susan stiffly, suddenly feeling very vulnerable with two rough men in her house and her son out of earshot.

"Hey, Mom!" Jenny called out. "Are you gonna join us for dinner?"

"That must be your daughter." Cutthredge smiled.

Susan hesitated for a moment, but there was really nothing else she could do, so she looked up at both men and asked, "Would you like something to eat?"

Disregarding her, Rob Marcus pulled off his wet jacket, hung it on the hook by the door, and moved past her, only to stop at the entrance of the dining room and stare at the young woman who was seated next to Jenny.

"Be still my heart," Marcus said in a voice dripping with interest. "I didn't know we'd be dining with cute little Pocahontas."

Teresa sat frozen, not sure what to say. Marcus pulled a chair up next to her and offered his hand. "Robert Beauregard Marcus, m'lady."

An uneasy tightness drew Teresa's shoulders together, but, out of respect, she shook his hand and forced a smile. "Teresa Songbird."

"Of course you are. A sweet song for my heart, little darlin'."

"Wow, you are one creepy dude," Jenny blurted out, a look of absolute disdain darkening her face. "Where do you get your pickup lines? Turds "R" Us?"

Marcus was taken aback by an attack from an obviously sick child and straightened up in his chair, but he did not let go of Teresa's hand.

Jenny placed one hand on her cheek as if she were a damsel is distress and looked up through fluttering eyelashes. "If you were a booger, Teresa, I'd pick you first. Blah, blah, blah."

Cutthredge let go a loud belly laugh at Jenny's wisecrack, which only infuriated Marcus more. He held firm to Teresa's hand.

"Back off, kid. I'm just havin' a li'l fun with your sister."

"She's not my sister. Unlike you, she's my friend."

Marcus glared at Jenny, who glared right back. A forty-three-year-old mercenary of war on three different continents trying to stare down a fourteen-year-old girl with failing kidneys. Jenny held his gaze icily, as if daring him to speak.

"You men ready?" said a voice behind them, low but firm. It was Sam, who had entered the dining room, tracking bag over his shoulder. His face was cool, dark brown eyes riveted on Marcus, whose glare remained focused on Jenny.

"Knock it off, Robbie." Cutthredge slapped his friend on the side. "Let's eat and go kill us some deer."

Finally, Marcus did let go of Teresa's hand, but he leaned in close and whispered something that seemed to send a chill up her spine.

"I'll get your dinner," Susan said in a tone that was more of an order than a suggestion. She pushed past both men to the kitchen. "I'll make it to go."

* * *

The wind was howling on the drive up to Pargin Mountain, trees and bushes a rabid whirl as the sleet pounded down on Billy Cutthredge's truck. Sam was driving, for only he knew the now icy trails and switchbacks that would take them up to his favorite hunting grounds. It was the sort of wild night that was bitter cold and empty, empty of any living thing along their path. There would be no hunters out in this weather, or deer or elk or even rabbit, for all would be seeking shelter from the type of storm that could kill.

They reached their destination by ten o'clock, on the edge of a forest of pinyons, junipers, and ponderosa pines. Sam had said nothing on the trip. He pulled the bill of his baseball cap lower as he opened the door and headed out into the storm. The winds were fiercer at the higher elevation, and the clouds were low. The truck's lights illuminated what would have been complete darkness.

"Get our gear out of the back," Cutthredge said as he leaned against the side of the truck. "Take 'em over to that dead tree for a wind break."

Sam did as he was told, hauling their packs up against a decaying ponderosa.

"You think this is dangerous?" Cutthredge asked.

"The safety of our clients is SJ Outfitters number-one responsibility," Sam answered.

"My buddy and I like it wild," Cutthredge said, his white teeth gleaming in the light of the truck's headlights. "It makes the kill that much more satisfying."

Sam didn't answer, his face calm, dark eyes giving no sign of recognition.

"You don't like us, do ya, kid?"

"It's not my job to like our clients," Sam said as he headed back to the truck to collect his own gear. "It's my job to track."

"And that's what we're paying you to do. Find us a big buck. Tomorrow. Five a.m. sharp." Marcus unzipped the side of his pack and pulled out a small tent. "Unfortunately for you, boy, this is only a two-man tent."

Sam threw his pack over his shoulder and reached into the cab of the truck. "In that case, gentlemen, I shall bid you good night." He then snapped off the lights, and like a ghost of the forest, disappeared into the pitch black of Pargin Mountain.

* * *

It was dark when Cutthredge and Marcus came out of their tent the next morning. The winds were still howling, but the sleet had let up, revealing a soft glow from the now-departing half moon. Cutthredge squinted toward his truck and reached for his knife. He was sure he saw something, something dangerous. It was his old Army instinct letting him know trouble was near, but as his eyes adjusted to the dim light, he saw, leaning against his truck, Sam Carson.

Cutthredge cleared his throat, perturbed by the disquiet he felt in the presence of this boy. "You . . . uh . . . ready for action, kid?"

Sam stood up and swept his day pack onto his shoulders.

Cutthredge turned back to Marcus. "I'll get our rifles and ammo. You pack the tent and bed rolls and throw 'em in the back of the truck."

Sam stood off to the side, a long stick dangling off the side of his pack.

"I love this time of day," Cutthredge said as he lowered the truck bed and reached for a long metal locker. "Wakin' up with the critters." He spun the combination lock and pulled open the top door. Inside were two AR-15 rifles. They were mainly used by the military, but lately were becoming more popular with hunters.

The side of Sam's mouth twitched, and Cutthredge felt his contempt. He watched Sam's eyes travel down the barrel to the cartridge and pistol-grip and noticed the tension of Sam's jaws as he watched him load the weapon. Billy felt a sense of power at Sam's revulsion.

"You don't approve of our choice of firearms?" he asked.

Very slowly, Sam's head rose up, and his eyes fixed on Cutthredge. "I believe in hunting to feed one's family—not destroying for pleasure."

* * *

They kept to the forest for the first mile, the pines heavy with sleet, helping to break the still-high winds that roared down the western slope of Pargin Mountain. Sam jogged slowly ahead, wooden stick in his right hand, stopping occasionally to study some track or marking in the now-dim sunrise. The temperature had dipped into the teens, but Sam seemed unaffected by the cold, almost indifferent when a shear of wind bit through the pines.

"What's that stick you keep poking with?" Marcus asked through a scarf that covered his face.

"Tracking stick," Sam said.

"What's it do?"

"Measures track." He held up the stick, pointing to the rubber bands fitted around the shaft. "I mark the lengths of footprints, the deer's stride, and the width of the feet."

"Where the hell you takin' us?" Marcus snorted with amusement. "Famous footwear for Bambi?"

Sam didn't answer. He stared down at the track for a long moment and then moved on through the trees.

"So are you locked onto our kill?" Cutthredge called after him.

Sam stopped and slowly turned back to Billy. "No," he said with cold formality. "That last track I saw was a buck that passed through about two days ago." He paused and looked directly at Cutthredge. "The only way this works is if we're quiet."

Billy gave an irritated nod, and the rest of the trip was in complete silence as they followed Sam for two more miles, until there was a break in the forest. The sun had now crested Pargin Mountain, a blinding light streaming directly at them, and seemed to calm the winds a bit. Sam jogged ahead casually as if every element he passed was telling him where to go. He stopped and went to one knee to study scat droppings and then continued on across a sleet-covered field.

His head was up, no need to study track, for he knew where the buck was going. He swept around a rock crag, through a stand of scrub oak, and circled back past a small bluff. The sun was behind them now, and as they rounded past a granite boulder, Sam nodded toward an open meadow.

There alone, enjoying the fresh mountain grass, was a spectacular twelve-point buck. Handsome and proud, casually munching away. with no worry in the world of any hunter invading his morning. For a moment, Cutthredge and Marcus stood frozen themselves, admiring God's brilliance, and then slowly their egos began to rise, demanding they take what they came for. The wind died as Cutthredge unslung his AR-15 and brought the stock up to his shoulder. He calmed his breath, closed one eye, and peered through the scope with the other, crosshairs on the buck's heart, when the wind picked up again. The buck raised its head, took a brief whiff, and then bolted toward the forest. Cutthredge aimed in haphazard pursuit, firing once, then twice, both shots missing their mark, until finally the stag was lost in the woods and gone.

"Dammit!" Cutthredge grumbled. "I had that sucker."

Sam smiled inside, his mission accomplished as he had purposely circled around the boulder to get upwind of the buck, giving the deer a chance to catch their scent. Despite the fierce winds, Sam tracked four more deer that day, all upwind, all with the same result: the deer catching their scent and bolting into the forest. As Sam had told them the night before, it wasn't his job to like his clients, it was only his job to track.

CHAPTER ELEVEN

Bagram Air Base, Afghanistan

March 2007

"Good things come in threes!" Army Colonel Bart Tomlinson said as he dropped three letters on the table in front of Daniel Carson. "I was at DiamondBar, visiting with your boss, when they had mail call."

Carson separated the letters in the order he always read them. "My wife and children."

Tomlinson sat down across from the DiamondBar tracker and watched him place his hands on the letters, close his eyes, and say a brief prayer.

Carson was different from the other members of the private security firm. It was as if he wanted no part of DiamondBar; he didn't hang out at their trailers, which were next to Bagram Air Base, or join his fellow security crew at Aziz's Cafe on Saturday nights. Instead, he always seemed to wind up at the Army Commissary, relaxing with Tomlinson's Special Forces team. They respected Carson, respected his instincts in the field, how he silently, almost invisibly, moved through the mountains without dislodging one single rock. For any sound, however small, could give away their position and bring the fury of the Taliban down upon them.

It was Tomlinson's duty to make sure everyone got along, but the tension between the military and private contractors remained: from the difference in pay to DiamondBar employees barreling through military areas without making radio contact or alerting US Forces. Things had improved a bit ever since DiamondBar CEO Drake Dixon removed Billy Cutthredge and Rob Marcus from Afghanistan, and Tomlinson noticed that Carson was also glad that they were gone. The Ute tracker had been furious when Cutthredge and Marcus ignored his reconnaissance and gave the okay to have the CIA launch Hellfire missiles at a target near the Pakistan border. Unfortunately, that decision cost the lives of ten innocent Afghans, but it also cost Cutthredge and Marcus their jobs with DiamondBar.

Now, as Tomlinson studied Carson, whose warm smile brightened as he opened the first letter, he thought the time was right to ask a question that had long been on his mind.

"Hey, Dan, why are you here?"

Daniel slowly looked up from his letter. "What do you mean?"

"Most contract men are here for the money or the adventure. What about you?"

"Insurance," Carson said.

Tomlinson raised both eyebrows and scratched his chin. "You came all the way to Afghanistan for insurance?"

"My daughter has a serious kidney disease. It's tough to get insurance for preexisting conditions when you operate a small hunting-and-fishing business. We needed insurance for hospital visits, treatment, dialysis, and hopefully, a transplant."

"I'm sorry."

Carson stared at his daughter's letter for a long moment. "She's a great girl. Despite missing a lot of school time, she still got straight A's and even started a help-line program to counsel other kids suffering with kidney disease."

"How did DiamondBar get involved?"

"I took their management team on a hunting expedition, and soon after, Dixon started recruiting me."

"Damn." The colonel flinched. "Drake Dixon? The man himself?"

Carson nodded, but there was a coldness behind his gaze.

Tomlinson had only met Dixon once and thought him to be a hustler, a man who preached about pride and patriotism, sacrifice and service, but likely the only one he served was himself. He decided to change the subject. "How's your family doing now?"

This time, Carson's eyes lit up, and he pointed to a third letter. "My son's a freshman at Mesa State in Colorado. Starting pitcher and outfielder on their baseball team."

"Starting as a freshman? That's pretty strong."

"He's a strike-thrower."

"My son plays baseball," the colonel said proudly. "He's only fifteen, but he made the junior varsity team at Blue Valley High in Kansas."

Carson cocked his head to the side. "Royals fan?"

"My entire life." Tomlinson grinned. "Although we haven't had much to cheer about the last few decades."

Carson tapped the letter with pride. "One of the Royals scouts was at my son's first game. Same guy who's been following him since his junior year in high school. I've never met him, but my wife says he's a great guy."

"Your son must be pretty good if pro scouts are after him."

Carson nodded, but his eyes seemed to dim, as if the conversation suddenly pained him.

Tomlinson decided it best to leave the man alone. "Well, I've got some paperwork to finish up. I'll let you get back to your family."

*   *   *

Daniel opened the first letter from his wife.

> *Good day, my sweet husband,*
>
> *I pray this letter finds you in good spirits. Our cold winter continues on Pargin Mountain. Another blizzard arrived yesterday with snow drifts all the way up to our front porch.*

Jenny keeps a shovel next to the front door and wakes up early, shoveling a path to the end of the drive, making it easier for me to drive her to school. I fought her the first four times to let me do it, but as you know, when Jenny makes up her mind . . . well . . . she makes up her mind.

She finishes exhausted, but happy, her cheeks bright red with a sense of accomplishment.

Because of the bad weather, I've only seen a few of Sam's games.

He's had a good start: 3-1 as a pitcher and hitting over .300 as the Mavericks left fielder on the days he doesn't pitch. Unfortunately, baseball has limited him to leading only two hunting parties this semester. The first was a team of insurance executives from Phoenix while the other was the same two men who booked Sam in November. I'm not crazy about them. They're rather crude, but they pay double and insist on having Sam lead them.

When I offered Joseph Blue Hill to track, they said no, they only wanted Sam.

Our son never complains, but I know he's not a fan of Mr. Cutthredge and Mr. Marcus.

Daniel didn't make it to the end of the letter. He stared down at the two names, as if the conscious part of his brain couldn't register what he was reading. He blinked once. Twice. Cutthredge and Marcus. Dear God, no. It couldn't be. That son of a bitch, Drake Dixon, was now stalking his son. He had to get to a phone. Right now. He had to call his wife and warn her. He had to—

The distant sound of sirens pierced the air, and then shouts and footsteps came from the other side of the commissary. The door opened. It was Colonel Tomlinson, out of breath.

"Taliban forces have opened fire on one of our PRTs north of Mihtarlam! Afghan police and DiamondBar Security are holding them off, but the road has been mined. We need you to find us another trail to support them."

Daniel stood up quickly and glanced about. With this new knowledge of Cutthredge and Marcus, the last thing he wanted to do was leave his letters at his DiamondBar facility.

There was an office mail sorter bolted to the opposite wall. He hurried over, found Tomlinson's slot, and tossed them inside. Then Carson was gone to get his gear at the DiamondBar Armory trailer and head to Tomlinson's waiting Black Hawk helicopters.

* * *

Colonel Tomlinson strapped himself into his seat and spread out the map of the Laghman Province in front of him. There were three UH-60 Black Hawks in the air, roaring to the east at 180 miles an hour over the Afghan valley. He couldn't see the enemy, but he knew, on that dry, rocky terrain below, there were people who wanted to kill him. They had been raised to hate. For almost two centuries, Afghanistan had been under siege from Russia, Great Britain, Pakistan, and America, leaving behind a parched land full of mines, death, and distrust of any outsiders.

Carson's chopper was to Tomlinson's right, four of his best Special Forces with him, armed to the teeth, ready to defend the man who would find a trail to where the Afghan police and Provincial Reconstruction Team were pinned down.

The Black Hawks veered right, into the steep, jagged, rough terrain, the road now in sight. Carson's chopper was in the lead, the tracker likely studying the stony mountain cliffs and crevasses for the best place to drop. His chopper swept low, to maybe fifty meters above the valley, speed down to sixty, ready to land, when suddenly a volley of flashes spit from a nearby cave. The first flash missed Carson's Black Hawk, but the second caught the back rotor, sending the chopper spinning to the ground, slamming sideways against the dust-colored rocks. Out of the cave came one more flash, heading directly at the downed Black Hawk.

CHAPTER TWELVE

Grand Junction, Colorado

March 2007

"Stee-rike three!" the umpire yelled.

Jose shook his fist before firing the ball back to the Mesa State freshman pitcher. Sam was totally locked in, his face a cool, expressionless calm, like a falcon, perched on the limb of a ponderosa pine, hunting its prey. Twenty-three up, twenty-three down. Seven and two-thirds innings. Seventy pitches. Perfection. The event had simply become an elevated game of catch between Sam and his catcher, as if the baseball knew exactly where it was supposed to go. Down and away. Cutting in. Rising. Late fade. As if on a string attached to the end of his right hand. Perfection.

Sam nodded and drew in a deep inhale as he raised his arms over his head, brought them back down, separated his hand from his glove, and let fly a two-seam fastball that barely touched the outside corner.

"Stee-rike!" barked the ump. The batter from Regis University shook his head in frustration.

Sam had tunnel vision, drawn only to Jose's sign for pitch and location, completely unaware that Mesa State's associate dean had entered the dugout to talk with the Mavericks baseball coach. But those on the bench saw Coach Elba's jaws tighten as he listened intently to what the associate dean had to say. Elba nodded out of courtesy, then his eyes flickered up to watch his pitcher throw a perfect slider for strike two.

The young man from Ignacio High was the best player Elba had ever recruited. After fifteen years of building a powerhouse in the Rocky Mountain Conference, Elba had finally found a player who could take the Mavericks all the way to an NCAA Division-2 title. A talented, competitive, focused, fearless, unselfish leader. Even though he was only a freshman, Sam Cloud-Carson was like a magnet with his teammates. They were drawn to him, drawn to his work ethic, drawn to his fire to compete, to play the game right, and his absolute loyalty to every Mesa State Maverick.

Yet there was also a sadness about Carson that concerned Elba. It was as if he cared too much . . . felt too much. There were times in the clubhouse when his fellow Mavericks would be laughing and teasing each other while Sam sat alone in the corner, a controlled smile on his face, distant, as if he was unable to surrender all of himself to joy.

And here they were, a darn good team, fourteen and three on the young season and about to sweep their first conference opponent. A jolt of guilt stung Coach Elba, his selfish thoughts of his first NCAA title now overshadowed by his concern for the boy on the mound.

Carson's next pitch was a changeup that had the Regis batter reaching, punching a soft grounder to third for the final out of the eighth inning. As Sam jogged off the field, he gave his third baseman a thankful pat on the back.

*　　*　　*

Sam sat down next to Jose and opened his notebook. Inside was his personal scouting report on every Regis player. Their strengths, their weaknesses, how he had pitched them the first two times through the order. He would be facing hitters seven, eight, and nine in the top of the ninth. Certainly not the Rangers' best hitters, but they had a bat in their hand, so they were dangerous.

"We threw Jameson a first-pitch fastball low and away first two times up," Sam said as he studied his book. "I was thinking of curve, but with a five-nothing lead, why show him a pitch he hasn't seen when we play 'em again in Denver next month?"

Jose said nothing. He stared through the chain-link fence.

"Jose, did you hear me?"

Still nothing.

"Jose . . . you're kind of my catcher. I'd like to discuss the last three outs."

"Scoreboard," Jose mumbled.

"Yeah, it says, five-nothing, bottom of the eighth–" Sam paused and turned to face his catcher with a grin. "Are you thinking of all the other zeros on the board?"

"Shut up, turd. You're gonna jinx it."

Sam chuckled and turned to his coach. "Hey, skip, I was thinking fastball away to start Jameson and then coming in hard with four-seam. What do you think?"

Elba nodded, his eyes distant, faraway, which confused Sam.

"All right." He looked back down at his notebook. "I guess I'll be like the Little Red Hen. I'll have to do it myself." He tapped Jose on the leg. "Ya might wanna take off your shin guards. You hit third this inning."

*   *   *

With just three outs to go for perfection, Sam's teammates treated him as if he had a disease. They stood at the opposite end of the dugout, occasionally glancing his way to study their pitcher. As soon as he would raise his head, they'd look away.

Mesa went three up, three down in the bottom of the eighth. Sam grabbed his glove and headed to the field. He was unafraid, no doubts or fears about pitching or not pitching a perfect game. His only job was to help his team win. And he liked being alone on the mound. He felt a union with the dirt, the pitching rubber, the wind, the temperature, every element that he would need to throw the next pitch. He felt the same way when tracking. He let the natural world guide him, visualizing in his mind where the animal came from, when it stopped, how long it paused, and where it would go next.

Out of habit, he drew his father's initials in the dirt, then sought the seams of the baseball and let loose his first warm-up throw. Eighty percent effort but one hundred percent focus. The warm-up was just as important as the game pitch. Jose never moved his glove as the baseball found its target nine straight times.

The crowd of just over two thousand at the beginning of the game had swelled to almost five thousand as word had spread at the student union and via the campus radio that the Mavericks freshmen pitcher was close to making school history. Fans were now lined along the chain-link fence from home plate to the end of both foul lines, cheering every strike and groaning at every ball.

Down by five runs, the first Regis batter took a first-pitch strike. Sam came back with a four-seamer on his hands and got him to pop up to short. Two outs to go.

The Regis coach called back his number-eight hitter and, in his place, sent up a pinch hitter. It was the same big, husky first baseman, from Burlington High, who homered off Sam to win the Colorado State Championship the year before.

Sam touched the bill of his cap as a salute to his old nemesis, who replied with a quick nod back and stepped into the box.

"You and me, big boy," Sam whispered to himself and then stared to get the sign from Jose. Fastball in. Same first pitch as the title game. Windup, delivery—

"Strike one!" yelled the ump.

The big hitter called time. He, too, remembered the sequence. Fastball in, followed by a changeup away. A slight smile lit the hitter's face as he stepped back in.

Jose wiggled four fingers, and Sam shook his head. The Regis hitter, confused by Sam's shake, called time again and stepped out. The slight smile faded to doubt as he glanced at Sam, who gave no tell. The hitter dug back in, took two practice swings, and readied himself for whatever may come.

Sam shook no again, then nodded with a smile, and let go a four-seam fastball up and in that had the Regis hitter bailing out of the box, his helmet flying off his head. The crowd "ooooed."

Next was the changeup for a swing and a miss, followed by a fastball in for a called strike three. The crowd screeched their delight and, sounding like a thousand jazz drummers skittering their brushes across a thousand cymbals, they shook the fence. But not one of his fellow Mavericks said a word as Sam was now one out away from perfection. His teammates pounded their mitts and tightened their laces to make sure no ground ball made it through the infield.

First pitch to the number-nine Regis hitter was a curveball, taken for strike one. The second was a fastball, swung on and missed. One strike away from perfection.

The crowd hushed, but the nerves at Mesa State field were deafening. For a split second, Sam thought about his family and wished they were here, sharing in this moment. Then just as quickly, the thought was gone, his attention again locked onto his catcher. He loved this. On his own. Free. Unrestricted. An ability to hyperfocus, where his body almost became separate from his mind. It was called Good Medicine in the Ute tribe. Good Medicine was a mystery, but it was also a sign that the natural world was allowing you to be part of something special, something magical.

He bent low at the waist and stared in to get the sign from Jose. His face calm while his deep brown eyes bore in on something beyond Jose's glove. It was the same look he had when he was closing in on a track. The absolute concentration. The heightened awareness. He was somewhere else, perhaps in that other world, as he nodded to his catcher's sign, reached into his glove for the baseball, his mind, body, and spirit all coming together in an almost ethereal windup as he let fly the white orb one last time. The ball came out of his hand effortlessly, straight for about fifty feet, then biting down at the end. The hitter had no chance as he swung futilely over the top of Sam's signature pitch.

Sinker. Strike three. Game over. Perfection.

The crowd erupted in delirious joy, and a slight grin finally began to crease across Sam's face. Jose gave a war whoop and tossed his mitt high in the air. He joined his teammates in racing to the mound to mob the Maverick who made Mesa State history. Good Medicine.

*   *   *

Hair tousled, uniform top untucked, dirt and grass stains on his pants from when his teammates knocked him to the ground in celebration, Sam walked off the field, a Cheshire grin lighting his face and Jose's arm around his broad shoulders.

"Sam Carson"—Jose brought his hand up to Sam's mouth as if he was holding an imaginary microphone—"you just threw a perfect game! What are ya goin' to do now?"

Sam laughed and shook his head.

"You're supposed to say, 'I'm going to Disneyland!'" Jose shoved his friend toward the dugout.

"You're crazy, dude." Sam chuckled. "The only thing that matters is we're three and oh. First place in the Rocky Mountain."

"Enjoy the moment, Sam Bam! You're a rock star today!"

Coach Elba and the assistant dean were waiting for them in the dugout. Both wore proud smiles, but their joy seemed a bit forced.

Elba gave him a warm hug and whispered in his ear, "That's the best pitching performance I've ever seen. We're absolutely blessed to have you on our team."

"Thank you, sir." Sam sensed discomfort in his coach and wasn't sure why. He extended a hand to the assistant dean. "Thanks for your support, sir."

"Brilliant performance, young man. Just brilliant."

Elba put his arm around Sam. "I want you to come to my office. You need to call your mom."

Sam's head jerked up. "Jenny?"

"No." A tremor ran down Elba's throat as he tried to swallow. "Jenny's fine."

CHAPTER THIRTEEN

Southern Virginia

March 2007

A cold March rain pounded down from the early evening sky as Drake Dixon opened his umbrella, stepped out of his black limo, and ran up the steps to his DiamondBar office. The front door opened, and his lawyer waved for him to hurry.

Dixon arrived out of breath. "What have you heard?"

Barry King took Dixon's umbrella and shook the rain off. "Every damn liberal in town is blaming you for the tragedy. Not enough security for the Afghan police, who were defending the road, not enough cover for the Special Forces chopper, and all after our DiamondBar guys declared the road safe."

"How were we supposed to know they had a rocket launcher inside a cave?" Dixon followed his lawyer through the lobby, up a flight of steps, and down the hall to a private conference room. DiamondBar's top public-relations man, Archie Newton, was the only man in the room and immediately stood up in front of a dry-erase board.

"Ready to go to work, sir?"

"This is why I pay you the big bucks, Arch." Dixon clapped his hands and sat down. "How do you want to handle it?"

Newton pointed to the first line under the heading *As DiamondBar Security goes, so goes America*. "Get out in front of the critics. Talk about how tough it is in Afghanistan. Let 'em know that, if not for DiamondBar, they could have lost twice as many soldiers in this tragedy."

Dixon smoothed an errant strand of his jet-black hair away from his eyes and winked at Newton to continue to work his magic.

"I think you should tell America what they want to hear." Newton pointed to the second line. "Tell them that, because of DiamondBar, the Taliban has less control of Afghanistan. Tell them that, because of your company's security, more Afghan girls are being educated than ever before and that fewer women are dying in childbirth."

Dixon cleared his throat. "Is there any truth to those statements?"

"The truth isn't important, Drake. The only thing that matters is getting people to believe what we tell them is the truth."

"What do the polls say?"

"Not as bad as we thought. Sixty percent want us to get out of Afghanistan, and thirty percent want us to blow it to hell and turn it into a parking lot."

Dixon leaned back in his chair and clasped his hands behind his head. "Good stuff, boys. We might be able to get out of this with just a slap on the wrist."

Newton raised his hand tentatively. "If you really want to shine a positive light on this, Drake, I think there's something you need to do."

Dixon cocked his head to the side.

"I think it would be great PR if you went to Carson's funeral this weekend. His body's on the way back to Colorado. It'll look good if you're seen comforting the family, offering your condolences, perhaps speaking at the ceremony."

The side of Dixon's mouth twitched slightly. The last thing he wanted to do was attend the Carson funeral, but Newton's plan was pretty smart. Great photo-op, children by his side, a grieving widow crying on his shoulder. It could be a real tearjerker to pull at the heartstrings of America.

"I can quietly let the press know that you'll be attending," Newton said. "It's important the nation see what a caring, compassionate leader you truly are."

CHAPTER FOURTEEN

Pargin Mountain, Colorado

March 2007

Jenny wiped a tear from her cheek as she watched her brother lift their father's body onto the back of the painted horse. Sam's jaw was set, his face browned from hours on a baseball field, yet gaunt, as if hiding the pain he kept inside. He stood alone, holding the buffalo robe that cloaked their father's burned corpse. The horse jerked forward, but Sam held firm, following alongside. Jenny could feel her brother's suffering, could hear the raggedness of his breathing as he led the family to Ouray Memorial Cemetery. She glanced up at their mother, head bowed, eyes swollen from a week of grieving, and touched her arm. Jenny wanted to say something, offer some form of comfort, but instead she clamped her lips tight.

There was a fine crowd offering support, not only from their tribe, but also from neighboring towns, whose hunters and fly-fishing enthusiasts had been taught by Daniel Carson. The sun was high, and as the funeral procession moved forward, the ceremonial colors shimmered off the waters of the Los Pinos River.

Susan screamed, a haunting, strangled sound of a widow's desperate grief. She fell against the side of the painted pony, sobbing uncontrollably as Sam finally let go of his father's robe and gently stroked his mother's back.

Jenny stood behind but shed no tears. It was as if she were watching the scene from outside her body, her mind somewhere else, searching for words of understanding from the ancients, from her father, or perhaps from the truth that connected all humanity. As she raised her vision, she thought of the old Ute story, of Father Sky, who created the sun, moon, stars, and Earth; and of Mother Earth, who asked only for reverence and respect. Jenny knew their answers were sometimes gentle—and sometimes severe.

As the funeral column continued on toward the cemetery, Jenny looked up to see two television news vans parked in front of the entrance, one from a Durango station and the other from Denver. Photographers were busy setting up, and a writer from the *Durango Herald* was visiting with a man in a tailored black suit.

"Mama?" The word was barely out of her mouth when she saw her mother straighten up and glare at the man in the black suit. Susan turned away, as if pretending he wasn't there.

"Mrs. Carson!" Drake Dixon called out as the procession turned into the Ouray Cemetery. "I'm so sorry for your loss." He hurried over and put a hand on her shoulder.

"Don't touch me," she said in a hushed tone and continued on through the gate.

For a moment Dixon froze, but then he glanced back at the cameras recording his every move.

"Please, Mrs. Carson," he said again, his voice softening in an attempt at compassion. "I want you know that we did everything we could to save your husband."

Sam dropped the horse's reins and started back toward Dixon, fists clenched.

Jenny stepped between the two men, one hand on her brother's chest, the other on Dixon's. "Please go," she said to Dixon, striving to remain courteous. "This is a private ceremony. You are not welcome here."

* * *

The country rock band's rendition of The Allman Brothers' "Ramblin' Man" was beginning to annoy Dixon. He fired down the last of his scotch and motioned for Cutthredge and Marcus to join him at a back booth in Durango's Club Finale.

"Talk about an ungrateful bitch." Dixon's voice was sharp with agitation as he sat down. "I flew all the way from DC to Denver on a red-eye, rented a car, and drove like hell to make it to the funeral, only to be told I wasn't welcome."

Cutthredge gave a bored nod and wisely poured his boss another glass of the bar's finest whiskey.

"Then the media grilled me about why the family wouldn't let me be part of the ceremony. Unless they believe my side of the story, this could be a PR disaster." Dixon seethed.

"You're a smooth talker, Drake. I'm sure that PR firm you hired will spin it to make it sound like you're the grieving widow."

"They'd better, Billy. The last thing we need is for the liberal media to say I'm some jerk who doesn't care about his employees."

Cutthredge looked over at Marcus, who rolled his eyes, but kept his mouth shut.

"Everything was fine until that sick kid interrupted the conversation I was about to have with her brother. His dad was a damn good tracker, but the boy's better. Everybody I've sent to check him out says he's the best tracker they've ever seen."

"Overrated, if you ask me," said Marcus. "Dude took us out three times, and we bagged nothing."

Dixon's thin lips curved upward in a condescending smile. "The kid worked you, Rob."

"What are you talking about?"

"Billy told me what happened. He said Carson tracked you plenty of deer, but they all ran off." Dixon chuckled. "It took me a while to figure out what he did."

Marcus raised one curious brow.

"He took you upwind of the deer. He made sure they caught your scent."

Marcus's expression changed from one of curiosity to a look of fury.

"I told you he was good, but what the hell did you do to piss him off? I didn't have any trouble with any of the other hunting parties I sent to test him."

"Robbie hit on a cute friend of Carson's," Cutthredge said.

"Dammit, Rob! What did I tell you after Sierra Leone? You're gonna ruin everything if you keep chasing after girls half your age."

Marcus glared over the rim of his glass but said nothing.

"I'm serious. This is a big year for me. I'm gaining power in Washington."

"But you just buried your project," Cutthredge said. "Who's gonna replace Carson?"

"I'm working on it. We're training some men at our Virginia complex."

Cutthredge gave his boss a look of doubt. "You found guys who don't mind being *alone* in the Afghan mountains?"

"No," Dixon replied reluctantly. "I'm training teams of five or six men to do the job."

"Who won't be seen by the locals?" Cutthredge snorted. "Good luck with that."

"It has to work, Billy. More and more politicians think private military companies are the future of war. The ratio of contractors to troops in war zones is increasing every year. I'm just tapping into the DC money train."

"How are you selling it?"

"With the same thing that won the West." The side of Dixon's mouth twisted into an evil grin. "Good old-fashioned fear. Tell our citizens to be afraid. That only we can save them from the bogeyman who lurks behind every tree. Back then, we told 'em to be afraid of the red man. Today, it's the Taliban or Communists or anyone else who gets in our way." Dixon tossed down the rest of his whiskey and winked. "Governing doesn't matter, boys. The only thing that matters is winning."

*   *   *

After five days of round-the-clock visitors, the Carson home was finally quiet. Yet the sudden calm only seemed to amplify every sound in the house: the ticking of the wall clock, the crackling of the last embers in the fireplace, and the humming of the kidney-dialysis machine, all reminders that everything in life would eventually end.

Jenny opened the refrigerator and stared. It was bursting with expressions of Tupperware kindness from the Ignacio community and beyond. The shelves were stacked with venison-and-buffalo chili, fish casseroles, Southern Ute posole, beans, squash, corn, and pumpkin pies. *All this food and no appetite.* She couldn't remember the last time her family had eaten. Her mother had constantly busied herself making sure everyone else was taken care of. Now, all of them were gone.

Jenny closed the door and turned to see her mother by the dining room table, head down, eyes locked on the Durango newspaper someone had senselessly left for the Carsons.

Why did they have to show it to us now?

It was a story about the funeral, a tribute to her father, but it only included quotes from Drake Dixon after her mother and brother declined to talk with the press. It was all Dixon saying how blessed he was to know Daniel Carson, a man who had served his country admirably and died trying to save others. Dixon told the media how he had discovered Carson on a simple hunting trip, had personally experienced his brilliance, and how he had helped him become the greatest tracker he had ever known. He said he had broken down in tears when he had learned of Daniel's death, and that he had come to Ignacio as quickly as he could to support the grieving family. He completely understood the Carson's request for privacy at the funeral. Of course, Dixon then told them of his tireless effort to find Jenny Carson a healthy kidney and of his generous donation to the Kidney Foundation in Daniel Carson's name.

What a load of crap, Jenny thought. *He's using my lousy health and my father's death to promote himself. Geez, how disgustingly low would this creep go to make himself the hero?*

Sam came through the front door, his arms loaded with wood to stoke life back into the fire. The temperature had dropped twenty degrees since the funeral, and the March winds were again howling down Pargin Mountain, but the cold didn't seem to bother Sam, who was only wearing a cotton T-shirt.

"You need to eat," he said to his mother.

She didn't respond.

"Please, Mom."

Nothing.

Jenny watched as if detached from her mother and brother, observing their misery, their torture. They seemed to dread these moments when the house was empty, and they would be forced to look at each other's agony. The same heavy grayness was inside Jenny as well, but it was claustrophobic. She had to leave the room, to get away from the suffocating sadness. In that instant her father's voice came to her. Old words from when she was a child and had asked him about the differences in people.

"We're all the same. We all come from the same God, yet not all of us accept our purpose here. It's as if we are waiting for the dream to end and finally wake up. We are spiritual beings having a human experience, and until we grasp that truth, there will be difficulty among the people. But the Great Spirit is within all, making harmony a very real possibility."

Jenny closed the door to her room and stood alone, listening to the incessant hum of the dialysis machine. It was getting ready to beep, to let her know that the time was now for the artificial kidney to clear wastes and extra fluid from her blood. Her mother and Teresa were her home-care attendants, but she didn't want to bother her mom. Not now. She could do it herself. She lifted her blouse and cleaned the area around the catheter near her belly button. Next, she connected the catheter to the bag of dialysis solution, prepared the cycler, placed the drain tube in its proper slot, sat back on her bed, and turned on the machine.

With nothing to do for the next few hours, she placed her hands in her lap, palms turned upward, closed her eyes, and inhaled a deep breath. She imagined the cleansing air as a spoon scraping any negative thoughts or cells out of her mind, her neck, her shoulders, her lungs, her stomach, and finally her kidneys. As she exhaled, she let it all go. Everything . . . all the pain that ravaged her body, along with the grief she had suffered since learning of her father's death. She inhaled and exhaled another long breath until she was finally gone. Gone, somewhere else.

The first time it had happened she was only four, sitting in the rocking chair on their front porch, staring up at a ponderosa pine swaying in the mountain winds. Visions of the past came to her that day; some were beautiful, of children laughing, fishing, playing games. There were terrible visions as well, of disease and death, of a line of people walking with heads down through a field of dead buffalo, stripped of their hides, the prairie a bright crimson from the slaughter.

Jenny had awakened in tears, wanting to rid herself of the vision, pleading for the Great Spirit to take the images away. They stopped, for perhaps a year, but then they returned in her night dreams as if to tell her she was needed to bring a new message. A message of hope, a calm voice for love in a world of chaos and fear. The dreams reminded her that kindness would be her conviction, gentleness would be her strength, and service would be her way.

Now, those voices came floating back into her consciousness. Her father was among them. It was as if he and all the ancients were speaking directly to her. She heard Chief Seattle: *Dead, did I say? There is no death, only a change of worlds.*

She heard Black Elk: *And I say the sacred hoop of my people was one of many hoops that made one circle, wide as daylight and starlight, and in the center grew one mighty flowering tree to shelter all the children of one mother and one father.*

She heard Mammedaty: *You see, I stand in good relation to all that is beautiful. You see, I stand in good relation to you. You see, I am alive.*

She heard her father: *It's as if you are waiting for the dream to end and to finally wake up.*

Jenny was lost in the dream, her face blank, her forehead serene. Her heart rate had slowed to barely a whisper. *There is no death, only a change of worlds. One circle, wide as daylight and starlight. You see, I am alive.* She felt a hand brush hair from her face, fingers on her wrist. Then a cry of anguish. Her eyes flickered open. Her mother and brother stood over her, frantic with fear, her mother's hand on her forehead, her brother's fingers seeking her pulse.

"What's wrong?" Jenny asked, and her mother collapsed by her side in relief.

"You set the dialysis machine incorrectly. It started beeping. We thought you had . . ."

"I'm fine, Mom." Jenny shrugged. "I was just meditating."

"But you were careless with the clamps," Sam said, his eyes dark with worry. He let go of her wrist with more than a hint of disappointment. "You didn't completely seal the catheter again, and it started leaking."

"I said I'm fine."

He drew in a deep breath, as though to reply, then let it out again, shaking his head and muttering something under his breath.

Jenny looked at both her mother and brother. They looked older. Their skin was brown, but there were harsh lines of exhaustion about their mouths and eyes. She wanted to say something, anything, to snap them out of their misery.

"Dad spoke to me," she finally said, and her mother inhaled a startled gasp.

"He said that we needed to wake up from the dream that we created and know that the Great Spirit is within all of us—that harmony is a very real possibility."

Her mother stared at her for a long moment, mouth still open, but the pain seemed to lift from her eyes. "That does sound like something he would say." She smiled for the first time since hearing of her husband's death. "He always sought the good in everyone."

Sam stood off to the side, head bowed, hands gripping the handle on the dialysis machine, a look of confusion etched on his face, as if not understanding the release that Jenny and her mom were now feeling.

"Will you look at this?" Jenny blurted out as she flipped open her cellphone. "Twenty-three texts. Almost all of them from kids at my Kidney Bean Help-Line." Her finger scrolled through the numbers. "This one's from a ten-year-old girl in Morristown, New Jersey, who just started dialysis. And this one's from a twenty-two-year-old senior at Dine College in Tsaile, Arizona, who I've been talking with about the best diets for people with kidney disease." She paused and glanced up at her brother. "Here's one from Jose. He said you haven't been answering your phone, so he texted me. He wanted to make sure we were all right and to tell us the team has been praying for us."

"I'll have Sam take a thank you note to Coach Elba for sending us flowers," Susan said.

"I'm not going back," Sam responded, his face grim, hands still gripping the handle of the dialysis machine. "I'm needed here—with our family"

"You'll return tomorrow," his mother said firmly. "We all have jobs to do, and yours is to get your degree and be a loyal teammate."

"But we don't have Dad's money coming in anymore, and with you taking the second job at the hospital, Jenny will need my help."

"I don't need your help. I can take care of myself."

"Like you just did when you put the clamps on incorrectly?"

"Stop it!" Susan snapped her hand against her leg and turned to face Sam. Her eyes were moist with tears. "I said you will go back to school tomorrow. I want you there, and your teammates are counting on you."

Jenny muttered something under her breath that Sam didn't hear.

"What did you say?"

Jenny raised her vision and looked directly at her brother. "I said baseball doesn't need you. *You* need baseball."

CHAPTER FIFTEEN

Grand Junction, Colorado

April 2007

It had been a rough two weeks for Sam when he finally returned to Mesa State. There had been a thousand awkward moments: "I'm so sorry for your loss; Is there anything I can do for you?; I'll keep your family in my prayers." *But where was God in all this? Was his father,* as one of his teammates had said, *in a better place? Was he at peace? If so, what made him so sure?*

Sam believed in God, even thought he felt the Great Spirit's presence when he was in the mountains; he was grateful for the beauty of the forests, the lakes, streams, and creatures who inhabited them. Yet for all of it, there would be an ending. The mountains and streams would eventually erode, the forests would burn or decay, and predators or age would end the lives of all creatures. He tried not to feel his father's death, didn't even want to talk about him with others, and was thankful that he had a friend like Jose, who knew when to talk but also knew when to shut up.

Being back on campus had been two weeks of strained conversations, two weeks of "I'm sorrys," two weeks of anguish. So he did what he had always done with his sadness. Suppress it. Retreat into himself. Push the pain to some back corner of his mind and deal with it later.

It wasn't until the fourth inning of a game against Colorado Christian when the gray cloud of grief finally began to lift. After three innings of struggling to get comfortable with the mound—his breathing, his balance, his delivery—it suddenly clicked in. It wasn't any one thing he did; it was something he didn't do. He didn't think.

He had been distracted while warming up in the bullpen as images of his father, of the funeral, of Jenny flew through his mind. Consequently, he gave up four runs on six hits and two walks in the first three innings. Two walks! He never walked anybody. Yet here he was, constantly 2-0 and 3-1 in the count. He had always felt his strength wasn't his velocity or movement. It was his ability to absolutely block everything out. He could twist some internal dial, similar to the way a microscope worked, that would bring together every part of his mind, body, and spirit to throw the baseball exactly where it needed to go.

He had been in trouble, two on, two out, in the fourth inning. Coach Elba had a left-hander warming up in the bullpen. Sam threw a fastball on the inside corner to a Cougar batter that he thought was strike three, but the ump called it a ball. Three and two. But, instead of showing any negative body language, he just stepped off the mound.

It was a natural movement, something he had done countless times in the past, but the step-off seemed to get him back into a rhythm as he took a deep breath and exhaled very slowly. Perhaps he was releasing more than just his breath. Every other thought except executing the next pitch left his mind. The fans in the stands began to blur into a myriad of colors, and their chatter became white noise as the internal microscope lens began to twist inside Sam, to a tunnel of intense focus on Jose's glove.

He stepped back on the rubber, bent forward to get the sign, nodded, and went into his old instinctive, loose, organic delivery that sliced a curve on the outside corner. The sharp break completely locked up the Colorado Christian hitter, who started back to the dugout even before the ump called strike three. A soft smile lit Sam's face as he walked off the mound. Damn. His sister had been right. Baseball didn't need him. He needed baseball. Yes, indeed.

The Mavericks won that chilly April afternoon in Lakewood, Colorado, 6-5. It was the day Sam rediscovered his groove; his two-seamer once again had that late sink, his slider and curve hissed as they spun home, and his change looked like it was falling off the end of a table.

A perfect fifth inning with two strikeouts finished his afternoon, but more importantly, his teammates were smiling again. Their freshman ace was back. After losing six of their last seven, a renewed optimism permeated the team bus as the Mavericks headed home.

CHAPTER SIXTEEN

Grand Junction, Colorado

May 2007

"Let's go, Mavericks!" *Clap, clap–clap, clap, clap.* "Let's go, Mavericks!" Jenny squealed from the seventh row of the bleachers at Suplizio Baseball Field in Grand Junction, Colorado. The sky was a bright blue with soft, thin clouds barely touching the tops of Capitol Peak beyond left field. There was still a crest of snow atop the mountains, but the black tern and bluebirds were busy announcing that summer was just around the corner.

It was the first round of the Rocky Mountain Conference Tournament. Mesa State had fought back from seventh place to win eight of their last ten games and grab the third seed in the postseason tourney. The Mavericks would face the number-four seed, CSU-Pueblo. Despite his freshman status, Sam would pitch game one.

"Well, look who's back, trying to steal my job?" Roberto Francisco grinned as he walked up the aisle of the stadium steps toward Jenny and Susan Carson. It was the first time the Royals scout had seen the family in almost two months, and he reached out to shake Susan's hand.

"I'm very sorry for your loss, Mrs. Carson. Your family has been in my prayers."

"Thank you for the flowers," Susan said and then inhaled a deep breath. "That was very kind of you."

Jenny saw her mother's lower lip begin to quiver and was determined to change the subject.

"It's nice to see you again, Mr. Francisco, but it's hard to believe there were fifteen hundred players in last year's draft who were better than my brother."

The Royals scout bit his lip to keep from laughing. "You are correct, Ms. Jenny. But our management team believed you and your client were determined to go to college."

"You could have at least made him a token offer with one of your last five selections. I mean, will any of your forty-six through fifty round picks make it past A-ball?"

Francisco snorted a laugh and motioned to a seat next to Jenny. "May I join you?"

"Please do"—Jenny slid closer to her mom—"because you have some explaining to do."

He sat down and took off his sunglasses. "We discussed your brother at our draft headquarters, but there was a consensus that his agent would be tough to deal with."

That got all the scouts surrounding them chuckling. But not Jenny.

"Don't treat me like a little girl. I know what my brother's worth, and you obviously didn't do a good job of scouting the intangibles."

Susan put her hand on Jenny's arm to quiet her, but her daughter was on a roll.

"If Sam threw ninety-five, you would have drafted him, but noooo, all you scouts are addicted to your radar guns."

A Giants scout in row five winked back at Francisco. "That girl's throwing you some high heat early in the day, Roberto. Better back off the plate."

The comment drew more laughter from both scouts and fans seated close by, including Susan, who was now stifling her own snickering laugh.

Their reaction only fueled Jenny's wrath. "It's true. You drafted that BDH in round seven. Sure, he threw ninety-nine, but then he blew out his arm only four weeks into his first pro season."

Francisco's brows came together as if puzzled by her statement. "B . . . D . . . H?"

"Brain. Dead. Heaver," Jenny said defiantly, and the entire section exploded in laughter.

Their silly conversation quieted when the public-address announcer asked everyone to stand for the playing of the national anthem. As soon as the young woman in the tight white jeans finished singing, the Royals scout leaned close to Jenny and whispered, "You're a very strong young lady. I admire the way you protect your mom and brother."

It was a comment Jenny was not expecting, and she swallowed hard to calm the emotions that suddenly welled up in her. She was fine when the subject was about someone else, about anyone else, for her entire life had been surrounded by the oversympathetic: her parents, her brother, doctors, kidney specialists, teachers, and coaches, hovering over her as if every ache or back pain was some sign of death. Sure, she wasn't happy about having a crappy kidney that coughed and sputtered like some old broken-down furnace, and she would have given anything to be like the other kids . . . but she was not. She had accepted her fate, had even accepted death, which no longer scared her. But to have the spotlight of compassion suddenly shine on her? No thank you.

"So . . . you'll draft Sam?" she asked softly, attempting again to change the subject.

Francisco scratched his chin reflectively, and then said in a voice that only she could hear, "What's special about your brother?"

She paused for a long moment, and then as the Mesa State team broke from the dugout to prepare for the top of the first inning, she watched her brother jog out to the mound.

"Are you a man of faith, Mr. Francisco?"

He sat up straight. "Why, yes, yes, I am. Even though I'm on the road a lot, I'll find a church to sit down and pray. Sometimes it's one of those mega churches you see on TV, and other times it's just a little one-room chapel in some small town."

Jenny stared at her brother as he threw his first warm-up pitch, a smooth, effortless delivery as inherent as breathing in and breathing out. She pointed to the field. "You see that mound?"

Francisco nodded.

She then pointed to the Rocky Mountains far off beyond left field. "And those mountains?"

He nodded again.

"Those are my brother's churches. That's where *he* feels closest to God. I know people who are afraid of being alone in the wild, and I've seen pitchers who are afraid of being alone on that mound. But not Sam. He may have other doubts and fears, but never on the mound or in the mountains. That's where he's most comfortable. That's where he unites with his higher power."

Francisco turned to face her. "What about you, Ms. Jenny. Where's your church?"

A bright smile began to light her face as she spread her arms wide. "Here. There. Everywhere. Because of my illness, I have limitations. I can't do things my brother does, so I've made wherever I am a holy place. If it's in a bed at the dialysis center, or sitting on the front porch of our house, or watching my brother pitch here in Grand Junction, that becomes my holy place. My church is anywhere and everywhere." She cocked her head to the side and looked directly into the Royals scout's eyes. "Now, back to my original question. When my brother graduates, are you going to draft him?"

Francisco laughed out loud and put his arm around Jenny. "I'd not only tell my general manager to draft your brother, but I'd tell him to hire *you* to inspire the team!"

* * *

Sam pitched a perfect first inning, needing only eight pitches to get three outs. Two groundouts on fastballs and a pop up to the CSU-Pueblo number-three hitter.

"Pretty efficient, huh?" Jenny said to the Royals scout as she marked a P-3 in her homemade scorebook and then listed the pitches that Sam threw underneath.

Francisco showed her the gun reading on the last pitch at seventy-nine and raised an eyebrow.

"That change had a ten-mile-an-hour separation from his fastball. That's what you guys are looking for, right?"

He leaned forward toward the Rockies scout, "Hey, Carl, what's the best ya got Carson that inning?"

"Eighty-seven," came the reply.

"I'll bet all of 'em were two-seamers," Jenny said as she showed Francisco her book that displayed seven fastballs and one changeup.

"She's right." The Rockies scout winked back at them.

"Sam won't bring his four-seamer or slider into the mix until they show him they can hit his number one and number two." Jenny gave the scouts a serious, general manager look as she tapped her scorebook. "No need to get his pitch count up if he's goin' for a CG."

Francisco bit the side of his mouth and glanced over at Jenny's mom, whose hand covered her mouth as if to keep from laughing. "So you're letting your brother go nine today?"

"If he keeps his pitch count under a hundred, I am."

Shoulders silently shook in the rows in front of them as no scout wanted this little girl to shut up. Jenny had become the entire section's entertainment for the afternoon as she continued to give her scouting report not only on her brother, but for every hitter who stepped to the plate, talking about their strengths, their weaknesses, and of course, how her brother would, or should, get them out.

Sam did his part, stifling the CSU-Pueblo offense for a nine-inning five-two victory that day, needing only ninety-seven pitches for his CG. When the game ended, Jenny stood up and stretched.

"Hey, Mr. Carl," she called out to the Rockies scout. "What'd ya get Sam's four-seamer that last inning?"

"Got one at ninety and another at ninety-one, Ms. Jenny."

"Did I tell you scouts that my brother just turned nineteen in April?" She inhaled a deep, thoughtful breath. "Just thought you should know that there's a lot more 'velo' in that right arm."

The scouts could take it no longer and, for the second time that day, exploded in laughter.

*　　*　　*

As they headed down the steps of Suplizio Stadium, the Royals scout nodded to Susan Carson. "May I buy the two of you dinner? I hear they have a good eggplant parmesan at Pantuso's."

Susan smiled. "That's very kind of you, but Jenny has a dialysis treatment scheduled at Kidney Care in one hour."

Francisco paused at the bottom step as if searching for the right words to respond.

Jenny saw his discomfort and immediately went into her best zombie impression, head slumped over, arms draped at her sides, dragging one foot behind the other like the walking dead.

"Not enough red blood cells to carry oxygen to brain and muscles . . . must get dialysis . . . must move fluids through body . . . Arrrgghhh."

Her mother rolled her eyes and glanced over at Francisco. "She's like this twenty-four seven. Serious when it comes to defending her brother, but a complete looney tune when it comes to taking care of herself."

*　　*　　*

They had just started dialysis when Sam arrived, carrying two huge bags for dinner.

He's probably gone to every health food store in Grand Junction for me, thought Jenny as she gave her brother a quick kiss on the cheek and then opened the first bag.

"Grilled cauliflower–yum." She dug deeper in the bag. "Bell peppers, shiitake mushrooms, onions. Oooh, what do we have here? Skinless chicken—double yum." She dug to the bottom. "Where are the Shiitake Snickers?"

Sam laughed. "No sweets for you, AJ. The doc says sugar's inflammatorily wicked."

"Yeah, yeah, yeah—no phosphorous or potassium, which means no pretzels, chips, crackers, soda, or Snickers. All stuff normal kids eat." She pushed the bag to the side. "I'm not hungry."

Then he gave her that look. That anxious look of fear that something was wrong with his kidney-diseased sister. *Oh God, she's not hungry, there must be something desperately wrong!*

Jenny exhaled and pushed the bag toward her brother. "I don't feel like eating right now. Why don't you guys dig in, and I'll eat when my treatment is over."

He sat down on the edge of the bed next to her, a grim look on his face as he silently reached in the bag.

Geez, get over yourself with that damn look, Sam. She fumed for a second, trying to figure out how to respond so he wouldn't take it personally. Finally, she did what she always did. Talked baseball.

"Why did you throw a changeup on that 1-2 pitch in the fourth inning to their number-eight hitter?"

The question did seem to snap Sam out of his *look*. "Wh-what?"

"Man on first, one out, eighth-place hitter who swings at everything—and you throw him a changeup?"

"I got him to pop up."

"But the number-nine hitter got you on a cheap opposite-field flair that scored the guy from first. If you throw your sinker on the outside corner to their overeager number-eight hitter, he likely hits into a double play. Bam. Yer outta the inning."

Sam gave a sheepish grin and shook his head. "Is baseball and God all you ever think about?"

"No, there's a boy in my math class I also have my eye on."

"You're unbelievable."

Jenny reached in the bag for a shiitake mushroom and brought it up to her nose. "This stinks. Do people actually eat these?"

"Don't change the subject. But yes, they're said to boost your immune system."

"Oh, joy." Jenny rolled her eyes. "Tasty brown rubber immune boosters."

Her dialysis machine beeped that it was finished filtering her blood and clearing toxins from her body. A nurse quickly entered the room, and Jenny sat up in bed to make it easier for her to detach the solution from her catheter. She wanted to leave. It had been a long day. The drive. The ballgame. Dialysis.

She looked up at her brother and saw fear on his face. *Again.* For a guy who was so cool on the mound and in the mountains, he sure had a tough time accepting her fate. She was dying. She knew it. Her back hurt. She was urinating more. She had trouble sleeping, and her hands and feet were constantly swollen. It was likely Stage Five, and unless she got a new kidney, it was only a matter of time. She saw it on the doctor's face when he examined her. Her mother probably knew it too. But Sam wasn't ready to let her go. He was too competitive and believed they could cure her illness through sheer willpower. Unfortunately, his pain had become her pain.

When the nurse finally finished and left the room, Jenny reached for her brother's hand. "I think about God and baseball because they give me peace. They're two places I can go where no one asks me how I'm feeling, or what can I get you, or do you need help changing your dialysis solution? It's a time when I invite the Great Spirit to interpret my experiences and let Him take me to a place of peace and goodness. A place where I'm able to dream about walking in the woods or by a stream or in the mountains." She squeezed his hand and smiled up at him. "Or I think about how, if you'd just thrown that sinker on the outside corner to their number-eight hitter today, you probably would have thrown a shutout."

CHAPTER SEVENTEEN

Washington, DC

November 2007

Dixon stepped out of the black limo with his lawyer and waited for two Marines to escort him into the huge five-sided building that housed the Department of Defense. He had just returned from a hunting trip in Oklahoma and was feeling pretty good about the power he was gaining in Washington. Even though Dixon wasn't military, just about every individual he passed on his way to the briefing room seemed to recognize him. Colonels, captains, sergeants, National Security Agency officials, all rushing by until they slowed and nodded respectfully at the new darling of DC. Drake Dixon, multimillionaire founder of one of the top private security companies in the world. A man to be both admired and feared.

When he entered the briefing room, Senator Ed Richardson and Secretary of Defense Bill Clifford nodded for him to take a seat.

"The intel is still coming in, but it doesn't look good. Your people opened fire on unarmed citizens." Clifford was the first to speak. He pushed a folder with the words *Confidential Information* on the cover in front of Dixon.

Dixon's mouth fell open in shock. "What are you talking about?" He thought this meeting was to praise him for his company's recent success in protecting NATO convoys.

"Six hours ago, one of your private security details was scouting in the Nuristan Province when a group of insurgents opened fire. Your contractors gave pursuit and tracked what they thought was the enemy into a valley east of Parun. A warning shot was fired over the heads of the alleged insurgents, who then retreated into a mud hut near the river. DiamondBar fired two rounds from a grenade launcher and killed four people. But, instead of finding the Taliban inside, your boys killed a goat herder's family."

Dixon bit down hard on the side of his mouth to keep from showing any outer emotion. *Shit. This can't be happening. This is a half-billion-dollar deal I can't afford to lose.*

"Over the last six years," the Defense Secretary said, "DiamondBar has been accused of negligence, lack of control of your workers, smuggling drugs and weapons—"

"That's bullshit!" Dixon snapped. "None of it was proven!"

Richardson glared at Dixon to shut up.

Dixon said nothing more, but his mind was racing a hundred miles an hour, trying to find a way to defend Clifford's attacks.

"You had your run." Clifford shook his head. "Eighteen months of good luck. High-performance, low-budget success in Afghanistan. But this is the second screwup in the last six months: the helicopter crash that killed five of our Special Forces and one of your contractors, and now this murder of a farmer's family."

"It wasn't murder," Dixon said, his voice low. "Every business makes mistakes—"

"That's the problem," Clifford cut him off. "DiamondBar is a business. You're in the business of war. If there's peace in the world, your company doesn't make money."

Dixon bit down again on the side of his mouth, this time almost drawing blood. He wanted to lash out at this political hack. *How dare he? His men were loyal Americans, many of whom had fought in Desert Storm and the Second Persian Gulf War. And now, this former general, who had probably led many of DiamondBar's employees in Iraq, was dishonoring their service? Fuck him.*

The Secretary of Defense stood up and headed for the door, stopping only to glance back at Dixon and Richardson. "Instead of running off on a hunting trip, Drake, why don't you take the money Congress gave you and clean up your mess? Because if you don't, I'll go over Ed's head and do what several Afghan leaders are calling for—I'll pull your contract."

Then, Clifford was gone, out the door, down the hallway, his footsteps fading away on the black tile floor.

Richardson's, King's, and Dixon's expressions said it all. Frustration, anger, disgust.

Stupid fucking generals, Dixon seethed. *No one in this room, and probably the world knew more about what was going on in Afghanistan than he did. So what if a few towel-heads got greased while his company was protecting America's interests. The government owed him, owed DiamondBar. There was no way the fucking Defense Secretary was going to break their contract.*

Senator Richardson clapped his hands which broke Dixon out of his trance.

"This crisis may present us with a great opportunity." Richardson turned to Barry King. "Can Drake's company be prosecuted for making a mistake?"

"It shouldn't be," King said. "Status of Forces Agreement should protect us. Collateral damage. Mistakes are made in war. We may have to pay off a few people, but at least we won't lose our contract."

"Good. Very good." Richardson flashed a condescending smile. "This is where you become a politician, Drake. Defend everything you do and attack your critics. Act like you're an open book. Totally transparent. Tell US and Afghan investigators you'll give them whatever they need to get to the bottom of this tragedy, when actually you're only giving them some vague intel that includes all of DiamondBar's past accomplishments."

As Richardson and King continued to strategize, Dixon gazed out the window at a red maple swaying in the brisk November wind. It had lost all its leaves and seemed frail, almost as if the next breeze might knock it over, but the maple held firm to its foundation, its roots always seeking stability. It reminded him of growing up in Oklahoma, going on hunting trips with his father, the man who had given him his own foundation.

No one will give you anything, son. This world is for you to take. It's like hunting white-tailed deer. They know you're coming. They know you're going to kill them. It's time for you to be their champion. Now, go and take what's yours.

"Hey, Drake," Richardson called out. "What was the common denominator of the eighteen-month-stretch of success you had in Afghanistan?"

"Daniel Carson."

"That's right," Richardson said. "When you had a human tracker who was giving accurate intel to our Special Forces."

Dixon exhaled, long and low. "Carson and a Colonel Tomlinson hit it off and did some solid work in the province. But Tomlinson has since distanced himself from my security team after Carson was killed."

The Senator rubbed his chin thoughtfully, his eyes distant, and then very slowly his gaze returned to Dixon. "How do you get back in the good graces of this Tomlinson so DiamondBar can get back in the good graces of Afghanistan and America?"

"I need to find men who are as skilled as Carson." Dixon's brow was furrowed, thinking it all out. "Men who aren't afraid of being alone in dangerous country . . . men who can become invisible . . . who can find safe trails to our mountain. I thought that I had them with the new team we trained, but obviously, they screwed up yesterday."

Senator Richardson pointed a finger at Dixon. "Make this work, Drake. We're in this together. No more mistakes. Check out every retired Special Forces soldier, Navy Seal, and tracking guide in America, and I'll make sure Congress doesn't pull your contract."

CHAPTER EIGHTEEN

Ignacio, Colorado

November 2007

Sam knelt down on the bent brome grass and studied the track. "Old Mel." He smiled. "I haven't seen this old boy's track since—"

He didn't finish his own sentence. It still pained him to speak about his father. The two of them had first discovered the big buck's track when Sam was ten years old. But they had never even seen a flash of the deer that was now a legend to local outfitters. Old Mel was smart, crafty, and wary from years of being hunted. Most mules lived for nine to eleven years, but Sam believed Mel had to be at least fifteen and weigh over three hundred pounds. His track was large yet chipped and fractured from years of crisscrossing the granite and limestone of Pargin Mountain.

His mom had called him on the drive home from college, asking him to stop along the way to pick up dinner. The Carsons' version of *picking up dinner* was different than most families. Their grocery store was Pargin Mountain. He always kept his bow in his truck, and there was still time left in rabbit-and-turkey season. Turkey was his goal today with Thanksgiving less than a week away, but he'd love to track Old Mel just to see if he could finally catch a glimpse of the big guy. Sam studied the track for a spell and then took off up the hill. The track told him not only where Old Mel was going but where he'd been and why. Sometimes it was food, sometimes danger.

As he followed the track through a stand of scrub oak, he noticed a change in the buck's gait. He had gone off his natural trail and moved close to a fallen pine, then leapt away and hurried farther up the hill. Something had startled the buck. Sam knelt down again to analyze the track. Old Mel had been here recently, probably only thirty minutes before.

Sam tightened his moccasins and took off up the hill, almost at a full run. He had learned to track that way with his father, trusting his senses to know where the hunted were going. His focus was extreme now, blotting everything else out; no thoughts of baseball or school or his dad or worries about Jenny surfaced as his entire being was concentrated only on the track.

He moved like a lone wolf, nose to the ground, then lifting to survey the surroundings. A spiderweb connecting two ponderosa pines had been broken, telling Sam that Old Mel had made another drastic turn off the easier path and deeper into the forest. The buck knew he was being followed, but it wasn't Sam who was his stalker.

The track continued through the trees, across a stream, and then up a trail to the left. Sam stopped suddenly, sensing some disturbance nearby, and let his attention wander across the bed of pine needles that covered the forest floor. There it was. A slight depression in the needles that showed something had passed by recently. He walked over and found a track the size of a man's boot. Ten feet away he found another track. Two men. Big. Size thirteen or fourteen boot. It wasn't until he came to an exposed patch of dirt at the base of a pine that he recognized the track. Yeah, it could be a coincidence, but one of the tracks showed a multitiered lugged sole that was similar to the boots Billy Cutthredge wore, and the other revealed a feathered-toe lug pattern that looked just like Rob Marcus's.

Sam smiled slightly and shook his head. Cutthredge and Marcus weren't tracking Old Mel. It was dumb luck that brought them across his path. But they were on to him now, and Sam better hurry up if he was going to save his phantom of the mountain.

The evening sun was just beginning to crest atop a southwestern ridge as Sam broke free of the forest and crossed a stretch of limestone and medium-sized boulders. The track was now easy to follow with both buck and humans following the same path. As he came around the biggest boulder, he froze. There, in the middle of a field was Old Mel, head bent down, grazing in grass that was lawn short in places.

For a moment, Sam thought about his father, how the two of them had searched for this giant mule deer for seven years and had never seen him, but now, here he was, barely ninety feet away. His moment of reflection was broken by movement to his right. In a rock crag about a hundred feet away were Cutthredge and Marcus, carefully raising their AR-15s to their shoulders.

A sudden fury lit in Sam. He had to stop them. But, instead of yelling out, he moved back behind the boulder, placed his bow and arrows on the ground, and found a medium-sized stone. He leaned forward to catch sight of both men and deer. Cutthredge was lining up his rifle toward his target and just beginning to stare through his scope. Sam knew he'd likely only have this one chance as he inhaled a deep breath, rocked back on his right leg as if he was pitching in a key Rocky Mountain playoff game, and let fly the stone. The rock soared through the air on a perfect line, drilling the side of the buck's left hip just before Cutthredge's rifle barked, the bullet missing its mark by inches as Old Mel shot off into the darkness of the forest. A string of expletives erupted from the rock crag.

*   *   *

"I feel fine," Jenny said to her mother as she lay back in bed. "I just need to catch my breath for a second."

"You need to eat something," Susan replied and then moved the tray of food closer to her daughter. "You haven't eaten anything since yesterday."

Jenny twisted her face away from the plate of cooked cabbage and raw apples. "Gross, Mom, you're going to make me throw up. I said I'm not hungry."

"How long have you been nauseous?"

"Ever since you came into the room."

"When was the last time you went to the bathroom?"

"2006."

"Please, Jenny. This isn't funny. I'll call Dr. Goodman and take you to the hospital if you're not honest with me."

"It's Thanksgiving break, Mom. I want to smell turkey and stuffing and mashed potatoes cooking, not that lemon-bleach-antiseptic, nursing-home stink."

They paused when they heard the front door open and the familiar voice of Sam boom out, "Hello, the house! Where's my family?"

"Sammy!" squealed Jenny as she rose up from bed a bit too fast and had to wait a beat to let the dizziness settle. Her mom helped her to her feet and together they headed to the living room, where Sam was waiting with a dead wild turkey in one hand and a plump rabbit in the other. His bright smile dimmed when Jenny walked into the room. She had lost more weight, her skin was a dull gray, and her breath was coming in short, labored gasps.

"Now, that's what I'm talking about," she said in a hoarse, husky voice and looked up at her mother. "Pretty cool, Mom. Real food. Meat. I think it's worth investigating."

Sam didn't laugh. He stared at his sister's withered frame for what seemed like an eternity, making Jenny uncomfortable.

"Let me help you clean those critters. I haven't plucked a bird since—"

"I've got this. You get back in bed."

"You're not the boss of me. I want to bless this food and thank the Great Spirit for His offering just like you did on the mountain. Why should you get all the fun?"

"I didn't end their lives for fun, AJ."

She walked over and snatched the rabbit out of his hand and started for the door. "That's not what I meant, Sammy, and you know it. Come on, let's skin Br'er Rabbit and pluck Tom Turkey. I haven't been this fired up about anything since Mesa State finished second in the Rocky Mountain

Tournament." She turned and winked up at him. "The Mavericks probably would have won the whole thing if their best player would have thrown more sinkers."

Sam stood dumbfounded, still holding the turkey in his left hand as his mother quirked a smile of surrender as if to say, *She's all yours, Sam. Good luck trying to win this argument.*

* * *

"Did you know back in 700 AD the Germans prayed to Saint Hubert, the patron saint of hunters, after their kill?" Jenny said as she pulled three tail feathers off the turkey. "And the Austrians would break a twig and pull it through the animal's mouth to honor its last bite."

Sam laid the rabbit on his cutting board and reached for his skinning knife as his sister continued to jabber away. "I was reading where the Cherokee, here in America, would ask the Great Spirit for forgiveness after taking an animal's life."

Sam raised a hand to quiet his sister.

"This is not something we get from books, Jen. It must come from the heart." He placed the knife on the table, took her hands, and placed one on the rabbit's chest and the other on the breast of the bird. "We close our eyes and inhale deeply. Exhale slowly and say, Thank you, Great Spirit, for this gift of food for our family. Teach me how to trust my heart, my mind, my inner being to honor and bless all your creations. Teach me to walk in balance in Your world. Thank you, God."

Jenny opened her eyes and glanced up at her brother, whose eyes were still closed, his forehead serene, a peaceful calm about his face. Finally, his eyes fluttered open, and he smiled down at her.

"You went to the spirit world again, didn't you?" She grinned.

He gave her a puzzled look.

"Yes, you did. I could tell. It was the same look you had on your face at the Sun Dance. It was only for five or ten seconds, but you went there."

"You're weird," he said with an exasperated exhale. He picked up the skinning knife to work on the rabbit and then nodded at the turkey. "Finish plucking Tom while I do Br'er Rabbit."

*   *   *

It took Sam no more than ten minutes to prepare the rabbit, and then he helped Jenny finish plucking the small hair-like feathers off the bird. For every part of the turkey would be used in the future: the primary wing feathers would be made into arrow fletchings, and the secondary and body feathers into fishing flies. Their mother would turn the smaller feathers into earrings, necklaces, pins, and holiday flower arrangements for friends.

Jenny sat down on a bench to catch her breath and watched her brother hang the bird on a hook to begin the cleaning.

"A penny for your thoughts?" she said.

He paused, knife in hand, ready to cut off the first wing. "All right . . . I want you and Mom to be completely honest with me. It's as if both of you are trying to protect me when it's *your* health that's declining. As soon as you get that new kidney, everything will be better—"

"I'm dying. I know it and Mom probably knows it."

All the color drained from Sam's face. "Don't say that. We'll get the kidney. Drake Dixon promised. Mom said you're on the list."

"But I know my body. I have all the symptoms of end-stage renal disease. I'm not sleeping, my joints are swollen, I don't have any appetite, and I haven't pooped in days."

"No." Sam's voice was sharp with conflict, and he drove his knife deep into the cutting board. "This is a battle we can win. With a positive attitude. With dialysis. With a new kidney."

"This isn't *we* anymore, brother. This is about *me*. This is about me being at peace with walking on. In our culture we believe that when someone passes on they don't die, but that they simply *walk on* and continue their journey."

His mouth opened, but no sound came out as he searched for words to make his sister fight on.

"I'm tired, Sam. Dr. Goodman said the dialysis machine is having a tougher time pushing fluids through my body. I may not have a year left."

"That's why we need to get that transplant. When was the last time Mom called the foundation? When was the last time she talked to Dixon? He has the power and money to speed things up. I—I know it."

She inhaled a deep breath and made a poor attempt at a lopsided smile. "Let me go."

"No."

"You hold onto me even when I don't belong to you. Please. I'm tired. Let me go."

He didn't respond. He just stared at the ground, arms at his side, fists clenched as if afraid that, if he did open his hands, some invisible spirit might abandon him forever.

"I'm not afraid of death, Sam. I'm actually looking forward to it. I'm looking forward to being with the Great Spirit in every moment, not just these brief moments of consciousness when I'm not in pain." She struggled to stand up, but finally did, and put her arms around her brother. "I need you to let me go. Please . . . give me your blessing."

He stood frozen, head bowed, unable to raise his arms to comfort her as a tremor of fear shuddered down his spine. "I can't, Jenny," he said, his voice scarcely audible. "There's still time. I promise you, I'll find a way."

CHAPTER NINETEEN

New York City, New York

November 2007

The United Nations briefing room was crowded with members of the media and those in town for the United Nations International Justice Forum. Drake Dixon was just finishing up a talk on the recent problems America was having in Afghanistan. He stood confidently at the podium, hands clasped at his chest, making sure he made eye contact with every camera in the room.

"My goal as CEO of DiamondBar Security is to find the most peaceful solution in everything we do. As you all know, I've spent much of my life protecting our great country and American interests abroad. That is my never-ending quest." He then pointed to a reporter from one of the major networks.

"What can you tell us about your company being involved in the death of Afghan civilians?" the reporter asked.

"That investigation is still going on," Dixon said with the most compassionate look he could muster. "So legally, I can't say anything at this time, other than to tell you that I made a generous donation to the Afghan Relief Fund and that I've been praying for those families as they go through this difficult time."

He had to choose his words carefully because the UN Working Group on the Use of Mercenaries had been very critical of private security contractors being used in overseas projects. Still, the UN was requesting more help from the private sector, and Dixon wanted to make sure those bids kept coming in.

"Have you talked with those families?" another journalist called out.

"God bless America"—Dixon shook his fist to the crowd—"and God bless the peacemakers who are keeping America safe!"

Then he was gone, ignoring the deluge of questions from the rest of the media as he left the stage and followed his security down the hallway and out a side door into his waiting limo. The door closed, and Dixon gave a proud exhale as he sat down next to his lawyer.

Barry King was on the phone, a serious look on his face.

"The event couldn't have gone any better." Dixon winked. "Why the sour face?"

King cupped his hand over the mouthpiece of his phone and whispered, "It's your secretary. She has that kid from Colorado on the line. He's called her four times in the last hour, demanding to talk with you."

Dixon leaned back in the plush leather seat and closed his eyes as the limo rocked forward, following two motorcycles up First Avenue.

"What do you want me to do?" King whispered again.

An annoyed Dixon opened his eyes and turned to his lawyer. "Put him on speaker phone. I know what this is about and want you to help me handle it."

King touched the speaker on and said, "I've got Drake here, Marsha. Patch the kid through."

There were a couple of clicks on the phone, and then Dixon inhaled a deep breath and said enthusiastically, "Hey, Sam! You must be home for Thanksgiving break. How did your fall-ball season go?"

For a long moment there was no answer. But Dixon knew Carson was listening. He could feel him, could hear his breathing on the other end of the line.

"My sister's dying. You promised my father you would get her a kidney transplant if he worked for you."

"And we will, Sam. I was just on the phone with the Kidney Foundation yesterday," he lied. "They're working on it, but as you know, your sister is a tough match."

"What's my sister's name?"

Dixon gritted his teeth and looked to his lawyer for help. King mouthed the name Jenny.

"Well, Jenny, of course—darling little girl—always lookin' out for you."

"She's dying, Mr. Dixon. What are you going to do about that?"

"I'll call the foundation as soon as we finish this call."

"Give me the number to your contact. I want to talk with them."

"Why, sure, Sam. I'll have my lawyer text it to you. By the way, how did you get my number?"

"I checked my mother's phone when she left the house. There were over fifty calls in the last three months to this number. Only two of those calls were ever returned."

Dixon swallowed hard. He had to take control of this conversation if he ever was going to get Carson to work for him. Every DiamondBar investigator he had sent to evaluate the kid said he was a better tracker than his father. And the Mesa State professors Dixon's staff had spoken to said Carson was the most intuitive student they had ever had in their Adventure Leadership Program. Dixon needed to keep this call short, throw the kid off balance, and, most importantly, let him know who was running the show.

"Like I said earlier, Sam, I'll call my people as soon as we end this call. Now, tell me about fall ball. How's your team doing?"

For a second there was no answer, and then Sam said more firmly, "Text me your contact with the Kidney Foundation in the next thirty minutes, or I'll go to the press and tell them about the promise you made to my father."

Then, just as Dixon was about to respond, the line went dead.

Dixon looked at his lawyer and then shook his head in anger. "What an arrogant little prick. Who the fuck does he think he's talking to?"

King was already scrolling through his phone, searching for the Kidney Foundation contact Dixon had never communicated with. He was too damn busy for such bullshit and had expected King to take care of the problem. His lawyer looked uncomfortable.

"When was the last time you talked with them?" Dixon asked.

Without looking up, King said, "Uh . . . last year."

"What did they say?"

"She's a difficult match, but . . . uh . . ."

"Well?"

"I'll call them right now and text Carson the number."

"I'm already having a tough time with the press, Barry. I don't need some punk kid going to them with an attack on my character, but I also don't want to piss Carson off. He has a unique talent that we can use, particularly as we get closer to wrapping up our mineral-rights deal with the Afghan government." He paused in thought. "Tell our contact with the foundation that they'll get a big donation from me if they can schmooze Sam Carson and find his sister a damn kidney."

* * *

Sam clicked his flip-phone shut and turned to face his best friend. "They're going to text me the contact info within the next thirty minutes."

"Do you think your mom will find out you called him?" Jose asked. "She wants you out of it so you can focus on school."

"I don't care." He hesitated, unsure how to best express his next thoughts. "I love my mom more than anything, but it's—it's as if she's already accepted Jenny's death."

Jose didn't answer. He sat silently on the couch of his living room.

"I don't know what the Western docs have told her. I just know that we can't give up. Jenny's a fighter. She's way tougher than me. But the look in her eyes when she told me to let her go just killed me."

"Let's wait for the text, make the call, then get things going," Jose said.

Sam looked at his watch. "Teresa and Jenny should be done with the doc and dialysis soon. Mom gets off work at five and said she'd meet us at Foothill Grill at 5:30."

* * *

Billy Cutthredge's phone pinged that a text had just arrived. He took a look and said, "Time to move, Rob. Boss says we gotta check on the chickens."

The old chair creaked under the weight of the huge man as Marcus raised to his feet, unsteady after an afternoon of drinking, and fired down the last of his scotch. "What the hell's happened to us? We've gone from hunting down terrorists to babysitting a college boy and his little sister."

"Pay's the same," Cutthredge said as he opened the door of their double-wide and headed for their truck. "My guess is that somebody spooked Dixon. He wants us to see if the little girl looks like she's dying."

* * *

Cutthredge checked his watch and then casually rubbed the week-old growth of beard covering his face. 5:30. Susan Carson's 1992 white Datsun pickup rolled into the parking lot of Mercy and stopped in front of the patient-checkout circle. Two girls came out of the hospital, one covered head to toe in a down coat despite the mild temperatures and wheeling a small oxygen canister.

"Will you look who's with her?" Marcus stared out the window. "My sweet li'l Injun girl, Teresa Tom Tom."

Cutthredge shook his head, put the truck in gear, and giving the Carson truck plenty of distance, followed them out of the lot.

* * *

The Foothill Grill was nothing fancy. It was owned by a couple of retired cowboys who had decorated the restaurant with an Old West flair. There were spurs and horseshoes and lariats dangling from the ceiling while classic Western movie posters of John Wayne, Roy Rogers, and Clint Eastwood adorned the walls. It was a diner many of the hospital staff frequented after work to grab a beer and a burger before heading home to their families.

Jenny sat down at a table in the back and adjusted the nose buds to her oxygen tank. It was just one more indicator of her deteriorating health. Dialysis required work, work required energy, energy required fuel, fuel was oxygen, and her body was working overtime to find that oxygen. She opened the pamphlet Dr. Goodman had given her entitled, "What to Do When You Have Chronic Kidney Disease." It was a happy book with a cartoon teddy bear smiling as she received her daily dialysis from a joyful Dr. Owl, who proudly put his wing on his grateful patient's shoulder. The book was complete with information about all five stages of kidney disease and updates on her personal profile of Stage Five ESRD, end-stage renal disease. The results of the test that calculated her glomerular filtration rate were all in dark depressing colors, showing how poorly her crappy kidneys were cleaning her blood. She closed the pamphlet, pushed it as far away as she could, took her nose buds out, and sipped her 7UP.

"How do you feel, honey?" her mother asked.

Jenny shrugged and took another sip.

"Dr. Goodman said it's important that you're honest with me."

"I don't want to talk about kidneys anymore, Mom. I don't want to become my disease. *Little Miss Stage Five!* Geez, shoot me in the head."

"Well then, what do you want to talk about?"

"Baseball winter meetings are only two weeks away," Teresa teased, trying to hide her grin behind her own 7UP. Teresa didn't know a thing about Major League Baseball's annual event, but she'd overheard Jenny quizzing Dr. Goodman about it at the hospital.

"Now, that's what I'm talkin' about!" Jenny slapped her hand on the top of the table so sharply that several heads turned to see what the commotion was about. "Who do you think the Rockies should protect on their forty-man? The Rule 5 draft could really help them this year if they find a lefty reliever who can hit that outside corner."

Both Teresa and Susan broke up in laughter until the front door to the restaurant opened. Silhouetted in the soft glow of the streetlights were the imposing figures of Billy Cutthredge and Rob Marcus. Both walked to the bar and ordered drinks, but Marcus's eyes never left the Carson's table. Teresa moved closer to Susan. Only Jenny remained unfazed, straightening up in her chair, folding her arms across her chest, and staring back at the two men. They picked up their drinks and walked over.

"Well, if it isn't Tweedledee and Tweedledum," Jenny said with more than a hint of sarcasm. "The two lamebrains who went hunting in the middle of the worst November storm in years and came back with nothing."

Cutthredge stopped abruptly, seemingly surprised by the sick girl's comment.

There were times when Jenny would use her illness to her advantage. Even the roughest of men could be shaken by her anemic frame, gray skin, yellow eyes, and the bruises on her arms from the countless needles she had endured through the years.

"I think there's a table out on the patio that has your name on it." Jenny pointed to the door.

Marcus ignored her and pulled up a chair directly across from Teresa. "May I buy you a drink, mademoiselle?"

Teresa kept her eyes low as she shook her head. But Jenny raised her nose buds in front of Marcus's face. "May I offer you a bit of oxygen, mon-sewer?"

Her mockery drew concealed laughter from her mother and Teresa, which infuriated Marcus.

"Back off, kid."

Susan raised her hand. "Don't you talk to my daughter that way. We came here for a quiet dinner. I would appreciate it if you would respect our privacy and find another table."

Cutthredge pulled out his wallet and slapped it on the table. "I got yer dinner, Ms. Carson." He glanced down at her left hand, which still donned her deceased husband's wedding band. "It is still Ms. Carson, ain't it?"

Susan held her chin up and glared at Marcus.

"Yeah, I heard your husband was killed in Afghanistan," he said in a condescending tone. "What a shame . . . and you with a sick daughter and all."

Marcus reached across the table and touched Teresa's hand. She tried to pull away, but he pressed down hard and she reluctantly softened. "Let me buy you a drink, sweetheart?"

"Get your hands off her!" Jose stood by the front door, a look of absolute fury on his face. He started over, Sam right behind, matching his friend's every step.

Marcus let go of Teresa's hand and rose up out of his chair, a slight smile on his face, eager for a fight.

All eyes in the bar turned their way, but just before Jose arrived, Jenny stood up and stepped between the two men.

Marcus lunged past her and punched Jose in the face. Jose collapsed to the floor. The commotion knocked Jenny off balance, and she tumbled backward over a chair, her oxygen canister following her path.

Moving by reflex, Sam dove and caught his sister with his left arm, then twisted around and caught the oxygen tank with his right just before it smashed into her face.

"Police!" a voice shouted from behind the bar as two officers rushed in, right hands on their holsters, just in case.

Cutthredge raised both hands to the sky. "Sorry, man. We'll go quietly."

"Jose and Sam were only protecting their family from these two thugs," said the man behind the bar to one of the police officers. "I could tell they were trouble as soon as they walked through my door, Gabe."

The bartender's words seemed to sober up Cutthredge, who grabbed his wallet and then nodded to Marcus that it was time to leave.

"Hands behind your back," ordered the officer named Gabe.

"What?" a suddenly incredulous Cutthredge glared. "You're gonna arrest us for a little disagreement?"

"I'm not gonna ask you again," Gabe said, his voice lower.

"This is small-town bullshit," Cutthredge grumbled, but they followed orders, were cuffed, and led outside.

As soon as the door closed, all eyes turned to the little girl who was still sitting on the floor with her eyes wide open.

"That was awesome!" Jenny squealed, and the entire bar exploded in laughter.

Sam's mouth twisted into a sheepish grin as he helped his sister up.

"That had to be the greatest catch you've ever made!" Jenny gushed, and then returned her oxygen buds to her nose. "You caught me in one arm and the canister in the other. I'm filing that in my next scouting report."

* * *

Dixon clicked off his phone and turned to his lawyer. "What did I tell them to do? Just watch them. See how sick the Carson girl really is. That was it. Nothing more. Instead, they start a fight in a bar, get arrested, and almost give away our cover."

"I'll take care of it," King said. He quickly pulled out his phone and began texting. "I'll transfer money from one of our off-shore accounts to bail them out."

"My life would be so much better if the girl just died and took Billy and Rob with her."

King's mouth fell open in astonishment.

"I'm just kidding, Barry. But that sick kid is just another rope tying Sam Carson down. Until she's gone—"

"You have to find a way to get rid of Cutthredge and Marcus. Those guys are bad news."

"I know. But they could blackmail us. They know about my insider trading and that I overcharged our government for a few security projects. I just need to stay on top of them and make sure they follow orders."

"All it takes is one dumb mistake, Drake. That *one* could have been today."

"Calm down. Billy and Rob are more dangerous to me unemployed than employed."

"Why? Because they also know about the bribes you've given the Afghan government?"

Dixon froze and slowly raised his vision to meet his lawyer's. "That's enough, Barry. The money I gave Almeida Zubair is simply a down payment on an investment. The Minister of the Interior knows the mountain we want is filled with riches. He just wants in on the action."

"Unfortunately, it's a region that's still being watched by our military."

Dixon slowly nodded. "That's why we need a stealth operation where every move we make is watched only by allies of DiamondBar."

CHAPTER TWENTY

Grand Junction, Colorado

February 2008

It was Mesa State's season opener. The Mavericks were everybody's pick to win the Rocky Mountain Conference. But now, only three hours before first pitch, their starting pitcher and preseason pick for Player of the Year was staring down at his phone, praying for it to ring. Sam had called his mom ten times since they had last talked, but no answer. She and Jenny had been on Highway 550, just north of Silverton, anxious to watch Sam pitch game one.

"Your sister has gone to great lengths preparing for this trip," his mother had said on the last phone call. "She actually followed her nurse's instructions."

"They finally said something that helped me," he heard his sister say in the background. Sam chuckled as he listened to their banter.

"She named her new oxygen tank Mav," their mother said.

"For the Mesa State Mavericks!" Jenny cheered.

"Her skin color has a rather effervescent glow."

"Yeah, a lush oyster gray."

"And she had a nice and relaxing dialysis this morning."

"It wasn't relaxing, Mom. I was online the whole time trying to find information on West Texas A&M to give Sam a good scouting report."

He had laughed. "Yo, AJ! Coach already gave me a—"

"Sammy! Guess what color my new tank is?"

He bit his lip to keep from laughing again. "I'm guessing maroon, white, and gold?"

"Go Mavs! Kick Buffalo ass!"

"Jenny!" *Susan scolded her daughter, but there was joy in their mother's voice. For just a moment. Only a brief moment. Until, of course, Jenny started to cough. Not one of those little tickles in the back of the throat coughs. But a desperate, heaving, tortured, apocalyptic, painful hack that had Sam staring at the phone as he listened to his sister search frantically for something that was so readily available to everyone else. Air.*

"Jenny!" *his mother cried out.* "Jenny! Dear God, no! Sam, I have to go. I'll call you—"

Then the phone clicked off.

*   *   *

Sam waited another five minutes and called his mom for the seventh time. This time a metallic voice recording came on saying her mailbox was full and to call back later.

"What the hell's going on?" he muttered to himself as all the worries and fears he'd been pushing to the side came screaming back into his mind.

Where are they? Are they in a bad cell area? They couldn't be for this long. Why didn't Mom call back? Why did she say 'Dear God, no'? Please, phone, ring. Please, God, make the phone ring.

He flipped his phone open again and scrolled through his contacts. If his sister was in trouble, he needed to pull out all the stops. He first called Mercy Medical. The emergency-room nurse knew all about Jenny, but hadn't seen or heard from them since they'd left almost two hours ago. He called her personal doctor's number, but it went straight to voicemail. In near panic, he grabbed his baseball glove off his bed and flung it against the wall so hard it knocked over a picture of Sam and his dad returning from a hunting trip on Pargin Mountain.

Jose opened the door and peeked inside. "You okay, dude?"

Sam shook his head. "I was on the phone with my mom. Jenny started to cough. Mom sounded scared—said she'd call back. That was forty minutes ago."

"Maybe they're in a bad cell area," Jose said stiffly then picked up the fallen picture and hung it back on the wall. "We need to leave, Sam. Coach wants us in the clubhouse by ten thirty."

Sam didn't speak for a long time, his gaze fixed on his phone until Jose tapped him on the shoulder.

"Okay," he said in a voice barely above a whisper. "I don't want to disappoint Jenny."

*   *   *

Only the sounds of the grounds crew finishing the Mesa State field and Sam flipping open and then closing his phone could be heard in Coach Elba's office. Coach was busy studying his scouting report before handing it to his starting pitcher. Spring was still six weeks away, but Colorado was given an early tease with a beautiful February day. Blue skies, temperatures in the upper sixties, and thin white cirrus clouds with their tips curling high above left field.

Coach Elba finished his writing and turned to face his starting battery.

"All right, let's go over the West Texas lineup. Only four returning starters from last year's team that finished under .500. All four hit one through four. First two hitters are right handed, have speed but no power. Both love to go opposite field. Sam, how do you want to work 'em?"

Sam sat at the desk, motionless.

Elba cleared his throat. "Sam? May I have your attention?"

He straightened up in his chair. "Yes, sir, I'm sorry."

"How do you want to pitch their first two hitters?"

Sam glanced at the scouting report and then out the window at the centerfield flag, which showed a westerly breeze about ten miles an hour. "Four-seamers up and in, two-seamers down and in. If they don't adjust, I'll stay with it. If they adjust, I'll go away with a slider."

"Three hitter's got power from the left side. Ten homers last year, but eight of 'em in West Texas, where the wind always blows out."

"I'll stay down and away early with fastballs, and if it looks like he's on my heater, I'll go changeup down and away."

"How about their cleanup man?"

Sam's phone suddenly rang, and he jumped as if snapped by a teammate's towel. "Can I please get this, sir? My mom and sis are on their way to the game."

His coach gave a reluctant nod as Sam hurried to the far side of the room. It was Mercy Medical. "Hello? . . . No, ma'am, I haven't heard from them yet . . . I will . . . yes, thank you . . . and if you hear anything, will you please call me? . . . Thank you, I appreciate it."

He flipped off his phone and walked back to his pitcher's meeting.

"Is everything all right?" Coach Elba asked.

"I don't know, sir . . . I don't know."

"Are you good to go, Sam?"

"Yes, sir, I'll be fine."

*   *   *

Sam's first warm-up toss in the bullpen was in the dirt. His second sailed over Jose's head and clanged off the chain-link fence.

"C'mon, Sam Bam!" Jose barked as he grabbed another baseball and fired it back to his pitcher. "Season opener, dude. Let's go!"

After a promising finish to the 2007 season, Suplizio Field was beginning to fill with students coming over after classes to watch the Maverick who was named preseason Division 2 All-American.

Sam inhaled a deep breath and glanced over at the phone on top of his equipment bag, which immediately brought Jose out of his crouch and jogging to the mound. "Dude, you've gotta lock in." He tapped Sam on the chest. "Believe they're okay and focus. Team needs you. You the man. Let's go." Jose jogged back behind the plate and gave a good low target. "Now bring it, brother. Don't let me move this mitt."

Sam did, the next seven warm-up pitches perfectly centered in the middle of his catcher's glove. "That's it baby!" Jose grabbed their equipment bags and headed to the field. "Time to grill us some Buffalo!"

"Did you get my phone?" Sam asked.

"It's in your bag and staying there. New conference rules say no telecommunications equipment allowed on the mound."

Sam gave his friend a playful shove. "You're an idiot."

"Yeah, well, I'm the idiot you're workin' with today, and I want you to turn off that stressed-out brain of yours and trust me to call a good game."

* * *

Sam's warm-up pitches were absolute precision: fastballs moving, sliders biting, changeups fading. Then, just before the first pitch, he glanced at the stands. They weren't there. His mom and sister weren't there, and panic gripped him again. A cloak of fear was thrown across his body, and the comfort of his earlier throws was now gone. The ball felt uncomfortable in his hand. He had trouble maintaining his balance. Couldn't calm his breathing. He was thinking about separating his hand from his glove too quickly, or was it too slowly? And, before he could catch his breath, Mesa State was down 6–0. Sam lasted an inning and a third. How he got those four outs was a miracle, but his final line of six runs on six hits, with two walks and one hit batter, was the worst of his career.

"Freshman of the Year, my ass," mumbled the West Texas on-deck hitter as Sam came off the mound and sat alone at the end of the bench. Coach didn't even switch him out to finish in left field, the position he played when he wasn't pitching. He didn't care. It was the season opener, and he didn't care. He took a quick glance back at the crowd. Still no Mom and Jenny. Shit, where were they? When he turned back around, Coach Elba was sitting next to him.

"Jose told me to answer your phone if it rang," his coach said softly.

Sam's head jerked up.

"Your mom called. Jenny's at Mercy in Durango." Elba put an arm around Sam's shoulders. "Go on home, son. Take care of your family."

* * *

He was just past Ouray when his phone finally rang. He snatched it off the passenger's seat and clicked on. "Mom?"

"Jenny's in ICU," his mother said, trying to hide the distress in her voice. "They have her stabilized."

"What happened?"

"I'll tell you when you get here. Just know that she's in stable condition . . . hang on, the nurse is calling me . . . I have to go."

"Mom!"

"Be safe, Sam. Please."

"Mom!"

But she had already clicked off.

Sam slammed his phone down on the passenger's seat and pressed the accelerator to the floor. "Please God—if there is one—help my sister."

He waited thirty minutes and called his mom's number again. Straight to voicemail. *Shit.* Fear and worry gripped him. He turned on the radio as loud as it would go, then snapped it off. Fear turned to frustration, and frustration turned to anger. He pounded his fist down on the steering wheel. He had to call somebody, anybody, just to talk. He dialed Mercy Medical again. The admitting nurse would only tell him that Jenny was in ICU and that she couldn't find his mom. He called Jose's parents. No answer. He called Teresa. No answer. He scrolled through any numbers that connected Jenny to the outside world. His finger stopped at Drake Dixon.

"Screw it," he muttered and dialed the number. It rang only once, and he heard a sweet female voice on the other end. "DiamondBar Security, Keeping America Safe. May I help you?"

Sam inhaled a deep breath through his nose. "This is Sam Carson. May I talk with Mr. Dixon?"

"I'm sorry, sir, but Mr. Dixon is in a meeting right now. If you'd like to email us your question or concern—"

"Get me Dixon's executive secretary, Marsha Byers. Tell her that Sam Cloud-Carson wants to talk to Dixon immediately."

There was a long muffled silence as the woman appeared to be talking with someone else in the room. A couple of clicks later a new voice was heard.

"Hi, Sam, this is Marsha. How are you?"

"Not good."

"How may I help you?"

"How many times has my family called Mr. Dixon for help? One hundred? Two hundred? You've done nothing."

"Our staff continues to work on finding—"

"My father made a deal with your boss. He did his part and made the ultimate sacrifice. He died for your damn company."

"We're very aware of your father's patriotism, Sam, and we've honored his name with a plaque in our DiamondBar Hero's Room at our Virginia training complex."

"My father didn't go to Afghanistan because he was a patriot, ma'am. He went there because he made a deal with Dixon. Now, it's time for him to pay up."

"And we're making every effort to help Jenny."

"Yeah, well, you can tell your boss that I'm going to the press and tell them how he screwed our family. He broke a promise. I'll tell them that Drake Dixon's a lying piece of shit."

"Now, just calm down, young man!" It was Dixon's voice. Sam knew he had been on the line the whole time, and he wanted the man who had caused his pain to hear his wrath.

"My staff has been calling," Dixon continued, "and . . . uh . . . I've been calling everyday around the globe for a match for your sister."

"Who have you called?"

There was a bit of hesitation before he answered. "The National Kidney Foundation, which has bureaus all over the world and—"

"Don't bullshit me."

"I'm not, Sam." Dixon's voice took on a more mild and understanding tone. "I admire your heart, Sam. I love how much you care for your sister and am here to help you. Trust me. We need to work together on this project. Why, Marsha told me the other day that they may have a match for little Jenny from an organ donor in . . . Portland, Oregon, I believe. Yes, it's Portland. Now, I'd like to change the subject for a bit. I've been following your career, and I believe in you. I believe in your special gifts, and I want you to know that, when you graduate, I'd like to offer—"

"Fuck you! I'm calling the *Durango Herald*," Sam said before clicking off his phone and slamming it down on the passenger's seat. He tried to calm himself but failed. Drake Dixon had gotten to him. Again.

Dixon was so damn typical of men in power. Hell, the history of the world was a history of control. Control of the masses by the few. His own culture had been persecuted by the US government for centuries. Even their Native American religion had been outlawed for almost a century because the power brokers knew that seizing someone's soul was the ultimate form of control. He remembered his sister telling him about the importance of exercising his own spiritual muscle, because, as she had said, *"Without your soul, you have no true power."*

He looked out the window and down the road. Pargin Mountain was now in sight, a broad, proud sierra of dark green pines and oaks and gray granite imploring him to follow. That was indeed where he wanted to go, but not until he satisfied the rage in his heart. He knew he was in a dark place, for a mind filled with hate was dangerous.

* * *

The parking garage at Mercy was practically full when Sam arrived that night. He had finally talked with his mom a half hour earlier and found out what happened. How Jenny's coughing fit on the drive had brought up blood, then vomiting, forcing them to turn around and race back to

Mercy. His sister's temperature had soared on the drive, followed by feverish chills and difficulty breathing. By the time they arrived at the hospital, Jenny was near catatonic.

Sam sprinted across two parking lots and shoved open the lobby doors.

"Jenny!" he called out to a nurse he remembered from his sister's countless trips to the hospital.

"Still in intensive care, Sam." The nurse pointed down the hallway, but Sam was already gone, his running shoes echoing off the tile floor.

His grandfather and mother were in the far corner of the waiting area. Grandpa Douglas was asleep, but his mother was not. She was slumped over, head in her hands, the fluorescent lights overhead seeming to deepen the lines of fatigue on her face.

"Mom."

Susan slowly rose up and came to his waiting arms. "The doctors are with her right now. She won't eat anything and has had trouble breathing."

Sam didn't speak for a long time. He held his mother, his gaze fixed on the double doors of the ICU that separated him from his sister, separated him from her spirit. He tried to push the bitterness out, but the feeling remained. Behind those doors was a soul of pure love struggling to survive, while two thousand miles away a man in power was given so much. *Where was the Great Spirit's fairness in this?*

He had to do something to right the wrong. Tomorrow morning he would take the Carson's entire story to the press. Yes. Revenge would be his satisfaction.

* * *

Sam woke up on the waiting-room floor. His grandfather must have gone home, but his mom was still there, sleeping on a nearby couch, curled up with her face buried against a pillow to shut out the light. He pulled a blanket over her shoulders and went to talk with the ICU nurses. No change. Jenny was still sleeping, medicated but sleeping. He checked the clock on the wall. 7:14. Still too early to call the writer he knew at the *Herald* who had covered his high school games. He'd been a friend of his dad's. Good guy. A fair, honest family man who had covered southwest Colorado sports for over twenty-five years.

He fixed himself a cup of coffee and wandered the Mercy Medical halls, listening to the antiseptic sounds of the hospital: the constant beeping of monitors, muffled sounds of TV sets, and a child's cry from a distant room. He checked the clock again. 7:33. *I'll bet he's up. I'm calling him.*

He went back to the waiting room and sat as far away from his mom as possible. He called the *Herald* writer, who answered on the third ring.

"Hi, Mr. Williams, this is Sam Carson from Ignacio High," he said in a voice soft enough not to wake his mom. "Thank you, sir. I'm at Mercy Medical with my sister, Jenny." He paused to listen and then whispered, "I'm sorry to say she's not doing well, sir, but I needed to talk with you about why she's not doing well—"

"Sam, we can't do the story. Some DC lawyer called the publisher of the *Herald* last night and threatened to sue us if we wrote anything about DiamondBar Security and your father's death."

"But the only reason my father took the job was because of a promise Dixon made—"

"I know. Your father was one of my best friends. He told me that he took the job for insurance."

"It was more than insurance, Mr. Williams. Dixon promised to get my sister a kidney transplant. He said he knew all the right people to make it happen."

"There's no written agreement, Sam. It's your word against his. And with the money DiamondBar has, they could bankrupt our paper if we wrote a story about an accusation without proof."

The rest of the conversation was a blur for Sam as he listened indifferently to Mr. Williams attempt to make small talk about hunting and fishing and a basketball game Sam had against Bayfield three years ago. When he finally hung up, Sam sat alone, a numbing grayness pulling his mood lower. He turned to find his mother sitting up on the couch, staring at him.

"Who were you talking to?"

"Mr. Williams at the *Herald*."

Her eyes went wide. "What did you tell him?"

"I wanted them to write a story about how Dixon screwed our family." She stood up and stormed over. "And what good is that going to do?"

"I want justice."

"Justice? Or are you consumed about 'just us'?"

He took a step back, unsure of what she meant.

"Your sister needs you now, Sam. She's dying."

"She's not dying. Don't say that. Jenny's a fighter."

His mother paused, as if to make sure Sam understood her next words. "You're not here all the time, son . . . I am. You have no idea how hard Jenny works to make herself look healthy, feel healthy, when you come home. That's why we tried to come to your season opener. She wanted to see you pitch one last time."

"Don't say it's the last time."

His mother's entire body softened as she reached out and touched his shoulder. "Jenny's dying, Sam. I know it. The doctors know it. They said that even if she got the transplant now, she probably wouldn't make it through the surgery."

He stood frozen, staring at the doors to the ICU, his hands clenched together.

"Your sister's in terrible pain. She's been in pain for several months. She long ago accepted her fate and is ready to walk on."

The waiting room was silent, save for the beeping of someone's heart monitor and the raggedness of Sam's breathing. His hands were still clenched together as if holding onto the grief and sadness and fear that choked him.

"Sam," his mother whispered. "Jenny is only still here because she has been preparing *you* for her death."

* * *

It was just before noon when Jenny woke up. Her entire body ached from all the vomiting she'd done yesterday and now all the machines that were attached to her body, trying to keep her alive. Dr. Williams told her what she knew already.

End-stage congestive heart failure . . . your heart's ability to pump blood has decreased . . . kidneys are only functioning at 10 percent of their normal capacity . . . blah, blah, blah.

She hit the red call button, and a nurse hurried through the door a few seconds later.

"Hey, sleepyhead! How are you this fine morning?"

"Cheerio," Jenny said, forcing a weary smile.

"How about some ice chips for breakfast?"

"Is . . . my mom . . . here?"

"She never left," the nurse said, and then gave her a roguish wink. "And that cute brother of yours is here as well. All of our nurses were checking him out while he slept on the waiting-room floor."

"Sammy's here?" Jenny tried to sit up, but the pain in her chest was too much. "He shouldn't . . . have come." She paused to catch her breath. "This was . . . Mesa's . . . opener."

"Well, he's here. And if you're up for it, I'm sure they'd love to see you."

She nodded. "Can I have . . . some guacamole . . . with my ice chips?"

The nurse snorted a laugh. "It sounds like you're almost back to normal."

*　　*　　*

Their mom was first through the door, followed by Sam, who made a passing-fair attempt at a smile.

"Do I look . . . that bad?" Jenny asked.

"No, uh, you look great," he stuttered, his smile slipping a bit.

"You've always . . . been a bad liar." Her breathing was a struggle, but she had the strength to raise one brow. "How did . . . you pitch?

"Lousy. Six runs in not even two innings."

Jenny leaned back on her bed and let go a low groan. "Geez, Sammy . . . your inability . . . to focus . . . is killing me."

He sat down in the chair next to her. "I had a lot on my mind."

"So did Bret Saberhagen . . . in the '85 World Series . . . when he won game seven . . . the day after his wife . . . gave birth to their first child."

Sam's mouth fell open, a look of astonishment on his face. "Are you some kind of crazy human computer that just spits out Wikipedia baseball information?"

She struggled to raise both arms to display the tubes that kept her confined to a bed. "I have plenty . . . of time to research . . . the most important moments . . . in our country's history."

Their mother choked back a laugh. "This is what I'll miss most. The two of you going back and forth like some Wimbledon tennis match."

Sam froze at his mother's words while Jenny's face brightened with joy.

"Sam with the lob," she croaked, trying to mimic the voice of some overdramatic play-by-play announcer. "Jenny with the overhead smash . . . into the corner . . . she beats her brother . . . again." She turned to see the grim look on Sam's face, eyes staring at the tubes in her upturned arms, bruised by years of countless needles. How could such a fearless competitor in sports and tracking be so soft when it came to her? She touched her brother's hand and said, "We'll continue . . . this match later . . . I'm tired."

"Yes," he said, his voice scarcely audible. "May I stay in the room while you sleep?"

Jenny gave an appreciative nod, lay back on her stack of antibacterial pillows, and closed her eyes.

* * *

She dreamed of walking with her family on Pargin Mountain. Her hand in her father's as he pointed out the different wildlife that frequented the foothills near their home. She saw a coyote watching them from a meadow, an elk bugling near a stream, and a mule deer, ears raised, listening for some nearby predator. They passed by bear, buffalo, and wolf, then humans and wagons and automobiles, wildfires and thunderstorms and floods until they finally came upon a trail of celestial forms, ghosts from some other time, proud warriors, eyes fixed on an exquisite white light in the distance.

Her father joined the line, then she did the same, followed by their mother, leaving Sam alone. Her brother sank to his knees in fear, wanting to follow, but something held him back, frantic hands grabbing at him, wicked, bony fingers pulling him to some dark abyss. For a moment Jenny saw Sam's future. She saw suffering, depression, loss. She saw her brother giving up. She cried out to him, cried out again . . . and then her eyes fluttered open to find Sam next to her, rubbing a cool washcloth across her forehead.

"I'm here, Jenny. I'm here," he whispered.

She was sobbing uncontrollably as she reached up and pulled him close. She wanted to, but couldn't, tell him. She could never tell him what she saw. She would tell her mother tomorrow or the next day about her vision, but not Sam. She knew from the very depths of her soul that the only way for her brother to learn what he needed to learn was for her to go away. But she wanted to say something, give him some warning, some hopeful message that he could use on his journey.

"Do you believe in the Great Spirit?" she finally asked, a sudden surge of strength coming over her.

He couldn't bring himself to tell her that he wasn't sure.

"Yes," he said softly.

"Do you believe He sends the Holy Spirit to help guide you?"

"Jenny, what's with all the God talk?"

She grabbed him by the shoulders. "You need to ask the Holy Spirit anytime you need help, Sam. Rely on that spirit to interpret everything that will take place in your life. Not just some things . . . but *everything*."

He looked uncertainly from his sister to her heart monitor. "Are you okay?"

She rolled her eyes. "Yes, I'm okay. Totally lucid. Rock solid. In the zone." She paused for a long moment as she looked out the window at the heavy storm clouds beginning to build over the San Juans. "You've heard of Black Elk."

"The medicine man of the Lakota?"

She nodded. "He believes the power of the world is done in a circle." She pointed out the window. "Look outside. The Earth is round; the sky is round; the stars are round."

He gave his sister an absolutely bewildered look but said nothing.

"Black Elk said that the wind, in its greatest power, whirls. Birds make their nests in circles, for theirs is the same religion as ours. The sun comes forth and goes down again in a circle. The moon does the same, and both are round." She had to pause to catch her breath, but there was excitement in her voice. "He said even the seasons form a great circle in their changing, and always come back to where they were. The life of a man is a circle from childhood to childhood, and so it is in everything where power moves."

Sam blinked, entirely confused now. "What does all this mean, Jenny?"

She took his hands in hers and looked directly in his eyes. "It means, even when I get rid of this physical body, I will still be with you, always. It's the cycle and power of giving and receiving, maintaining the circle of life. I will be with you . . . *always*."

* * *

According to Mercy's official records, just two hours after their conversation, Jenny's kidney function fell to below 10 percent, which led to a seizure. She slipped into a coma. Her system was working so hard to clean the wastes from her body that it taxed her other organs until finally her heart gave out. Jenny Cloud-Carson died at 4:37 that afternoon.

CHAPTER TWENTY-ONE

Southern Virginia

February 2008

Drake Dixon held the phone to his ear and listened as a representative of Mercy Medical Center told him of the passing of Jenny Carson.

"What a shame," he said as he winked at the pretty brunette who placed a cup of espresso in front of him and then left the room. Dixon motioned for his lawyer to close the door to the DiamondBar conference room, which Barry King immediately did.

"When's the funeral?" Dixon asked the hospital rep and then paused to listen to her answer. "Yeah . . . uh huh . . . It is very sad . . . I'm sorry too. Jenny was a wonderful little girl, an inspiration to everyone she touched . . . Yes, ma'am . . . Thank you for taking my call . . . I will, ma'am . . . God bless you too."

He clicked off the phone and turned to his public-relations chief, Archie Newton, "Well, the kid finally died, and the funeral's next week. How do you want to handle it?"

Newton leaned forward and opened his folder. "First of all, I'm glad that you went along with our idea of making a donation to the Kidney Foundation and the Ute Cultural Center. That makes you look compassionate. We got great press after the speech you gave at the UN. Genius of you to show pictures of your DiamondBar guys handing out candy to smiling Afghan children." He tossed an eight-by-ten photo of Dixon at the

UN press briefing. "You've got the look, boss, the look of both power and compassion. That's a big plus. There was a moment during your speech when you were talking about friends you've lost in Afghanistan, and I actually saw you tear up."

Dixon glared at his PR man. "Those tears were real. We're talking about men who died for our country. They're called patriots, Arch. I feel blessed whenever I'm in the presence of soldiers."

Newton clapped his hands enthusiastically. "Damn, you did it again! You're a natural! Just like at the UN. You paused for just the right amount of time, squared your shoulders, and looked directly into the camera as if you were talking to every American. That was awesome, my man. If you ever want to get into politics, you're gonna kill it."

"Politics? No way. I'm the one who pulls their strings. Now, let's get back to how you think going to this funeral helps me."

"Let's double down on empathy, Drake. We got great coverage from the press the last time you went to a Carson funeral." Newton flashed a condescending veneer smile. "Even though the family didn't let you be part of the ceremony. But hell, that wasn't your fault. You showed them respect by acting like you were honoring Southern Ute customs . . . you know, the way they like to send their dearly departed to the happy hunting grounds."

Newton placed a sheet of paper in front of Dixon. "Here's what we want you to say to the press before the funeral"—he then handed him another sheet—"and here's how we want you to respond when it's all over."

Dixon looked it over. There were plenty of cool catchphrases like, "We don't want to just treat a disease, we want to treat people," and "Nurses may not be angels, but they're the next best thing," and "Jenny was generous in her service to others, which inspired me to make this generous donation in her name." And his favorite: "If you want to understand Jenny Carson, you have to walk a mile in her moccasins."

"Good work." Dixon flashed a confident smile. "Now let's take this act to Colorado."

* * *

Walks With the Wind

It wasn't true that Sam spent all his time thinking about his dead sister. There was too much to do following Jenny's passing. There were funeral arrangements. Death certificate. Writing the obituary. Deciding who would speak at the ceremony. Flowers. Songs and music. Cremation.

Unlike her father, who had received a traditional Ute burial, Jenny wanted to be cremated and have her ashes spread on certain areas of Pargin Mountain. All places that Sam had taken her on their hikes when she was healthy. And, because of her popularity, there was now the challenge of how would they handle the forty or more Kidney Beans and their families who were coming from out of town to pay their respects to the girl who had started the kidney-disease support group. Through it all, his mother was upbeat, seemingly unaffected by her daughter's death. She had told Sam that it was because Jenny had prepared her the last two years for this time. That her daughter had taught her there was a difference between life and the body, and that while the body may be limited, the life, the spirit, would live on forever.

"Jenny visited me last night," his mother had told him the day after her passing. "She was happy and said that her walk on was beautiful. She also said that she would watch over us, be a guardian angel to lift us up in times when our spirit was low."

Sam didn't buy it. How could he? How dare the Great Spirit take a soul so pure as Jenny? How dare He give his family so much pain? Sam knew that death happened every day, and that many had experienced so much worse, which made him question the very existence of the Great Spirit. *Why would He do this? Why did He make grief so painful and feel so much like fear? Why did He promise suffering and demand sacrifice?*

Sam made it through the days by staying busy, but his nights were absolute agony. Alone. Suffocating. His father and sister now gone. Who was next on the Great Spirit's tablet?

CHAPTER TWENTY-TWO

Durango, Colorado

February 2008

"It's been paid for?" Susan Carson's voice was curious as she looked around the empty Holiday Inn conference room. She'd slept fitfully the night before, wondering how she'd pay for a room to host the celebration-of-life party for all of the Kidney Beans who had flown in from around the country to honor its founder. Now, some Good Samaritan had picked up the bill for the room along with all of the flowers and refreshments.

"Do you know who wrote the check?" she asked the hotel manager.

"Why yes," the manager said as she flipped through her notebook to find the name. "It was a Mr. Dixon. He stopped by this morning."

Susan's mouth fell open in shock. She wanted to cry out in fury, but instead, she held it all in. How dare he? Dixon had come to Durango to use her daughter's funeral as a way to inflate his own image as some caring, compassionate business leader. And now, he was using their family again. But she couldn't turn him away. Not after the way he worked the press the last time she saw him. Dixon had controlled the narrative at her husband's funeral, and now he had returned to try and do the same at Jenny's ceremony.

"Mrs. Carson, Mr. Dixon was hoping he might be able to say a few words about Jenny at today's ceremony," the hotel manager said.

Her face tightened but she remained stoic. "Mr. Dixon may talk with me, but he will not speak at my daughter's Celebration of Life."

* * *

Susan walked arm in arm with her son across the Holiday Inn conference room, thanking everyone she met for coming to celebrate her daughter's life. The room seemed to glow with love as complete strangers offered their condolences and then a story of how Jenny's words had inspired them or a family member. There were flowers from several Major League scouts who had been the target of Jenny's barbs at high school and college ballparks. Even Royals scout, Roberto Francisco, had driven all the way from his home in Arizona. He walked over with a bouquet of daisies.

"I'm so sorry." Francisco bent his head courteously and then handed Susan the daisies. "Jenny told me once that daisies were her favorite. She thought they were the most free and cheerful of all flowers."

"That was very thoughtful of you." Susan inhaled the bouquet and her face brightened. "She liked the way they danced in the wind."

"I . . . " he paused for a moment as if to collect his thoughts. "I don't know how to explain it, ma'am, but your little Jenny was special. I would often drive to my next game thinking about something she had said."

"The elders in our tribe believed that she was an *old soul*."

His mother's words pained Sam, and his smile vanished, replaced by a look of regret.

Francisco seemed to notice and put a hand on his shoulder. "Jenny was your biggest fan, Sam. No one could sell your talent better than she—"

Francisco looked past them to the entryway of the conference room, where a television camera light was flipped on. "Wow, your Jenny is even more popular than I thought. Isn't that the new power broker in Washington, Drake Dixon?"

Both mother and son stiffened at the name but didn't turn around.

"Thank you again for coming to support us, Roberto, but Sam and I need to thank several other people who came today."

"Of course," Francisco said, mildly startled by her reply.

Susan, still pale at the mention of Dixon's name, stared down at the daisies for a long moment and then looked back up at Francisco with a forced smile. "I would be honored if you would join us at our table today."

* * *

Dixon was in the hallway, his back to the room so the TV cameras could get a good view of the ceremony behind him. He answered every reporter's question with a thoughtful and sympathetic cliché, nodding graciously to well-wishers who wanted to shake the hand of, or have a selfie taken with, the prominent private military CEO who flew all the way from Washington to pay his respects to the grieving Carson family.

Susan glanced back to watch him, and for just a moment their eyes met, a contemptuous smile creasing the corner of his mouth. She gripped Sam's arm tighter and moved deeper into the room, fighting back the urge to confront Dixon. She knew why he was here. This was a business trip for him. Nothing more. Nothing less.

* * *

Although Dixon didn't speak at Jenny Cloud-Carson's Celebration of Life, he ingratiated himself with every person he met, treating them as if they were long lost friends. As soon as the final speaker finished, Dixon and his security detail were out the door and gone.

Susan breathed a sigh of relief when she saw him leave and reached for her son's hand. "Let's go home. Let's go help Jenny walk on."

* * *

Susan was met by a blast of cold wind when she opened the door to their backyard. After being teased by Mother Nature with a mild early February, the weather had suddenly changed, with heavy gray clouds moving swiftly over the San Juans toward the Carson property. Jenny had requested a traditional Ute service, so her mother had changed into her deerskin skirt, white blouse, beaded belt, and blue gourd dance shawl. Sam was next to her, wearing a simple buckskin jacket and jeans with tan buckskin moccasins that came up to his knees. He had made the mocs the way his father had taught him, with soft soles, because he liked the feel of his foot to the ground when he was tracking.

"Would you prepare Jenny's horse?" Susan asked.

He gave a brief nod and headed to their corral. As Jenny's brother, it was his job to place the spiritual urn of his sister's ashes on the back of her horse and cover it with a buffalo robe.

The wind picked up again. Susan pulled her shawl tighter and turned away from the rush of arctic chill only to look full into the face of arrogance.

"Bad weather's coming fast, ma'am," Dixon said with a glance at the clouds as he walked, flanked by his two imposing security men, around the side of the house. "May I help you set up?"

She blinked twice, as if not understanding him. Then, as her surprise was replaced by anger, she balled her fists at her side, resisting the urge to run over and slap him in the face. "This is a private family and tribal ceremony. You are not welcome here."

He gave an amused look. "I figured my generous donation to the Kidney Foundation and paying for your room at the Holiday Inn was a ticket to the show."

"This is not a show. We are here to honor my daughter's life."

"And I came a long way to pay my respect to your family. As we both know, your husband died a patriot, a hero to our nation. I will never forget his service to my company and to our country." He then paused for a long, almost rehearsed moment, before adding, "Your son has similar skills that our country needs—"

"You stay away from Sam!" she snapped and pointed down the hill. "Get off my land! Now!"

The first snowflakes began to fall, big thick wafers fluttering softly to the ground. Dixon caught one in his right hand and showed it to her. "Like I said earlier, Mrs. Carson, bad weather's coming fast. It's too dangerous to be going back down your hill right now." With that, he motioned for his two guards to join him on the back porch, and he sat down on a wooden bench.

She glared at him, trying her best to figure out what to do while also attempting to calm her boiling fury. She was already late in setting up for her daughter's funeral.

Jose and Teresa came around the side of the house, carrying chairs. Both stopped when they saw who she was talking to. Jose glanced from Susan to Dixon and back again.

"I'm sorry to interrupt, Mrs. Carson," Jose said tentatively. "Where can we put these?"

Susan didn't answer, only glared one more time at Dixon, and then hurried over to help set up.

*   *   *

Within fifteen minutes, the snowfall became heavier and Susan called for everyone to take their seats so the funeral could begin.

"It's time, Papa." She nodded to her father, who walked to the fire and began to chant.

A line of dancers joined him, classmates of Jenny's, all adorned in their finest Ute dress, shaking gourd rattles and pounding drums to a slow melodic beat. There was a pause, then three hard beats as Susan stepped to the center of the dance ground and called for Jenny.

Sam came forward, guiding the horse with his sister's urn of ashes on its back. The pony was prancing, blowing steam into the cold mountain air.

Susan took a step back and smiled. *It was perfect,* she thought: the wind sweeping the snow and bright ribbons and eagle feathers that adorned the horse around her Jenny. Sam handed the reins to his mother and took a seat.

*   *   *

The rest of the ceremony was a celestial blur, a whirl of sights and sounds as if the mountain and clouds were part of the ceremony. The mountain inhaling the wind and the clouds exhaling the snow, circling around them, both ancient and present memories, gifts of Jenny's spirit.

Sam felt it first, for his sister had told him about this dream the day she died. The wisdom of Black Elk. The cycle of giving and receiving. No beginning and no end. The life of a human was a circle from childhood to childhood, and so it was in everything where power moved.

His sister was free. She was free from pain and disease and suffering. Jenny was finally free . . . free to walk on.

And then, much like life, the peaceful, poignant, idyllic moment was gone as quickly as the millions of snowflakes that rushed by them. It was severed by the frantic cry of a mother.

"Mary?" a friend of Susan's cried out from the edge of the ceremony. "Mary!" Her head jerked from right to left as she searched for her five-year-old little girl. Friends and family scattered to the grounds, the house, the garage, the corral, hunting for Mary, but only Sam saw the fast-fading impressions of a little girl's boots leading to the forest. He sprinted into the trees and then quickly returned.

"Mom!" he called out, and Susan spun back around. "Get my tracking bag and coat."

She raced inside as Sam went to a knee to study the track. Mary's mother hurried over to find out what the Carson boy saw.

"Mrs. Juarez, do you have anything of Mary's?" he asked. "Scarf? Doll? Blanket?"

She combed through her backpack and purse and found an old sweatshirt of her daughter's at the bottom of the pack. Sam took it and pushed it down the front of his jacket.

His mother came with his tracking bag and his down winter coat. Jose was next to her, a worried look on his face.

"We'd better go now," Jose said as he handed his friend a canteen of water. "There's probably only another hour of light. I called Sheriff Red Sky. He said there's no way they can get vehicles or choppers up in this weather and that it's gonna get worse."

Sam glared at his friend to shut up, knowing his words would only frighten Mrs. Juarez more. "You stay here," he said, and then he zipped up his down coat and tossed his tracking bag over his shoulder. "I need you to communicate with Sheriff Red Sky."

"Your mom can do that."

"No," he said in a voice that made Jose take a step back. "I need to go alone. I need to concentrate on only one thing."

The storm was roaring now, the wind whipping snow and ice crystals around them as Sam pulled on his gloves. He wore a look of calm, the look of one who was born for the wild, born for tension, cold, even terror. Then, like a lone wolf with eyes fixed only on the fading track, he disappeared into the blizzard.

* * *

Mary sat on a rock and wrapped her arms around her knees to warm herself. She was cold, scared, and confused. She remembered following the bunny, and then had lost sight of him and turned back, but nothing looked familiar. She cried out again for her mom, but no answer. As the blizzard swarmed around her and the sun settled lower in the west, she started to cry, a desperate teeth-chattering sob that scared her.

* * *

Sam went to one knee to read the tiny, almost invisible tracks. They were haphazard in the way the little girl had zigzagged back and forth, following a rabbit. Now, the rabbit track was gone, but the zigzag remained as Mary must have realized she was lost. *That was dangerous,* thought Sam. A lost hunter would usually travel in a straight line, but a child would wander aimlessly with no sense of where to go or of the danger that surrounded her.

Sam lost her track for about five minutes, but as he raised up to study his surroundings, he noticed that an Englemann spruce, about seventy feet to his left, had been disturbed. Snow covered the entire tree with the exception of a low branch where the white powder was gone. He hurried over and found her track. Mary must have ducked down when she hit the branch and crawled on all fours to the other side. The track showed that she had lain on her back for a spell and then was up again, but this time her track showed fatigue. Sam was now a good mile and a half from his house. He knew the area well, but his concern grew as he imagined a little girl lost, scared, and alone in a snowstorm.

* * *

Mary continued to cry as she pushed past branches and briar and snow. It was deep now, over her knees, but she trudged on, crying out again for her mother through a roaring wind that inhaled every sound. Bone tired, she sat down and slipped on an icy rock. She slid down a hill to a ledge. The exhaustion of her journey finally overtook her, and she lay back in the snow, letting the blizzard wash over her.

* * *

It was almost dark, the sun's fading light a soft glow pushing through the storm. Sam moved on, running lightly up the trail, eyes focused on the ground, making sure he didn't lose Mary's fast-fading track. The temperature was dropping again, low twenties, he figured, but the wind made it worse. He was only minutes from last light, which of course meant lost track.

He saw a footprint near a stream and continued on, down a hill and into a stand of blue spruce covered in snow. Pushing through branches to the far side, he looked down but couldn't find her track. He reached inside his coat and pulled out the little girl's sweatshirt. Closing his eyes, he brought the sweatshirt to his nose and inhaled deeply, letting his instincts guide him. He moved forward twenty steps and stopped as if some presence told him to go no farther. He opened his eyes and scanned his surroundings . . . there . . . over by a small slope, he saw a slight depression in the snow, then a displaced rock and a scuffed mark on stone. Something or someone had fallen.

This was familiar territory to Sam, barely two miles from home, a place he called Toenail Ridge because of the way a rim of granite curved out from a hill some forty feet above the forest floor. He sat on the ground and slid on his back down to the edge of the ridge. Something was here. He felt a living thing's energy nearby and flipped over onto his hands and knees. Was Mary still on the ridge, or had she fallen below? He knew there was about fifty yards from where he was to the north side of the ridge, so he peeled off his right glove with his teeth, crawled forward, feeling under the snow for anything that would lead him to the little girl. His hand found rocks, a stick, more stone, and then . . . something soft. Was it the polyester of a down jacket? He scrambled forward.

Yes! It was Mary! He swept the snow off the little girl and felt for a pulse in her neck. She was still alive, and her heartbeat was strong. Now, it was time to move, to find cover, get her away from the storm, and check her fingers and toes for frostbite. He remembered a rock overhang on the ridge that was not far away. Inhaling a deep icy breath through his nose, he pulled Mary's cold body to his chest, slithered forward, and collapsed against the back wall, only a small relief from the blizzard that raged on.

* * *

Susan sat next to Cynthia Juarez, staring out at the darkness and snow that whipped against the kitchen window. It was now seven o'clock. Her son had been gone almost three hours in search of Mary, and each minute that passed seemed like an eternity.

"Sam will find her," she said as she took Cynthia's hand and forced a smile. "There's no one better."

With a trembling hand, Cynthia made the sign of the cross.

"We have everything ready for Mary when Sam brings her in," Susan continued. "I've warmed the bath water again, and I have aloe vera and sage tea in case there's frostbite."

"Your boy's worth his weight in gold if he can find her in this storm." Dixon held his phone above his head, searching for any kind of a signal. "Have you ever thought about moving closer to town or at least closer to a cell tower?"

Susan heard him but didn't turn around, attempting to ignore the man's impatience.

"Can I use your landline? I need to make an important call back to DC."

"No, we need it available for emergency calls."

"This is an emergency."

Susan took a deep breath and turned to face him. "You may use the phone when we know my son and Mary are safe."

* * *

Sam took off Mary's jacket and boots and slipped the little girl underneath his cotton T-shirt, leather buckskin, and down jacket. He wanted Mary's cold body as close to his skin as possible. All he cared about was 98.6. Get her body temperature up anyway he could. He sat her bottom on his stomach, with her facing him, and curled her feet up into his armpits. Using his teeth, he pulled off one of her gloves and put her hand in his mouth. The skin of her hands was hard, waxy, and white. Not a good sign. A muffled whimper came from inside his coat, and he peeked in to find Mary looking up in fear at some man who seemed to be gnawing on her hand.

He released her hand and smiled. "Hi there, sweetness. It's me, Sam. I hope you don't mind me warming up your fingers. They were very cold." He put her hand back in his mouth.

"That hurts," she groaned.

"Thasagoosiiy."

She crinkled up her nose as if not understanding, and he took her hand out of his mouth again. "I said that's a good sign—sometimes healing can hurt a little bit."

She nodded, and then rested her head against his chest and went back to sleep.

*   *   *

When Sam felt that Mary's hands and feet were warm enough to travel, he wrapped them in wool cloth that he had in his travel bag and gently lifted her up. She was still inside his buckskin and down jacket to keep her warm, but carrying her up the icy hill was going to be a challenge. He unclipped the ice axe from the side of his bag and headed back out into the blizzard.

Whiteout was his first thought. The ground was a blanket of white, the clouds were a whitish gray, and the wind swirled the snow at a speed that made it appear as if Sam were looking into a translucent abyss. He couldn't see a thing. One wrong step could send them tumbling off the ledge. It was time to trust something beyond the physical. To be very still and trust his gift, trust his instinct. Words came to him that were not his own. *You do not walk alone. I am with you always. You are blessed and protected on this journey.*

With his right arm cradling the girl to his chest and his left hand against the wall of the ledge, he took a step forward. Then another. And another, until he returned to the steep slope where he had slid down and found Mary. He raised the ice axe over his head, slammed it deep into the snow and pulled them up, gaining only a foot. He did it again, barely advancing a foot each time. For some reason, he thought about pitching.

Balance. Separate hands. Throw. In this case it was an ice axe he was pitching down through the snow, over and over, until they reached the top. His shaking limbs gave way, and he collapsed on his back, gasping for air. He rolled to his side, lifted the still-sleeping child to his chest, and stood up. It was only two miles to his house, but the whiteout would make it tough.

Trust was now his only thought. He knew the trees. The trees would lead him home. He waited a moment to get his bearings. The slope was behind him. From where he was standing, the blue spruce stand he'd gone under earlier was to his right at two o'clock. He closed his eyes and walked into the wind and snow that lashed at his face until he felt the sting change to the needles of the spruce. On hands and knees, he crawled through and stood up.

Trust. The creek was to his left at ten o'clock. He closed his eyes again and continued on, stumbling when he hit a rock that bordered the creek, his left leg sinking all the way to the knee in the icy water. Two long steps took him to the other side. He struggled up the embankment and found his tree. He knew this old lodgepole pine. Had climbed it many times growing up. About twenty paces ahead would be another lodgepole. With the canopy of pines cutting the wind and snow, he could finally see about ten feet ahead. He moved on, using each pine as if it was a mile marker on the road, letting him know how close they were to finding home.

* * *

Susan placed another log in the fireplace and stoked the coals. It was now ten o'clock. Cynthia Juarez had never left the kitchen, her chair turned toward the window, her shoulders hunched over in despair as she prayed for something, anything to come out of the darkness. The rest of the funeral party was resting in various rooms or curled up on the floor, hopeful that the storm would let up so they could help. Dixon and his bodyguards were next to the fire, one of them asleep in a chair, head back, mouth open, oblivious to the worry that gripped the house.

"They've been out there almost six hours," Dixon said softly so only Susan could hear him. "Wind chill is now minus five degrees. If that girl's body temperature drops below ninety, she won't make it."

Susan raised an index finger to her lips to quiet him.

"Mrs. Juarez can't hear us, but those are the facts. I'm a hunter whose been out in bad weather before. Almost lost a toe to frostbite ten years ago, hunting elk in Montana. I've never seen a storm like this."

"Your facts chip away at faith." She tapped the side of her head. "Why don't you try and change the way you think?"

"Blizzards don't give a shit about faith, Mrs. Carson. They'll freeze anything in their path. Your son had a chance in daylight. But when darkness came and the wind picked up, well, you better hope Sam hunkered down in some cave to save himself."

She let go a deep sigh as if she were releasing more than simple fatigue. "Perhaps Black Elk was right."

He raised a curious brow, wondering what she meant about the Lakota medicine man.

"It's not the darkness outside we get lost in." She nodded to the window, where the storm was still wildly blowing. "It is in the darkness of *their eyes* that men get lost."

It was then that her father rose up from a chair on the far side of the room. He was still dressed in his Ute ceremonial finery from earlier in the day: fringed buckskin tunic over a simple blue cotton shirt and beaded moccasins. But there was something different about his face, as if a kerosene lamp had turned from dim to bright. There was no longer the look of fear and worry that had consumed all of them much of the day. Despite cataracts that blurred his vision, his eyes went wide, drawn to something outside.

"Papa?" Susan asked, but he didn't respond. He shuffled into the kitchen and on toward the back door.

"Papa!" she called out again and hurried after him. "It's still storming. You'll need your coat if you're going outside."

By then, others were interested and followed them to the kitchen, but as Susan reached for his hand on the doorknob, he turned to her and smiled in a way that made her pause.

"I feel him," he said, and then opened the door. A rush of cold and snow poured in, but the Ute elder stepped out onto the back porch and pointed toward Pargin Mountain. "I feel him," he said again as both Susan and Cynthia Juarez followed him outside and stared into the blizzard.

"What do you feel, Papa?" Susan asked.

The storm continued to roar, snow and ice and cold biting their faces, but the old man seemed unaffected. He stood erect and pointed a bony finger into the darkness. "It is my grandson," he said in a proud voice. "The one who walks with the wind."

And then, like a phantom coming out of the shadows, Sam Cloud-Carson stepped out of the storm.

* * *

There were shrieks of both joy and relief when Sam collapsed on the kitchen floor and unzipped his jacket to reveal little Mary inside. The girl beamed a bright smile as she reached up for her mother.

"You found her! Praise God!" Cynthia pulled her daughter up to her chest and began to sob uncontrollably. "My baby . . . my sweet little Mary . . . baby girl!"

There were plenty of hearty pats on the back for Sam as his mother pulled off his snow-covered ski cap and kissed him on the forehead. "Your father and Jenny would be proud."

He gave an appreciative nod and then glanced up at Mary, whose red face was streaked with ringlets of sweaty hair after being inside Sam's jacket the last two and a half hours.

"I know she looks fine, Mrs. Juarez, but we should probably soak Mary in a warm salt bath for at least a half hour."

"I'll take care of that." Susan put her arm around mother and daughter and led them to the bathroom.

Jose and Teresa helped Sam to his feet, peeled off his still snowy down jacket and buckskin shirt, and handed him a towel.

"Where the hell did you find her?" Jose asked.

"Just past Oak Creek," Sam mumbled. The exhaustion of the day hit him full, and he crumpled down in a chair. His hands shook as he wiped the ice crystals from his eyebrows and the ends of his hair. "She slipped down the northern slope onto Toenail Ridge and passed out."

Teresa's eyes went wide. "She was asleep when you found her?"

He nodded.

"God, Sam—she would have died if you hadn't found her."

He continued to mop at his hair and face with one trembling hand while struggling to untie his moccasins with his other frozen claw. It was his pitching hand. Jose must have noticed because he knelt down to help Sam pick the frozen leather laces apart and slide his snow-covered moccasins off.

Grandpa Douglas placed a cup of hot spiced tea in front of his grandson and sat down next to him, a proud smile lighting his face.

Sam nodded a weary thanks, and with shaking hands, brought the cup to his lips only to look directly into the dark hooded eyes of Drake Dixon.

The DiamondBar owner was leaning against the doorframe of the kitchen like a cobra studying its prey. He glanced at the others in the room and said, "I'd like a word with Sam . . . alone, if you don't mind."

Jose, Teresa, and the others did oblige, but Sam's grandfather did not.

"I'll stay," Douglas said in a voice that made Dixon pause. "Someone needs to make sure you don't lie."

Sam stifled a grin as he took a sip of tea.

Dixon cleared his throat and stepped into the room. "You have incredible gifts, Sam. Gifts our country needs."

Sam took another sip of tea.

"I've spent much of my life serving our country. That's why I created a company of service. DiamondBar is all about integrity, discipline, dedication, and honor in trying to create a safer world."

"Honor?" Sam eyed him coolly. "You have no right talking about honor and integrity."

Dixon's face tightened, but he did a good job of hiding his displeasure. He put his hands together behind his back and moved a step closer to his prospect. "I was once your age, Sam. Young and idealistic, chasing a dream. You're chasing this baseball dream right now, but I want you to think about *your* future—beyond baseball." Dixon's smooth voice took on a blend of compassion and superiority. "How many college kids do you know who get paid two hundred thousand dollars a year when they graduate? That's what I'm offering you if—"

"Sam not for sale." Grandpa Douglas interrupted and pointed toward the door. "Time for you to go now."

Dixon raised a hand for quiet. "I'm trying to make life easier for the entire Carson family, sir. Sam will get a good salary, insurance, retirement benefits. You don't get those things working as an outfitter on an Indian reservation."

Grandpa Douglas continued to point toward the door. "Go now."

The howling of the wind against the house let up for a bit, and Dixon glanced out the kitchen window. The snow was still falling but nowhere near the blizzard-like conditions of just fifteen minutes earlier. White drifts were heavy against the sides of the house, and icicles hung like sharp daggers from the gutters on the roof. There was no way Dixon and his security team could get their Range Rover down the hill until the emergency road crew cleared the road. He leaned back against the wall and crossed his arms over his chest as if to let them know he wasn't going anywhere until *he* said so.

"Your grandson has a chance to be paid very well while serving his country." Dixon stayed with his strategy of appealing to their sense of national loyalty. "What we saw today was a young man who risked his life to save another . . . much like his own father did when he died trying to save others in the mountains of Afghanistan."

Sam's brows shot up, and his eyes seemed to darken, but he remained quiet.

"Daniel Carson was a hero," Dixon said respectfully. "A hero who made the choice to serve his country while also helping those suffering terrible human-rights violations in Afghanistan. I believe that is a call of the highest good."

"More like serve your highest good," Grandpa Douglas grunted.

Sam snorted back a laugh and spilled most of his tea on the kitchen table. As he grabbed a towel to wipe up the mess, he winked at his grandfather and then looked firmly up at Dixon. "Perhaps you didn't hear my grandpa right—Sam not for sale."

CHAPTER TWENTY-THREE

Durango, Colorado

February 2008

Two miles south of Durango, a black Ford F-150 was parked in the shadows of the dimly lit Sky High Nightclub. The driver held a cell phone to his ear with one hand while inhaling a line of cocaine off the blade of a pocketknife with the other.

"Did you hear me, Billy?"

Cutthredge wiped his nose. "Yeah, boss, I got everything. Find more trackers and stay out of trouble."

"I'm serious," Dixon said from the office of his Georgetown home. "Have you met any trackers worth recruiting?"

"Not really. We went on five trips the last two months. Most of the guides are old enough to be my daddy, and the one young dude we booked near Steamboat Springs would be tough to break. He comes from money, so he don't need no insurance like the Carsons did."

There was a long pause on the line. "All right, it's getting late. Keep after it. I want twice monthly updates from you."

Dixon clicked off, but Cutthredge continued to glare at the phone. "God, I can't wait to finally be rid of that egomaniac."

"Our first day of independence starts tonight," Marcus said as he stepped out into the cold Colorado night.

They opened the door to the Sky High Club and searched the bar and dimly lit booths for their new business partner. Tommy Sherman. Durango drug dealer who had connections. He was in the last booth, next to the bathroom.

Cutthredge walked over and sat down across from Sherman while Marcus remained standing, eyes on the door, just in case there was trouble.

"I hear you've got friends who work the railroad?" Cutthredge asked.

"They still can't believe how easily you got the smack here," said Sherman.

"It's easy when opium production is protected by both the Afghan government and the Taliban."

Sherman chuckled lightly. "Everybody wants in on the deal."

"And our CIA and military have been turning a blind eye to the farmers who grow it. It's okay to drop bombs and kill their people, but God forbid we do anything to hurt their economy." Cutthredge grinned.

"All that drug money going straight to the Taliban." Sherman rubbed his palms together. "No reason why you and I can't get a slice of that cake."

CHAPTER TWENTY-FOUR

Grand Junction, Colorado

March 2008

"**B**us leaves in one hour," Jose said and then flipped a letter onto Sam's desk. "You got more mail from DiamondBar."

It was the second piece of correspondence that he had received from Dixon in the two weeks following his sister's funeral. The first had been a personal note, thanking Sam for sharing Jenny's funeral and Celebration of Life. There was the typical sweet-talking sales mumbo jumbo, praising Sam for being a man of service, someone who was making his Southern Ute, Mesa State, and Colorado communities proud.

Then, there was the obvious shift toward his future and the benefits of working for DiamondBar, a family-run organization that cared about both their employees and their country. Dixon's final strategy was to grab at Sam's heart. He had included a photo of the DiamondBar Hero's Wall at their Virginia training facility with his father's plaque front and center. Sam remembered wanting to throw up when he saw the picture and had torn it into shreds before heading out to baseball practice.

What has he written this time? Sam thought and finally opened the envelope. He had never met a person who so easily could rob him of his peace. He hardly knew Dixon, yet the man seemed to have this unique ability to get under his skin, like a tick burrowing inside an animal and sucking their very life away, taking, always taking, never giving.

He read the letter and cringed. It was a litany of his father's accomplishments while working for DiamondBar Security: teamwork, sacrifice, loyalty, service, patriotism; there was even a letter from an Army Colonel Tomlinson, praising Daniel Carson's help while tracking for his Special Forces team in Afghanistan.

He stared at the letter for a long time and then crushed it in his hands and fired it into the trash. Drake Dixon had done it again. The man seemed to know every button to push to make Sam feel lost.

*   *   *

Tucson in March was perfect baseball weather. Most days not a cloud in the sky, temperatures in the seventies, and soft breezes blowing at Hi Corbett Field. The only real trouble might be a sun so bright it could turn routine popups into blind adventures for outfielders.

With Pac-10 favorite Arizona hosting the non-conference invitational that also included perennial powers Cal-State Fullerton, Oklahoma State, Minnesota, and Tennessee, it would be a difficult mountain for Division Two Mesa State to climb. There were also more than thirty Major League scouts in the stands to evaluate the talent.

Sam's pregame bullpen session had gone well. Command and movement were there, evidenced by a confident wink from Jose, his catcher, when Sam completed his throws. This would be his first game since Jenny's death.

There were moments, most coming unexpectedly, when thoughts of his sister would lock him up: memories of her laughter, her wit, her confidence in him that gripped his heart. Was there still something he had yet to release since Jenny's passing? Some spiritual weakness his sister had warned him about? His strength in baseball and tracking had always been his ability to block everything out and focus on the present. He had done that at Jenny's funeral in his search for Mary, but lately, his mind was burdened by a thousand random thoughts: of his sister, his mother, SJ

Outfitters, baseball, school, midterms, and now, the second letter from Dixon. He shook his head to rid himself of those images.

"Time to rock and roll." Jose smiled, and together they jogged to the main field.

Sam went down his mental checklist for the Oklahoma State lineup. Leadoff batter, lefty hitter with speed, vulnerable to an above-average fastball inside. *What were his father's last moments like in Afghanistan?* Number-two hitter, righty, trouble with the curve. *Is Jenny watching me right now?* Number-three hitter, right-handed power, don't make a mistake with a fastball middle in. *Isn't Wasson Peak beautiful today? I'd love to hike that mountain. Geez, Sam, get your head back in the game. Focus, dammit, what's wrong with you?*

His first pitch missed by a foot outside. Second was in the dirt. Third, he threw right down the middle for a called strike, and fourth was a flat fastball lined just past his left ear for a single. He stepped off the rubber, trying to calm both his body and mind. Everything seemed like it was on fast forward. The baseball, which always was like an extension of his fingertips, felt foreign. He wasn't sure where to grip the seams or where to place his foot on the pitching rubber.

"C'mon, Sam, bring it!" Jose barked out to him.

He bent down to get the sign, nodded, and came set. He glanced at Wasson Peak and delivered another poorly located fastball that the Cowboys' number-two hitter absolutely demolished. The Mesa State outfielders didn't even move as the ball took off in an arc some fifty feet beyond the left-field fence. By the time the inning was over, Mesa State was down 7–0 and Sam was done for the day.

* * *

Two days later, he sat alone in the last row of the bus, somberly looking over the stat sheet of the Arizona Invitational. No wins, three losses, outscored 31–4. The Mavericks worst tournament showing in fifteen years.

Sam's line was even worse. Nine runs allowed in three innings on the mound and 0-8 as a hitter with four strikeouts. He even hit the last batter he faced on purpose, which led to a screaming match with the opposing dugout. He was frustrated, angry, lost, searching for the right path in a dark cave with no flicker of light to guide him. He tossed the stat sheet aside and stared out the window, mentally replaying his failures on the field.

"You okay, man?" Dennis Martin, his first baseman, sat down next to him.

Sam didn't respond, still absorbed with his final at bat, a swing and a miss strikeout on a slider that was a good two feet off the plate.

"Do you want to talk about it?" Martin asked.

Sam sat up straight, jaw tight, and glared at his teammate. "I don't need your help."

Martin's mouth fell open. He glanced down at the stat sheet on the floor and then back up at Sam. "We're a team, ya know."

The glare deepened in Sam's eyes. "I said, I–don't–need–your–help."

Martin stood up and shook his head sadly. "Whatever, dude. But eventually, we all need each other."

Then Martin was gone, down the aisle of the bus to join his fellow Mavericks, leaving Sam Carson very much alone.

* * *

The next two weeks saw no improvement. Three starts, three more losses with an earned run average over ten. He continued to distance himself from his teammates. Midterms were a struggle too. As became Bs and Bs became Cs. His mind was like a squirrel's, screeching and scratching, leaping from limb to limb with no apparent destination. His strength had become his weakness. His ability to focus was now wandering haphazardly in every direction.

As the bus drove away from Las Vegas, New Mexico, after another humiliating loss, this time to Rocky Mountain Conference favorite New Mexico Highlands, Coach Elba walked down the aisle and sat next to him.

"How you doin', Sam?"

He shrugged his shoulders.

"You've been through a lot in the last year. I don't think you've given yourself enough time to recover."

Sam turned in his seat, a sudden heaviness of suspicion etched on his face.

"Spring break starts tomorrow. I'm giving the team two days off. I want you to take the entire week," Elba said.

"I'm fine, sir . . . please."

"I've already called your mom. Our bus should go through Durango about eight thirty. She's gonna meet us in the hardware store's parking lot to pick you up."

His mouth grew dry at the thought of leaving. He couldn't. He had a responsibility to his team, through good times and bad, through wins and losses, he had to grind through this temporary struggle. Stepping off this bus while his fellow Mavericks continued on to Grand Junction would be both an embarrassment and his greatest failure as a man.

"I–I can't go, Coach. Please. I need to battle through this."

Elba stood up and put his hand on Sam's shoulder. "This isn't a suggestion, Sam. I think it's best for you—and best for the team."

* * *

It was a quiet drive back up the hill to the Carson home, Sam staring out the window, his dark brown hawk's eyes dull with the weight of disappointment. His mother had only said hello when she picked him up, obviously knowing how he would feel after leaving his team. He gave her a brief, distracted glance when she parked next to their house, pulled his travel bag out of the back, and headed inside.

"I want to show you something, Sam."

"Tomorrow morning, Mom. I'm tired."

"No. Now." Her voice was sharp.

He let out a long breath, dropped his travel bag in the living room, and followed her to Jenny's old room.

It was much the same, as if her bed was still waiting for Jenny to pull back her pink blanket and climb inside. Her throw pillows perfectly framed against the headstand tightened Sam's heart more. There was a red, white, and black Bobcats pillow from his high school days; a maroon, white, and gold Maverick pillow of Mesa State; and one the shape of a baseball in the middle. All made by his sister. His gaze went to the wall where Jenny's dreamcatcher art reminded him of a past conversation.

"Our physical bodies need sleep," Jenny had said. *"But our spirit never rests. It constantly moves and wanders about when we sleep. That's why we need the dreamcatcher to catch our nightmares and allow the good dreams to float over us to comfort our minds and bring us peace."*

Susan opened a drawer to Jenny's nightstand and pulled out two spiral notebooks. One was a neat green seventy-page notebook; the other was a ramshackle, overused two-hundred-page monstrosity, overflowing with scraps of paper and dog-eared from years of reading and writing. Sam opened the green notebook and his chest tightened. It was Jenny's scouting reports of every high school and college game he had ever played.

December 1, 2002: Ignacio v Delores, Bobcats won 57-50, Sam Carson 6-1 150 lb. sophomore 11 pt. (4-7FG, 1-3trey, 2-2FT) 3Reb, 4Ass, 2TO Good defensive footwork but got pushed around inside by stronger guards. Needs to get in weight room if he's going to avg more than 3 rebounds per game. 2 turnovers, including one crossover where he dribbled it off his foot. What's that all about?

Sam flipped forward about twenty pages.

May 11, 2005: Ignacio v Bayfield, Bobcats win 4-0, Sam Carson 6-3, 180 lb. senior, CG shutout (fifth this year!) (7IP-3hits-0runs-0ER-0w-8k) 4-seam avg 86, 2-seam avg 84, curve 73, change 75. 11-GO, 8K, 1-FO. Good command, both sides of the plate, LH 0-12. My brother rocks. On to postseason!

Sam wiped the tears from his eyes and looked up at his mother, who nodded for him to open the second notebook. He had to sit on a chair to make sure none of the many slips of paper inside the journal fell on the floor. He opened to the first page.

May 17, 1999

"Wow," he whispered. "Jenny was only seven years old when she wrote this."

Be kind to everyone. Even those who are mean to you.

He turned the pages to later years:

The Great Spirit is always with me . . . I am as God created me . . . I will not fail to hear you, Father. I will choose your happiness today.

There were all kinds of quotes from Jesus and Buddha to Muhammad and Black Elk, from Chief Seattle and Luther Standing Bear to the Torah, from the Bhagavad Gita and Eddie Box to A Course in Miracles. All were words of inspiration, peace, and unity.

He read a quote from Gandhi: *The essence of all religions is one. Only their approaches are different.* Another from Romans 12:16: *Live in harmony with one another.* One from A Course in Miracles: *By grace I live. By grace I am released.* Another from Buddha: *The root of suffering is attachment.*

He turned back to his mom. "May I take these with me?"

"They're yours, Sam. Jenny wrote those books for you."

* * *

Sam lay back in his bed and returned his attention to his sister's notebook. There was so much he still didn't know about his sister. Yes, the elders had said Jenny was an old soul, someone who completely trusted the Great Spirit to direct her thoughts and actions. But there was a vigilance in her quest that was different from the other holy men and women of their tribe.

How was she able to find joy and peace when her body was being ravaged by disease? And why was he depressed when he was given so much? Was it, as Jenny had said, his lack of discipline to exercise his spiritual muscle that was holding him back? He had the ability to quiet his mind in the natural world, and until recently, on the mound. But was he in some way refusing to let the Great Spirit enter?

He took a deep breath and randomly flipped open Jenny's notebook to a quote from nineteenth-century Ponca Chief White Eagle:

When you are in doubt, be still, and wait; when doubt no longer exists for you, then go forward with courage. So long as mists envelop you, be still; be still until the sunlight pours through and dispels the mists, as it surely will. Then act with courage.

He placed Jenny's journal on his nightstand, turned off the light, and settled back into the silence.

*   *   *

That night was his most restful in months. He dreamed of the past, of hunting and fishing with his father, of long walks with his sister when she was healthy. He dreamed of taking Jenny's hand and leading her to a stream to teach her how to live in the wild.

"This is watercress," he said. "You can make it into soup or tea. It's good for the liver, heart, and kidneys." They walked to a meadow filled with sunflowers. "Every part of the sunflower is beneficial to our health, Jenny. I can mash the root to heal blisters and spider bites; the flower can help with arthritis or rheumatism; and the seed can be eaten raw or boiled into tea to help with bronchitis, rheumatism, or to help clean the waste from your body." He taught her the benefits of alfalfa and alumroot, goose grass and wild lettuce, juniper and oak.

Her innocent eyes smiled up at him as she said, "What plant can one eat to heal the mind? To help you surrender. To let go of the pain *you* are holding onto."

He came awake suddenly. It was still dark, but he felt a presence in the room, some vibration that was near him. His eyes were open wide now, like an owl searching for some nearby mystery. Was he awake or was he still dreaming?

"Sam." He heard a whisper, gentle as a soft breeze. He sat up straight and looked around. Was there someone sitting in a chair in the far corner of the room?

"Brother," came the soft voice again.

He squinted through the dark. "Jenny?"

Whatever was in the chair seemed to glow brighter. It was her. He felt her. And then, he caught a glimpse of his sister's face in the glimmer of soft ethereal light emanating from the chair.

"You are needed," the voice said.

He stared at the faint light.

"Go to the mountain."

He finally found his voice. "Where?"

"You will know."

"Is someone lost?"

"Only release . . . will give you peace."

He turned to flip on the light switch, but when he turned back, the image was gone.

* * *

He stopped to catch his breath. His heart was still racing, and sweat poured off his forehead as he tried to make sense of what had just happened. Was it real, or was it a dream that he was now remembering? Despite his confusion, he dressed, wrote his mother a note, and went to get his tracking bag. But where would he go? The voice said he would know. And what did "only release will give you peace" mean? He got in his mom's truck, drove down the hill, and headed east.

It was a foggy March morning. The sun had yet to break, making visibility difficult. As he stared into the mist, he calmed his breathing and focused on each breath. Slow inhale, slow exhale. Words came to him that were not his own. *Inhale peace, exhale release. Inhale peace, exhale release.* What did that mean?

About a mile from Salt Canyon, he felt an urge to stop near a trailhead. He hiked north, into the forest, staying on the trail for a good mile, wondering who or what he was looking for. As the fog began to lift, he found that there was plenty of track to see. Coyote and raccoon, fox and turkey, possum and deer had all passed last night, but nothing stood out. Nothing . . . until he saw the big track of Old Mel. The ancient mule deer's track looked tired, and the fracture on the front left hoof had widened a full inch and a half. The track also showed he was dragging his back right leg a bit. A half mile farther, he noticed there had been a scuffle. Old Mel had spun around several times to ward off some predator. Sam found the culprits. Three coyotes had attacked Mel this very morning. A broken point from the right antler was on the ground, blood and fur on the end, showing that Mel had scored in the fight.

The sun had come up now, tossing a soft pink glaze against the thin clouds in the east. Sam continued on through the woods. The track was easy to follow as Mel's track showed signs of severe fatigue with the coyotes in pursuit up the mountain. Sam crested a hill and caught scent of blood. Hurrying through a stand of junipers, his heart sprang to his throat. There, in the middle of a meadow, was Old Mel, laying on his side, breathing hard, his neck ravaged by teeth and his stomach and hind legs torn open. The coyotes had won. Much like the circle of life, nature's cycle of giving and receiving, the coyotes were now feasting on the Phantom of Pargin Mountain. The old buck raised his head and looked at Sam, as if pleading for help. Was this it? Was this the help that Jenny had told him about?

Without thinking, Sam charged at the coyotes, his bow in one hand, his tracking stick in the other, raised over his head. "Get away from him!"

The coyotes did scatter, but stayed close, growling back at Sam in anger. He knelt down next to Mel and cradled the old deer's head in his lap. The buck was too tired by now, having accepted his fate to the coyotes. But there was no reason for him to be in pain and have to suffer. For a brief moment their eyes met, and Sam saw in Mel's soft brown gaze his sister. This wasn't just about Mel. It was also about Jenny. *Only release will give you peace.* It was time for both Mel and Jenny to walk on without him.

He turned his face to the sky, searching for some reason, some answer to why Jenny, or a dream, or some damn invisible spirit would request him for this task. Why him? Why not the coyotes or a bear or another hunter?

"What more do you want from me!" he screamed to the heavens as he pulled the knife from his belt and placed the blade against Mel's jugular vein and carotid artery. Tears streamed down Sam's face. "I don't want to do this, Jenny. Please!"

But he knew what had to be done, or the old buck would suffer.

"Damn you, God!" he screamed again, and then thrust the blade into the deer's neck, blood spurting over the knife and his hand, pumping several times until it died away along with Old Mel.

The mountain was silent, save for the wind swishing through the pines and the weary, strained, heavy breathing of a brother who had done what was asked of him. He struggled to stand up, his chest still heaving, his shirt drenched with both blood and sweat. For a moment he glared at the coyotes, who were moving closer, then with a loud sigh, he nodded for them to take their prize.

CHAPTER TWENTY-FIVE

Grand Junction, Colorado

March 2008

He came back to school six days later, still depressed, confused, and distant. His efforts at reconnecting with his teammates were mostly awkward and forced, and the team played accordingly. Despite warm weather returning to Colorado in late March, it did little to thaw the deep freeze that continued to grip Mesa State baseball. The Mavericks had lost seven in a row to fall to ten and twenty, dead last in the Rocky Mountain Conference, and Sam had yet to pitch since his fiasco at New Mexico Highlands two weeks before.

"Dang it," Mavericks backup catcher Keith Nelson grumbled as he sat down next to Sam in the dugout. "We're letting a six-run lead slip away. Can't we just get two more measly outs?"

Sam's left leg shook restlessly, like a sprinter waiting for the sound of the gun to let him run. For the first time in his life, he had been moved to the bullpen, and now he desperately wanted to be part of helping his team win. He looked down the bench at Coach Elba, hoping he might look his way. Instead, Elba continued to study his lineup card.

Michael Sanchez was struggling on the mound and peeked out at the scoreboard because he forgot the count. *Never a good sign.* Three balls, one strike. Sanchez stepped off the rubber a second time and asked for another set of signs from his catcher.

"C'mon, Mikey!" barked Sam. "Finish it!"

Sanchez's pitch missed his target by about three feet, with Lopez having to leap out of his crouch to keep the ball from going back to the screen. Bases loaded.

"Carson! Get loose!" Coach Elba called out. Sam grabbed his glove and sprinted out to the bullpen.

Sanchez's first pitch to the next Kearney hitter missed outside. Ball one. Second pitch bounced in the dirt. Ball two. Jose asked the ump for time and walked slowly out to the mound in an effort to give Sam as much time as he needed to warm up. With one eye on his coach and the other on the bullpen, Jose barely said two words to Sanchez before getting a pat on his shoulder from the ump.

"Let's go."

Jose nodded but kept a watchful eye on the bullpen as he went back behind home plate and dropped another sign for his pitcher. Sanchez delivered another fastball way outside. Ball three. "Damn," Jose mumbled and peeked over at his coach. Nothing.

He asked for another fastball and set up right down the middle of the plate. Sanchez missed badly again, ball four, forcing in a run. The Mavericks lead was now 8–7.

"Time!" Coach Elba shouted as he walked to the mound and then pointed to the bullpen.

Sam clenched and unclenched his right hand as he jogged to the mound. Heart racing, eyes wide, jaws tense, he reached for the baseball that was still in his catcher's glove.

Jose swept the ball behind his back. "Are you okay, dude?"

"Just give me the ball."

Jose chuckled and took a step back. "Not until you answer me a question."

"Give me the fucking ball, Jose."

"Not until I get an answer."

"C'mon, guys," the ump interrupted. "We ain't got all day."

Sam let go an irritated exhale and glared at his catcher. "What?"

The corners of Jose's wide mouth curled up as if he was enjoying his friend's discomfort. "Who lives in a pineapple under the sea?"

Absolutely befuddled by the random stupidity of the question, Sam stared at Jose for a long moment.

"Who lives in a pineapple under the sea?" Jose asked again.

"SpongeBob," the umpire answered, and then clapped his hands. "Now let's play ball."

Sam bit the side of his mouth to keep from laughing as he finally understood what his friend was trying to do.

"Keep her down, meat." Jose popped the ball into Sam's hand.

"Just give me a good target . . . SpongeBob." Sam chuckled, his earlier tension finally draining from his body.

The rest was like old times for Sam and Jose. Eight perfectly located warm-up pitches followed by his signature sinker, biting low and away to the Kearney right-handed hitter, who lunged for the ball and topped it back to the mound. Sam snatched it with his glove, threw home for the second out, and Jose fired to first for the double play. One pitch. Two outs. Game over. The home dugout erupted in joy and then raced to the mound to celebrate with the man who ended the Mavericks seven-game losing streak.

*   *   *

Three weeks later Mesa was back to .500. With Carson back in the starting rotation, the Mavericks won eight of their next ten games. Whether it was drowning his grief in baseball or his team simply winning, Sam became more relaxed with his teammates, and more outspoken.

He had always been a quiet encourager, but now, if an outfielder overthrew the cutoff man, he spoke up. If a baserunner forgot the number of outs, he reminded him that was not the way they played Maverick baseball. And, if a teammate was disrespectful to another, he gave them the Carson look. Head cocked to the side, eyes narrowed, jaws clenched.

No words. Just a penetrating knock it off, are you kidding me, would your mom approve of your behavior stare. It worked every time.

*　　*　　*

"Hum baby it in there, Sam Bam." Jose pounded his fist into his mitt as he awaited the first pitch of the sixth inning. Mesa led Metro 4–0, with Carson tossing a two-hit, no-walk, six-strikeout gem in the first five innings.

Sam delivered a first-pitch fastball, perfectly located on the outside corner for a called strike one.

"Way to paint, Sammy! Paint that black!" Jose yelled again, much to the dismay of the toothpick-thin left-handed Roadrunner hitter.

"Shut up," he said under his breath, but Jose heard him.

"Ya gotta appreciate good art, dude," Jose teased as he dropped two fingers for a curve.

Sam spun a curve that looked like it was falling off a table. Metro's hitter reached for it but came up with nothing but air.

Jose snorted back a laugh, knowing he owned the Metro hitter if he'd gotten under his skin. "The Medicis had Michelangelo, and we got us Samalangelo."

"Would you shut the hell up?"

"Check out this next pitch." Jose dropped an index finger inside his right thigh. Sam threw a fastball that cut in on the left-hander's hands, splintering his bat as the ball rolled weakly out to the mound. He was thrown out by forty feet.

"Better luck next time, meat." Jose winked and the hitter started back toward the plate.

"Calm down, fellas." The umpire stepped between the two opponents but only looked at Jose. "Back off a bit, kid."

"Yo, Metro!" Kenny Alvarez yelled from shortstop. "Grab some pine!"

The outburst brought both benches to the top steps of the dugouts, screaming obscenities at each other until Sam stepped off the rubber and gave his teammates the look. They quieted and settled back into their respective positions as peace was restored.

Coach Elba watched the entire scene from the corner of the dugout and smiled. His sophomore sensation was back. He knew that championships were not won in a vacuum. A coach needed every player pulling on the same end of the rope. And when the best player was braiding the line, well, Mesa would be a formidable team to beat.

Sam went nine that day, shutting out Metro 7–0 and pulling Mesa within three games of second-place Colorado Christian in the Mountain Division.

CHAPTER TWENTY-SIX

Durango, Colorado

May 2008

"You ready to go?" Susan called out to Teresa as she hustled across the lobby of Mercy Medical Center. "We have a long drive, young lady. Game one of the Rocky Mountain Tournament starts in five hours. Don't want to miss our two favorite Mavericks."

Even though there was a twenty-four-year difference between the two women, Susan had always felt a deep connection with her son's childhood friend. She'd known Teresa since the day she was born, and Sam, Jose, and Teresa were darn near inseparable growing up on Pargin Mountain. When Susan had taken a second job, working two days a week at the Mercy gift shop, she had grown closer to the nineteen-year-old girl who was in her first year of nursing school at Fort Lewis College. On this day, Teresa was relieving the emergency-room triage nurse while she went on break.

"Almost ready," Teresa said, but she seemed absorbed in another matter as she closed the admittance book and looked up at Susan. "I didn't think we had much of a heroin problem in Southwest Colorado, but our hospital alone has treated three overdoses in the last two weeks."

"Is one of them Valerie Quintana?" Susan asked.

"I can't say . . . HIPAA laws." Teresa answered, but the surprise in her face told Susan she had guessed correctly. She had seen Valerie's father, Mauricio at church the previous week, remembered him kneeling by the votive candles, head bowed in prayer, shoulders slumped as if some weight were pulling them even lower. There were rumors that his daughter had fallen in with the wrong crowd, first drinking, then marijuana, then meth.

"How is Valerie?"

Teresa glanced about the lobby and then whispered, "Still in ICU."

Susan slipped her arm through her friend's and pulled her towards the parking lot. "I'll visit with her when we return . . .but right now we've got to hit the road and cheer on our Mavericks."

* * *

The sky above Suplizio Field was a brilliant blue. The sun overhead cast long shadows across the field for the one o'clock start. The Mavericks were just beginning to loosen up in the outfield when Susan and Teresa found their seats on the home side. As Susan watched the players long toss, she noticed a difference between her son and the rest of his teammates: the way he glided to receive the baseball and then pivoted smoothly and returned the throw. While the 120- to 180-foot tosses looked to be an achievement for his fellow Mavericks, the ball seemed to explode effortlessly off Sam's long fingertips, gaining speed as it made a perfect path to its target. That target was chest high, sternum. The recipient never moved his glove.

She began to count his throws. One. Two. Three. She stopped counting at ten, but every single throw was absolutely perfect. She then watched his teammates' throws. Some were high, some low, and some skipped on the ground before reaching their destination.

She looked down at the row of scouts in front of her. They were all watching the same thing. They were watching her Sam. It was the first time she realized her son's baseball talent and instincts were that much different than everyone else's.

Her eyes teared up as she suddenly realized that this was the first time she'd been to a game without her daughter, without worrying about how

Jenny was feeling. Was she hot or cold or tired? Did she need a nutritious drink or snack?

Before returning her gaze to her son, she whispered, "Jenny, if you're watching now, take care of your brother."

* * *

It was a pitchers' duel until the sixth inning. Then Sam opened the bottom of the inning with a sharp single up the middle. A teammate's bunt moved him to second, and first baseman Martin roped one off the left-field fence, barely missing a home run. Sam scored easily for a 1–0 lead.

The Colorado Christian pitcher snatched the rosin bag off the back of the mound and fired it down in disgust. He then walked the next two hitters on eight pitches to load the bases.

"Right man, right time!" Sam yelled from the dugout.

Jose Lopez twirled a weighted bat over his head in the on-deck circle and then winked back at his friend. "I live for these moments."

"Big hit. Right here, big boy. Big hit."

Jose stepped to the plate, took three practice swings, and readied himself.

The Cougars' pitcher threw a first-pitch changeup that completely fooled Lopez, his big swing lunging for the baseball as it died just out of the zone. But somehow, the very end of Jose's bat barely touched the baseball, sending it spinning toward first base like a drunk snake. Unsure of whether to charge the ball or wait, the Cougar defender stood flat-footed as the ball zipped in and out of his glove, off his right shoulder, and rolled away. Jose ran. As fast as he could. Which was only a hair quicker than teammate Mike Hymer, who had been sidelined the last month with a broken foot.

"Run, Jose, run!" the entire dugout roared. And Jose ran.

The Cougar first baseman stumbled in his desperation to find the ball, clutching at it as if it were a trout escaping a fisherman's grasp. He dropped it once, twice, then recovered and threw off balance to the pitcher covering. The ball sailed over the pitcher's head toward the Mavericks' dugout. The Cougars' catcher made a nice backhanded stop, popped up, and as the Maverick runners flew around the bases, he let fly a throw to third that would have been perfect had the third baseman been positioned in the eighth row of the stands beyond the visitors' dugout. By the time the play was over, three runs had scored, and Jose was standing on third base, panting as if he'd just run a marathon.

"Ricky Henderson got nothin' on you!" Sam yelled from the top step of the dugout.

"Way to get all of it, meat!" another teammate roared.

"Absolutely crushed it!" a third belted out.

Jose grabbed his ample belly, jiggled it like a bowl of Jell-O, then kissed each of his biceps and smiled back at his fellow Mavericks.

Mesa would score three more that inning and go on to win 9–0. Coach Elba lifted Sam after six shutout innings to make him available if the Mavericks made it to the championship game.

* * *

"Hottest team in D-Two!" a Maverick shouted when they were back the clubhouse.

"Sixteen and two the last month!" another yelled back. Half the team was dancing around the food table with joy while the other half was peeling off their uniforms to shower and eat.

"Hey, hey, hey!" Jose's eyes went wide when he entered and saw a gift basket on Sam's chair. "Looks like today's winning pitcher has a secret admirer." He pulled off the card that was taped to the top and held it just beyond his friend's reach. "Come and get it, *mon cherie*."

"It's probably from my mom. She usually brings me good-luck cookies." Sam snatched the card back.

"These are brownies shaped like hearts, loverboy." Jose picked up the basket and held it over his head. "Hey guys, check out this pink puppy holding a red rose."

His teammates howled in laughter, which only made their star pitcher's face burn a brighter shade of red as they egged him on.

"Who sent it?"

"C'mon, man, come clean!"

"Who's the babe, Sammy?"

He tried to walk away, but his teammates tackled him, grabbed the card, and flipped it to Jose, who read it aloud in the most feminine voice he could muster.

"This little doggie says: Thinking of you." He opened the card. "Just sending a little warm and fuzzy your way for today's big game. It was wonderful getting to know you this semester. I hope it's not the last time we see each other." Then Jose's eyes went wide. "Holy shit, guys! It's from Lindsey Ellison."

"Runner-up to Miss Colorado Lindsey Ellison?" a teammate asked.

"Heir to Ellison Ford in Denver Lindsey Ellison?" another said.

"Have you done it with her yet Lindsey Ellison?" Jose grinned.

"Give me that card, you . . . moron," Sam said.

"Moron?" Jose rolled his eyes. "That's the best you got, meat?"

"Lindsey's in my Global Sustainability class, and she's . . . uh . . . very nice."

"Very nice?" a teammate called out from across the room. "Dude, Lindsey's got some globes I'd like to sustain."

The room broke up in laughter again until the door opened and Coach Elba entered the clubhouse.

"All right! Enough celebrating!" Elba clapped his hands. "Time to focus on tomorrow and Nebraska-Kearney. We get their top lefty, Jimmy Howell, at three thirty."

Elba then turned and nodded across the room. "Michael Sanchez will start for us. Keith Nelson will catch. Scouting reports on my desk." Elba looked over at his regular catcher. "Jose, you haven't had a day off in a month. I want you ready for the semifinal and title games. So you'll DH tomorrow, and Sam will be in left, hitting second." He then nodded to the dry-erase board next to the trainers' room. "The rest of the lineup is as posted. Be here no later than one tomorrow."

* * *

"Yeah, Mom, Jose and I are just pulling into the parking lot right now," Sam said into his phone as he searched for an open spot at Las Marias on Seventh Street. "We'll be right in." He clicked his phone off and parked his truck.

"Nice of your mom to invite me and Teresa for dinner," Jose said as they walked to the restaurant. "I've been goin' out with that girl since seventh grade, and she still makes my heart skip every time I see her."

"Dang right you're lucky," Sam teased. "You're lucky she's got poor eyesight."

Jose gave his friend a playful shove and opened the door. "I'm gonna ask her to marry me when we graduate. Ya know, before she needs glasses and—" Jose suddenly stopped and looked to the far corner of the room where Teresa and Susan were sitting with none other than Lindsey Ellison.

Sam had already found her and felt himself flushing. Lindsey Ellison was beautiful. Blonde, blue-eyed, with those pouty lips, and . . . and . . . he put on his best smile and walked over.

"Great win!" His mom was first to greet them with a hug before nodding to Lindsey. "This young lady introduced herself at the game. Said she's a classmate of yours, so I invited her to join us for dinner."

Sam hesitated for a moment, unsure of what to say, and then cleared his throat. "Thank you for the brownies. My teammates enjoyed them."

"I'll say we enjoyed them." Jose rubbed his belly. "They now gone too. Dee-licious."

Sam was relieved that his friend didn't go further in revealing what else was said inside the clubhouse.

"You were amazing today. It's like you're two different people: so shy in class, and then you become this fierce warrior on the mound." Lindsey paused, eyelashes fluttering up at him. "I told your mom, I want to know that person on the mound . . . where does he go? What is he thinking about? Who is *he*?"

Sam didn't know what to say. Her compliments made him feel good, almost giddy, but he didn't have an answer for her questions. He didn't think it was any big deal to throw a five-ounce sphere where he wanted to. It was all muscle memory. Finger pressure. Balance. Breathing. Delivery. Just make sure to do it the same way every time. It wasn't that hard.

"Well?" his mother said, teasing him. "I think it's a very fair question, son . . . who are *you*?"

He let go a loud exhale of surrender and sat down across from his mom and Lindsey, mimicking his glare on the mound. Eyes focused, jaws clenched, right hand in an imaginary glove.

The table got a good chuckle at that with Sam breaking out into a huge, idiotic grin, ears burning red as he glanced at Lindsey, who seemed to be watching him closely.

"What?" he asked.

"You"—she smiled—"are too cute."

"I'm just a dumb jock."

"You're anything but that." She reached over and touched his hand, sliding her index finger down his. The warmth of her lingered even after she withdrew her hand.

"What are . . . uh"—he paused to both calm his heart and change the subject—"what are your plans this summer?"

"I have an internship with DPF Energy in Denver, working with their environmental-specialist team, dealing with water, waste, and land use. What about you?"

"Haven't decided yet."

"C'mon, man." Jose put his arm around Sam. "Tell her you got three offers from wood-bat leagues in Alaska, Cape Cod, and Denver."

"I'll probably accept the invite from the Mile High Collegiate League because I can outfit for Mom on the days we don't play."

"Oh, please do accept the Denver offer. I'd love to watch you play," Lindsey said.

"We have clients in the Denver market. I know they'd love to have Sam take them hunting or fly-fishing," Susan said.

"That sounds like fun." Lindsey looked directly at Sam. "I've never been fly-fishing."

"Well, Sammy here's the best." Jose squeezed his friend's shoulder. "His reputation is so feared in fast water that the trout just surrender when he shows up. Why, just last summer, we were fishing the Animas, and a ten-pound rainbow leaped right outta the water and into his arms. It was amazing."

Sam rolled his eyes at his friend and then turned back to Lindsey. "A really big rainbow is only two to five pounds. Biggest I've ever caught was four, near Weasel Skin Bridge."

Lindsey thumbed a loose strand of blonde hair off her shoulder and smiled up at him. He wanted to take her hand but felt everyone watching him.

"Baseball and backwoods," Jose chuckled and put his hand on Sam's head. "That's all that's inside this simple melon. Those are his safe places . . . his home bases." Jose then winked at Lindsey. "Maybe you're the one who will expand Bigfoot's horizons."

That brought another laugh from the table and a brighter shade of red from Sam.

"But right now, Bigfoot's ours. He's our meal ticket to winning the Rocky Mountain Tournament." Jose grinned.

* * *

Bigfoot's track was large in Mesa's 11–4 quarterfinal win over Nebraska-Kearney. Three for five with two doubles and five RBIs. He was even better in the Mavericks 6–3 semifinal win over Metro State. Four for four with a double and a three-run homer that gave Mesa the lead for good in the sixth inning. His moon shot carried well beyond the deepest part of left-center field, and got lost in the muted colors of the Rocky Mountains, before settling fifteen rows up in the bleachers to pit Mesa against number-one seed Regis.

* * *

Suplizio Field was packed for the conference championship game. Students stomped the bleachers, cheerleaders danced atop the dugouts, and scouts scribbled in their notebooks as Michael Sanchez trotted to the mound in the bottom of the eighth, attempting to protect a 7–5 Mavericks lead.

"What's Elba thinking?" groaned Lindsey. "Why isn't he bringing Sam in?"

Susan inhaled a deep breath and shook her head. Lindsey was beginning to get on her nerves. Sam's new friend had joined them for nearly every meal the last three days and had sat next to Susan every inning of the tournament, relentlessly questioning just about every decision the Mavericks coach had made. But it was the happiest she'd seen her son in a long time, so no reason to dampen his joy. Instead, she put on a happy face and said, "Tournament rules only allow Sam to pitch one more inning."

"Well, this could be the inning they need him. Sanchez has an ERA over five."

"Sam's was over ten the first month of the season," Susan said sweetly and then turned back to the field.

Lindsey clasped her hands in prayer but said no more.

Sanchez allowed two baserunners but got out of the inning with a double play. The Mavericks still led by two.

* * *

Mesa went three up, three down to start the ninth, and Elba pointed to the bullpen. It was time to bring in his best player and finish the job Mesa had set out to do four months earlier.

As Susan watched her son warm up to start the ninth, there was a different energy about Suplizio Stadium. An undisciplined mind may not have been able to see the difference between doubt and confidence, but it was there. She saw it in the way the Mavericks took the field to start the inning, the chatter, the enthusiasm, the way they bounced on the balls of their feet when taking infield, and she saw it in the way the Regis players paced the visitors' dugout, mustering whatever dwindling hope was left to overcome their fate. Each Ranger twisted his upside-down rally cap on his head, urging lady luck to smile their way one more time.

And then she did. The Regis leadoff batter chopped a slow roller past the mound and reached on an infield hit. The next batter struck a tailor-made double-play ball to the Mavericks second baseman that took a bad hop and was booted for an error. Sam struck out the next man on three pitches but gave up a bloop single to the fourth Ranger. Bases loaded, one out.

Coach Elba jogged out to the mound for a visit with his pitcher and catcher.

Jose knew his friend. Had seen this look before. Now was not a good time to talk.

Elba must have seen it too as he simply patted Sam on the back and said, "How about that old super-sinker here?"

Sam nodded, his focus already tightening. The rest of the world seemed to fall away as the only thing that mattered now was this instant—the target or the track, eye to glove, nose to trail, like a wolf catching scent of its prey or a trout locking on to a fly above the water's surface. The score was no longer important. The past was gone. Everything that had happened in the first eight innings was immaterial. The only thing that had any significance was executing the next pitch.

* * *

Susan stood up, a sudden awareness lighting her face. She wanted her son to see confidence if he glanced her way. As she watched Sam look in to get the sign from Jose, she saw her husband's face: intense yet calm, connected yet free, completely aware of his surroundings yet focused on a singular target. She wanted to take in every moment of these final two outs. Her son, who, just two months earlier, had been a shadow of the young man she watched today.

His first-pitch sinker bit down and in on the right-handed batter, who fouled it off his front foot. Strike one.

From grief to contentment, from depressed to determined, from fearful to fearless, this was her son's rebirth.

Slider, outside corner, strike two.

Breathing in, Susan focused on calming her body. Breathing out, she smiled.

Sam's next pitch was a tease, a curve, three inches off the plate that buckled the knees of the hitter when he checked his swing.

"First!" Jose barked and pointed to the first-base ump, who signaled no swing, bringing a groan from the Maverick faithful. One ball, two strikes.

I know this is a wonderful moment, thought Susan as she inhaled another deep breath. *Be present and simply enjoy this experience.*

Fans were on the edges of their seats. A scout was writing in his notebook. A child sat on the shoulders of their father, shouting, "Let's go, Mavericks!"

Sam knifed a sinker on the outside corner. The Regis hitter swung and pulled it to shortstop Alvarez, who underhanded to second baseman Lyle to start the double play. Lyle's relay was close, but . . .

"Safe!" yelled the ump, and the Rangers' runner scored from third.

"No way!" screamed Jose and started toward first with a wild-eyed, how dare you steal this game from us glare.

Sam sprinted in to cover the plate, yelling, "Home! home! home!" but the Regis runners held at first and third. 7–6 Mavericks, with one out to go.

"Terrible call!" Maverick fans booed. "He was out!"

"C'mon, blue!" Lindsey yelled. "Get your head in the game!"

As if a mirror image of each other, Susan and her son raised both hands as if to say, *Settle down, everyone. Let's just finish the game.*

Teresa caught the duplicate movement and playfully elbowed Susan in the side. "He's just like you."

Susan cocked her head to the side and grinned back. "He's his father."

Teresa pointed to the mound, where Sam had also cocked his head to the side and was grinning at his catcher.

"No, he's you."

Susan watched her son put his arm around Jose and guide him back to home plate. There indeed were similarities in mother and son. Similar strengths and weaknesses. Loyal to a fault. Both driven to achieve yet completely relaxed in the arms of nature.

Sam delivered a strike on the outside corner to get ahead of the Regis cleanup hitter. The Rangers' first baseman had doubled twice already and was hitting over .500 in the tournament. Sam tempted him with a slider away, but the big man didn't bite. Another slider missed outside for a 2–1 count.

Base open, Sam, Susan thought. *Don't give in.*

He didn't, staying with the slider and getting a swing and a miss. 2–2.

For some reason Susan thought of her totems. The wolf and the deer. Were they Sam's too? Both of them enjoyed being alone. She, hiking and running SJ Outfitters, and he on the mound and in the mountains. Despite the dire situation, tying and go-ahead runs on, conference championship on the line, there was a peacefulness, a gracefulness about her son. No frenetic movements, no shortness of breath. He was lost in some otherworldly baseball universe, relishing this moment.

She inhaled along with him as he came set, and exhaled as her son let loose a fastball that was a good three inches above the zone. But the location and change in velocity so surprised the Rangers hitter that he desperately swung in an effort to at least foul it off.

He missed. Strike three. Game over. Bedlam.

The Mesa State Mavericks were Rocky Mountain Champs.

CHAPTER TWENTY-SEVEN

Southern Virginia

June 2008

Dixon turned off his computer and dropped his head into his hands. His professional and personal life had become an absolute mess. In public, he and wife, Liz, were the perfect picture of a loving couple, but behind closed doors they were anything but. They slept in separate bedrooms, took separate vacations, and had no interest in suffering the permanence of having a child.

Liz was addicted to the physical, a workout fiend who spent three hours a day in the gym. He had bought her all the new personal upgrades too: new lips, new cheeks, new boobs. She looked fabulous for forty-one. Unfortunately, there was little connection beyond the physical.

And now, their financial empire was crumbling. The market was a mess, their personal stock portfolio was down 23 percent, DiamondBar's contract in Afghanistan was in its final months, and now politicians were asking him for support in the November election. It was going to be tough to write big checks to lawmakers who had supported private military companies in the past.

"Senator Richardson's counting on you, Drake," Barry King said from across the room. "We have to pat Ed's back so he'll pat ours and get that contract extended."

"He owes us," Dixon grumbled. "He still gets money from my family's old company."

"Both of you got deferred money after you sold Dixon Industries in 2000."

Dixon didn't speak for several moments. His mind was occupied with all the ramifications of what might happen if someone blew the whistle on what he was planning in Afghanistan. Richardson supported his efforts to control the mineral rights of a mountain in the Nuristan Province. What he didn't know were the illegal tactics Dixon was taking to seize the property. Beginning construction without permission from the local warlord or securing a contract with the Ministry of Mines and Petroleum was more than risky. But his ally inside the Afghan government said he would make it happen if Congress renewed DiamondBar's contract to handle security in the Nuristan Province.

"How much did we give to Ed's campaign last year?" he finally asked.

"Fifty thousand."

Dixon pinched the bridge of his nose. Another headache was likely on the way. He needed Richardson's support. Even though Ed, who was one of the most powerful men in Washington, had given him preferential treatment in DiamondBar's previous contract in Afghanistan, the three-year deal would end in November.

He sighed. "All right, write him another check for fifty, but cut back on every other senator and congressman we grease by ten grand." He smacked the wall so hard a picture of Dixon with his father on a pheasant hunt in Oklahoma fell to the ground. "And put a note inside telling them they'll get a raise when they fix the damn economy!"

"I'll leave that last part out." King said. "We'll need those guys when Richardson pushes for our new deal."

"He'll give it to us, Barry. He'll give it to us because he still gets stock options from our old company. He knows that for every road grader, backhoe, and bulldozer he ships for one of our construction projects, he gets a better payday."

"We're still talking about digging in a very remote region of the Nuristan Mountains. We're going to need help finding the safest path. How are Cutthredge and Marcus doing recruiting new trackers?"

"I don't know." Dixon let go a frustrated exhale. "I haven't been able to reach them lately."

* * *

Grand Junction, Colorado

Marcus checked his image in the rear-view mirror of the Ford F-150. He liked the look of a man who was finally doing well. The one-hundred-grand-a-year contract he continued to receive from DiamondBar was always helpful, but the drug money that was now pouring in took both he and Billy to another level.

It was easy too. They still had contacts in Afghanistan who wanted to make a quick buck. Those contacts were part of the Counternarcotics Unit who knew how futile it was trying to slow the opium trade in a lawless country. The US had poured billions into reconstruction projects throughout the country, improving roads, deep-well technology, irrigation, and agricultural assistance, which had led to arable land and an explosion in opium cultivation.

The DiamondBar contact knew a guy inside the Afghan government, who knew a guy with the Afghan Border Patrol, who knew a farmer who had a one-thousand-hectare poppy field in southwest Afghanistan. Even though the US had an alliance with Pakistan, there were a significant number of soldiers in the military and Pakistan Intelligence who supported the Taliban and al Qaeda and wanted in on the easy money. The opium trail came through southwest Afghanistan, across the Pakistan border, and south to freighters on the Arabian Sea.

"Whistle stop," Marcus said when he saw the train begin to slowdown as it rolled southeast toward Grand Junction. "Henry's never late."

Cutthredge got out of the passenger side of the truck and walked up close to the tracks. The railroad worker would toss a twenty-pound cardboard container off the side of the railcar. Tommy Sherman's associate, Henry, would get five grand for dropping off the box, which contained four bricks of pure white heroin, valued at about $4 million on the street. The train would continue on to town.

"There he is," Marcus said when he saw a man wave from a distant railcar.

The train slowed, and Henry tossed the package to Cutthredge, who calmly walked back to the truck and covered his investment under a canvas tarp.

"Let's find Tommy." Marcus put the truck in gear and headed south. "He'll want his cut."

Cutthredge's easy expression hardened. "He'll get half right now because he knows all the rich kids. But as soon as we connect with his buyers, we'll cut him out."

CHAPTER TWENTY-EIGHT

Denver, Colorado

July 2008

Lindsey cocked her head to the side and smiled at Sam as they drove away from All-Star Park in Denver. His summer league Cougars had beaten the Express 7–2 with Sam tossing three shutout innings and going one for three as a hitter.

He felt her staring and playfully nudged her in the side. "What are you looking at?"

She leaned against the door and eyed him fondly. "I'm looking at the guy who all the scouts were talking about."

"Game's over, Lindsey. How was your day at DPF Energy?"

"Don't change the subject. All the scouts were wondering why you don't let 'er rip?"

"Because that's not pitching."

"Two of them said you might be taken in the first three rounds next year if you threw a little harder. They topped you at eighty-eight."

"This is only a summer league. I'm just trying to stay sharp for Mesa. We have a chance to do something special next year. Seven starters and the entire rotation return from a team that went all the way to the Final Four."

"Do you know what a first-round bonus got this year?"

He grinned down at her. "No, but I'm sure you'll tell me." He was smitten by her questions, for they were endearing reminders of the times when Jenny used to tease him with her myriad of scouting reports and suggestions on how he could improve as a ballplayer.

"The first pick got over six million, and the first pick in the second round got one point five million."

He slowed for a stop light and turned to face her. "I don't play for the money, Linz."

"Perhaps you should."

He sighed. "My dad used to tell me that if I focused on money, I'd lose myself, but with talent, hard work, and being a good teammate, I'd probably get a shot."

"That may be true, but now's the time we need to build your brand—"

Before she could say more, he leaned across the seat, took her chin in one hand, and kissed her on the lips. It was the first time he had kissed her, and for a moment, he felt self-conscious about what to do next. He didn't have to wait long because the car behind them honked, and he drove on through the intersection.

She looked up at him sideways. "Five dates and I finally get a kiss."

"Just trying to build my brand."

She laughed out loud. "Yeah, well, I'm not waiting another five dates for my next kiss. What are you doing this weekend?"

"No games scheduled, but Mom booked me a fly-fishing trip on the South Platte." He gave her a hopeful look. "I should be finished Sunday afternoon if you'd like to go to dinner Monday."

"When's your next game?"

"Not till Tuesday."

She smiled.

*   *   *

The black-speckled back rose out of the foam and then dove under. Sam cast hard but low across the water with his fly but never let it touch, then whipped his line back over his head to come in again, teasing the rainbow where he had last seen it dive. He cast another six times until he saw a circle appear on the surface, signifying that either small fish were attracted to the fly, or hopefully that big rainbow he'd been courting.

The fish leaped, caught the fly, and dove back under. Sam gave some line, then tugged back swiftly. The rainbow jumped again, and Sam pulled at the line with his left hand to let him know who was boss. Then he let him go again, like a child teasing a kitten with catnip, and worked the rainbow to the shore two more times. When it came to the surface, he pulled high with his rod, and the fish was his.

Letting go a victorious exhale, he turned back to shore to find Lindsey, by a lodgepole pine, watching him.

"Hey!" he called out happily and waved her over. "What are you doing here?"

She took off her flip-flops and waded into the cold water. "You told me that you were teaching a couple how to fly-fish until today, so I thought you might still be on the river,"

"How'd you find me?"

"I stopped in Deckers and asked some fishermen at Flies and Lies if they'd seen you, and they told me where you like to fish."

He gave her a quick kiss and then knelt down to take the fly out of the rainbow's mouth. "I taught a nice couple from Golden the last two days. Yesterday was instruction, and today they fished. Caught two browns and two rainbows between sixteen and twenty inches. Pretty good."

"Did they camp out here with you?"

"Naw, they rented a hotel room in Castle Rock. Wanted a soft bed after being on the river all day. They left about an hour ago, but I don't have a game until Tuesday so I thought I'd stay." He smiled up at her. "Are we still on for dinner tomorrow night?"

"Of course." She looked over her shoulder to the shore. "Where's your tent?"

"A tent?" He gave her a look of absolute astonishment. "No way. That would spoil my view of the night sky. I just spread a tarp and a blanket and climb inside my sleeping bag. No moon until late. No lights from the city dulling my view of the heavens. It's awesome."

"Sounds beautiful."

"It is." He placed the rainbow in his basket, took Lindsey's hand, and led her back through the shallow water to the riverbank. "Why don't you join me for dinner? Trout, raw carrots, and water is all I have, but you're more than welcome."

"As long as I don't have to fillet the fish, I'm in," she said with a mischievous smile.

* * *

The sun was barely touching the top of Cheesman Mountain when they finished their meal, the smell of cooked fish and campfire mingling with the scents of pines, sun-warmed leaves, and damp moss. Sam told stories of past adventures on Colorado rivers: of matching the hatch, of splashing a grasshopper down on calm water, and of pulling in a four-pound cutthroat the week before. The air was full of the sound of rushing water, and the sun's final rays reflected off the tops of trees when Sam stood up and took a whiff under his arm.

"Yikes," he winced. "Why didn't you tell me I smelled this bad?"

She laughed. "You smell like a man. Musky and locker-roomish."

He reached into his backpack for his castile-liquid soap and headed to the river. "I'll be right back. I wanna wash the stink off before I walk you to your car."

* * *

Sam found a private spot downriver, stripped his clothes, and dove into the cold South Platte. It wasn't until after he'd finished bathing that he realized his mistake. He'd forgotten a towel and clean clothes.

"Idiot," he muttered to himself. He shook like a dog on the shoreline and put his fishing shorts back on. With his dark hair and upper body still dripping with river water, he walked back to camp and suddenly froze.

Lindsey was no longer by the campfire. Instead, she was inside his sleeping bag, staring at him straight-on, her blue eyes dark and tempting.

"Hey," was all he could manage as he searched but failed for any combination of words that might form a coherent sentence.

She smiled sweetly and lifted the cover of the sleeping bag.

He gasped.

Lindsey was completely naked. The light from the fire shimmered off her golden skin, full, soft breasts, and flat belly, all the way down to her very being. It was the first time he had seen a woman undressed, and all he could do was stare. Stare at the most beautiful art he had ever seen. His mouth opened and closed, but no sound came out. His heartbeat echoed in his chest, but he could not move, could not even swallow.

Finally, she broke his ice by giggling, and then waved him over.

"Why don't you take off your shorts and join me?"

He did.

CHAPTER TWENTY-NINE

Washington, DC

November 2008

November smacked Drake Dixon hard. The recession ripped another $30 million from his stock portfolio, a Democrat was elected president, the government had yet to approve his Afghan contract, and his personal life was a charade. He hadn't seen his wife in more than a week as she was attempting to perfect her tan at their British Virgin Island villa.

It's not as if he missed her. They didn't have much in common. Liz didn't like to fish or hunt, and she rarely stepped foot in Drake's trophy room in their Aspen chateau. It was his man cave, a room of pride and conquest. The heads of bear and wolf and cougar and ram adorned one side of the room, while his international wall boasted lion, zebra, leopard, and crocodile. The only thing missing was deer. Oh, he had killed plenty of deer in his lifetime, but none with an impressive set of antlers, and there was no way he was going to put a measly six-point buck in his trophy room. He wanted at least ten.

Now, on a misty Washington, DC, evening, he sat alone in the waiting area of Senator Richardson's office. It had been two months since the Vice Chairman of the Appropriations Committee promised him that DiamondBar would again be given the contract to handle all security for the Provincial Reconstruction Teams in the Nuristan Province. Right now, he wasn't so sure.

Richardson's office door opened, and he motioned for Dixon to join him.

"Drink?" The senator asked as he reached for a bottle of Four Roses Kentucky Bourbon and poured them both a glass.

Dixon took a sip but remained quiet.

"I've been going over the money Congress has already spent in Afghanistan," Richardson began. "We spent thirty-one billion last year alone, and that was with twenty-five thousand troops."

Dixon already knew those numbers and had a ready answer. "Rumor is we're going to add more personnel in 2009."

"Fortunately, our top economists believe that our never-ending war has little to do with the recession. As a matter of fact, the global slowdown hasn't affected Afghanistan."

Dixon raised a curious brow.

"Even though they've been ravaged by three decades of war, the Afghan currency has remained steady. The Afghani is still fifty-two to the dollar," Richardson said.

"Why?"

"It was an election year in the States. We had to stay engaged, politically, militarily, and economically to win those votes. That's why we continue to prop up the Afghan Central Bank."

"America doesn't need another headache with the market crashing."

Richardson raised his glass in the air. "Thus, the importance of winning the war on terror has never been greater. Congress won't make any aid cuts this year because we believe any cut might weaken the Afghan economy and strengthen the Taliban."

Holy Shit, thought Dixon. *Is this Ed's way of saying that DiamondBar's going to get the contract? Yeah, baby, I'm finally getting a break.* He took a long drink to not only steady himself, but to convey the sense that he was taking every word that the senator said very seriously.

"Maybe you're right, Ed. Maybe now would be the perfect time to take advantage of Afghanistan's economy and help them rebuild."

The senator took a sip of bourbon, and then his eyes slowly came back to focus on Dixon. "How's the investigation into your company going?"

Dixon almost spilled his drink as he jerked up to meet Richardson's penetrating glare.

"I wasn't born yesterday, Drake. I know your lawyer slowed any real inquiry into the deaths of those goat herders."

Dixon remained silent as Richardson opened his briefcase and pulled out a folder with the heading *Top Secret*. "And now this. I received this report from Pakistan Intelligence this morning. I'll give you the Cliffs-Notes version. Afghan diplomat escorted through the Helmand Province into Pakistan last night by none other than two DiamondBar Security guards. They're stopped and searched at the Port of Karachi." He shook his head. "Police found four hundred pounds of white-powder heroin in the trunk of the diplomat's vehicle."

Dixon's back stiffened. "Why wasn't I told about this?"

"It's not like America, where you get a phone call, Drake. I'm sure you won't be surprised that both of your employees insisted they had no idea what was in the diplomat's trunk."

"I'll get to the bottom of it."

"You'd better, because I'm the guy who got you your last no-bid contract. I'm the guy who sold Congress on funding your company and then protecting your ass every time you've screwed up."

"I said I'll get—"

Richardson's right hand shot up for quiet. "You know how much I'm indebted to your family, Drake, but I'm in the results business now. And your results lately have been making me look bad." He leaned forward to make sure Dixon's eyes stayed with his. "I'm not a man who likes to look bad. Fix this problem—or I'll have to find another private military company to work Afghanistan."

* * *

Durango, Colorado

"Pleeeeease!" Valerie Quintana sobbed and curled up in a fetal position on the bed inside the Durango motel room. She had gone two days without her heroin fix and now was frantic for any kind of high. She wiped her nose and moved closer to the man who was gently stroking her sweat-drenched hair.

"Here you go, baby." Rob Marcus tied a rubber tube around her upper arm to swell the vein on the inside of her elbow.

Valerie's arm was tracked with bruises and cut marks where veins had collapsed from overuse. She reached for the needle on the nightstand, but he pushed her hand away.

"Patience, sweetie, almost there." Then he picked up the plunger and pushed the needle into her bloated vein. Valerie lay back on the bed in euphoric ecstasy, her glazed-over eyes staring up at the ceiling.

* * *

Billy Cutthredge wanted no part of watching some junkie get shot up. But he did enjoy the money and control that came with selling heroin. Billy had become the enforcer. If a new contact or junkie didn't pay, he'd let his fists encourage them to find the cash, and he took a perverse joy in watching an addict grovel at his feet to get their fix.

"Let's go, dude." Cutthredge knocked on the motel-room door. He never called Rob by his real name for fear that it might get back to the police. Just sell the smack, pick up the money, and get the hell out before anyone else recognized them. He waited another minute and was getting ready to knock again when the door suddenly opened and out came Marcus, counting his money.

Cutthredge shook his head, a cold expression masking the vicious satisfaction of completing another chapter in his plan. The plan to start his own drug cartel. When the time came that they'd made enough money, they could break from Dixon, even blackmail him, and set up their own personal kingdom.

CHAPTER THIRTY

Pargin Mountain, Colorado

November 2008

Happy laughter resonated through the Carson house as Lindsey pushed Sam down on the couch, tickled his ribs, and slid her right hand down to the waistband of his jeans.

"Hey, hey, hey, knock it off." Sam laughed again and pulled her hand away. "My mom can see us from the kitchen."

Rejecting his request, Lindsey straddled his waist, swishing her blonde mane against his face and then peppering his neck with light kisses. "I can't get enough of my All-American," she giggled. "I won't see you until after Thanksgiving break. Why don't we go for another stroll on Pargin Mountain?"

His face burned red as the very thought of yesterday stirred him. He had taken his girlfriend on a hike northeast of their property, an easy one-mile trek through pine and oak to a quiet spot near a stream. Lindsey had been the aggressor, playfully pulling him down onto a soft bed of pine needles and immediately removing her top. Even after four months of dating, her beauty still took his breath. He remembered every detail: the scent of vanilla on her skin, the tiny birthmark underneath the curve of her left breast, the sun shimmering off her blonde tresses when she climbed on top of him. He did want to go on another hike, but . . .

Walks With the Wind

"No," he blurted out, and then as if she were as light as a sparrow, he lifted her up and sat her comfortably next to him. "Your grandparents are already upset that you're not in Santa Fe. I don't want to get you in any more trouble."

"I only missed one day of a boring week-long family tradition." She stuck out her lower lip and looked up through fluttering eyelashes. "One more day with my superstar shouldn't bother them."

They were interrupted when Susan loudly cleared her throat from the kitchen and then slammed the pantry door.

Sam gave a shrug of resignation and kissed Lindsey on the cheek. "Sorry, Linz, I have work to do. I need to prep for tomorrow's hunt, so let me walk you to your car."

* * *

"Hey, Mom!" Sam called out as he opened the front door.

"In the kitchen, Samuel."

"Samuel?" He raised one inquisitive brow and casually sauntered in to join his mother. "You never call me Samuel unless you're mad at me."

She stood quietly, as most mothers do when they're disappointed in their cubs: jaw set, face unflappable, dark yet loving gaze locked on their guilty offspring. In this case, the target was one Samuel Cloud-Carson.

"Do you have a problem with Lindsey?" he asked.

"No." She crossed her arms over her chest. "She's not my child. But you are . . . and I do have a problem with your behavior."

"What did I do wrong?"

"Did Lindsey sleep with you last night?"

He took a step back, embarrassed by his mom's query. "No . . . uh . . . yes . . . uh . . . she . . . um . . . didn't feel comfortable sleeping in Jenny's room, so she . . . uh . . . came to my room. Geez, Mom, why the fifth degree?"

"I know you've been sleeping with her, and I don't want you to make a mistake that could change your life."

Sam was completely stunned by his mom's words.

"Are you using protection?"

Now, the tips of his ears were really burning.

"I hope you're using protection because it only takes one time."

"Yes . . . uh . . . um . . . we both are."

She shook her head in motherly relief and motioned for him to sit down at the kitchen table across from her. "You're a good boy, Sam. I know you'll do the right thing." She waited for him to sit and then asked, "Are you reading Jenny's journal?"

The question jolted him even more than her previous cross-examination. "What?"

"Have you been reading the journal your sister wrote specifically for you?"

He heaved a heavy sigh and stared down at his hands. He tried to answer, but he could only shake his head.

She reached across the table and touched his hand. "Where do you think she is?"

"I don't know. I don't know what I believe anymore."

"You've never had closure over Jenny's death."

His shoulders slumped.

"Has Jenny come to you in your dreams?"

He kept his head bent, as though in thought, and then finally nodded.

"Do you think you're responsible for her still being in this earthly realm, rather than walking on?"

He didn't answer.

"Do you really believe that you have that kind of power, Sam? That through your sheer willpower Jenny could still be alive?"

"Don't, Mom."

But a kind of joy seemed to light in Susan's voice as she squeezed his hand. "I think Jenny chose to stay here. I think she's watching over us . . . watching over *you*." She paused for a long moment as if waiting for her son to look up. He did.

"Tell me about your dreams."

"I"—he paused to compose himself—"I've had the same dreams ever since Jenny died. She's healthy, eyes clear, skin brown, and she's riding the horse from her death ceremony. I asked if I could go with her. She said no."

"The horse, the owl, and the deer are her totems."

He nodded as if he already knew. "I also saw her as an owl, far off in the forest, circling above the trees. I chased after her, down a dark path into the woods. But she flew ahead and blocked my way. I tried to go around her, but she blocked me again, her face stern, warning me not to follow."

"What else?" his mother asked.

"She came to me in another dream, not as a body, but as a white light, free of her pain and suffering. She waved for Papa and Old Mel to join her . . . but there was someone else too." He paused again, but he couldn't, or wouldn't, tell her the rest of the dream. "I don't want the dreams anymore, Mom. I just want to live my life."

"Don't do that. There's a reason she's revealing herself to you now. You must have more to learn from Jenny for her to still be in your dreams."

He stared down at their intertwined hands, two souls forever linked by both blood and spirit. Jenny's spirit. Was he again denying his sister's vision? Was he pushing her away even though her final words to him had been, *I am with you always.*

"Sam," Susan said softly. "Let Jenny speak to you. Don't deny her the power to be part of your life."

CHAPTER THIRTY-ONE

Washington, DC

November 2008

Dixon studied the man on the computer screen he was having a conversation with, who was some seven thousand miles away. Fahad Bukhari looked like an honest man, but he certainly wasn't the guy in charge of this investigation. Bukhari was likely just a lowly officer in the Pakistan Intelligence Agency who was chosen to communicate with Dixon because he was the most fluent in English.

"I assure you, Mr. Dixon, we will find out who is smuggling the heroin out of our port," Bukhari said in a clipped tone with a definite Urdu influence. Urdu was the official language of Pakistan, but English was widely used in the executive, judicial, and legislative branches. That's what bothered Dixon the most. Why wasn't he talking with the general of InterServices Intelligence instead of some junior officer?

The Pakistani government owed him. He was part of the US political machine that was aiding his country, pouring millions into Pakistan so that they would keep their massive nuclear arsenal quiet. Unfortunately, most of that money wound up in the hands of an army and intelligence unit that still supported who the US was fighting. The Taliban.

"We made the arrest at the Port of Karachi last night," Bukhari continued. "The two men who are employed by your company are being held at Central Prison."

"What about the Pakistanis they were working with? Were they detained?"

"No, they were questioned and released."

"Let me get this straight. You arrested five men at your port and only put the Americans in jail?"

Bukhari swallowed hard and looked down at his hands. "I'm very sorry, sir. That is all the information I was given."

Dixon shook his head slowly but didn't respond for a long moment. He wanted the ISI officer to feel his displeasure. He knew what was going on. The Pakistan Intelligence Agency was corrupt and had too many cliques. It wasn't unusual to have one faction chasing a particular terrorist or drug cartel while another group paid to get them released. It was likely that the Pakistanis who worked with his men had paid off the arresting officers. Quite frankly, he didn't give a shit if his employees were dealing drugs. All the power brokers in this part of the world seemed to be getting some kind of kickback from the cartels. But the fallout could be irreparable for DiamondBar.

"Here's what I want you to do," Dixon finally said. "Let my men stew in your prison for a couple of weeks, and then interrogate them again. Tell them you're not letting them go until they give you the names of who they're selling to in the States."

* * *

Durango, Colorado

Susan sat in room 254 of Mercy Medical, typing her contact information into Valerie Quintana's cell phone. It was the second time in the last six months that the eighteen-year-old had been admitted for a heroin overdose, and Susan wanted to do whatever she could to help her friend's daughter. The poor girl's arms were pocked with needle tracks and scars along her veins, a heartbreaking reminder of how many times Valerie had relapsed in the past.

"I remember watching you play softball. You were a good infielder," Susan said with a kind tone.

No response.

"My son, Sam, was your assistant coach one summer. I believe the name of your team was the Goldfish."

Valerie's hollow eyes stared out the window to the heavy gray clouds building over the San Juans. Cold weather was on the way.

"Your father and I would sit together, cheering you on."

"He hates me," Valerie finally spoke, her voice ragged with despair.

"No. Your father prays for you—he aches for you—but he doesn't hate you."

That was when Valerie finally turned her head and looked Susan's way. The dark circles under her eyes seemed a gothic frame to the bloodshot orbs above, pinpoint pupils empty of any emotion. But then, for just an instant, Susan saw past the darkness to a flicker of hope.

"I talked to Jenny," Valerie mumbled. The mere mention of her deceased daughter's name made Susan sit up straight.

"It was about this time last year," Valerie continued. "Holidays always depress me. I called her Kidney Bean Help-Line." She paused to peel a scab off her left arm. "I know it's for kids with kidney disease, but I wanted to talk with someone . . . and Jenny was a good listener."

This time it was Susan who couldn't speak. Her daughter had never told her about any conversation with Valerie. But then again, Jenny had rarely revealed what she talked about with her Kidney Beans, who were suffering both the physical and emotional pain of a chronic illness. It was a club that moms and dads were not invited to.

"She told me I had to forgive myself."

"That sounds like her." Susan smiled.

"The elders believed she was some kind of holy woman." Valerie said. "They said she had this wisdom and strength to shine a light bright enough to inspire others out of their darkness."

Susan beamed at the revelation only to see the hope in the addict's eyes dim into bland nothingness again.

"If your daughter was such a great healer, then why is she dead?"

CHAPTER THIRTY-TWO

Washington, DC

December 2008

Dixon shook the sleep from his head and tried to comprehend the words on the other end of the phone. It was six o'clock in the morning in the nation's capital, making it four in the afternoon in Pakistan. He had told the Pakistani police officer to call him at any time if he had information on who was transporting heroin to the States.

"Are you absolutely sure?" he asked Fahad Bakhari for the second time.

"That is the intelligence our investigating officers were able to gather," Bakhari said. "We finally broke your men this morning, and they revealed that Billy Cutthredge and Rob Marcus are their contacts in the United States."

Dixon leaned back in bed and closed his eyes. *This can't be happening. Not now. I've got too much invested in Afghanistan. We're so close to securing one of the richest mineral deposits in the country. But Senator Richardson will only push for another no-bid contract for DiamondBar if I clean up this problem. If this story about my employees dealing drugs goes public, it could cost me hundreds of millions.*

He inhaled a deep breath and opened his eyes. "Did they give the US port of entry?"

"Harbor Department of Long Beach, California." Bakhari paused. "But they did not know the dockworker's name who unloads the heroin, nor where it is networked after it leaves the port."

Dixon didn't speak for a long time, his mind completely overwhelmed by his countless problems: His wife, Liz, was back in the BVI with God knows who; the man he needed to track for him was just named preseason All-American, making it extremely difficult to leverage his services; and now, the two men he had personally hired when he started DiamondBar, had double-crossed him.

"Thank you, Officer Bakhari. Please keep this information between your leadership and me. Neither one of us can afford for it to go public."

* * *

Four hours later, Dixon was at Dulles Airport, waiting for his pilot to do the final prep of his Learjet before flying to Durango to deal with Cutthredge and Marcus. It would take a team of his best men to convince these two freaks that their services were no longer needed. He had three of his most loyal bodyguards with him and Barry King. There, of course, would be an expensive buyout to keep Cutthredge and Marcus quiet, but now, Dixon had them by the balls.

"I tried to warn you," King grumbled as he sat down across from Dixon in the cabin of the jet. "I told you they were trouble. They're like land mines waiting to be stepped on."

Dixon glared at his lawyer, but he did remember his words from some two years before. *Those guys could take down your entire empire.* Even though it was only nine in the morning, he opened up a bottle of scotch. "I never thought they'd do something as reckless as this."

"They're damn mercenaries, Drake. Hired guns. Whoever puts the most money in their hands gets their loyalty."

"I'm paying them each a hundred grand a year to do nothing but hunt and fish and find me some trackers." Dixon took a sip and leaned back in his chair. "Speaking of trackers, when we clean this up and Senator Ed signs off on our deal, we're gonna need the absolute best men to track for us. I'm gonna stop by SJ Outfitters and sweeten my deal for Sam Carson."

King shook his head. "The Carson deal is over, Drake. I mean, c'mon, All-American, his college team is picked to win it all, and he'll likely be a high pick in June's draft. There's no way he's working for you."

As the Learjet door closed and the turbine blades began to spin, Dixon looked out the window, to the heat rays shimmering off the engines, a reminder that he'd been in hotter spots before. He'd find a way out of this mess. He always had, and he would again. This was personal. Nobody screwed with Drake Dixon—and nobody told him no. He buckled his seat belt and leaned toward his lawyer. "The Carson deal is *not* over."

CHAPTER THIRTY-THREE

Colorado

As Sam drove home for Christmas break, he couldn't stop smiling. The last twenty-four hours had been absolutely magical. It began with yesterday's press conference at the Mesa State Student Union after two of the most respected college-baseball magazines selected him as their preseason Division Two Player of the Year and picked his Mavericks as the team to win the 2009 National Championship. Then today, he was sure he aced his Geology final and impressed three Major League scouts at a throwing session. And the prettiest girl in school, Lindsey Ellison, told him she loved him. It was all more than awesome. He was drunk on smiling as he picked up his phone to call his mom.

She answered on the third ring.

"How's my All-American?"

"High in the Rocky Mountains!" he sang out happily. "Oh, Mom, I wish you could have been there. It was so much fun. The student union was packed. My whole team was there, and they even put my ugly mug on TV. It was IN-CRED-UH-BUL!"

Susan laughed out loud. "I wish I could have been there too, sweetie, but we have two pheasant hunts to prepare for and your fly-fishing trip tomorrow—"

"What are you doing tonight?"

"Just dinner with you and Teresa. She's been helping me prep for the trips. Is her boyfriend with you?"

"No, Jose has one more final this afternoon, so he's coming home tomorrow." He paused in thought, and then exclaimed, "We don't have to wait on that moron! Let's have a preparty tonight. I'll take you and Teresa out to the finest dining spot in all of Dooo-Rango."

Together they laughed, and then Sam belted out the school fight song. "Mesa Mavericks, Mesa Mavericks! Long may you live! Show us that spirit! Fight for the win! See you tonight, Mama. Love you soooo much!"

He clicked off the phone and, with a bright smile still lighting his face, drove down the mountain pass, flashing by blue spruce, juniper, ponderosa pine, and aspen, all seeming to smile back at him on this most glorious day.

* * *

Valerie Quintana lowered her nose to the straw and inhaled the line of cocaine. It was the second best thing she could get to bring her relief from the evil she'd brought into her life. Rob Marcus was the devil. She had known it from the first day she had met him, but he had something that was essential for her very existence. White-powder heroin. And she needed it now.

Unfortunately, Marcus refused to give her any until he had his fun. Only this day, his fun was violence. She never should have pushed him away when he tried to kiss her.

Marcus slapped her hard across the face and slammed her against the wall of the hotel room. She tried to fight back, but he grabbed her by the hair, pulled her down on the bed, and ripped open her blouse. She scratched at his face, but that only seemed to excite him more as he forced open her legs. She gave in, and let him have his way with her. When he was finished, he rolled over onto his back, his breath slowing, and he fell asleep.

It is time to end this nightmare, Valerie thought. *It is time to get help.*

Slipping away from the bed, she picked up her phone and tiptoed into the bathroom. What was the woman's name she had met in the hospital? The one who knew her father? Scrolling through, she found it.

Susan Carson. She pressed call. It rang several times and then went to voicemail.

"This is Valerie Quintana," she whispered. "I need help. I'm at the Mesa Motel with Rob Marcus and—"

The door was kicked open, a fist smashed her face, and everything went black.

*   *   *

It was an unseasonably warm winter day on Pargin Mountain as the bare cottonwood and Gambel oak branches twisted in the breeze. A soft morning rain had settled the dust on the Carson driveway, darkening the color from a pale yellow-brown to a burnt umber.

Teresa was busy packing extra fingerless fleece gloves, long underwear, insulated socks, and wading boots into a waterproof footlocker. The family from Albuquerque had a history of forgetting important items when booking a fly-fishing trip with SJ Outfitters, so Susan had made a run to a Durango store to buy extras of just about everything.

"Jose called me from Sam's press conference." Teresa laughed as she slipped a pair of socks inside a boot. "He said Sam was so nervous he probably drank a gallon of water during the five minutes."

"He was singing on the phone when he called me!" Susan beamed, her smile widening at the memory. "I don't think I've ever heard him so happy."

As Teresa closed the footlocker and snapped the latch shut, Susan reached into her purse to see if there were any messages from her son, who should be near Durango by now. Instead, she found a message from an unfamiliar number. She clicked on to listen, and the color drained from her face.

"This is Valerie Quintana. I need help. I'm at the Mesa Motel with Rob Marcus and—" The next sounds she heard were an obvious scuffle, a woman's muffled cry, and then the message clicked off.

She called 911, but the signal was bad. She moved closer to the house and tried again. Nothing.

"Teresa! Get in the truck! Right now!"

* * *

"I told you not to mess with junkies," Cutthredge hissed as he sped down the dirt road toward the Carson drive.

"We don't have to worry about the girl anymore," Marcus said. "I shot her up with so much smack she won't last two hours. She was choking on her own vomit when I left."

"But she was still able to call the Carson woman, who could take us down. We gotta find out what she told her."

"We shouldn't have to wait long." Marcus pointed ahead. "Ain't that her truck?"

* * *

"Dear God, no!" Susan gasped when she saw whose truck was fast approaching. She turned off her drive and floored the accelerator.

"What's going on?" Teresa pleaded.

"Not now!" Susan fishtailed the truck around a bend, dust and rocks flying behind, and then glanced over to make sure Teresa had her seatbelt fastened. "Call the police."

"You're scaring me, Susan."

"Just call them!"

Teresa's fingers were shaking as she tapped in 911. "There's no signal!"

They were on a straightaway now. Susan pushed the truck past sixty, then glanced in the side mirror. Cutthredge and Marcus were still on her tail.

* * *

"Bitch acts like she knows what she's doin'." Cutthredge grinned and gunned his Ford F-150 within five feet of Carson's rear bumper.

"Tag her, Billy!" Marcus pounded his fist on the dash. "Tag her!"

Cutthredge braked and turned the wheel, the tires skidding on the dirt road. "Shut the fuck up!"

"No! Tag her! C'mon! Ride that bitch!"

Cutthredge floored it just as they were approaching a right turn and hit the Carson truck on the back-right corner. The truck spun clockwise, flipped once, twice, before the driver's side slammed into a big pine.

Cutthredge roared past and then pulled over some forty yards down the road. The two men leaped out and raced back to the Carson truck. There was broken glass everywhere, and gasoline leaked out on the road.

"You tagged 'em good!" Marcus gave Billy a maniacal smack on the back. "Let's find out what they know."

Cutthredge was already peeling back the broken passenger door. He felt for Teresa's pulse. "Your squaw's still alive." He unbuckled her seat belt, dragged her out of the cab, and handed her to Marcus. "Put her in our truck. I'll check the old lady."

Cutthredge reached back in and touched the woman's shoulder, whose head rolled sideways across her chest, a half-opened eye staring lifelessly up at him. He jerked back.

"Oh shit, man . . . she gone." He checked her pulse to make sure and then headed back to his truck. He stopped suddenly in the middle of the road.

"Someone's comin', Robbie! Let's get outta here!"

*   *   *

"Nobody's home, Mr. Dixon," one of Drake's security men said when he returned from banging on the trailer door. "But they have to be close. Coffee pot was still warm."

Dixon made one more call to Cutthredge's phone and then clicked off as soon as it went to voicemail. He'd left four messages already. No reason to leave one more. These renegades were obviously onto his investigation, but unless he found them first, they might divulge his background to both the press and the Senate investigative committee. He had to bring them in quietly, pay them off, and set them up somewhere outside the country.

"No use staying here," Dixon said. "Let's at least make our time worthwhile and stop by the Carson place."

*   *   *

Sam stood alone by the side of the road, staring at the broken glass, the fuel stains on dirt, the twisted metal, and the lifeless body of his mother. He wanted to look away from the horror, even closed his eyes, trying to convince himself that what he saw had not happened. He remembered the sirens wailing as he drove home, remembered pulling over to the side when he saw the flashing lights, first a police car pursued by an ambulance, then a fire truck. He remembered following, remembered getting out of his truck, remembered words that made no sense now as he watched people he'd known his entire life pull a sheet over the bloodied head of his mother.

Their neighbor, John, had first come across the accident and had immediately gone to a spot where there was cell service and called 911. Sheriff Red Sky had told Sam what they believe had happened. His mother must have been traveling at a high rate of speed when she came to the right turn on the road and flipped her truck. He was so sorry.

It was a familiar feeling. The desolation of loss, of despair, of grief. It was as if his mind was paralyzed and that he was viewing this tragedy from some otherworldly place. It was impossible to move, difficult to breathe. Dark clouds blocked his senses, stifling his ability to think, to hear, to understand the sympathetic chatter that he wished would stop.

"... *corner too fast* ... *dirt road* ... *I don't think she suffered* ... *why don't you sit in my squad car until* ..." Sheriff Red Sky's words dissolved into nothingness as Sam bent over, fighting the bile that was rising in his gut. For a moment he remembered his father's and sister's deaths plunging him into extreme sadness, but this nightmare was like throwing hot coals on an open wound, burning deep toward some dormant flame, a simmering rage of vengeance that needed someone or something to burn that might end this pain.

It was only when they carried his mother's body to the ambulance that Sam saw the track on the road that others might miss. A slight depression in the dirt, surrounded by the myriad of tracks from John and Sheriff Red Sky and the EMT officials. But this track was moving away from the accident. He bent down to study it. Why was it familiar? Then, like a laser finally locking on its target, he recognized Billy Cutthredge's boot. Ten yards farther, he found Rob Marcus's print. Marcus's track was different, heavier on the right side, as if he was carrying something . . . or someone.

Sam walked on. Another vehicle had been here. It made the same print as Cutthredge's Ford F-150. Then, he found one more track, much smaller, as if Marcus had rested a body against the side of the truck before opening the passenger-side door.

They have Teresa. He walked slowly back to his truck, head down, mind consumed by his objective, completely unaware of the black Ford Tahoe that was parked some one hundred yards down the road.

*   *   *

There was only one dirt road that led to the Carson property, so it wasn't difficult for Dixon's team to come across the accident. They pulled over to the side, and Dixon brought his binoculars up to his eyes.

"Holy shit! That's the Carsons' truck." He panned right to see a paramedic pulling a sheet over a person's body. "And that's Susan Carson . . . what the hell happened?"

"Drake," King cut in. "Who's that down the road?"

Dixon swept his gaze past the emergency vehicles some forty yards away. There was a man on one knee, head down, as if studying the dirt. The man raised up, and Dixon almost dropped his binoculars. "That's Sam."

They watched Carson move away from the accident, get in his truck, and slowly drive away.

Why would he leave his mother? Dixon leaned across the front seat, squinting into the distance, making sure not to take his eyes off Sam's truck. "Stay a good distance back. Just don't lose him."

* * *

The first track could be like the beginning of a baseball game. The first inning was a mystery, getting comfortable with the mound, the release point, the umpire's strike zone, searching for a rhythm, a pattern, pitch by pitch, track by track, until the mystery began to reveal itself to the pitcher, or tracker, and they became one with the quest, lost in the breath, completely immersed in an energized hyperfocus that took them to some higher level of consciousness and allowed them to accomplish feats that others would consider impossible.

Sam slowed his truck at every dirt road or trail, checking for a turn or an adjustment by the driver of the F-150. It wasn't until the third dirt road that led north up the mountain that he found it. It was a trail he was familiar with, and he knew it ended in less than two miles. He drove some three hundred yards up the road and parked between two pines.

* * *

Teresa woke up with a pounding headache. Her eyes fluttered open to find blue sky and the gnarly branches of a Gambel oak overhead. Where was she and what had happened? She tried to raise up on one elbow, but the pain in her head was too much. She pressed her hands to her temples for relief.

"Well, look who's finally awake?"

She turned in horror to find Rob Marcus sitting next to her. He rested the back of his hand against her left hip and slowly slid it across her belly to her ribcage, and then to the curve of her breast. "No reason to be afraid of me, darlin'. I just need to ask you a few questions."

She shuddered as he leaned in close, his revolting cigarette breath hot on her face.

"What did the Carson lady tell you?"

The very mention of Susan's name had Teresa twist away from Marcus and search for her friend. "Wh-where is Susan?"

He raised one greasy brow. "You don't know what happened?"

Teresa tried to swallow but could not.

"You were in an accident." He smiled wickedly. "She didn't make it."

Teresa dissolved into tears.

* * *

Dixon lowered the Tahoe's window, his eyes never leaving the tiny speck that was Carson far in the distance, beside his truck. Dixon brought his binoculars up in time to watch Sam pull a bow and a quiver of arrows out of his cargo bed. *What the hell did he find?*

* * *

It was an easy trail for Sam to follow. Tire patterns on a dirt trail that no other vehicle had been on for weeks was clear for even the most novice tracker. He knew that Cutthredge and Marcus might see him approaching, so he cut through the forest and followed an old deer trail, his footsteps as silent as snowflakes falling on wet ground, no broken twigs, no rustle of dry leaves, no birds scolding him for invading their space. He had become part of the terrain, visible only to the trees and bushes he passed by. His breathing slowed, his eyes focused, sights, sounds, smells, and intuition all amplified, telling him where to go. A blue jay called out and he froze. He heard another jay, and then another. He was close.

* * *

"Hey, Robbie!" Cutthredge waved Marcus over to a distance where they could keep an eye on Teresa but she couldn't hear their conversation. "I found a good spot about a hundred yards up the hill. Small cave covered by shrubs. No one will ever find her body."

"We better get moving then," Marcus said as he held up his phone. "I finally got cell service, and Dixon left a message sayin' he's in town to recruit Carson."

"I got three." Cutthredge gave a disbelieving frown. "Dixon didn't come for Carson."

Both of Marcus's brows drew together in interest. "You think he's onto our Afghan poppy party?"

"Yep, and I'll bet he even brought muscle to help convince us that our services will no longer be needed."

"When do you want to leave?"

Cutthredge looked up at the sun and then back down at his watch. It was just past four. "We'll wait until after sundown, circle back to Durango, get our money, and split."

Marcus smiled wickedly and glanced back at Teresa. "Then, I have time for some fun. She's too pretty to just gut and bury."

* * *

Mentally, Sam was gone. The hyperfocus that had always been his ally in baseball and the outdoors had become dangerous. It had blurred everything in his mind except for two objectives . . . finding Teresa . . . and avenging his mother's death.

With bow in hand and arrow ready, he raised up slowly and peeked over the top of a fallen log. Cutthredge and Marcus were in conversation fifty meters away

Where was Teresa? He needed to move closer, so he slithered on his belly around the log and through a stand of chokecherry. He saw her. Next to a small Gambel oak, head in her hands, obviously crying.

He glanced back at Marcus, who had just finished his conversation with Cutthredge and started back to Teresa.

* * *

Teresa sobbed as she looked up at the hulk of a man standing over her. He was laughing as he pulled his sweatshirt over his head and sat down next to her.

"Please . . . no," she whimpered, but her cries seemed to excite him as he looped his index finger in her hair and twisted it away from her face.

"Don't . . . " she begged again as he climbed on top of her. She kicked her legs and screamed, but Marcus was too strong. He pinned her arms down and covered her mouth with his. All she could do was cry.

* * *

Very slowly, Sam rose up from the chokecherry bush, eyes focused, hand steady as he notched an arrow and raised his bow. He always said a prayer before hunting another animal, but this time he did not. He calmed his breathing and drew back the bowstring. His target would be just below the back of the skull. But he needed Marcus to raise up, allowing a better target and less risk to Teresa.

Finally, Marcus did, and Sam let fly, a quiet *thwish* from his bowstring as the arrow shot forward. It takes only one second for an arrow to reach a ninety-meter target, but Sam was half that distance and the arrow's accuracy was true, splitting between C1 and C2 of Marcus's cervical vertebrae, severing his spinal cord. The dead man's eyes involuntarily lurched wide as he collapsed on top of a still-sobbing Teresa Songbird.

* * *

Billy Cutthredge chuckled as he watched his friend dominate the girl. He, himself, always had a desire to control, to enforce, to overpower anyone weaker. There was a certain thrill that came with watching her cower, knowing full well that this would be the final hour of this girl's life. But when he saw the arrow penetrate the back of Rob's neck, he stood frozen for just a second, mouth open, staring, and then he jerked toward the truck to get his Ruger semiautomatic pistol.

That split second of hesitation was all it took for Sam to let loose his second arrow. Cutthredge screamed as the arrow ripped through his ribcage and shredded his aorta. He clutched at his chest and fell to his knees just before Sam's third arrow found its bullseye, just above Cutthredge's right ear, burrowing through cartilage and bone before coming to a stop in the middle of his brain. The big man fell over on his left side, dead.

* * *

Sam raced to Teresa and pulled Marcus's dead body off her. At first she didn't recognize it was Sam, and she continued to scream and cover her face.

"It's all right, Teresa! It's Sam. I'm here now. Everything's okay—he can't hurt you anymore."

She flinched like a scared, beaten dog, and then reached up and pulled Sam to her, sobbing uncontrollably against his chest.

* * *

Dixon's crew had followed Sam up the footpath and saw everything. Drake had quickly motioned for one of his security men to videotape it all on his cellphone. This was a dream come true. He couldn't have written a better script than what he had just witnessed. The two biggest land mines threatening his financial future, Billy Cutthredge and Rob Marcus, had been taken out, eliminated, problem solved, and if he played his cards right, he might also be able to accomplish one other goal.

"What the hell have you done?" Dixon called out, and Sam's head jerked around in shock.

Dixon, his lawyer, Barry King, and three security men walked up the hill, one man continuing to videotape on his cell phone.

"I'm very sorry about your mother," Dixon said with the most empathetic tone he could muster, "but what did that accident have to do with you murdering these two men?"

Sam's mouth fell open, a look of absolute astonishment on his face. "I–I–didn't murder anyone. These men kidnapped my friend."

"Why didn't you tell the sheriff?"

Sam didn't answer.

"We saw you leave the scene of the accident, Sam. Were these two men, the men you claim were kidnappers, were they coming on to your girlfriend?"

"She's not my girlfriend."

Dixon turned to Teresa. "What's your name, sweetie?"

Teresa wiped her eyes and sat up. "Teresa Songbird. I've known Sam my entire life. He saved me."

Dixon's lawyer leaned forward and whispered something into his ear that brought a slight smile.

"I can help you, Sammy"–Dixon paused–"as long as you don't lie to me."

Sam gave a look of confusion.

"Did you know these men before today?"

He nodded cautiously. "They hired me to guide them on hunting trips."

"Did you have any problems with them?"

He hesitated, a look of guilt on his face, and then nodded.

"Let me get this right." Dixon smirked. "Your mother is killed in a car accident, yet you leave the scene, where police and EMT personnel are, to chase after men you've had problems with in the past, and accuse them of kidnapping your friend." He turned to Teresa. "Did you know these men?"

She nodded reluctantly.

"Were you in a *relationship* with one of the deceased?"

"No!"

"Do you have any proof that you weren't having a little fun on the side?"

"I did not!" Teresa exclaimed, her voice shaking, "Marcus came on to me!"

* * *

The emotional enormity of the day hit Sam like a concussion, as if a heavy stone was slammed against his chest in a wash of grief and loneliness. His father, his sister, now his mother, all gone. He withdrew into himself, pulling his knees up against his chest, and closed his eyes, Dixon's words drowning him in an ocean of hopelessness.

"I have no idea if you were or were not in a relationship with one of these dead men," Dixon continued to lie to Teresa. "Unfortunately, we must deal with the facts we do have. Sam killed two unarmed men."

"Who kidnapped me!"

Dixon raised a hand to calm her. "*Allegedly* kidnapped . . . but Sam didn't even warn the men. He just killed them in cold blood. We have the videotape that shows the men were unarmed. Even if it's second-degree murder, or voluntary manslaughter, we're still talking fifteen years to life in prison."

Sam couldn't breathe and thought he might be sick as the bile rose up again in his throat. Grief was still there, but also the horrible sense of failure. He began to shiver, a cold, wicked, uncontrollable shake in the very pit of his stomach.

"But I may have a solution to Sam's problem." Dixon looked at Teresa. "Do you know if these men had families?"

"I–I don't think so."

"Then, maybe they won't be missed. My people can completely clean this up by burying the bodies in these hills—no trial for Sam, no prison time, no damaged reputation." He paused as if waiting for Carson to raise his head.

Sam kept his head bowed, though his eyes were now open.

"But if I'm going to risk my career and reputation by covering up Sam's predicament"—Dixon cleared his throat—"well then, Mr. Carson has to do something for me."

Sam glanced up, his eyes dark with pain.

"Track for me in Afghanistan, and if you do well, maybe I'll give you your life back."

CHAPTER THIRTY-FOUR

Ignacio, Colorado

December 2008

Three days later Sam stood next to the same quarter horse that had carried his sister's ashes during her funeral ceremony. Only this time the horse held his mother's body, which would be laid to rest next to her husband at Ouray Memorial Cemetery.

He was numb, empty, lost in both grief and guilt. His nights were restless, and when he did sleep, old dreams haunted him, the same visions he'd had since his sister's death, dreams that he had finally revealed to his mother before Thanksgiving. He had told her that Jenny had come to him not as a body, but as a white light, seemingly free of the pain and suffering she had experienced in the physical world. Jenny welcomed their father and Old Mel to join her, but there was someone else in the dream his sister had also invited . . . someone Sam didn't, or couldn't, reveal. That person was his mother. And now the guilt of that revelation pulled his head so low his chin rested on his chest.

The horse moved forward and Sam followed, one hand on the reins, another on his mother's body. He glanced up to catch Lindsey's gaze, disappointment etched on her face for his loss, but for hers also. He had shocked everyone at his mother's Celebration of Life when he announced his decision to join DiamondBar Security instead of returning to school to lead Mesa State in their quest for a national championship. The color had rushed from Lindsey's face, Jose sat dumbfounded, and Teresa had collapsed in an avalanche of tears. Only his grandfather showed no emotion, sitting stoically in the corner, jaws clenched firmly, knowing there was something his grandson was withholding.

As Sam led the horse to his mother's final resting place, he kept his eyes low, not wanting to see the somber looks from his friends, his tribal family, and from his college teammates. He wanted to disappear, to retreat into his own misery, and not have to listen to any more sympathy and pity.

The funeral was a blur of sounds and colors and sadness, from words of inspiration to Ute chants and songs about the Great Spirit and afterlife. Sam didn't know what he believed anymore. So much had been taken from him, his parents and sister gone, and now the chance to chase his lifelong dream of baseball. It too was dead.

* * *

Three hours after the funeral he was on his way to the Durango Airport to begin his journey to the DiamondBar training facility in rural Virginia. It was quiet for most of the drive with only his grandfather, Jose, and Teresa to see him off. Lindsey and her parents were already gone, having said their goodbyes when the ceremony ended.

As Jose pulled the car up to the departure drop-off, Sam stared out at Pargin Mountain, certainly no rival to the impressive peaks of Colorado, but Pargin was his. He knew every rock and crag and tree and stream on his beloved sierra, and walking its trails had always given him peace. He wished he was there now.

"I'm sorry, but I gotta say something before you leave." Jose's booming voice snapped him out of his melancholy. "Outside of my mom, the two people I know the most in my life are sitting in this car. My girlfriend and my best friend. Yeah, we all suffer differently, but I can't get it off my mind that something happened to you two the day Susan died."

Teresa shrank back against the passenger door, head down. Sam, sitting directly behind her, said nothing. He rested his hand on her shoulder as a reminder to stay silent.

"Dammit," Jose snapped. "We can't help you if you don't tell us! What the hell happened?"

Grandpa Douglas, sitting next to Sam in the back seat, reached over and touched Jose's shoulder to quiet him down. But Jose would not.

"Shit! I'm sorry, but your mom's gone. I know she'd want you to give baseball a go. Our season begins in six weeks, and the Big League draft is in June. Mr. Francisco, from the Royals, was at the funeral. He told me their staff loves you and hoped that you'd be available when they pick. Please, Sam . . . tell me what happened?"

Sam couldn't look at him. He stared out the window as Jose continued to rail on.

"You hate Drake Dixon. Why the hell would you work for that bastard now? It makes no damn sense."

Grandpa Douglas squeezed Jose's shoulder harder, bringing pain, and finally, Jose did shut up and turn off the engine.

"You stay here," Douglas told Jose and Teresa. "Say goodbye to Sam now. I'll get his bags."

As soon as Grandpa Douglas left the vehicle, Teresa grabbed the hand that was still on her shoulder, clutching at Sam as if he was the last rock on the edge of a steep cliff.

"Please, Sam." Teresa choked back tears as she held his hand to her cheek. "I have to tell Jose. I–I can't keep this from him."

Startled, he glanced at his friend and then back at Teresa, whose eyes were desperate with pain. He drew back, but she clenched his hand even harder.

"Please," she pleaded once more.

He sat frozen, head bowed, breath heavy. Then, he reluctantly squeezed Teresa's hand and placed his other hand on Jose's shoulder.

"All right, but not until after I'm gone." He raised up, making sure that Jose heard his next words. "You have to promise me that you'll never repeat what Teresa tells you."

His best friend's mouth hung open. He glanced from Sam to Teresa and back again, a look of absolute confusion on his face. Finally, he placed his hand on his heart and nodded.

*   *   *

Grandpa Douglas was waiting by the entrance to the airport, Sam's backpack in one hand and his Mavericks travel bag in the other. He put them down and put his hands on his grandson's upper arms. He squeezed, waiting for Sam to raise his vision.

"I don't know what happened," his grandfather said when Sam looked up, "but the past is gone. Use it as a lesson to make you stronger, to make you a better man."

Sam swallowed hard but said nothing.

"Don't ever forget who you are. You are not *Southern* Ute. That was the name the government gave the people when they pushed us off our lands. You are *Ute*—never forget that." Then he paused for a long moment and stared directly into his grandson's eyes. "You don't belong to this *Dixon*. He is just another lost soul trying to steal yours, thinking it will give him greater power. Don't give it to him. One day you will understand why it was important that you didn't give him your power . . . and that you didn't give up. Stay strong. Be courageous. Blessings are coming. Believe that. For you are *Ute*. You are *Walks with the Wind*."

CHAPTER THIRTY-FIVE

Bagram Air Base, Afghanistan

September 2009

The US Air Force C-5 Galaxy began a lazy bank to the south. Sam looked out the window at the largest military base in Afghanistan. Bagram Air Base. Home to the Army, Air Force, Navy, Marines, and Coast Guard in the Parwan Province. Located nearby was the Afghan headquarters of DiamondBar Security.

As the plane swept through thin clouds, Sam leaned back in his seat, closed his eyes, and thought about his last nine months. Of training in the rugged hills of southwest Virginia, learning about weapons, self-defense, and military tactics. DiamondBar had immersed him in everything Afghanistan from the clothing he wore to the food he ate, to the languages he spoke. Tutored by Afghans employed by Dixon, he studied the country's history, geography, and culture, and he was only allowed to speak Dari, Pashto, and the Nuristani languages as he trained.

Languages had always come easy for him, but depression had not. His past haunted him with insane thoughts of death and suffering, of a meaningless world where no God could ever exist. In those dark times he dreaded being alone, as if any connection, or really, any human interaction, could distract him from his loathsome self-hatred. Twice, when he was alone in the Virginia hills, he had almost taken his life. There were times he could still smell the gunpowder from the barrel of the pistol he had placed in his mouth.

He had received letters nearly every day, from Lindsey, Coach Elba, and Maverick teammates, but the only ones he could relate to were from Jose, Teresa, and his grandfather. The raw honesty of Teresa's pain and memories of that horrible day on Pargin Mountain moved him, and he was able to reply with his own personal desolation, yet he always reminded her that, outside of Jose, she could never, ever reveal their secret. Teresa had, of course, told her boyfriend, and he had responded as Sam had expected.

My dearest brother,

Teresa told me everything. I went crazy when she first revealed what happened and I wanted revenge for you. I wanted to kill Drake Dixon. Teresa was scared of what I might do and pleaded with me to go with her to visit your parents' graves. It was there I realized that I was allowing Dixon's venom to poison my spirit. If my brother had the strength to stay quiet, then I must too. I am now grateful. I am grateful that Teresa wasn't killed in the crash. I am grateful that you saved her from those evil men, and I am grateful that the Great Spirit gave me such an honorable friend as you.

I love you, Jose

His grandfather's words were always short and to the point, reminding him to *search for the lesson in everything.* He ended each letter with, *Are you reading Jenny's journal?*

Sam was not.

*   *   *

"Mr. Dixon bought us brand-new trailers after Congress gave him another three-year contract," said Operations Chief Charlie Whitson as he gave Sam a tour of their DiamondBar compound. "We have eighty men at our Bagram facility. Some train police. Others escort and guard diplomats. You'll be part of an eight-man unit doing recon for the Provincial Reconstruction Teams in the Nuristan Province."

Sam nodded.

Whitson pointed to a flat-green trailer. "That's where you'll bunk." He opened the door to an adjoining trailer. "And here are your teammates and the Army Special Forces colonel we'll be sharing your intel with."

Sam followed Whitson into a bigger structure that obviously doubled as a rec room. Men were relaxing on couches and chairs, all looking just like him with long hair, most with beards, and dressed in rugged gear the color of desert sand, urban gray, and foliage green.

The only man who stood up was the Army Special Forces colonel, who immediately stepped forward and extended his hand.

"Colonel Bart Tomlinson. It was an honor to work with your dad."

Sam flinched. The mere mention of his father pained him. Still, he shook the man's hand.

"Daniel Carson made life easier for both DiamondBar and my Special Forces team. He was always out front, finding trouble before it happened or safe roads to get diplomats from one end of the province to another."

Sam didn't respond.

"He told me you were quite the baseball player . . . had pro aspirations. My boy plays ball for Blue Valley High in Kansas. He's had some junior-college offers."

Sam nodded but remained quiet.

"Haven't you heard, Colonel Tommy?" One of the DiamondBar Security men snickered. "This here Carson boy led his school to the Final Four."

"Ain't we lucky!" another man teased. "We gotta bona fide All-American on our team now. Taliban better watch out, or they'll get a fastball right on the kisser."

The room broke up in laughter, save for Tomlinson, who seemed to sense Sam's discomfort and changed the subject.

"That's enough, fellas. Maybe we should give Mr. Carson a few days to get settled at DiamondBar, and then he can come over to Bagram, check out the base, and meet the recon unit he'll be communicating with."

Charlie Whitson put a hand on Sam's shoulder. "This is a fine group of men you'll be working with, Sam, showing them how to track, finding safe trails, helping the Provincial Reconstruction Teams—"

Sam cut him off. "I work alone."

Whitson chuckled lightly. "That's a good one. You don't make that call. Now when do you want—"

"I said I work alone. I can't track if I'm thinking about protecting other people."

Another security man jerked out of his chair. "Who the hell do you think you are! We've been doing security in this shithole for two years, and all of a sudden some college punk—"

Whitson stepped between his man and Sam. "Let's calm down, fellas. I'm sure as soon as Carson gets a look at the threats we deal with, day in, day out, he'll understand the importance of working together."

"I'll work with my teammates here at the base, but when I'm in the field, I work alone." Sam's face remained serious.

"That's not possible."

Sam pulled his cell phone out of his jacket pocket. "Then let's call Dixon."

Whitson's eyes widened in surprise. "I'm not calling the CEO about something so foolish."

"Then I'll call him. Because Dixon told me if I had any trouble getting what I needed, I was to call him immediately."

"You won't last one fucking day out there!" a security man snapped.

A slight, almost maniacal twist curled up at one corner of Sam's mouth as he slowly turned and looked directly at the man who spoke. "That, sir, would be a relief."

CHAPTER THIRTY-SIX

December 2009

It was late, and Sam should have turned in long ago, but he was intrigued by what he saw on two different satellite photos of the same mountain, some sixty miles northeast of Bagram. He also found that, if he kept himself busy, he wouldn't have to think about the past. Three more letters had come this week. Reading what Grandpa, Jose, and Teresa were doing always made him smile for a short time, but it was soon followed by a deep sadness and longing for home.

He shook his head to rid himself of dark thoughts and turned his attention back to the pictures. The map from last year was slightly different than the satellite photo that was taken one week ago. Sliding a magnifying glass across both pictures of a bluff about two-thirds of the way up the mountain, he saw it. There was a soft discoloration in the second photo, as if two trees had been removed.

"I'd like to get a closer look at that bluff," he whispered to himself as he wrote down the coordinates and slid the paper in his shirt pocket.

He had been in Afghanistan only three months, scouting the rural lands northeast of the air base one week, then returning to Bagram to compare his findings with maps and satellite imagery the next week. He did his best to dissolve into the landscape when near a village, playing the part of a homeless man, carrying a dirty canvas bag, and picking up bottles and cans along rivers and streams while mentally recording every bit of his surroundings. With his brown skin, long black hair, and *perahan tunban*, he easily passed for a local. Not even his poor attempt at facial hair gave him away. This would be his disguise once he convinced both Whitson and Colonel Tomlinson that it was time to get answers to the questions he found on the maps.

"Well, look who's still up?" It was Frank Weber, the DiamondBar guard who had confronted Sam when he had told his teammates that he worked alone in the field. "The punk who thinks he's so much damn better than the rest of us."

Sam didn't turn around. He slid the magnifying glass off the maps.

"I'm talking to you, college boy!" Weber kicked Sam's chair around to face him. He had coworkers Scott Thornton and Ed Morrow with him, and all three had obviously been drinking. "Get up," Weber growled.

"No thanks," Sam said politely. "I still have work to do."

Weber grabbed him by the collar and jerked him out of his chair. "I said get up!"

The door to the adjacent recon room suddenly opened, and a young Army intelligence specialist looked in. "Is everything okay in here?"

"Close the door. This is none of your damn business." Weber turned back to Sam and shoved him out the back door into the cold December night.

"Time for a little rookie hazing." Weber slammed him up against the side of the trailer and then stood back, feet set wide, fists ready.

Sam leaned back into the shadows of the trailer, arms limp at his sides, a look of complete defenselessness on his face.

Weber faked a punch but drew no reaction. That simple act of passivity seemed to ignite a rage within Weber, who then slammed his fist into the right side of Sam's face, dropping him to one knee.

Sam slowly raised up, a line of blood dripping from his lip to chin. He offered no resistance, displaying the same unflappable, detached, apathetic gaze.

"What the hell is wrong with you, boy?" Weber pulled his Glock 31 out of his holster and pointed it directly between Sam's eyes. "All-American, my ass."

"Put it away." The order came from Colonel Tomlinson, who was by the open door with the Army intelligence specialist they had seen earlier.

Weber chuckled as he lowered the pistol and clicked open the base to show an empty magazine. "Wasn't even loaded, Colonel. Just having a little fun with the rookie."

"Not on my base," Tomlinson said firmly. "If you want to haze at DiamondBar, that's your business, but not inside Bagram."

Weber turned a cold blue gaze on Sam and motioned for him to join them on their trek back to DiamondBar quarters.

"Carson stays," Tomlinson said.

"He's not your property, Colonel."

"He's on *my* property. I want a word with him—alone."

Weber swore under his breath and glared back at Sam, who still had not wiped the blood off his face. "We'll take this up later, kid."

As Weber and his coworkers left, a snowflake fell between the colonel and Sam.

"Big storm's headed this way." Tomlinson handed Sam a tissue. "Right now it's in the Hindu Kush, near the Pakistan border."

Sam nodded thanks and then wiped the blood off his face.

"Let's get some ice on that, so it doesn't swell."

"I'm fine."

Tomlinson cocked his head to the side as if trying to crack the code of this most perplexing young man. "What are you doing here, Sam?"

"I was hired to find trouble."

"That's not what I asked. Why are *you* here?"

He gave the colonel the same indifferent gaze he gave Weber.

"Your father was a friend of mine. I could tell he didn't like working for DiamondBar. He told me he took the job for insurance." Tomlinson paused, as if waiting for a reaction from Sam, but when none came, he said, "What is Drake Dixon holding over your family? Your father didn't like him and didn't hang out much with the DiamondBar staff. He spent most of his time at Bagram with my Special Forces team."

Sam's jaws clenched, but he remained quiet.

"I can't help you if you're not honest with me."

Sam relaxed and glanced up at the sky as more and more snowflakes fell. "You can help me by sending one of your men over to get my gear. I may not make it by Weber and his goons if I go alone."

Tomlinson raised a curious brow. "Did you find something?"

Sam reached into his pocket and pulled out the geographic coordinates he had written down earlier. "Can one of your choppers drop me a few of miles northeast of this location?"

Tomlinson studied the paper and then looked back at the DiamondBar tracker. "You want to go out in this weather?"

"Best time," Sam said matter-of-factly. "Not even the Taliban will want to be out in a blizzard." He motioned for the colonel to follow him back into the map room, where he pointed out the difference he found in the two prints. "It might be nothing, but this road ends at a bluff where two trees were cut down recently."

The wind picked up outside, whipping more snow flurries up against the window.

"Then we'd better not wait." The colonel looked directly at Sam. "But remember, this is just a recon mission. Your job is the same: be invisible, report what you find, and we come pick you up."

Sam wore a look of calm, but also the look of a man who was eager to get away, away from the base, away from civilization, and be in a place he felt most comfortable . . . *into the wild.*

*   *   *

It was midnight when Sam hopped off the UH-60 Black Hawk helicopter in the mountains, sixty miles northeast of Bagram. The worst of the blizzard was still about an hour away, but three inches had already fallen along the pass, adding to the two feet that had dropped in November.

Sam took one last look at the sergeant's compass and headed off into the night. He had only two items he would carry that would tie him to the Western world: a small monocular and a satellite phone, both of which he could easily discard if he was spotted by the enemy. Everything else he had was tied to local culture; his clothes, coat, mittens, food, utensils, twine, toiletries, even snowshoes were all Afghan. His only weapon was a locally made Gurkha kukri knife with an eleven-inch blade. He hoped that he would only need it to skin critters for food rather than for self-defense.

As he moved down the mountain, he let go a sigh of relief, happy to be away from mankind. While others may dread being alone in a snowstorm, on a foreign mountain, in a violent country, it was peace to him: away from his past, away from loss and depression, away from Diamond-Bar and his dark thoughts of Drake Dixon. Now, all of his senses were fixated on only one goal, finding the blurred image he had seen on the map. As his eyes adjusted to the darkness, he looked over his shoulder at the clouds gathering thicker over the eastern sierra, foreshadowing heavier snow was on the way. He'd make camp in an hour.

* * *

He tapped his boots against the frozen ground to get the feeling back in his toes. Even though he was wearing three pair of wool socks, it always took his body a few days to get acclimated to this kind of cold. The wind picked up as the storm grew close. Snowflakes breaking up into tiny ice crystals peppered his face. He quickened his pace, found cover underneath a stand of small juniper, and set his pack down against the trunk of the biggest tree. The sound of a diesel engine in the distance made him pause.

* * *

"Whose side are you on?" Frank Weber tried to keep his voice low so his coworkers sleeping in the adjacent room couldn't hear his conversation with DiamondBar's operations chief.

"I'm on the side of keeping my damn job." Charlie Whitson moved his chair closer to Weber. "Dixon called last week to remind me to share Carson with any service team that wants his expertise—Army, Navy, Air Force, Marines, doesn't matter who—as long as DiamondBar gets the credit."

"That arrogant prick is goin' home in a box. He doesn't even have the guts to come get his own shit . . . sending some Army flunky to pick it up." Weber bristled.

"Tomlinson texted me about getting Carson's stuff and said he needed to prep the kid for this mission."

"Bullshit! He's Dixon's fucking bonus baby. Stealing money from guys who've been grinding it out for years, and then this college boy comes in making more than us—"

Whitson raised a hand to quiet his man. "Carson has certain skills that Dixon needs, and the recon he's done while alone in the field is pretty impressive."

"C'mon, Charlie, he hasn't been close to any hot spots."

"No, but he's been in the Nuristan Province, finding good terrain in unpopulated areas, where a Provincial Reconstruction Team might be able to start building a road."

Both of Weber's bushy eyebrows rose in interest. "Sounds like Mr. Dixon is close to starting his little project?"

Whitson nodded. "And he doesn't want the military looking over his shoulder watching his every move."

"Then why are you letting the kid work with Tomlinson?"

"Because Dixon wants Carson to see all the satellite photos and intel the military has of the Nuristan Province. Only then can we make the best decision on where to build." He winked. "He also wants to make sure DiamondBar gets credit for any success the kid has."

*　　*　　*

Sam raised the monocular to his right eye to get a closer look at the lights in the distance. He had moved to within fifty meters of the sound of diesel engines and then waited for the storm to let up. This was precisely the location of the blurred image he had seen on the map, and he wondered what was so important for a truck to plow through a snowstorm in the middle of the night? There was no way a satellite could see through heavy clouds, so perhaps now would be the best time to move weapons.

The wind died for a spell, and Sam caught the headlights of the truck shining into an opening in the mountain. It looked like the entrance to a cave big enough for a small car to enter, but not nearly large enough for a truck this size. He swept the monocular to the left to watch two men peel back the canvas cover, revealing precisely what he had expected. Plywood boxes the size of a rifle.

One of the men took a crowbar from the truck and ripped open the top of one of the boxes. He pulled out an automatic weapon. And not any automatic weapon, like the old Kalashnikov, but the new Kalakov that soldiers back at Bagram had been talking about. The Taliban liked it because its bullets had the ability to pierce American body armor.

Sam followed the men as they carried the boxes into the cave and then brought his monocular back to the second truck. They didn't have wooden boxes big enough for the next weapons he saw.

"BGM-71 TOW," Sam said under his breath. "American-made anti-tank missiles—where the hell did they get those?"

* * *

Colonel Tomlinson paced the reconnaissance quarters at Bagram Air Base. He had not heard from Sam Carson since the day he had dropped the DiamondBar tracker in the mountains east of Pukh. Carson had called him on the secure Special Forces satellite phone only five hours after his Black Hawk chopper had dropped him off. His message had been no more than ten seconds: *I discovered weapons cache. Need to get more intel.* Then he had turned off the power to the phone, making it impossible to track him. That was two days ago. At first Tomlinson had been angry that some rookie had cut off his ability to communicate, but the more he thought about it, the more he thought it was a good idea. There were rumors that the enemy now had the technology to track radio-frequency emissions, and if they locked onto Carson's GPS location, he was as good as dead.

Tomlinson admired the kid; he was just like his father—patient, analytical, inquisitive, and self-reliant—yet there was something about the son that troubled him. He saw it in the young man's eyes when the Diamond-Bar Security guard had challenged him, saying he wouldn't last a day in the mountains if he tracked alone. Carson's response had been chilling and dangerous, veiled in some cryptic despair, when he replied that dying on the first day *"would be a relief."*

* * *

The sun finally peeked through the clouds on day three of Sam's reconnaissance mission in the Hindu Kush. It wasn't as if he minded the low clouds that hovered around his mountain snow shelter. It made it easier to hide the smoke from his fire and hide himself from the rabbits he had trapped for dinner. His body and mind had also adjusted to the extreme cold, with temps during the day in the teens and below zero at night. There was no more shivering in his down sleeping bag at three a.m.

Like every morning, he had hiked to the top of a nearby peak, not only for exercise, but to get a good view of the valley below. Most of the mountain was cold granite, but there were stands of juniper and birch at the nine-thousand-foot level, near the opening to the cave he'd been watching. He brought the monocular up to his right eye to check the road. Still no traffic since day one, when three trucks dropped off the shipment of automatic rifles and anti-tank missiles. There were only two armed guards at the cave. One near the mouth, another somewhere inside. It was time to get a closer look.

* * *

Walks With the Wind

As with most satellite photographs that he had studied of hideaways in the mountains of Afghanistan, this site was intentionally bland. A blanket covered the cave opening, and there was a metal chair for the security guard out front. But with the bitter cold December winds picking up, Sam had only seen a guard out front one time.

Moving as if he were one with the snow, Sam hiked a good mile away from the bluff and then circled around and cut through boulders that faced the opening of the cave. He crawled on his stomach to a rock crag only sixty meters from the enemy and brought the monocular up. Nothing. Only the wind flapping the blanket against stone. He glanced up at the sun. One hour till sundown. He would wait. There was something he still needed to make sure of before he called Tomlinson.

* * *

As soon as the sun slipped beyond the western ridge, Sam took off his boots and stepped out onto the snow-packed road. The last thing he wanted to do was leave any marks in fresh snow, where the Taliban guards could track him back to his shelter. Wool socks on tire tracks would be less visible than boots. He stepped lightly inside the tire track, ball of the foot down first, front to back, front to back, from sixty meters to fifty, to forty, ready to dive for cover if he saw a guard.

At last, he was directly in front of the blanket covering the cave. There were plenty of footprints near the opening, making it easier for his track to go unnoticed, so he swiftly moved left behind a rock and peeked inside. Both guards were sitting twenty meters away, their backs to him, one warming his hands at their campfire while the other stirred a pot of what he presumed was their dinner.

Slowly, cautiously, he stepped between stone and blanket and slipped behind two large crates of weapons that had been stacked to the ceiling. The wind suddenly whipped outside, the blanket fluttered, and the two Afghans turned but found only darkness.

Sam shook his head, knowing he had been lucky this time. He slithered on between the crates to the deepest part of the cave.

Despite its small entrance, the cavern was of good size, carved out to a room of some fifty meters deep and wide, and to a height tall enough to stack two crates.

He stayed close to the stone wall, searching for an open crate. He found one a good distance from the Afghan guards and peeked inside. It was filled with American-made bullets. He remembered reading that some Afghan National Security Forces, armed by America, were likely selling weapons to the Taliban. In another crate he found AMD-65 Hungarian-made machine guns, in another Russian Kalashnikovs, in another American M60 machine guns, and in the deepest part of the cave, he discovered what he had feared most. Three old American-made Stinger anti-aircraft missiles, more than likely given to the Taliban during their fight with the Russians two decades earlier. He turned on his satellite phone, took several pictures, and then powered off. It was time to get the hell out of this cave and make that call to Colonel Tomlinson.

CHAPTER THIRTY-SEVEN

Nuristan Mountains

"You went where?" Colonel Tomlinson, absolutely furious with the young man on the other end of the line, growled into the sat-phone mouthpiece. He had not heard from Carson in two days, and that was a simple text message of *still doing recon* before he again powered off his sat-phone. He was thinking about sending out a search-and-rescue team to find the DiamondBar tracker, and had even called Drake Dixon to express his concerns, but the arrogant owner had acted as if what the kid had done was exactly what he'd sent him to do.

Hell, Dixon's tracker hadn't even been in Afghanistan half a year before he went on a wild goose chase, and he, Bart Tomlinson, an Army Special Forces colonel, had helped him. Geez, he could be in deep shit. *Why had he trusted the kid?*

"I didn't want you to have to fire off one of those expensive smart bombs if it was just a small cache of weapons," Sam said.

Tomlinson inhaled a long breath, trying to calm his growing anger, and then asked, "What did you find?"

"I'm sending you pictures right now: mortars, anti-tank missiles, grenade launchers, crates of machine guns and ammunition . . . and three Stinger missiles."

"Damn"—Tomlinson's eyes went wide when the pictures came through—"you found the mother lode."

"The geographical coordinates I gave you last week are correct." There was a long pause from Carson. "How soon before you drop one of your forty-thousand-dollar guided bombs on the cave?"

"None of your damn business," Tomlinson seethed. He was now more than frustrated at this private military tenderfoot who was acting like he was in charge. "All I want you to do is get the hell out of there and go back to where we dropped you last week. I'll send a chopper to get you in thirty minutes."

"No can do, Colonel. I need to go back to the cave one more time to check on something. When I call back, I'll want the *exact* time of the strike." Then, he clicked off the power so the US military satellites couldn't trace him.

Tomlinson slammed the phone down on his desk, completely stunned at the audacity of Daniel Carson's son.

"Do you want me to call Tony and get a couple of F-15s ready?" his lieutenant asked.

He hesitated for a long moment, his jaws clenching in anger, and then simply nodded.

* * *

One hour later, Sam called back from his snow shelter, only a quarter of a mile from the Taliban cave. "What time's the strike?"

"Why do you need to know?" Tomlinson said.

"Because I don't wanna get blown up."

"What?" Tomlinson hissed. "Are you still near the cave?"

"What's the exact time of the strike?"

There was a long pause at the other end of the line, but Sam could feel the tension in Tomlinson's breathing. Finally, the colonel answered stiffly, "One-one-three-three. Now, get the hell out of there."

Sam clicked off the phone, checked the cheap Afghan wristwatch he was given at the DiamondBar training facility in Virginia, gathered his gear, and headed to the cave.

* * *

"It wasn't their fault," Sam said under his breath as he followed his earlier trail through the snow back toward the Taliban hideout. "They don't deserve to die. They're just doing their job, guarding this cave. They're somebody's father or brother or husband or son, just doing their job . . . just like me."

He checked his watch. *The F-15s should be in the air by now.*

He continued on, following his tracks around to the same rock crag he had been hiding behind every other day the last week, sixty meters from the opening of the cave.

It was a cold but clear day, not much wind. It was easy to watch the entrance from this distance. The guards were nowhere to be seen. *They're probably still inside by the fire.*

Sam checked his watch. 11:30. Time to move. He stood up and ran toward the cave, yelling out in Pashto, "Get out! Get out! American missiles are coming! Hurry! Hurry! American missiles!"

The two Taliban guards hurried from the cave, Kalashnikovs pointed at Sam, who was now bent at the waist, hands on knees, feigning exhaustion. He raised up and waved for them to follow, again yelling out in their native language, "Hurry! American missiles are coming! Get away! Get away!"

Both guards eyes went wide with fear as they stared at the intruder and then back at each other. Then, they dropped their weapons and ran as fast as they could, following the stranger up the road.

* * *

The smart bomb hit one minute later, a concussive blast that lifted all three men off the ground and deposited them haphazardly in the snow. At one hundred meters from the explosion, they were all safe.

The Taliban guards scrambled to their feet, mouths wide open as they stared at the destruction of their previous home. They turned back to thank their savior, only to find that he had vanished.

*　　*　　*

Sam continued to sprint down the road, away from the blast, curling left around a limestone boulder whose southwest slope was barren of almost any touch of the recent storm. He dove from the road to a rocky ledge, making sure he made no mark in white powder that could be traced, log-rolled up, and ran on, south along a sandstone outcrop until he came to a stream eighty meters from the road, where he'd left his gear. It was an escape route he had planned three days earlier, something he had learned when tracking coyotes on Pargin Mountain.

Coyotes were the ultimate tricksters, vilified by Europeans for their cunning and nerve, yet to Sam, they were the very definition of what man wanted to be . . . independent, mysterious, and smart. A coyote would fake an injury to draw its dinner close or enter a stream to throw off a predator.

He chose the latter, following the water for a good mile until it emptied into a mountain lake with a small waterfall that cascaded down to the valley below.

He stood by a tall Himalayan pine, admiring the view. It was beautiful. There were huge granite and limestone boulders carved smooth by millions of years of glaciers and rivers. The trees were tall and spaced wide along the river, leading directly to a tiny village about a mile away. He brought the monocular up to study the neighborhood and smiled. Not a smile of delight or joy, but a simple appreciation of innocence.

He had spent so much time at the Virginia DiamondBar training facility and Bagram Air Base that he had not seen children in a long time. Despite the cold and snow and threat of war, parents of the village had obviously cleared the snow from the dirt road that cut through the center of town, and children were playing soccer. A father even put down the Kalashnikov machine gun he was carrying and joined in the fun.

It reminded Sam of something Jenny had told him when she was healthy enough to go on hikes. They had been by a stream in the dead of winter; everything was frozen except the water that cut through the rock and ice.

"There is an old Chinese proverb: The soft overcomes the hard. The gentle overcomes the rigid. Everyone knows this is true, but few put it into practice."

Sam had never ventured to think about it further until right now. Whether it was water and ice, or love and kindness, the gentle would eventually triumph.

* * *

He gave a wide berth to the village and followed a wild goat trail through pines to the top of a ridge. Another lovely valley was on the opposite side, and he sat down against a gnarly old pine for a bite of jerky and to study the land he would be traversing. He looked at the sun setting in the west. Two more hours of light. *I'll make camp in the cover of pines by that small creek and call Tomlinson.*

* * *

"Where the hell are you?" the colonel snarled into the sat-phone. "We've had two crews on standby the last six hours waiting to rescue you."

"Sorry," Sam said from his mountain hideout. "I wanted to find a location that was safe for your Black Hawks, but I didn't find one."

"That's not for you to decide. Keep the power on the phone so we can track your coordinates."

"No thank you, sir. I'll find my way back."

"You'll stay right where you are, Sam!"

"It's too risky, sir. I'm near a village that might have insurgents. If you come to get me, they might shoot at you, then you'll shoot back, then innocent people might die—"

"Just stay where you are."

"Gotta go, sir. I'll avoid any human contact, do some recon in these hills, and see you in a week."

Sam powered off the phone, lay back in his sleeping bag, and fell asleep.

*   *   *

The closer he got to civilization, the heavier became his old thoughts. Each effect of war he saw, a bombed-out home, a starving child, a soldier with a lost limb, pulled his soul lower. The oppression, poverty, and fear were the results of thirty years of war. What had started as a Communist military coup in 1978 had never ended. The Soviets arrived in '79 to replace the existing Communist government, and Afghanistan resisted. The Taliban emerged, the fighting continued, 9/11 happened, and NATO invaded under the rallying cry Operation Enduring Freedom.

The heartache pushed him back to the foothills, setting snares for rabbit at night and boiling snow for water. He hiked down the Panjshir Kapisa at daybreak, the sun at his back, giving him a good view of the city of Golbahar and even jets taking off from Bagram. Sam smiled at a bit of fog at the lower levels because most citizens wouldn't be able to see some wayward backpacker coming out of their hills.

He descended into the city and changed his guise as he pulled a plastic bag out of a trashcan and filled it with anything moderately valuable he could find: metal, aluminum cans, and string. Then he hunched his shoulders low and shuffled into the city, once again imitating the look of some homeless man.

The streets were beginning to fill with workers heading to their jobs. Most looked away at the sight of a beggar holding a trash bag. Sam glanced at a shop window to see his reflection. Holy cow, he did look bad . . . like someone who had worn the same clothes for nearly two weeks, which he had.

*   *   *

"Just don't shut off your phone again," Tomlinson said as he tightened his grip on his own sat-phone. "Give me thirty minutes to scramble a chopper and pick you up."

"No need to send one, sir," Sam said. "I'm about a quarter mile from your northwest entrance. I figured, with DiamondBar wanting me undercover, it might be bad if I just walked up to your front door unannounced."

"I'm on my way," Tomlinson said firmly. "Where exactly are you?"

"Go straight out the northwest gate, make your first right, then first left. I'm under a stone bridge finishing my rabbit stew."

Tomlinson stifled a grin as he shook his head. There was something about this kid that he both admired and respected. Something that wouldn't let him stay angry.

"Rabbit stew, huh?"

"Wild onions, kale, what's left of a bunny I snared yesterday, and hot water. It needs a little salt, but it's not bad. I'll save some for you if you're hungry."

"Just finish your damn meal. Don't move one inch. I'll be there in ten minutes to pick you up."

Sam clicked off his sat-phone but made sure to keep the power on.

* * *

Colonel Tomlinson was conflicted. On one hand he appreciated the help from DiamondBar Security for offering his Special Forces team trackers as gifted as Daniel and Sam Carson, but this younger Carson was a mystery. And mysterious could be dangerous. Sam was a lone wolf, refusing any help in the field, seeming to have no allegiance to his DiamondBar unit, and wanting no one to rescue him. There was a fearlessness in the boy that he admired, but that also concerned him. Was it fearlessness . . . or something else?

He stood in the middle of the Bagram athletic center, waiting for Carson to finish his shower. The kid had been in there for a long time. Just as he glanced down at his watch, the door opened and out came Carson, in the robe and shower slippers Tomlinson had left for him.

"That was awesome," Sam said as he toweled his hair. "It took me a while to get the stink off. But I'm all thawed out, like a snowman on a hot, rainy day."

"Follow me," Tomlinson said.

There was a private room off of the gym, and Tomlinson motioned Sam inside and then shut the door. "Sit."

Sam sat.

Tomlinson sat on the edge of the desk and crossed his arms over his chest. "Your dad said you were a pretty good ballplayer. Team guy. Never put yourself first."

Sam shifted uncomfortably in his chair but said nothing.

"Well, here at Bagram, we put team first every time. Not just sometimes. But *every time*. If we don't, someone gets killed. Now, why the hell didn't you listen when I tried to send a chopper to pick you up?"

"I had to warn the guards."

"What guards?"

"The guys who were guarding the weapons."

The colonel's eyes went wide. "You warned the Taliban that we were going to bomb them?"

"They were just doing their job, sir. They didn't deserve to die."

Tomlinson swallowed his growing anger. "How the hell did you warn them?"

"Well, I got the eleven thirty-three arrival time from you. I went back to my lookout, near the cave entrance, then at eleven thirty, I told them that a missile was on the way and they needed to leave."

"Jesus, Mary, and Joseph! You're lucky to be alive. They could have killed you, or our smart bomb could have killed you."

Sam didn't respond, but the slight twitch at the corner of his mouth bothered Tomlinson. "What's going on with you?"

Sam looked down at the ground.

There was a very long silence as Tomlinson studied Sam, who sat with his head bowed, his dark, damp hair covering his eyes. Tomlinson had seen the same grim look on some of his own Special Forces. Fearlessness, yes . . . but desperation too. Here was a kid who reeked of success. All-American baseball player, straight-A student, rugged good looks. But what if, despite all that, he didn't like himself?

"Sam?" Tomlinson asked again. "What's going on with you?"

Sam's bowed head didn't move.

"Have you had thoughts about suicide?"

Sam sat frozen in his chair, his hands clasped together tightly as if he might fall apart if he separated them. Then, in a barely audible voice, he said, "I don't have the guts to kill myself."

"So you want someone else to do it for you?"

An eerie, tense silence filled the room as the clatter of soldiers lifting weights and running on treadmills could be heard outside.

Tomlinson reached across his desk for a notebook. "We have several great chaplains and counselors here at Bagram—"

"I don't need a therapist." Sam said, his eyes were open now, but filled with pain. "Just—just give me something to do. Please."

"Not until you talk with someone." Tomlinson paused for a second, remembering a conversation he'd had with Daniel Carson about his family. He knew they were close. "Have you talked with your mom or another loved one about your depression?"

"My mom was killed in a car accident last December, and my sister died of kidney disease the year before."

Startled, Tomlinson inhaled a deep breath to hide his surprise. There it was. The pain this young man was carrying. Sam Carson had lost every member of his family, and now someone, likely Drake Dixon, had convinced him to give up his dream of baseball and sign on with Diamond-Bar. But why?

He knew Sam was watching him, like a wounded coyote hiding behind the cover of brome grass. He was waiting for him to make the next move.

"I'm very sorry for what you've been through," Tomlinson said carefully. "I'll talk with Charlie about what's next for you."

Sam raised up slowly, his face still quite grim as he walked over to a map on the wall and placed his index finger on a spot near the Panjshir-Kapisa border. "On my hike back, I discovered two caves in this area you might want to investigate."

Tomlinson straightened up in his chair. "What did you find?"

He glanced once more at the map and then back at Tomlinson. "I'm not sure. But, if you let me do the recon, maybe we can answer those questions peacefully."

CHAPTER THIRTY-EIGHT

Washington, DC

January 2010

Dixon rose from behind his desk and accepted the congratulatory handshake from Senator Richardson.

"Hell of a job," Richardson said as he shook Dixon's hand and then sat down across from him. "Your team helped our military destroy a major weapons cache and then arrest a Taliban leader without any loss of life. You can't get any better PR than that."

Dixon smiled proudly. "It's a plan I've had for years, Ed. Use highly skilled trackers who can spot trouble that others might miss."

"I love the fact that they're low cost and high return. Damn liberals can't jump our shit about how much we spend on beating Islamic terrorists. One little smart bomb did major damage, and two weeks later, Special Forces captured four insurgents hiding in a cave."

"Yeah, but I have to rein the kid in a bit."

Richardson's brows came together as if wanting an explanation.

"My operations chief said they've had problems with Carson getting along with his coworkers and following orders from the Special Forces colonel. Apparently, he kept powering off his sat-phone so they couldn't track him, and then he just randomly showed up outside Bagram a week later."

Richardson frowned. "We don't need some wild hare we can't control."

"Part of what makes a brilliant tracker is their independence—"

"We've got a lot of balls in the air right now, Drake. We've changed our strategy in Afghanistan from a military operation to counterinsurgency. Instead of sending more troops to fight the bad guys, we're writing checks to build the country's infrastructure, connect their provinces, and train their security forces."

Richardson continued to ramble on about the Afghan leaders' addiction to US money, drug problems, and intersectional fighting among warlords. But Dixon wasn't listening. He was thinking about how this change could help him.

The roads and bridges that American money would now build were exactly what he needed to take control of a mountain rich in minerals in the Nuristan Province. He'd been preparing for this moment ever since DiamondBar brokered their first contract with the US government to provide security in Afghanistan. He had paid off local Afghan politicians to fight both the Taliban and a certain warrior who reigned over a remote area on the southern slopes of the Hindu Kush Mountains. Abdul Hazrat.

No one could find him in those rugged hills, or perhaps no other warlords wanted to reveal his whereabouts for fear of retribution. But one thing Dixon knew . . . he couldn't have his mountain until he eliminated Hazrat. Unfortunately, assassinating an enemy leader for personal profit could get him into hot water. Which was exactly why he needed to keep this part of his plan from Senator Richardson.

CHAPTER THIRTY-NINE

Nuristan Province, Afghanistan

March 2010

Sam was lost. Lost in a cave. Which way should he go? There was a faint light in the distance. He followed, but his fear expanded as the tunnel narrowed, forcing him to crawl on his belly toward the fading light. Suddenly, the roof gave way, and stone and sand covered him. He reached for the light. A hand touched his. It was Jenny's hand, he knew it, was sure of it.

"Help me . . . help me!" he called out, and then jerked up, gasping for air, eyes wide as he stared into the darkness. He shook his head to clear his mind, realizing it had only been a dream. He was safe in bed at Diamond-Bar's Bagram compound.

Thank God he hadn't spoken too loudly. The last thing he wanted to do was wake up one of his teammates. They already thought he was some kind of weird loner, who never joined them for a beer or a card game. The hazing had slowed though. Obviously, Charlie Whitson had ordered them to back off or Dixon might have them transferred to some more violent outpost, or even worse, dock their bonus pay.

His life at Bagram had become routine. The days were fine, studying maps, trying to get a tell or feel from the geography he researched, and then following up in the field. In this day of satellites, smart phones, and technology telling people where to go and how to get there, one might argue that man didn't need to read a map or topography anymore, but Sam knew differently. He loved improving his navigational skills, reading the land, water, and sky to best understand the past, present, and future. He thought that everything from politics to climate change and business were being shaped by geography.

He also believed he had an intuition that told him what to see and where to go. It was a subliminal ability to process information in the field that was too complex for rational thought or technology. It was simply the ability to *trust*.

His nights continued to be agonizing. Doubt, fear, and depression crept back in, like ice slowly splitting a canyon wall, sending stone tumbling into some dark abyss below. He would lay in bed, staring at the ceiling, wondering what death felt like. Was it like being lost in the cave, or simply snuffed out with no memory of anything? Ashes to ashes, dust to dust, blowing haphazardly away into oblivion. No form, no flesh, no nothing?

* * *

Four days later, Sam sat atop a rocky ridge some ten kilometers southeast of the city of Parun, studying the dirt trail that cut through the rugged Nuristan Province. The wind whipped again, fluttering the end of his *shemagh* head scarf, and he quickly tied it back down to the side of his head. He didn't want some local to spot a strange dude in the mountains, with a monocular, doing recon of their province. His job was to make sure these rural roads were safe for the Provincial Reconstruction Teams that were bringing heavy equipment in to build roads and bridges. The PRT had already built several schools and medical clinics in Nuristan, but this trail was a far cry from any town or village.

What are we doing here, he thought. He had only spotted one IED in the two weeks he had been in the field, and the Explosive Ordnance Disposal Unit had easily disarmed it.

He brought the monocular up to his eye again to search the trail for suspicious debris, digging, or any other abnormality that would hint at buried explosives. Nothing out of the ordinary, but something didn't feel right. The sat-phone on his side suddenly vibrated, and he clicked on.

"What the hell's taking you so long?" DiamondBar Security guard Frank Weber growled. "We've been parked forty-five minutes waiting for you to give us the green light. Have you found anything?"

"No."

"Then let's go."

"Just ten more minutes, Frank. I'd like to do one more sweep."

"You've done four already. No insurgents have been reported in this area, and management doesn't like it when we waste time."

"I'll do it quickly and—"

"Time's up, college boy."

Sam grimaced in frustration, then brought the monocular back to his right eye. He trusted his instincts, and something told him the road wasn't safe. But he couldn't find *what* wasn't safe. He scanned the roadside again and then a dry creek bed that would likely be the easiest path to the road.

The PRT convoy was now moving. He searched the creek bed once more and saw it. A break in the ice, at one edge of the creek bed, the size of a footprint. He followed where it would likely go and saw another print. Then another. The PRT was only a quarter of a mile away now. He swept the monocular down the bed and searched the road.

There! A swirl in the dirt, as if someone used their hand to push dirt up against some foreign object. Sam yanked the sat-phone off his side and called Weber. No answer. The lead PRT vehicle was now one hundred meters away. He called again. No answer.

He scrambled down the hill, frantically waving his arms, trying to get his coworkers' attention. Nothing. Fifty meters away. He picked up a rock and threw. It bounced off the front tire. Thirty meters. He picked up another rock, set his sight, raised up his left leg, left shoulder at target, and let fly. The rock smashed against the driver's side window, and the lead truck slammed on its brakes. The road grader and military vehicles behind them skidded to a stop. Weber jumped from the truck, his M4 carbine pointing up to where the rock had come from.

"There's an IED only fifteen meters in front of you!" Sam yelled down.

"It took you long enough to find it," Weber shouted back. "Now, get back on the trail! We can't have the Taliban taking pictures of our secret agent man!"

* * *

His team returned to Bagram the following week. He had found only one more IED, but it was an old one, probably worthless. It took the Explosives Unit only ten minutes to dig it up and disarm it. Now, it was time to file his report with DiamondBar's operations officer.

Colonel Tomlinson was in Whitson's office when he arrived.

"Good work," Whitson said as he closed the door and motioned for Sam to take a seat.

Sam hesitated, a bit confused, but he did sit. He thought their trip was worthless. They hadn't even been near a war zone. As a matter of fact, word was that the mayor of the region they had worked had not only cozied up to the US Provincial Reconstruction Team, but also to DiamondBar.

"Three IEDs in three weeks, good job," Whitson said.

"Two and a half. The last one was a dud. It looked like about a hundred vehicles had driven over it in the last five years," Sam said.

"Still, you found it, and that's all we asked you to do."

Sam's expression of respectful interest didn't change. But he remained quiet, hoping Whitson or Tomlinson might offer something valuable to help him understand why the construction team was in a remote, mountainous part of the province.

"I've kept Special Forces up to date on your field work, and because of the deal Dixon made with the military, the colonel would like to borrow you for some recon."

Sam nodded.

"We had trouble near the Pakistan border in October." Tomlinson finally joined the conversation. "Over three hundred Taliban assaulted Combat Outpost Keating."

"Battle of Kamdesh," Sam said. "I read about it."

"We suffered eight casualties."

"And the Taliban lost a hundred fifty."

Both of Tomlinson's dark eyebrows rose. "Whose side are you on, Sam?"

He glanced at Whitson, then back at the Special Forces colonel. "I'm on the side of no one getting killed."

That brought a slight smile to Tomlinson's face. "Hopefully, we're all on that side. But there have been rumors of more insurgents coming over from Pakistan and causing trouble."

"Why did we build a base there? Keating's in a valley surrounded by mountains and two rivers. It's hard to get to, dangerous to escape, kind of like a shooting gallery at a carnival."

Tomlinson stared at him for a moment, seemingly surprised at Sam's candor. He wasn't used to one of his soldiers asking these types of questions.

"The Afghan president wanted us there."

"So it was political?" Sam said matter-of-factly.

Tomlinson crossed his arms over his chest and straightened up in his chair. "You get right to the point, don't you?"

"I can't believe I'm the first one to ask that question, Colonel."

"When I signed up to serve our country, Sam, I gave up my freedom to question authority. My job is to follow orders."

"But I'm not in the military. I'm an independent contractor."

Whitson straightened up in his chair. "Show some respect, boy."

"I'm just stating facts, sir. Drake Dixon contracted me to help DiamondBar find safe trails through rural areas of Afghanistan and to aid the military for similar projects."

Tomlinson raised his right hand. "I can't order you to do anything, Sam. I'm only telling you what *my* responsibilities are as the leader for my

Special Forces team. I was given orders to check out some disturbances we've had in the hills southwest of Kamdesh, so that's where we're headed. Are you willing to help us?"

"If you're willing to listen to me when I get a feeling about something."

"Yeah, I heard you had some problems getting Frank Weber to heed your advice."

Sam nodded.

"Where do you get this *feeling* from, Sam?"

"Trust."

"That's rather vague."

Sam took a deep breath, bracing himself for what he would say next. "My little sister was considered a medicine woman by our Ute elders. She had this connection, this trust, to the spirit world." He stared out the window, a faraway look on his face. "She thought I had a similar connection to the natural world, an ability to find a path when none is there."

"Trust," Tomlinson said.

Sam nodded again. "My sister wrote a journal of daily inspirations to help me reconnect with something she thought I had lost. I hadn't read it in a long time, but I did this morning."

The colonel leaned forward in interest. "Do you remember what you read?"

"It was a Lakota prayer." Sam smiled at the thought of Jenny writing it down. "Wakan Tanka, Great Mystery, teach me how to trust my heart, my mind, my intuition, my inner knowing, the senses of my body, the blessings of my spirit. Teach me to trust these things so that I may enter my sacred space and love beyond my fear, and thus walk in balance with the passing of each glorious sun."

Tomlinson sat frozen, as if mesmerized by the Native American devotion. After a long moment, Whitson cleared his throat loudly.

"Those are real fine words"—he chuckled—"but words ain't gonna keep Special Forces alive, boy. Only you finding a safe path through Taliban land is gonna help them."

Still moved by Sam's words, Tomlinson didn't reply for a long moment. He drew in a deep, wistful breath. "If you don't mind my asking, Sam, what religion do you practice?"

Sam shook his head, a faraway look on his face. "I'm not sure what I believe in, sir, but it seems to me that most religions are for people who are afraid of going to hell. My sister's journal is for people who have already been there."

* * *

It was good to be away from Bagram again. Back in the mountains, a brisk March wind in his face, and signs of spring everywhere. Native grasses were beginning to show as well, as buds sprouted from mulberry, ash, hawthorn, and walnut trees. It was as if there were no war going on in the rugged hills of the Nuristan Province.

He'd seen deer, red fox, rabbit, porcupine, even black bear, but no sign of what he had been hoping for: the proud, magnificent, endangered snow leopard. The Ghost of the Mountain. Creatures of solitude, rarely seen, their smoky gray fur perfect camouflage for the Hindu Kush, they were loners, choosing cold, treacherous, bleak, isolated domains as high as seventeen thousand feet above sea level to make their homes. Sam felt a brotherhood as he scanned the mountains. He knew one was there. Perhaps it was watching him now.

There was some clues of human traffic, but most were hunters or poachers, searching for their family's next meal. No Taliban trouble. Not yet. But the closer he got to Kamdesh, he sensed unrest, much like a deer suspicious of a predator, feeling, rather than seeing or hearing, a nearby threat.

Tomlinson's Special Forces team was several miles back, four military vehicles switchbacking the rural road through the Landai Sin Valley, waiting for Sam's updates as they moved forward. The sun was high now, temperatures in the forties, and as Sam pulled back the *shemagh* headdress to cool his face, he spotted movement from across the valley. He hid behind a tree and brought the monocular up to his eye. Two men with bolt-action rifles. Likely hunters. He dropped to a knee and called Tomlinson.

"Two men at one o'clock, about two klicks away. I'll keep an eye on them. If they move up and away from you, they're probably just hunters, but if either of them pulls out a cell phone, I'll want you to halt."

"Roger, Eagle One," came the reply, and Tomlinson's party continued on.

Sam watched the two Afghans pause and then sprint up a hill and hide behind a fallen cedar. Sam's monocular locked on the Afghans as the Special Forces team drew closer, but neither man reached inside his robe for a cellphone. Just hunters. This time.

He called Tomlinson to let him know they were safe and then slipped back into the protection of the forest.

There were two more inconsequential encounters with locals as they drew within a few miles of Kamdesh before Sam called Tomlinson to stop.

"Stay where you are," he whispered. "I need to check on this village. You have good cover in the pines on the ridge you're on. I've surveyed your surroundings, and there's no structure or human for at least one klick."

"Roger, Eagle One."

"I'd turn off your engines too. From where you are, you should be able to hear any sound from across the valley."

"Roger that." Tomlinson's voice had a brusque edge to it. "Anything else?"

"I'm gonna track the perimeter of this farm. I saw a couple of dudes who don't look neighborly."

"How can you tell?"

"They're carrying Kalashnikovs."

"Keep the sat-phone on, Sam. I don't want you doing anything stupid."

"Yes, sir." Then he clicked off, but following orders, kept the power on.

*   *   *

It wasn't hard for Sam to understand Afghanistan. His own culture's history told him what happened when powerful outsiders invaded and pushed people off their land. Foreigners with strength in numbers, greater weapons, and a belief in manifest destiny were difficult to discourage. His grandfather and grandfather's grandfather had passed down the stories of a time when God was found in nature; a time when there were no environmental disasters or economic instabilities or nuclear weapons. There was only the blessed land, wildlife, and the people.

He stayed in the pines as he canvassed the village. It seemed to be a simple hamlet, only four stone structures and two barns connected by a wooden fence that held goats, chickens, and mules inside. There was a large vegetable garden in the back that spread from the farthest stone structure near a creek all the way to the forest.

A community farm, he thought, and continued on. It was dusk now, a good time to move, when the human eye was still adjusting to poor light. There were a few lanterns by the stone huts and a fire in the central square. As the sun disappeared beyond the Hindu Kush, the mountains became like black silhouettes ready to swallow up this tiny village.

Sam moved from pine to pine in a low, quick, semicrouch, only pausing when the wind stopped swishing the pine needles.

A door from one of the far huts opened, and a man was shoved out into the square. The left side of his face was bloody, and his nose had been broken. Two men with Kalashnikovs were screaming in Pashto, but Sam couldn't quite make out what they were saying. He knelt behind a pine and called Tomlinson.

"We have a situation," he whispered.

"We're watching it on our infrared scope. I'm sending a team to help you out," Tomlinson said.

"How soon can you get here?"

"They have to traverse down our side of the valley, cross the river, and then negotiate your hill. I'm guessing a good twenty minutes."

"I'll keep an eye on them, sir."

"How many bad guys?"

"I've only seen two, but there might be more inside the house . . . hang on, they're yelling again. I gotta get closer to hear what they're saying."

"No. Stay put," Tomlinson said, but Sam had already clicked off.

He moved five meters closer, behind a white pine, and strained to listen. It was a different Pashto dialect than he was familiar with. This close to the border, it could be Pakistani, and word was, the Taliban near the border were particularly brutal as they sought to gain control of the region. These were the fundamentalists, men, always men, who manipulated Allah's word to benefit themselves. These were murderers of fellow Muslims for their own personal power.

A man with a Kalashnikov pointed his weapon at the beaten man.

"You are a traitor to your faith!" the Taliban leader screamed in a Pashto accent Sam finally understood. "You don't deserve to be a father to these children!"

The father was sobbing as he knelt before the insurgent, his hands together in prayer. "I beg of you . . . please don't take my children. They are my everything."

"Your home and family show that you are an unbeliever. The boy washing dishes. Girls reading books. Infidel!"

The father's bowed head didn't move when he asked, "Where does it say in the Quran that girls should not be educated?"

His words seemed to inflame the Taliban leader's anger more as he stared down with an evil disgust.

"God is great," he said, and then shot the man in the forehead.

* * *

Shock more than fear brought a gasp from Sam, who continued to watch openmouthed from behind the pine tree. He fumbled for his sat-phone and called Tomlinson.

"He shot him."

"Get out of there, Eagle One. My team is at the river. Should be there in fifteen."

No answer from Sam as he stole a quick glance at the courtyard and saw that two more Taliban fighters had come out of another stone hut.

"There are four insurgents," he whispered to the colonel, and then he saw another man push a mother and three children out into the courtyard. "Wait, make that five."

"Get out of there, Eagle One. Move."

But Sam couldn't. Not yet. He had to see what the Taliban was going to do with this family. The boy looked to be in his midteens, and the two girls younger, perhaps twelve or thirteen. There were stories about Taliban atrocities, abducting women and girls and selling them into sex-slavery rings in Afghanistan and Pakistan.

"Talk to me Eagle One." Tomlinson's voice was calm but commanding. "I order you to pull back immediately."

Sam's complete focus was centered on the square. The Taliban leader was taunting the mother, chastising her parenting, knocking her to the ground. He grabbed the woman's oldest daughter by the arm and half-dragged her back toward her home. The girl shrieked in fear, reaching for her mother, who was on the ground, sobbing, held down by two Taliban guards.

"Get out of there, Eagle One! Now!"

But Sam heard nothing. He was back on Pargin Mountain, his mind filled with images of Rob Marcus leering at Teresa Songbird, twisting her hair around his index finger, and then climbing on top of her.

Now, seven thousand miles away on another mountain, it was happening again. This little Afghan girl's sobs sounded just like Teresa's. For a brief moment, he stared down at the sat-phone, the grief that he had held tight for so many months wound even tighter. He couldn't stop now. He couldn't leave that poor little girl with the man who had just murdered her father. As he stepped back behind the pine tree, he pulled his earpiece out, clicked the power off of his phone, and moved swiftly through the shadows of the forest.

* * *

"Eagle One . . . Eagle One . . . talk to me," Tomlinson growled into his mouthpiece. He looked over at the infrared-scope monitor of the Afghan village. He watched a man drag a girl into a stone structure while others near a campfire knelt on the ground. Tomlinson's recon specialist pointed to a blurred image on the edge of the screen, moving from tree to tree as if circling around to the back of the house.

"Damn fool," Tomlinson muttered. "He's gonna get himself killed." He turned back to his recon man. "How much time before our guys get there?"

The corporal shook his head. "Ten minutes."

* * *

Sam concentrated, his head sweeping slowly left to right, listening not just for the chatter in the village square, but for the forest. He stayed low, circling through the trees to the back of the stone hut, all the while hearing the soft cries of the girl inside. He crept through the garden to the back door and cautiously turned the knob. It was open. He peeked inside, and his jaws clenched in fury. The girl was on her back, dress pulled above her waist as she fought to keep her legs together. The man was shirtless and was just beginning to untie his baggy trousers.

For the briefest of moments, Sam froze, trying to calm the rage that was burning inside. But every time the girl cried out, he heard Teresa. It was as if he was drawing the bowstring back again, sighting the cervical spine of Rob Marcus, letting fly the arrow, killing men who deserved to be killed.

It's all right, Teresa! It's Sam. I'm here now. Everything's okay—he can't hurt you anymore.

His eyes locked on his target, tunnel vision, his face emotionless as he slowly inhaled a deep, settling breath. He drew the Gurkha kukri knife from its scabbard and very slowly pushed the door open.

The Taliban leader stood over his conquest, his breath heavy, a wicked smile creasing his face as he lowered his pants and wrenched the girl's legs apart.

Sam moved with sudden violence, his knife raised over his head, but at the last second, he twisted his wrist and slammed the butt of his knife down on top of the man's skull. There was a stifled gasp as the Taliban leader's big body went limp and fell on top of the shocked girl. Sam dropped his knife and covered the girl's mouth with his left hand to silence her.

"I'm here to help you," he whispered in Pashto. "Please don't scream. I'm here to help you."

The little girl continued to sob, her frightened eyes flickering back and forth between the stranger towering over her and the body of the Taliban chief who lay unconscious on top of her. At last she nodded, and Sam removed his hand.

"We must go quickly and quietly," he said softly as he rolled the man's body off the girl, who immediately pushed her dress down and curled into herself. She buried her head in her arms and shook uncontrollably as she whimpered for her mother.

"My friends will be here soon to rescue your family." He then lifted the girl off the ground and carried her out to where he knew she'd be safe, into the darkness of the forest.

CHAPTER FORTY

Bagram Air Base Hospital, Afghanistan

March 2010

Sam's eyes fluttered open, and he looked down at his left arm. There was an IV needle sticking out of the vein inside his elbow. He turned in bed to push the call button to bring a nurse. Why the hell was he in the hospital?

There was nothing wrong with him. No bullet holes in his body or stitches from some mishap in the hills. The last thing he remembered was being in the mountains, doing recon for Colonel Tomlinson. They had come across a few Afghan hunters, but nothing too dangerous. What had happened?

A pretty young nurse peeked her head into his room. "Hey, sleepyhead, it's nice to see you finally up. How are you feeling?"

He chuckled lightly. *Sleepyhead* was the endearing name he had called Jenny when she would wake up after one of her countless kidney-dialysis procedures.

"I'm fine, thank you, but why am I here?"

The nurse's face suddenly became serious. "Colonel Tomlinson is on his way over. He'll be able to answer that question."

"I don't understand. I feel fine."

She forced a smile. "I think we should wait for the colonel."

The nurse left, and Sam sat up in bed, curious about why she wouldn't reveal what had happened to him. He closed his eyes and searched his mind, going over every detail of his recent outing. He remembered the path, the tracks of deer and rabbit he'd seen, even the feel of the bark of the pine tree he had hidden behind when studying some Afghan hunters. But nothing after that. Why?

He remembered his mother telling him that he was blessed with a photographic memory, and that was why languages and tracking had always come easy for him. Yet he remembered nothing except seeing the hunters.

"Sam?" He opened his eyes to find Tomlinson seated next to him. "Hello, sir, I'm a little confused. I hope you can clear up some things."

Tomlinson hesitated before saying, "The nurse said you're having trouble remembering all of yesterday."

"I don't know. I remember tracking for you, finding a few hunters on our way to Kamdesh. It was pretty uneventful."

"You don't remember saving the girl?"

He straightened up in bed. "What girl?"

"You came across a small village that was being attacked by Pakistani Taliban," Tomlinson explained. "The leader killed a man and then dragged his daughter into a house to rape her. You went in—against my orders—and saved her."

Sam's mouth opened in utter surprise.

"My team arrived a few minutes later and secured the village. No shots were fired. The insurgents surrendered, and we transported them back to our military prison."

Tomlinson paused to see if any of it registered with Sam, but he saw only confusion.

"We found you a short distance from the garden, trying to comfort the girl. As soon as we reunited her with her family, you started shaking uncontrollably. The only thing you said was, 'Why did they have to kill her father?'" Tomlinson paused again, but Sam gave no response.

"Your shaking didn't stop, and then you passed out in the chopper on the way home. The medic thought you were having a heart attack, but the docs here thought it was some kind of breakdown or panic attack. You need to get some help, Sam."

Sam's eyes were all the way open now, but he couldn't speak as he stared past the colonel, out into the hospital hallway. He did remember. He remembered everything. Almost. He remembered the girl. The Taliban leader. His blind rage. He forced a swallow and turned back to Tomlinson. "I . . . I didn't kill anybody, did I?"

The colonel shook his head. "The Taliban leader you subdued is in our military jail." He stifled a grin. "But he has a pretty big knot on the top of his head."

"Thank God," Sam sighed.

"Hakim Khandowa is a bad guy, Sam. A real sicko who traffics young girls. Why are you interested in his well-being?"

"I don't know," Sam said softly, staring at the IV needle in his arm as if it were draining him of any ability to understand the madness that he had witnessed in this world. "I'm just relieved I didn't kill him."

"I'm glad you feel that way," said Tomlinson, "for I've seen many young men become numb to bloodshed."

Sam was moved by the colonel's words. In part it was because of the life he had spared, but also because of the life he had saved. "What happened to the Afghan family?"

"They're at a local mission just a few miles away. I didn't think it was safe for them to remain at their farm without our protection and with their father dead."

"May I see them?"

"Sure. I'll take you there myself whenever the doc lets you out of here. There's a cool hippie minister who runs the place. He's probably someone you could relate to."

One of Sam's dark eyebrows rose in interest.

"Both of you have trouble taking orders and seem to enjoy living on the razor's edge." The colonel grinned.

*   *   *

Two days later they entered the front gate of the Friends of Everyone Hotel. That's what Whiplash McCracken called his place, because the Taliban had made it illegal to practice any faith other than Islam in Afghanistan. From outside, the property looked like a prison with a ten-foot hurricane fence, topped with barbwire, surrounding the complex, and another eight-foot wall protecting whatever was inside. Beyond the thick wooden door was a carnival of colors. It was like walking into a time machine, back to the days of the Summer of Love, in the 1960s.

"Where the heck are we?" Sam exclaimed when he and Tomlinson walked through the gate into a playground square, bordered by four simple houses, painted with a wild variety of colors. One house was a mixture of blue and pink and red; another was green and purple and yellow. Children's artwork of flowers and birds and animals and peace signs were painted haphazardly on every outside wall. In the middle of the square was a dirt playground, a basketball goal on one end and a soccer/baseball field on the other, complete with a chicken-wire backstop.

Children played whiffle ball against their parents, men in traditional Afghan garb and women dressed according to their personal strict, or not-so-strict, Islamic tradition. The only adult who looked out of place was the pitcher, who was clad in flip-flops, torn jeans, an Arkansas Razorbacks sweatshirt, and a Kansas City Royals baseball cap. He flipped a plastic ball underhanded, and a boy no more than eight years old smacked it high in the air, the wind catching it, sweeping it into foul territory. Sam took two steps to his right and easily snatched the ball out of the air with his right hand. He whipped it back to the pitcher.

"Whoa, baby!" the pitcher roared. "We got another player! And he brought Colonel Tomlinson with him."

"Hey, Whiplash." The colonel grinned. "Ya got a second to meet your new prospect?"

McCracken held the whiffle ball aloft and winked. "Just one more pitch to my little slugger, Shahpur, and I'll be right over."

Sam chuckled with amusement. There wasn't much difference from this field than his Little League field back in Ignacio. Chicken-wire backstop, peppered with holes from too many foul balls, and hard-packed, sunbaked dirt infield. It was heaven.

As he stood admiring the field, he felt a tap on his back and turned to find a little girl smiling up at him. She looked familiar.

"Thank you for saving me," the girl said in Pashto.

Sam inhaled a startled gasp. "Hello, I mean, *Salam*," he stuttered and then extended his hand. She did not accept it, but she smiled, put her hands together in prayer, and gave a brief bow.

He bowed back and introduced himself. *"Ze nome gem, Sam."*

She covered her mouth, stifling a giggle. *"Ze nome gem, Nahal."*

"Nahal!" a boy who looked like he could be her brother shouted across the ball field. He had a stern expression and waved for her to join him.

She nodded and turned back to Sam. *"Ter bia ledolo."* Goodbye.

Sam placed his right hand on his heart and smiled. *"Salam Alaikum."* Peace be upon you.

*　　*　　*

"There are stories of girls and women being beaten by the Taliban if they were simply seen walking down the street with a man who was not a member of their family," Tomlinson explained as Nahal hurried off to join her family.

"I hope I didn't bring her trouble," Sam said, a look of concern following the girl across the playground.

"Don't worry about it. Whiplash has a unique way of cooling even the hottest of young tempers."

The words were barely out of the colonel's mouth when McCracken called Nahal's brother over to pitch so he could meet their new visitor.

The boy's face brightened as the children on the field clapped and teased him to throw them a pitch they could knock out of the yard.

McCracken jogged over and extended his hand. "You're the dude the colonel's been raving about. Way cool to meet ya, my man."

Sam felt himself flushing as he shook his hand. "Oh, it's nice to meet you too. I didn't know I came with a press release already attached."

McCracken laughed out loud and slapped Tomlinson on the back. "Colonel calls you Kid Carson, the best wilderness guide since the legend Kit Carson himself tamed the Rocky Mountains."

Sam wanted to change the subject. "Where did you get the name Whiplash?"

"You should know. I heard you pitched a little hardball?"

Sam nodded.

"Did you ever give up a homer?"

"Many."

"Well, I bet I gave up more than you." He gave a dramatic pantomime of delivering a pitch. "And when I'd give up a shot, my head would jerk around so fast to watch the flight of that ball that my teammates called me Whiplash." He gave a quick demonstration with a twist of his head, and then rubbed the back of his neck. "Heck, it took three chiropractors to get my vertebrae all straightened out." He threw his arms in the air and spun around. "So wadda ya think of the Friends of Everyone Hotel?"

"Is this a Christian mission?"

McCracken jumped back as if he'd been shot and raised an index finger to his lips. "Don't ever say *Christian* in this playground, brother. Or Muslim or Hindu or Jew. That's about the only law I have on this property." He placed his hand over his heart. "The only laws we have are respect everyone and *no* talk of religion. It's the IED of Afghanistan."

Sam cocked his head to one side. "I beg your pardon?"

Whiplash twirled his finger around the side of his head. "Religion makes everybody go cuckoo here. Muslims fighting Christians, Christians fighting Muslims, Fundamentalists fighting Not-So-Fundamentalists. It's like everybody's a walking IED with their detonators sticking out, daring you to touch them." He paused for effect. "Let me ask you, would it be best to touch those buttons and blow up, or do you think nonresistance might work better?"

"Does it?"

"A heck of a lot better than missionaries coming here to proselytize the name of JEEE-sus!"

"Aren't you a Christian minister?"

"I am, and nuthin warms my heart more than teaching the love of Jesus, but I choose do it through my actions and not my words."

"Ye shall know them by their fruits," Sam said softly.

"Matthew 7:16." McCracken's two wild eyebrows rose in surprise. "Are you a Bible dude?"

"Not really. My sister wrote a book of spiritual stuff that resonated with her. It didn't matter if it was Christian or Buddhist or Native American or New Age. She believed that truth is true, no matter who said it."

"I like her already." McCracken smiled. "Give me her address, and I'll send her some of my—"

"She died two years ago," Sam said abruptly.

McCracken put a hand on Sam's shoulder. "I'm sorry for your loss. But your sister's right. By our fruit, our service, people will know us. That's why I think it's time to get out of the conversion business. Just respect one another the way Jesus and Buddha and even Muhammad told us to. Be kind." He paused. "I don't think Jesus taught nonresistance as a kind of test to see if we were up to it spiritually. I think he was teaching us a way to avoid pain and suffering. If we fight life, life tends to fight back. So just don't touch those IEDs."

Sam grimaced at the memory of the last two years of his own life. "Sometimes the innocent are in the wrong place at the wrong time."

McCracken narrowed his eyes. "You're Native American?"

"Ute."

"So you know what happens when foreigners come in and force their religion on another culture?"

Sam frowned. "They even wrote laws at the end of the nineteenth century that made it illegal for us heathens to practice our godless ways."

"And our government boys didn't change those laws until 1978." McCracken shook his head sadly. "That was real neighborly of 'em."

Sam stared past McCracken to the ball field, where Nahal's brother was high-fiving a child no older than four for a solid hit to the outfield. Whiplash seemed to know what Sam was thinking.

"Ah, heck," he muttered. "I don't know if our politicians or ministers or parents and teachers intentionally steered us wrong. They taught us what they had learned. Maybe they were just afraid of the unknown. And fear often reveals itself in ugly ways."

Sam stood silent, watching the game and the family who, only days before, had lost their father and husband. It wasn't fair. This vicious cycle of attack and defend, attack and defend that was terrorizing Afghanistan had now infected this poor family. He bowed his head as if the sadness of the moment was too much.

"Fortunately, we know there's a better way." McCracken squeezed his shoulder. "Forgiveness may be necessary to leave the past behind, but I think we need God's help." He waited for Sam's eyes to raise up and meet his. "Who's your spirit guide, Sam Cloud-Carson?"

A tinge of color came back into Sam's cheeks as he suddenly brightened. "My sister, Jenny."

CHAPTER FORTY-ONE

Afghanistan

April 2010

Sam tossed off his covers and silently rolled out of bed. He picked up the small foot locker nearby and carried it out to the Diamond-Bar barracks common room. It was time to figure some things out. He opened the locker and pulled out his unopened mail. There were letters from Jose, Teresa, and his grandfather, Coach Elba and Maverick teammates, even two from Royals scout Roberto Francisco and General Manager David Wilson. But nothing from Lindsey.

Jose had revealed in a recent letter that he had seen her with the quarterback of Mesa State's football team and that she had asked about Sam. But she hadn't written him. Not even a Christmas card.

Much to his surprise, he found that the revelation didn't really bother him. It was as if he had always expected to be rejected by Lindsey. Why not? He had lost just about everyone else he cared for. Why get close to someone only to have them ripped away like some weed from a cold winter garden? It was much easier and less painful to be alone.

He opened his grandfather's letter and read:

Dear favorite grandson,

Ha ha, I only have one, so you are my favorite. I pray to the Great Spirit every day to give you the strength to get through whatever challenge you are facing. I do not know what burden it is you carry, but I know one thing . . . you are stronger than you know.

Your mother, my daughter, was the same. She was so stubborn as a little girl. I would call her Oakley, for she was as rigid as the bur oak in our front yard when she thought she was right. But the bur oak also adapts to its surroundings. It tolerates drought or bad soil to blossom every spring, giving us the most beautiful yellow-green catkins. Remember that, when sorrow visits you, Oakley loses her leaves every year and still stands tall because she knows better days will come.

You are the same. You are strong. You are my favorite grandson.

You are Walks with the Wind.

May the Great Spirit be with you today, and may you continue to read Jenny's journal.

Stand Tall,
Grandpa Douglas

He put the letter back in the envelope and stared deep into his foot locker. Jenny's journal was at the bottom. He had not opened it in more than a month, and that was just one time. He still didn't think that he deserved his sister's words of inspiration. His failure and guilt were too great.

He had failed his family, failed his tribe, failed his community, failed his team, failed his university, failed everyone who had believed in him when he made one myopic decision to kill Cutthredge and Marcus. Why hadn't he just told Sheriff Red Sky what he saw at the accident site? Why? Why? Why? The thought of that mistake haunted him.

Finally, he reached down and pulled out his sister's journal. A faint smile touched his face as he stared at the curvy lettering on the front: *Jenny's Journal of Inspiration.*

He flipped it open to a random page. There was a drawing of a dream-catcher and below Jenny's words:

Our physical bodies need sleep, but our spirit never rests. It constantly moves and wanders about when we sleep. That's why we need the dreamcatcher to catch our nightmares and allow the good dreams to float over us to comfort our minds and bring us peace.

How did she know what he was going through? He turned the page.

There are no accidents . . . all things are lessons the Great Spirit would have us learn so we can return to the home we never left.

He turned another page. At the top in bold letters was one word: *TRUST.*

Below she had written something specifically for him.

Think of what you do when you pitch and track, brother. You empty your mind and trust.

I remember watching you track deer. You followed their track until we came to a broad expanse of rock. You closed your eyes for a bit, then opened them, glanced about, went forward across the rock for a hundred yards, and immediately found the deer's track. How did you do that? Trust.

In baseball, think of all you do when you throw a baseball? Breathe, focus on target, leg lift, balance, hip rotation, separate hands, raise arm, stride, release. With all that going on, how do you throw the ball with velocity and movement exactly where you want to? Trust.

In both tracking and pitching, it's as if your body is bypassing the brain and trusting in some power greater than you. Am I being too esoteric? I hope so. Maybe that's the only way to get you to let go of whatever troubles you and get back to what I told you to do ten pages ago.

He flipped back ten pages.

Learning to Breathe Properly

A human being's life is consumed by movement and noise. We run, we talk, we watch TV, listen to music, and text our friends. But how often do we get completely quiet and listen to our breath? That is the time the Great Spirit can enter our minds. My advice on learning to breathe: sit down and shut up.

He chuckled softly. Jenny was right. He had gotten away from his true nature. He didn't think he was worthy of the Great Spirit's help. But . . . was he wrong? He turned the page.

A Course in Miracles says *God's will for you is perfect happiness, and I agree.*

He read on.

Repeat those words whenever anything is bothering you. Let all that other junk go, brother, and let the Great Spirit enter. If you find it difficult, think about something that brings you peace. Tracking. Pitching. Perhaps visualize the way you might pitch to Babe Ruth or Jesus.

He stifled a laugh. Baseball and spirit. It always got back to baseball and spirit with Jenny.

When you visualize throwing the baseball, also visualize throwing away any worries and conflicts that seem difficult to resolve. Then say, I let go and let God. Now breathe.

He put her journal down, found a comfortable seated position, placed his hands in his lap, inhaled deeply, and let go a long slow exhale. He repeated it over and over until he was lost in his breath, drifting into a world that seemed familiar, some kind of ancient peace he had felt before . . . a peace he had known in the wild and on the pitching mound. But, as soon as that awareness came to him, his eyes opened. He looked at the clock. Three minutes. *Is that all? Geez, I suck at this.*

He turned the page in Jenny's journal and read: *Good job, Sam. Now do it tomorrow and again the next day. You've done this before and quite well. You did it at the Sun Dance, and you did it when we cleaned that turkey for Thanksgiving. That is your true nature. Always know that if you are going be the very best you can be, you must first clear your mind so the Great Spirit can enter. This ends your first lesson in Learning to Breathe Properly.*

CHAPTER FORTY-TWO

Washington, DC

April 2010

"It's all coming together perfectly," Barry King said when his boss hung up the phone with Afghanistan's Minister of the Interior. "To have Almeida Zubair give us permission to build the road to our million-dollar mountain is beyond awesome."

"*Billion*-dollar mountain," Dixon corrected him. "The geologists who did the study ten years ago said the mineral reserves were off the charts. Then the war started, and Hazrat's clan ran everybody off."

"And because Hazrat's guerillas helped fight off the Russians in '89, the Afghan government left his mountain alone."

"Until now." Dixon smiled wickedly. "Zubair told us to go ahead and start construction, that all he wants is a cut of whatever we take." He looked at the clock on the wall. It was four o'clock. A little early for a scotch, but what the hell. He poured himself two fingers of Glenlivet and another for his lawyer. "I lost a quarter of a billion when the market crashed, and now everything is lining up to not only get that back, but a whole lot more."

"We have Saudi and Nigerian companies lining up to bid on whatever we carve from Hazrat's hill."

Dixon raised a glass. "And the US government will pay for all the construction."

King took a sip. "Thank you, Senator Ed."

Dixon raised his glass again. "And thanks to our boy, Sam Carson, who tied a bow around the whole project by capturing a warlord that everyone wanted dead."

King frowned. "Don't give him all the credit."

"But he was part of the team. Tomlinson's Special Forces heard of trouble on the border. They recruited Carson to track. He came across a village where Taliban warlord Hakim Khandowa was terrorizing the locals. They captured a scumbag with a history of raping and kidnapping young girls and selling them off as sex slaves. The US arrested Khandowa without one shot being fired, and our public-relations man, Archie, made sure all the networks knew it was DiamondBar who led this brilliant rescue. Hell, even CNN gave us love." He drained his scotch in one long swallow. "You can't buy that kind of PR, Barry. Sam Carson's been a damn fine investment. That boy's a big reason the good times are about ready to roll our way again."

*   *   *

DiamondBar facility, Afghanistan April 2010

"Well, look who finally showed up?" Frank Weber's voice boomed across the room when Sam returned from another visit to the Friends of Everyone Hotel. "Little Miss Vulnerable."

Sam stopped in the middle of the room and stared openmouthed at Weber. The man was sitting in a chair, his feet propped up on the table, reading Jenny's journal. There were pages torn out, littered haphazardly around where he was sitting.

Weber winked at his coworkers on the other side of the room. "Let me read you guys some of this crap." His voice rose as if mimicking a little girl. "Vulnerability is not a weakness, Sam. Vulnerability is your most accurate measurement of courage." He flipped a page. "The ones who have hurt you the most are your greatest spiritual teachers . . . waa waa, cry me a river." He tossed the book on the table and gave a condescending sneer. "Who wrote this shit?"

Sam stood stock still, his hands clenched at his sides, his fury beginning to boil. He couldn't believe it. This was Jenny he was insulting. His sister. It was as if this jerk was spitting on her grave. He had to do something, but he also knew his temper was dangerously close to reaching a level he couldn't control.

"I asked you a question, boy?" Weber tore another page out of Jenny's journal and crumpled it up in his hand. "Who wrote this shit?"

Sam's face flamed and his eyes narrowed. He wanted to run over and knock that smile off Weber's face. Instead, his gaze went to his sister's journal, a book he desperately wanted to save. The words of Whiplash McCracken came to him.

"I don't think Jesus taught nonresistance as a kind of test to see if we were up to it spiritually. I think he was teaching us a way to avoid pain and suffering. If we fight life, life tends to fight back. So just don't touch those IEDs."

Weber is one of those IEDs, Sam thought. There was nothing the DiamondBar Security brute wanted more than to have Sam charge him, so he could kick his ass. With that realization, his entire body relaxed, and he smiled back at Weber.

Sam's gaze seemed to irritate Weber, who rose up out of his chair. "What the fuck's wrong with you?" He stormed over and shoved Sam, who took two steps back and caught himself. He rose up with the same bland gentleness lighting his face.

"Answer me, ya goddamn pussy." Weber went to shove him again, but this time a DiamondBar coworker grabbed his arm.

"Knock it off, Frank," said Scott Thornton, a guy who had teased Sam when he first arrived, but lately had treated him with respect. "I don't need another dock in pay for fighting."

Weber looked around the room and saw that he had no support. He gave a disgusted snort and started for the door. "Good luck spending the money after he gets y'all killed."

Thornton waited for Weber to leave and then walked over and started picking up the pages from Jenny's journal that were scattered all over the floor. He straightened up and handed them to Sam. "Sorry about Frank. I should have stopped him when he broke into your locker."

"Thanks." Sam looked the papers over with a half smile. "I'll leave it unlocked in the future. There might be something in there that could help him."

Thornton chuckled at that. "No doubt. By the way, who's Jenny?"

"My sister."

Thornton scratched his head reflectively. "Pretty smart girl."

As he stared down at the stack of papers in his hands, he decided that he would commit himself to reading Jenny's journal. And not just read it, but *read* it. Immerse himself in it. Transcend it. Go deep within this book to see where it would take him.

Why had Jenny written all of this down? Was she simply interested in other cultures' religions and spiritual practices, or was she talking directly to *him*? Her brother. *Sam*. Was Jenny truly his spirit guide, not only in this lifetime, but perhaps others? It was time to find out.

*   *   *

He sat down cross-legged on a folded blanket in the corner of the DiamondBar dining trailer and opened up Jenny's journal. This was his fourth straight day of waking up at four a.m. and attempting to meditate on his sister's daily devotion. He made it a full three minutes on day one, five on day two, and was pretty proud of himself to go seven yesterday. Inhaling a deep breath, he looked down and read:

I love going to the Bear Dance every May. It represents a rebirth, a new start, a reawakening of the spirit. Perhaps it's as one of our shamans, Eddie Box, once said, "You come to learn from the past in order to arrive at the present with an understanding of the harmony of things." Harmony. I like that word. May all things be blessed by harmony.

Sam rested his upturned hands on his knees, closed his eyes, inhaled a deep breath, and slowly let it all go.

"Harmony," he whispered. *Harmony.* He then released that thought and emptied his mind, concentrating on the inflow and outflow of his breath. His face muscles relaxed and his back rounded as his entire being surrendered into the breath.

Despite having his eyes closed, he could see a soft white light appear between his eyebrows, and with each breath, it grew brighter and brighter until he was sure that he saw his sister's face. She was smiling back at him with one of her *I told you so* looks she always gave him whenever he had struck out a batter on a pitch sequence she had written down on one of her countless scouting reports. The light was indeed his sister. She was happy. Filled with joy. At peace. And so was he.

* * *

He discovered that the more he meditated on Jenny's daily inspirations, the more he carried her thoughts with him throughout the day.

The Great Spirit made you perfect. May your eyes see through the darkness to a world that has forgotten love. The world is like a spider web. Everything is connected. Live your life so the fear of death can never enter your heart.

He could feel his change particularly when he was alone in the field. The tightness of his grief slowly unwinding to the raw beauty of the Hindu Kush. Of rugged granite mountains disappearing into clouds, of spring wildflowers turning toward the light, of fast whitewater rushing down through evergreen and oak onto the valley floor.

Harmony. For much of his walk, it was harmonious, but the closer he got to civilization, that harmony quickly dissolved into the reality of Afghanistan: pain, loss, suffering, starvation, and families torn apart by the country's seemingly endless wars. There were times Sam could step back and view the horror as if he were in a theater watching a movie. He had never seen such hatred in the eyes of both the Taliban and NATO forces. Both sides were determined to win, to be right, to be in control of all decisions and all people. There were other times when the horror was too much.

* * *

A soft breeze shimmered through the pines at the top of the tree line, sixty kilometers east of Bagram. Sam wanted cover, but he also wanted a good sight line of the trail his crew was traveling as they provided security for the Provincial Reconstruction Team. His rules of engagement were completely different than the rest of the DiamondBar team's. He was to steer clear of both the enemy and the construction detail he was guiding. Be invisible. Just track from the hills, at least two kilometers ahead, and call back if he saw any possible threat. But who and what was a threat? It was nearly impossible to differentiate between civilians and Taliban fighters because they all looked just like Sam, like Afghan farmers.

Charlie Whitson had told him these mountains were ruled by some warlord named Abdul Hazrat, but his secrecy was so well kept that no one knew if he was loyal to the Taliban or simply a ruler protecting his land. Sam believed that if given the chance, he could find Hazrat's hideout, but Whitson had given him strict orders to stay away from any villages or camps. He would have to do all of his reconnaissance through the lens of his monocular.

To his right was the valley, the river, and the mountain road the PRT was building, an ominous gray line cutting through the green of fir and pines. He was two kilometers away as a hawk flies, in a much more difficult terrain to traverse, loose shale and stone splintering down the sides of the slope despite each soft step.

What the heck are we doing here? Sam thought. *We're surrounded by mountains. They've brought in two more road graders to build this highway to nowhere.*

Hearing voices ahead, he froze. Nuristani. He slid back into the rocks, becoming one with the colors, muted gray, brown, and tan. The men soon passed by, oblivious of the ghost only twenty meters away.

When he felt it was safe, Sam reached into his sidepack and pulled out his sat-phone. "Purty Six, this is Eagle One, over."

"Roger, Eagle One, what up?"

"We have a band of five Afghans, my side, headed your way. They should catch sight or sound of you within minutes."

"Are they armed?"

"Three are, one with a Kalashnikov and two with old rifles. Looks like a hunting party."

"Roger, Eagle One. We'll alert Chopper BamaBear for support."

"Roger that," Sam said softly and then clicked off. He moved off the broken shale and back into the forest, thinking now was the time to see if these men were Taliban or simple locals out hunting for food. He followed their trail for a good two hundred meters until he saw a heavier depression in their track. They had paused, likely hearing the diesel road graders building the road on the other side of the valley. Then, they had changed direction and hurried up the hill. But why? To set up a defensive position? To alert Taliban leaders? Or simply to escape the threat of the PRT security?

It was deathly quiet in the forest as Sam followed, stopping every twenty feet to catch sound of broken twig or conversation. Instincts on high, he caught the shift of the wind and the voices that came with it. He pressed up behind a white pine and listened to the slightly unfamiliar dialect of Nuristani.

"Zubair thinks he owns our land," one man said. "He's making deals with infidels."

"He never talked to Hazrat about PRT being here," another man said. "They just show up, cut down our trees, and build their road."

"What can we do?" a third voice asked. He sounded young.

"Hazrat sent a messenger to meet with Zubair, to find out why PRT is here. He told us to leave PRT alone until he finds out."

Sam crept back down the hill and into the forest a hundred meters away from where the Afghans were hiding. He clicked on his sat-phone.

"Purty Six, this is Eagle One. I have location of Afghan party. Don't think they're insurgents. Just locals wondering why we're on their property."

"Roger that, Eagle One, but BamaBear has already made two drops east and north of where they are, and your security team just crossed the river to cover the flank. Thanks for keeping your sat on so we could follow your signal."

"What? I just said I don't think they're insurgents."
"You said they had weapons."
"Yeah, one old Kalashnikov and two hunting rifles."
"Then they're dangerous, Eagle One. Just hunker down and wait for your team."

Sam squeezed the sat-phone in anger and clicked off.

Shit. If one of those men even raises a weapon in surprise, he's dead.

The words were barely out of his mouth when he heard shots fired to the north.

"Dammit," he hissed. Then he disobeyed another order and ran back up the hill.

* * *

By the time Sam arrived, the two Army squads had the Afghans surrounded. Four frightened men, arms raised in surrender, save one, who was lying on the ground, holding onto what was left of his right arm. He'd taken a direct hit from a 5.56mm bullet through the inside of his elbow, and now his lower arm was dangling grotesquely off to the side.

"I said they weren't Taliban!" Sam screamed as he came out of the woods, looking himself very much like an insurgent, his loose-fitting light-brown linen pants and shirt, filthy from days in the field, his scraggly black hair dangling from his turban, and eyes wild with fury. "Why did you have to—"

Those were his last words as suddenly everything went black.

* * *

He woke up in the back of a military vehicle with his hand pressed against his forehead. His head throbbed with pain, and each breath only brought more. As his mind began to clear, he reached back and felt a lump on the back of his head. There appeared to be several stitches on top of a layer of dried blood, and as he raised up on one elbow, he heard a familiar voice.

"What the hell's wrong with you?" Frank Weber glared at him from the other side of the transport. "You're supposed to be undercover, dude. Shit, word could get out what you're up to, and the Taliban will put you on their hit list."

Sam didn't care. He was trying to make sense of what had happened on the hill. "Why did they open fire on them?"

"One of our soldiers said the boy reached for his weapon, and he didn't want to take any chances, so he popped him."

"They were just hunters."

"It's damn hard to tell friend from foe in these hills." Weber lifted his M4 to show the blood stain on the butt of his weapon. "That's why I tapped you on the head to shut you the fuck up."

"You hit me?"

"Probably saved your ass. I mean, look at you, all dressed like Afghan scum. Army boys thought you might be playing for the wrong team."

Sam said nothing more, but continued to hold Weber's gaze until the big man looked away. *Wrong team? Right team? Who was the right team?* thought Sam as a flood of images of the Afghan on the ground flashed through his brain. The boy's face etched in pain, his destroyed right arm, which likely would have to be amputated, and the looks of hatred in the eyes of the Afghan men, stunned by one of their own being shot for no reason. The scene drew him back to a quote in Jenny's journal from Lakota medicine man Black Elk:

I looked below and saw my people there, and all were well and happy, except one, and he was lying like the dead. And that one was myself.

The Afghan boy is me, Sam thought. And he was Frank Weber, and he was the soldier who had shot him, and Drake Dixon, and Grandpa Douglas, and Jenny, and his mother, and on and on . . . there was no difference. There was only the belief that they were different. Another quote from Black Elk came to him:

And I say the sacred hoop of my people was one of the many hoops that made one circle, wide as daylight and as starlight, and in the center grew one mighty flowering tree to shelter all the children of one mother and one father.

"What the hell are we doing to each other?" he muttered softly.

"What'd you say?" an irritated Weber kicked Sam in the leg. "Don't tell me you're getting soft with the enemy."

Sam squinted up at his tormentor. "Why does there always have to be an enemy?"

Weber chuckled lightly. "Because without an enemy, we don't have a job."

* * *

Two days later, Sam was back at the Friends of Everyone Hotel. He had tried to meditate that morning, but his mind kept wandering back to what had happened in the mountains. The fear, hatred, and revulsion he had seen in the eyes on both sides played over and over in his mind as if a cassette on a nonstop loop. But with a cassette, one could always push stop.

He had a terrible feeling about the Afghan boy, whose arm had been amputated when they had returned to Bagram. What would become of the boy? What would his future be like? His comrades had been captured and brought to some holding cell, and were now likely being interrogated by an Afghan Intelligence unit. It was yet another example of the endless cycle of suffering for Afghanistan.

* * *

"Well, don't you look to be in good spirits!" Whiplash McCracken called out when he saw Sam enter the Friends of Everyone sports courtyard. "I see ya gotta new turban," Whiplash wisecracked as he pointed to the bandage that circled Sam's head.

"One of my own coworkers hit me," Sam said, and then shook McCracken's hand. "He said he was protecting me."

"Yeah, I read about it."

Both of Sam's brows rose in surprise.

"The Afghan government claimed overzealous Americans attacked a hunting party. The American general said his troops thought they were

Taliban. He apologized for injuring the boy, said American soldiers came here to protect the Afghan people, not to hurt them. He admitted that we could have made a mistake and that our intelligence teams are looking into it."

Sam sighed and looked down at the ground. "It was my fault. If I hadn't called in the intel, that boy would still have two arms."

Whiplash grabbed him by the shoulder. "Don't you dare do that to yourself. You were doing your job. This is damn cause and effect that goes back centuries."

Sam continued to stare at the ground.

"This trouble didn't start when we showed up, Sam. It began when the Brits and Ruskis fought to control trade in Asia over a hundred years ago. British writers called it the Great Game. The game was control. The effect was suffering for Afghanistan.

"The Ruskis returned in 1919 with a promise of aide. What was that aide? Guns, ammo, and a few rubles to fight the resistance. The effect was more suffering for Afghanistan. Then, after World War Two, the Commies returned, outsiders financed the resistance, and another two million Afghans were killed. The Reds came back in '79, but US, Saudi, and Pak money helped fight them off.

"Attack, defend, attack, defend, attack, defend. It's been one damn struggle, over and over and over. And then we wonder why they hate us."

McCracken's words only drew Sam's shoulders lower. When he raised his vision, he saw a grim look on Whiplash's face.

"But your people know all about suffering, don't they, Sam?"

He stood frozen, his breath heavy, as McCracken went on.

"We'll give you land . . . shitty land. We'll give you government handouts . . . not enough. We'll make you what you're not . . . farmers. And we'll justify it by saying we're civilizing you heathens with *our* form of education, religion, and government."

A familiar, numbing gray sadness crept back into Sam's mind, and he turned away. Why was McCracken saying these things? He wished he would stop. He wanted to get away. Tears trickled slowly from under his closed lids as he heard McCracken's voice soften.

"It seems overwhelming, doesn't it? The problem is too great. Too impossible to fix."

Sam bit his lip so McCracken wouldn't see it tremble.

"Have you ever wondered why you're here?" McCracken asked.

Sam swallowed hard and turned to face him.

"You're here for a reason, Sam. I believe it's to help."

"I couldn't help that boy," he said in a voice barely audible.

McCracken put his arm around him and turned him toward the baseball field. He pointed to a girl, wearing a hijab and a ball glove, who was playing first base, awaiting the throw from a teammate. She caught the ball and grinned broadly.

"You helped her. How would her life have been different if you hadn't saved her from being raped by that Taliban leader?"

"I couldn't save her father."

"But you saved her."

Sam wiped the tears from his eyes but said nothing.

"One at a time, Sam, one at a time." McCracken nodded for him to follow. "That's what I love about team sports. It's the great lesson that we can't do this alone; that you have to let go of your defenses, your ego, your personal goals, and buy into *team*. When we think that only our way is the right way, we fail. But, when we pull together, play for the dude next to us, amazing things happen."

McCracken inhaled a deep breath as he watched the Afghan children playing baseball. "Each one of those kids has been scarred, Sam. Each one of them has seen some horrible tragedy or the loss of a loved one. But if they can let go of their anger, drop their defenses for just a moment and focus on what's for the good of all, incredible things can happen. Just like baseball, do the simple things: move the runner, hit the cutoff man, execute the pitch to get the groundout rather than go for the strikeout." He clapped his hands as he watched a little boy running the bases the wrong way. "How do we do it? How about by first believing we're spiritual beings having this crazy human experience. I think we were designed perfectly by the Great Master Himself, but we didn't believe it, so we went off on our own and struggled. That Great Master, whether you call him God or Allah or the Great Spirit, never left us. We left Him. And I believe He's simply waiting for us to change our minds and come on home. Just like baseball."

Sam still didn't respond.

McCracken waited a long moment before saying, "Colonel Tomlinson shared something with me. He said that you've suffered. That you've lost loved ones."

"Please, don't," Sam said, despair in his voice.

"Do you ever wonder what I'm doing here?" McCracken said matter-of-factly. "What the hell is a forty-five-year-old dude from Arkansas doing in Afghanistan instead of on Wall Street, where my business degree should have taken me?" He waited a beat for Sam to answer, but when he received no response, he answered his own question. "My life was great, brother. Working for a big financial company in Little Rock, living the good life, married, two kids, happy as a clam in warm salt water. Then I get a visit from the cops, telling me that a drunk driver ran a red light and broadsided my wife's car when she was driving our girls back from ballet class." He snapped his fingers. "All three gone—just like that."

Sam's face went ashen, stunned by McCracken's revelation.

"It was dark for a long time. The grief was too much. I tried drinking. That didn't work. Went back to my job. Nope. So I quit life and wandered for a few years."

Sam's eyes were all the way open now as he stared at McCracken, who had a faraway look as he watched the kids on the ball field. "Probably like you, they still invade my dreams from time to time, but I had to get back in the game, had to live my life." He walked over to a metal box next to the dugout, lifted the lid, and pulled out two gloves and a ball. He flipped a glove to Sam and put the other on his left hand. "How about a catch?"

Without another thought, Sam slipped the glove on. It felt familiar, like an old friend he hadn't seen in years. Soft, worn leather, easy and smooth as his fingers stretched deep into the seasoned cowhide. He stepped back and looked up at Whiplash, who was smiling as he tossed the ball from no further than twenty feet. Sam caught it and looked down at the stitching. Eighty-eight inches of beautiful waxed red thread. Sewn by hand. He knew all 108 double stitches by touch, and as he placed his fingers along the seams, a tremor of excitement went up his arm. Two-seam fastball. His pitch. His dependable ally. He stepped back ten paces and threw the baseball. McCracken had to jerk his glove down to keep it from hitting his knee.

"Dang, Sammy, you got some movement." He tossed the ball back and then moved another ten paces away, to about sixty feet. "Lemme see what ya got, kid?" McCracken crouched down and pounded his fist into his glove.

Sam bent at the waist and stared in as if getting the sign from Whiplash. He came set, inhaled a deep breath, exhaled slowly, rocked back, raised his left leg, separated his hands, brought his arm up into an L-position, and let it fly. McCracken didn't even move his glove as the ball popped solidly into the back of the mitt.

Shouts of amazement erupted from the kids on the field, who had stopped to watch.

Sam whirled around and grinned at the children, then raised his glove for McCracken to return the baseball. He did.

"Be easy on me, Sammy. I need this hand."

Sam chuckled as he threw another perfect strike. It was only about seventy miles an hour, but to the children it was a near superhuman feat. McCracken waved the children over and had one of the boys stand in like he was a batter. Whiplash dropped one finger to signal fastball, and Sam brought it home. The boy jerked back in fear, sure that the ball was going to hit him.

The children giggled, and from the corner of one eye, Sam caught a faint glimpse of fascinated envy from the older boys, all watching him intently, mouths slightly open. He winked at the oldest boy and motioned for him to stand in. The kid grabbed a bat and hurried over. He had a look of determination on his face that said no matter how fast that ball came in, he would not back away. Sam motioned to McCracken that he was going to throw a curve and then let go a bender that buckled the boy's knees. But the kid did not back away.

"Ooooo!" the children squealed and clapped, amazed by what this man, who looked like one of them, could do with a baseball. Sam let each child stand in the imaginary batter's box and have a look. As he continued to throw, it was if he was releasing more than just the baseball from his hand. There was a freedom in playing catch again, a return to his youth, a surrender of all his worries and fears, tossing them out into the endless sky, imagining them floating off with the clouds into the faraway Hindu Kush.

He waved Nahal over, the little girl he had saved, and showed her how to grip the baseball across the seams; how to throw a pitch that would cut through the wind, and, if thrown properly, would arrive precisely at its desired destination. He showed her brother how to stay low and follow a ground ball all the way into his glove, then crow hop, line up to his target, and throw to his first baseman. He taught the children how to run the bases, cut the bag, and how to slide into second.

Two hours later it was time for dinner, and McCracken had to practically pull the kids off the field and into the dining hall.

As Sam gathered up the bats, balls, and gloves and tossed them into the metal locker, he let go a sigh and wiped the sweat from his brow. He was tired, a good tired, one of sweat and dirt and blisters, but also one of joy. The simple joy of seeing children smile, many of whom, most likely, had not smiled in a very long time.

"Isn't baseball the greatest game?" McCracken yelled out as he hurried over. "It's like life. It's hard. It ain't fair. You hit a line drive and somebody catches it."

"You throw the perfect pitch"—Sam grinned at a memory from his high school days—"and some .220 hitter nubs it off the end of the bat and wins the game."

"Hell, you fail most of the time, but does that mean you should quit?"

"Never!"

"I think Babe Ruth was right." McCracken mimicked the powerful swing of the great Hall of Fame slugger. "Never let the fear of striking out keep you from playing the game."

Sam grabbed the last baseball, stared down at it for a long moment, and then tossed it to McCracken, who caught it so gently it seemed as if it were a porcelain egg.

"I think God plays baseball." Whiplash winked. "He wrote about it in Genesis: in the Big Inning, He made the Heavens and the Earth."

Sam laughed out loud. "That sounds like something my sister would have said."

McCracken cracked a brow in interest. "You two were pretty close, huh?"

"Jenny was my best friend."

"You told me she wrote you a book."

"Jenny's Journal of Inspiration," he said proudly.

"What did she offer you today?"

He inhaled a deep breath and looked up at the mountains to the northeast, a magical ruggedness of tan, green, and gray, peaceful and inviting, but also a darkness hidden in its caves and villages with men consumed by fear and vengeance.

"God's will for me is perfect happiness," he finally said.

McCracken put his arm around Sam's shoulder and walked him to the gate that would lead him home. "Share that message with everyone you meet today, Samuel Cloud-Carson. You're here for a reason, brother, and I think it might be to share your happiness."

CHAPTER FORTY-THREE

Afghanistan

November 2010

Sam stretched up from his sleeping bag and pushed aside the pine branch to watch the sun rise over the Nuristan Mountains. He had always loved mornings. The soft orange glow shimmering above Pargin Mountain. The birth of a new day, from cold to warm, from darkness to light, the journey of the sun, a new beginning. The forest had been his home for much of the last seven months as he tracked the mountains northeast of Bagram for the Provincial Reconstruction Team. While many of his DiamondBar teammates complained of the isolation and boredom of being away from civilization, Sam cherished it. He felt he needed the solitude, the fresh air, and the ruggedness of the countryside to heal his soul.

The overnight temperature had dropped to near freezing, but Jenny's morning meditation had warmed him. It was the first part of an old Ute prayer:

May the Earth teach you stillness as the grasses are stilled with light. May the Earth teach you suffering as old stones suffer with memory. May the Earth teach you humility as blossoms are humble with beginning.

That thought was on his mind as he began his reconnaissance mission in a region so remote that he hadn't seen a human being in more than a week. *May the Earth teach you stillness as the grasses are stilled with light.*

Why was the PRT building this road to nowhere? A twelve-mile stretch had already been completed, and now, they were beginning to assemble a bridge across a pass to . . . more nothing. It made no sense. Yet every time he had questioned his DiamondBar Security manager about where this road was going, he had received a sharp retort of *just do your fucking job*. He knew there was more. Perhaps, it was time to find out.

* * *

Washington, DC November 2010

"How's our boy doing on our mountain?" King asked from the office of DiamondBar's Washington, DC, headquarters.

"Not one single problem since we put him on point." Dixon winked. "Carson's making sure the PRT doesn't get ambushed as they build our boulevard to big money."

"This is exactly what you predicted eight years ago, Drake. Low-cost, high-return trackers finding trouble before it could burn us. And now the recent election gave us greater power."

Dixon didn't speak for a bit as he thought about what his lawyer said. November had indeed helped his company. It was a perfect storm: a down economy, public anger over the Wall Street bailout and the Affordable Care Act, and the rise of the ultraconservative Tea Party movement all had resulted in Dixon's team winning both the House and Senate. Adding to the victory was the Supreme Court's passing of Citizens United, a law that gave corporations like DiamondBar unlimited ability to influence elections. There would be no more liberals double- and triple-checking his company's every decision in Afghanistan.

"We take that mountain," Dixon said in a proud tone, "bring in our heavy equipment to pull out the emeralds, rubies, lithium, coal, iron and uranium, and we're in fat city." He pulled a map out of his briefcase, spread it across his desk, and pointed to a red line along a rugged stretch of the Nuristan Mountains. "The PRT has completed twelve miles of road and needs just four more for us to get to the promised land."

"And we don't pay for a thing." King gave a smile like a Cheshire cat who had just been tossed another bit of tuna. "Courtesy of the US government."

"I told you, when we switched from this being a military operation to counterinsurgency, DiamondBar would win. The locals love having us build their bridges, roads, and hospitals."

"What about Abdul Hazrat? He sent one of his top aides to meet with the Minister of Interior, demanding we stop construction of our road. He has to know what we're up to."

"Screw Hazrat!" Dixon snapped. "He's a relic who refuses to come out of the Stone Age. He's ordered his people not to take any bribes. Said if they took American money, they'd become puppets of the infidels." Dixon paused to look down at the map, to his mountain of riches. "But now that I have Zubair in my back pocket, there's nothing Hazrat can do."

"Except fight us."

"And that's exactly what I'm hoping he'll do." Dixon smiled. "He may not have caused any trouble while his aide was negotiating with the government, but now that he's lost that battle, he'll turn his vengeance on us. And under the rules of engagement in a time of war, we'll be absolved of any wrongdoing when we have him killed."

They exchanged a glance and grinned broadly at each other.

"I told Zubair to put a bounty on Hazrat's head," Dixon said smugly. "He's told warlords and Taliban leaders as far away as Pakistan that whoever takes out Hazrat gets a one-hundred-thousand-dollar bounty."

"Does he have the power to do that?"

"He doesn't have a choice. Zubair knows that America's his cash cow. If he screws with us, the cash cow dies."

CHAPTER FORTY-FOUR

Nuristan Province, Afghanistan

January 2011

Sam jerked up from his sleeping bag, awakened by the sound of an explosion off in the distance. Instincts on high, he listened for where the low rumble of rock and dirt sliding down the side of a hill was coming from. It had to be at least two miles away and to the southwest. Certainly no danger to his DiamondBar squad, who was camped several miles up the road, protecting the PRT bridge crew. He quickly packed his gear, threw his bag over his shoulder, and headed out, cutting through a forest of white pine to the edge of a rocky ridge that overlooked the valley.

"Oh, geez," he whispered as he scanned the damage. "That's not good."

At least fifty meters of the road the PRT had built only months before was gone, likely blown away by a remote bomb that had been placed there the night before.

He scrambled down the side of the mountain, waded through the icy stream, and climbed up the far side to investigate. It didn't take long to find the source. Bits of metal and battery fragments strewn about proved it was a rudimentary but lethal IED, likely triggered from a distance of no more than a hundred meters.

He searched the perimeter of the blast, looking for signs of track or tell that might give him an indication of where the bomb had been triggered.

He crisscrossed farther up the hill and found it. A slight depression in the grass and an overturned stone. As he knelt down to study a clear footprint on dirt, he heard, in the distance, the gravelly sound of diesel engines coming his way.

A minute later, a DiamondBar truck came around the bend and slammed on its brakes, coming to a stop just inches from the edge of the bomb crater. Frank Weber jumped down from the cab and slammed the door.

"We give you one damn job!" he screamed up at Sam. "Make sure nobody messes with this road, and you let some fucking towel-head blow it up!"

Sam headed back down the hill but didn't respond. He actually had been surprised at how little resistance they'd come across in his time scouting for the PRT. It was his job to find potential threats and report them to DiamondBar, who would relay the intel to the Afghan military, who would look into the problem. In recent months, all had been innocent: goat herders, hunters, or locals out searching for stray livestock. Only one arrest had been made, and that was a teenage boy who had found a rusted old Russian military rifle in the woods and was carrying it back home. The rifle had been confiscated, but the boy was released.

"Do you know how long it's gonna take the PRT to rebuild this?" Weber continued to rant. "With winter here, it could take two or three months!"

Sam knew that defending himself to a man like Weber would be like tossing kerosene onto a smoldering fire. Instead, he pointed back up the hill. "I think I found the track of the guy who set off the bomb."

"What good is that gonna do us now, you worthless—"

"That's enough, Frank." Scott Thornton came up behind Weber. "The kid has about forty square miles on each side of the road to patrol."

"I don't give a shit. He's fucking up my bonus. Dixon promised five grand extra if we finished by the end of the summer."

This was the first that Sam had heard of a bonus. Those details usually didn't get lost on employees. Maybe he wasn't included.

"Why is Dixon so interested in this road?" he asked innocently. "We're supposed to be building it *for* Afghanistan's benefit, not ours."

Weber looked as if he had revealed too much. He glanced at Thornton, then back at Sam. "I don't know. That's above my pay grade. Dixon made a deal with the Afghan government, and this is where they want the road."

"But it's not connecting anyone to anywhere." Sam motioned up the road. "And there's no way we're going over that mountain."

Weber cleared his throat, recovering himself a bit. "I don't ask those questions, kid. I just do what I'm told and move on to the next job."

Sam flipped his backpack over his shoulder. "Then I'll move on with my job, and see where their track leads me."

* * *

It was an easy trail to follow. The people who had detonated the bomb had gone back up the hill and hidden behind a large fallen pine. He found the spot where a man had knelt on one knee, and the scuff marks on the mossy bark where he had likely placed the remote box to trigger the bomb. There had been two others with the perpetrator, for all three wore a different style shoe—one a moccasin, the others, athletic footwear—and their track was easy to follow with a light winter frost marking their trail.

It had been two hours since the explosion. Sam tracked swiftly, knowing where they were headed. Humans were much like animals, seeking the easiest passage, unless of course, they sensed danger in their path. These men did not.

The trees were thick, but the brush between had been broken and matted down. Likely a deer or mountain goat had carved this path the Afghans were following. Two miles later he reached the tree line close to a man-made trail heading northeast. If he followed it, he would likely be seen, captured, and questioned, and even though he looked and talked like one of them, he doubted the ending would go well.

Slipping back into the cover of the woods, he moved on, like a snow leopard who knew where his prey was headed. Another two miles brought him to a pass that looked down into a beautiful valley. He stretched his view beyond the now thread-like trail and saw three specks far off in the distance. They had to be the three men who had destroyed the road.

He took a chance and followed, down the path some two hundred meters. He scaled a hill to a cliff that overlooked the valley. He brought his monocular up to his right eye and smiled. A small village was hidden in the shadows of the mountain. No more than twenty-five to thirty stone huts. There was a mosque in the middle of the town square with one spire that needed repair.

This was not a terrorist outpost, and those men were probably not even Taliban. They were more than likely simple Afghan farmers, angry that the PRT was carving a road through their land without permission. How many of these little hamlets existed in the Hindu Kush, villages defending what was theirs while the jaws of both domestic and foreign governments slowly crushed their neighborhoods?

He knew it was his job to find the culprits and call the coordinates in to DiamondBar and the Afghan Intelligence team so they could come in and question the perpetrators. But as he eyed the men returning to their village and saw their children run out to greet them, he hesitated before turning on his sat-phone.

He knew what would happen. The Afghan military would search the town, confiscate every weapon, maybe come across a few explosives, and arrest some child's father.

He looked down at his phone, his index finger hovering over the power button, and then shook his head and put his phone back in his backpack. His decision to come back with no intel would get him in trouble, but could both sides possibly be wrong in this fight? Were both Afghan and foreign power brokers benefiting at the expense of the weak and the defenseless? The vicious cycle of attack and defend seemed to have no end when it came to man's ego.

It was time to head back, to reconnect with his DiamondBar team, and face the wrath of Frank Weber when he told him that he'd lost the track of the men who had blown up their road to nowhere.

* * *

"You know who detonated the IED and didn't turn them in?" Colonel Tomlinson's voice was sharp with irritation as he handed an ice bag to Sam.

"I said I *thought* it was them." Sam placed the ice bag on the back of his head. The wound was courtesy of Frank Weber, who was so angry at having to wait seven hours for his inferior to return with no intel that he had shoved Sam up against the side of the truck. Sam's head snapped back against the door frame, opening up an old wound. It could have been worse had his teammates not stopped Weber.

"I tracked them up the hill and across a trail, but I wasn't absolutely sure if they were the guys who detonated the bomb." He paused to adjust the ice bag. "If I'd told Weber, he would have sent in a hit team to get revenge on the whole village. That's why I came to tell you."

Tomlinson inhaled a deep breath through his nose. "You're putting me in a tough spot, Sam. My job is to take out insurgents, not to try and understand their inner feelings."

Sam stood up and closed the door to Tomlinson's office. "Be honest with me, sir. Why is the PRT building this road in the middle of nowhere?"

"I don't know."

"Don't you want to know?"

Tomlinson cocked his head to the side. "Are you going to make this personal, Sam?"

"Damn straight I'm going to make it personal. War is personal. It's personal anytime a country invades another. It's personal when we build a road on somebody else's property—"

Tomlinson raised a hand to stop him. "I get your point. And there are times I, too, have similar thoughts, but we're here to do our jobs."

"The hell with *we're here to do our jobs*!" Sam snapped and then sat down across from the colonel. "I've heard that excuse so many damn times it makes me want to puke. Families are being killed because we're here *to do our jobs*. What truly is *our job*, sir?"

"Finding bin Laden," Tomlinson said succinctly.

"Then go find him. Just don't kill thousands of innocent Afghans while seeking revenge on one asshole."

"Damn." Tomlinson gave an exasperated exhale. "Now I know why Weber hates you. You never know when to shut up."

"How many lives have we lost by not speaking up, sir?"

Tomlinson sat at his desk, studying the young man who asked questions that he couldn't answer. He shook his head sadly and said, "You're brilliant, Sam. You're the best tracker I've ever seen—even better than your dad—and whether you believe it or not, you've saved countless lives on both sides of this conflict in the short time you've been here. You know that too, or you wouldn't have protected those men yesterday."

Sam stared out the window to the mountains, a faraway look on his face.

"That reminds me." Tomlinson opened his desk drawer and pulled out three folded sheets of paper. "I came across these the other day. Letters from your family to your father."

Sam jerked back around but said nothing.

"Your dad was reading these the day he died." Tomlinson handed the letters to Sam. "He had been visiting me that morning when we got the call about trouble in the hills. He left them in my mailbox."

Sam swallowed hard as he opened the letters to his father from four years ago.

The colonel glanced down at the ground for a moment and then back up. "I'm not proud of this, Sam, but I read them. I felt I needed to know you better. I've been worried about you . . . thought you might hurt yourself."

"I'm over it."

"Yeah, well those letters say a lot about your family. You were raised by fine people. I'm very sorry for what you've lost."

"Thank you," Sam mumbled, a bit distracted as he read his mother's letter. His face tightened when he came to the part where she wrote about the two men who had changed his life:

When I offered Joseph Blue Hill to track, they said no, that they only wanted Sam.

Our son never complains, but I know he's not a fan of Mr. Cutthredge and Mr. Marcus.

"There's something I need to ask," Tomlinson said. "I know your dad took the job with DiamondBar for the insurance, but why did you? It's no mystery you don't like Dixon, so you probably didn't like the men he sent to recruit you."

Sam raised his head and blinked, taken aback. "What men?"

"The men your mom wrote about in her letter. The guys you took hunting . . . Billy Cutthredge and Rob Marcus. They were DiamondBar Security guys."

All the blood drained from Sam's face, and his mouth fell open in shock.

"Cutthredge . . . and Marcus . . . for Dixon?" he said in a clipped, monotonous tone.

"They were two of his top men until they didn't follow your father's intel. They got trigger-happy after they were told that a warlord they'd been hunting might be in a certain village. Instead, their missile killed two Afghan families, and the Defense Department ordered Dixon to fire Cutthredge and Marcus. I always wondered what happened to them until I read your mom's letter."

Sam's hand instinctively went to his mouth. This was unbelievable. Dixon had set him up. From the very beginning. Stalking him the way he would hunt a wild animal. Hire an outfitter who would do all the work: pack for him, set up camp, cook for him, track for him, find his prey, and then watch as Dixon raised his high-powered rifle and killed to decorate his wall.

Sam was no different. He was another trophy to Dixon. Just like one of the deer or lion or bear heads that hung over the fireplaces at one of his hunting lodges.

The room was silent, save for Sam's heavy, ragged breathing. With his head bent over, his long hair hid the fury on his face as he continued to stare at the letter.

Tomlinson stepped forward and put a hand on his shoulder. "Are you all right, Sam?"

The room seemed claustrophobic. As if the walls of Drake Dixon were again closing in on him. He had to get out. He had to leave before he said or did something he would later regret.

"I have to go, sir," he said in a strained voice. "I–I need to do some thinking."

*   *   *

He would be in trouble for heading to the hills without DiamondBar permission, but he didn't care anymore. Even the bitter cold January winds that rushed down the sides of the mountains did little to cool what was burning inside him. Drake Dixon had ruined his life. If it hadn't been for that narcissistic hustler, his mom and dad would still be alive, and he, Sam Cloud-Carson, might be chasing his dream, pitching in pro ball, on his way to the Big Leagues. Yet he had made that one impulsive decision to seek revenge on his mother's killers. Why hadn't he simply led the police to Cutthredge and Marcus? And now, to find out that he had been set up.

"Damn you, Dixon!" he screamed, his voice echoing off the sandhill bluffs overlooking the town of Mahmud-i-Raqi. He kicked a rock off his path and sat down on the edge of a cliff, staring out at the Darya-ye-Pamaher River as it slowly meandered south.

A myriad of questions flooded his mind. *Why was Dixon there that day? Why would he want to cover up me killing two DiamondBar employees he had specifically sent to recruit me? Had they done something wrong, or was there some kind of leverage that Cutthredge and Marcus had been holding over Dixon?*

The thoughts infuriated him, and he punched his backpack, sending the contents inside spilling out across the rocky bluff. Startled, he reached for them, but he only saved Jenny's journal, as the rest of the papers flew away, fluttering slowly down to the canyon below. He pulled his sister's journal close. Thank God it had been saved. It was all he had left of Jenny, his last link to his family, to connection, to peace.

He stared at the cover for a long time, its edges weathered from years of use, and opened up to the page he had read that morning. It was another line from a Ute prayer:

Earth, teach me courage as the tree which stands alone.

"Dammit, Jenny, what are you trying to tell me? Am I the tree? Am I the one standing alone?"

He turned a page. It was a prayer familiar to him, from Lakota Sioux Chief Yellow Lark in 1887:

Oh, Great Spirit, whose voice I hear in the winds, and whose breath gives life to all the world, hear me. I am small and weak. I need your strength and wisdom.

Why was he here? It couldn't be to do the bidding of Drake Dixon. Not anymore. The man had used him.

Let me walk in beauty and make my eyes ever behold the red and purple sunset. Make my hands respect the things you have made and my ears sharp to hear your voice.

Whiplash McCracken had told him he was here for a reason—to help people. Was he listening? Was he truly opening his heart to what the Great Spirit was trying to teach him?

Make me wise so that I may understand the things you have taught my people. Let me learn the lessons you have hidden in every leaf and rock.

I am a tracker, he thought. *A seeker. These are the gifts the Great Spirit gave to me. How will I use them? Will I use these gifts to bring me greater power? To seek revenge on those who have hurt me? Or will I use my gifts to help others?*

The prayer continued: *I seek strength, not to be greater than my brother, but to fight my greatest enemy—myself. Make me always ready to come to you with clean hands and straight eyes. So when life fades, as the fading sunset, my spirit may come to you without shame.*

Sam gazed out at the Hindu Kush, his face softening from his earlier tension. The sun was behind him, casting his long shadow across the rocks toward the mountains, as if drawing him home, to his one self, united with his Creator. It was then that he remembered his grandfather's words the day he had said goodbye at the Durango-La Plata Airport.

You don't belong to this Dixon. He is just another lost soul trying to steal yours, thinking it will give him greater power. Don't give it to him. One day you will understand why it was important that you didn't give him your power . . . and that you didn't give up. Stay strong. Be Courageous. Blessings are coming. Believe that. For you are Ute. You are Walks with the Wind.

With those words, Sam raised his vision. His grandfather had been right. He wouldn't give up. Drake Dixon may have hurt him deeply, but from this moment forward, he would refuse to give him power over his mind, his attitude, or his happiness.

Perhaps everything that had happened to him in his life, both good and bad, were lessons he had to learn: his father, his mother, his sister, his grandfather, his friends, coaches, and teammates, even Dixon, Cutthredge, and Marcus. As painful as those experiences had been, they, too, had been his teachers. Maybe he needed his past in order to change, to be broken down so that something greater could break through. But first, he had to believe. He had to trust in a power greater than him.

Earth, teach me courage as the tree which stands alone. Stay strong. Be Courageous. Blessings are coming.

CHAPTER FORTY-FIVE

Kunar and Nuristan Provinces,

Afghanistan July 2011

The alarm on Sam's watch vibrated, signaling the end of his meditation. He opened his eyes and looked down at the journal in his lap. *You are still the same person,* Jenny had written, *but you will now handle your situations more peacefully.*

To his great surprise, the last few months had been pleasant. He thought about Dixon from time to time, tossing from guilt and uncertainty to mild irritation, but he no longer thought about revenge. There was a part of him that wondered how he'd react if he saw Dixon again. What would he say? What would he do? But there was another part of him, newly discovered, that believed, if he held onto that grievance, he would shut himself off from knowing God and knowing himself.

He still saw signs of human aggression and suffering almost every day from the abandoned farms and villages he observed while scouting for the Provincial Reconstruction Team's project to the violence he read about when he returned to Bagram. On May 2, Osama bin Laden was killed, three weeks later a suicide bomber detonated a bomb at the Kabul Military Hospital that claimed six innocent lives, and one week after that a coalition airstrike killed a dozen children and two women in southern Afghanistan.

Yet, despite the fear and misery that gripped the country, he was handling those situations differently now. And he believed it was because of his new practice. Meditation. His daily devotions were disciplining his mind, guiding it to a gentler place from judgment to acceptance, from defense to defenselessness, from a place of condemnation to a place of freedom, the freedom to choose a better way.

Now, whether he was searching for IEDs, scouting for the PRT, or home in the DiamondBar barracks, he made time to get quiet, immersing himself in one of Jenny's inspirations, thinking about each one for a minute or two every few hours. Some were deeply personal, just for him:

Can you make peace with those who have hurt you? Without forgiveness, you will still be blind. What looks like an obstacle may be an opportunity. My kidney disease helped me to grow spiritually. Always remember that the world is not here to make you happy. You are here to help create a happier world. When I see you smile, I am happy. What makes you smile, brother?

He thought about what made him happy. When he first started at DiamondBar, he was filled with fear and loss, and he took that anxiety out on himself. Twice in the first six months after his mother's death, he'd almost taken his life. He remembered the last two years in colors. The suffocating blackness of grief, the oppressive gray of Afghanistan's suffering, and then the brighter colors when he was in the mountains, reuniting with nature, with Spirit, and with others.

Was that it? Was that part of his healing? Was saving the Taliban guards from the smart bomb, rescuing Nahal from being raped, and even teaching children how to play baseball all part of *his* healing?

What makes you smile, brother?

A walk in the woods did . . . the smell of pine boughs . . . the silence of a snowfall . . . sunset on a mountaintop . . . a two-seam fastball perfectly located on the outside corner.

Ah, baseball. He loved the game. Even made it his mantra while meditating. He would find a comfortable spot in some cave or under a tree, close his eyes, and sink into the pure consciousness of baseball. He would visualize the diamond, the bases, and the mound, executing each pitch with his breathing, throwing the perfect sinker, then curve, then slider, then change. His mind became one magical theater in union with the master magician himself. Breathing in, he imagined balance. Breathing out, he delivered the perfect pitch. Breathing in, peace. Breathing out, a smile. Then he was gone, dissolving into the beauty of nothingness.

* * *

He returned as often as he could to the Friends of Everyone Hotel, slipping like a shadow through the front gate to surprise the children. The contrast of energy was immediate, from the tension outside the walls to the unabashed joy of the sports playground. Sometimes they played baseball, but other times it was soccer, cricket, or volleyball, and everyone, both boys and girls, was required to play.

It dawned on Sam that he had become somewhat of a mythical figure to the children. Who was this man who came once every two weeks with gifts of chocolates or fruit or colorful beads and headscarves to play with the children? He would spend the day pitching batting practice, or playing goalie, or putting a bandage on a skinned knee, and then he'd be gone before dinner, leaving as silently as he had arrived.

Whiplash had revealed nothing to the children of his backstory, not even his name. He added to his legend by calling him by his initials, SC, saying he was the spirit of the hills, protector of all creatures, the one who lived in caves and trees.

"Look, children!" McCracken would cry out. "Look who's come down from the mountain to play with you!"

The children would come running with shouts of "EsssCeee! EsssCeee!" He would open his backpack of gifts, and then challenge them to a game of baseball.

The memory made him smile.

* * *

Sam hiked down the mountain, following an old musk-deer trail, and paused to inhale the gentle fragrances of the Nuristan wild. It was a beautiful summer afternoon, a time when the sun was melting the last of the mountain snow, when the yellow buttercups, white edelweiss, wild blue geraniums, and purple delphiniums glistened across the hillsides. From both sides of the valley, narrow streams slipped down from the melting snow, growing faster and wider each mile as they carved their way to the Kunar River.

It was hard to believe there was any trouble in these mountains, so alive was their beauty, the bright colors, the call of birds and buzz of bees, all evidence of nature's innocence. But Sam knew trouble was there. He felt its presence and had been warned by Charlie Whitson that, one week ago, more than seven hundred Taliban had crossed over from Pakistan and invaded the town of Barg-e-Matal. It was not likely that the insurgents would travel this far southwest, but one never knew in the wild Nuristan Province.

His side of the valley seemed clear, so he doubled back on his trail and followed a stream that would lead him to the bridge the PRT was now finishing four kilometers away. As he made his way through the valley basin, a flash of light to his left made him pause. He turned and saw the flash again, high atop the backbone of the mountain. It looked like metal reflected off the sun. He slipped his monocular out of his jacket and scanned the ridge.

"Damn," he whispered. "They're heading straight for the bridge."

He counted their numbers: at least twenty-five insurgents with rifles and two RPG anti-tank grenade launchers. He pulled out his sat-phone and dialed Frank Weber.

"PRT Seven Two, this is Eagle One. There's trouble headed your way about two klicks northeast of your bridge."

"Roger that. What ya got?"

"About twenty-five to thirty insurgents—all armed—and at least two RPGs. You need to leave immediately."

"And let them blow our bridge, Eagle One? No fucking way."

Sam brought the monocular back to his eye. He spotted ten more insurgents coming through the forest on the same parallel line as his DiamondBar team.

"PRT Seven Two, this is Eagle One. Ten more guys circling around, still two klicks away. Get outta there now."

"No can do, Eagle One. We got plenty of firepower to defend our bridge."

"PRT Seven Two, the bridge is a sitting duck. The enemy will be both above you and on the ridge directly across. Please get out of there."

"We got it covered, Eagle One. Why don't you call Emaw Eight Nine to give us some air support?" Then Weber clicked off.

"Dammit!" Sam hissed to himself. "They can't get here that fast. Weber's damn ego is gonna get somebody killed."

* * *

"Emaw Eight Nine, Emaw Eight Nine," Sam said when he finally connected with Bagram. "This is Eagle One—needing help."

"Roger that, Eagle One. What's goin' on?"

"PRT Seven Two is about to be attacked by insurgents coming in from the northeast. I suggested they pull back to Parun, but they chose to stay and defend the bridge."

"Roger that, Eagle One. Let me get the Captain."

There was a pause for about thirty seconds until the voice of Air Force Captain Doug Freeman came on the line.

"Eagle One, this is Emaw Eight Nine. We have the coordinates of PRT Seven Two and will send two Black Hawks for support."

"Thank you, sir. How soon can you get here?"

"Just scrambling a team now. Should be about ten before they're in the air. I'm thinking one-six-four-oh, best case."

Sam looked down at the clock on the sat-phone. That was almost forty-five minutes away. This entire conflict could be over by then.

"Thanks, Emaw Eight Nine. I'll keep you posted."

* * *

He watched the insurgents move for a short time. They were doing exactly what he had predicted. One group stayed above the PRT base near the bridge, and the other squad was about a half klick away in a rock crag directly across from the bridge. These guys didn't just happen onto this rural location. This was a well-coordinated plan to take the bridge. Why the hell were we building a road here anyway? It was more than stupid. Parun was the closest town and this road didn't even connect to it.

The thought had barely entered his mind when all hell broke loose. Taliban machine guns let loose a barrage from the ridge above, followed by the sizzling sound of a grenade being launched from the rock crag. Sam curled behind a tree and covered his ears. A split second later came the deafening sound of a grenade hitting the gas tank of a road grader, lighting the air in a brilliant flash of yellow and blue.

There was little Sam could do but watch. Watch as the battle raged on. He moved closer, up the hill and behind a cedar, straining to hear voices through the gunfire. Shouts in Pashto, others in English, small snatches of fear and anger. He heard Frank Weber's thunderous voice through the melee.

"Light up that RPG, Scotty! Good shot! Yeah, yeah, yeah, let 'em have it!"

Kalashnikovs and M4 carbines shattered the air, blaring, spitting up dust and rock shards all the way down to where Sam lay hidden.

Get out of there, guys, he thought. *You still have time to protect your flank and bust it to Parun. C'mon—go—aw shit.*

Another RPG headed his teammates' way, and again the horrific sound of metal on metal exploded, destroying another road grader.

He looked up at the trouble. His DiamondBar teammates were holding their own—better weapons, plenty of ammo, good cover—but how long could they hold out? A burst rang out from above, bullets slamming into trees and rocks. A DiamondBar man fell. It looked like Emmitt Berger, but he wasn't sure.

"Fall back! Fall back!" he heard Weber scream through the sound of gunfire. Two Taliban charged down the hill, but Scott Thornton took them out with a quick blast from his carbine. Five more took up spots on lower overhangs, peppering the camp with machine-gun fire as an enemy squad curled around to their flank and let loose a volley.

They were now boxed in on three sides. Weber, Thornton, and the rest of the PRT hunkered down behind two Humvee transports, their last chance at escape. Just as Weber opened the door and climbed in, a third RPG hit the middle of an already-destroyed road grader, flipping the frame and drawbar onto the back of Weber's Humvee. The Afghans who worked for the PRT threw up their arms in surrender, and without an option, so did the DiamondBar crew.

Sam slipped back into the cover of the forest and called Bagram.

"Emaw Eight Nine, Emaw Eight Nine, this is Eagle One."

"Roger that, Eagle One. What's your status?"

"PRT Seven Two has surrendered, sir. Not sure how many casualties. How soon can you get here?"

"We're still fifteen away, but we'll have to hold fire if the bad guys have taken prisoners."

Sam inhaled a deep breath. "Yes, sir. I'll head back and get you more intel."

"Be careful, Eagle One. They'll have scouts checking the perimeter to see if any of your crew escaped into the woods."

"Roger that." Sam headed back to the danger.

* * *

He heard voices and slid between two small spruce trees, no bigger than fifteen feet, and crawled on all fours to just below the ridge where his teammates were being held.

"Traitors!" a voice screamed out in Pashto. "You disgrace your country by working with infidels!" The accent was indeed different from those of the Nuristan Province, likely part of the Taliban who had crossed over from Pakistan to invade Barg-e-Matal. But why had they come to this rural part of the province? There was nothing here—nothing between Parun and Kamdesh—except for this bridge. What was here that drew so much interest?

There was a *pop* from above and Sam froze.

"He didn't do anything!" It was Weber's voice, obviously calling out the Taliban leader for shooting someone, likely an Afghan PRT worker.

"Silence! Or I shoot you!" the Taliban leader said in broken English, and then paused as if listening.

Sam had already heard it a full minute before, the low rumble of helicopter blades reverberating in the distance. The Army Black Hawks were here.

"Hakim!" the Taliban leader yelled out. "Take the Afghans with you. Mahmoud! Bring the Americans and come with me. Asad, you and Firash blow the bridge."

Sam crawled back underneath the spruce just a split second before the sounds of men scurrying for the cover of the forest swept past him. He waited thirty seconds before calling the Black Hawk commander.

"Emaw Eight Nine, this is Eagle One," he whispered. "Stay in the air. Insurgents are gonna blow the bridge. Don't want you guys getting caught in it."

"Roger that, Eagle One," the pilot answered, and then Sam heard the Black Hawks peel off to the west. He tossed the phone in his backpack and hunkered down behind a spruce tree, waiting for the inevitable. Ten seconds later, the explosives blew, sending shards of sand, rock, and concrete raining down on his cover, followed by the low rumble of the bridge collapsing down into the valley below.

He waited a full minute, then pulled his backpack out from underneath small shards of concrete and scrambled through the spruce boughs and up the hill to check on the damage. The Afghan PRT man who had been executed was lying on the ground, bullet hole to his forehead, blood still oozing out of the back of his head, onto the dirt road. Sam counted three more dead, including his DiamondBar coworker Emmitt Berger.

*   *   *

"PRT Seven Two was captured and split into two groups," Sam explained to the Army Black Hawk lieutenant when they landed ten minutes later. "The Afghans who work on the construction team were taken by one group of insurgents back up the ridge, and I'm guessing they're heading toward Kamdesh. There's only one trail at the top, so if you get after them now, you might be able to block any retreat with one squad on the ground while your Black Hawks can circle around about six klicks north and cut them off at a pass that leads back down to the river." He paused to study his surroundings. "The other group was led by the Taliban leader. He has my DiamondBar guys."

The lieutenant grimaced. "They want Americans for ransom."

Sam nodded. "I better get going, sir. I need to get on their trail."

"Take two of my men with you."

"No offense, sir, but they'll just slow me down. Let me find them, radio back, and then you can send a team in."

The lieutenant crossed his arms over his chest and stared at the young man who looked like one of the many farmers he'd seen throughout the rugged Nuristan Province. "Colonel Tomlinson said to follow your lead, Mr. Carson. He said you can track deer in a flash flood."

Sam snorted at the comment. "Colonel doesn't know deer very well. They're not like humans. They won't chase danger in a thunderstorm." He threw his backpack over his shoulder, his dark hawk's eyes already searching for any sign that would tell him which way to go. He found it. A yellow buttercup that had been crushed by someone's boot. He nodded to the lieutenant and headed into the forest.

CHAPTER FORTY-SIX

Washington, DC

Dixon slammed the phone down and glared at his lawyer. "Somebody blew my fucking bridge!"

King's mouth fell open, and he dropped his head into his hands.

"We were only a few months from completing the road," Dixon continued to rant. "Ready to dig. Ready to carve cash off that damn mountain."

King raised up slowly. "Did we lose anybody?"

"Four dead. Three Afghans who work on the PRT and Emmitt Berger."

King put his hand on his chest as he struggled to get his lungs working. "Do you want me to call his wife?"

"I'll do it." Dixon poured himself a glass of scotch. "It sounds better when it comes from the top." He paused to take a sip. "We have another problem too. Weber, Thornton, and a PRT worker were kidnapped by the insurgents who blew the bridge."

"What the fuck! Shit, Drake, this is bad. Real bad. You've pushed this mountain deal too far. Our government oversight committee could look into what we're doing."

"No, they won't. Zubair's taking care of it. He's going to blame it all on Hazrat. Hazrat's goons were the ones who took out part of the road months ago, so Zubair's going to accuse him of blowing up the bridge. Maybe this is just what we needed all along to fire up the Afghan Army and finally take out that bastard."

King stared at his boss for a long moment. He could barely believe what he was hearing. "What are we going to do about our guys who were captured?"

A smile spread across Dixon's face. "Our boy, Carson, is already on their trail. As soon as he finds them, he'll call in a rescue team and make us look like heroes." He motioned for King to follow him to the door. "Have Marsha get my plane ready. I want to be at Bagram to show my support when they recover my men . . . and I also want to let the Afghans know how much I love them."

*   *   *

It took Sam only five minutes to latch onto the track. There were seven of them. Four Taliban and three prisoners: Weber, Thornton, and a track he wasn't familiar with. Likely an American PRT worker because the Taliban would try and use these men as leverage. The Afghan workers would bring them nothing, but Americans could draw either money or media exposure on the international stage.

With three captives tied up, their wrists likely bound behind them, the group was easy to follow, and by nightfall, he'd gained a good hour and was close to his prey. Now was the time to be careful. He crouched down and studied their track. Each print told him a story, revealing a mystery, dropping a hint of where the track had been and where it might be going. He could almost see the next track even before he came to it.

One of the captives was dragging his left foot and was not in good condition. His prints showed that he had staggered a bit and had fallen near a stream, probably desperate for water. There had been a disturbance in the track near the stream, as if all three captives had fallen or been knocked down. There was blood on a rock, more on weeds farther on, and then they crossed the stream and went through more rough country along the side of a mountain.

Sam stopped suddenly and stared down. Right next to the track of the Taliban leader's boot was the track of a snow leopard—the Ghost of the Mountain. He was sure of it. The paw print was too big to be that of a simple lynx, and for a moment, he was so excited he forgot his mission. Ten meters farther, he found scratch markings on the ground, something big cats did with their hind feet before depositing urine or scat. This would be their time to hunt as well, dusk and dawn.

A twig snapped and Sam slipped behind a tree. Twenty seconds later, a man passed by, Kalashnikov ready, searching for any threat. The purpose of the man's stride told Sam he was likely checking the perimeter of the Taliban hideout.

It's a good thing I stopped to check that leopard track, or I would have been on open ground when the guard came by.

The insight made him think of his own Phantom of Pargin Mountain. Old Mel. The big buck he had helped move on some three years before. Had Old Mel's spirit come to warn him? The thought made him smile.

From the cover of a pine, he watched the guard for a full minute before following. He stayed low in the soft fern and deep-green summer grasses, never taking his eyes off his target. At nine thousand feet in the Hindu Kush, the nighttime temperature had dropped considerably, drawing the dust and moisture from the air, making it not only easier for Sam to see, but also to hear from a greater distance.

He stalked the sentry around a stand of wild hawthorn and froze. There was a soft glow in the distance, silhouetting three men warming themselves at a fire in front of a barn. Tied to a nearby tree were his DiamondBar teammates, all three with their heads hanging low in exhausted defeat.

Sam went to the ground and crawled on his belly as quietly as a snake through tall grass to better listen.

"We have all the leverage now," he heard the Taliban leader say. "The Americans will pay us for the hostages, or we will kill them. And the traitor inside the Afghan government will pay, or we shall continue to rain holy hell down on his road."

"But Abdul Hazrat controls the territory. We must eliminate him or we'll get nothing," another man said.

Abdul Hazrat? thought Sam. *He was the warrior Charlie Whitson had warned him about.*

"But now we have something Hazrat wants." The leader glanced at the barn. "As soon as we make the trade, our snipers will take him out. We'll collect the bounty and demand a cut of everything they take from the mountain."

Trade? Bounty? Mountain? Was there some bomb or weapons inside the barn that Hazrat had bargained for?

"Hazrat is a fool," a man said. "He could have it all if he would simply work with the government."

The leader snorted. "The Nuristani mountain people live in the past. They believe that only they can save the land. That if the forest and mountains disappear, they will disappear with them."

With that statement, the leader clapped his hands and nodded to where Sam's teammates were tied up. "It's time to question the infidels."

Sam remained low in the weeds and crawled closer.

The Taliban leader grabbed Weber's hair and jerked his head up. "I want the names of both the American and Afghan traitors who made the deal to build your road?"

"Water"—Weber coughed—"please, water."

"You will get water when you give us the names."

"I don't know."

"Wrong answer."

Weber screamed, but Sam resisted the urge to raise up from the tall mountain grass where he was hiding.

"Only the names will save your friend." The leader's voice was more demanding this time.

"I don't know the Afghan's name. Please don't—no!"

Sam heard a grunt and then coughing, as if someone was choking.

"Damn you," Weber said. "Why'd ya have to kill him?"

The night was silent, save for the liquid sound of a man gasping in vain for his last breath, suffocating on his own blood, desperate for life, until finally . . . silence.

Sam bit down hard on the side of his mouth and slithered through the mountain meadow, back into the woods, to where he had left his backpack. It was time to call the Army lieutenant to come rescue his team.

But he also wanted answers. He wanted to find out who this Hazrat was, and why was there a bounty on his head? What was in the barn, and what was in this mountain? But most of all, he wanted to find out who the American was who made some deal with the Afghan government? It had to be Drake Dixon. Who else could it be? It was time to find out and end this nightmare.

He reached into his pack for his sat-phone. "Aw, shit."

The phone was broken, obviously crushed hours earlier by debris from the bridge explosion. Now, there was no way to reach the lieutenant and get help.

For some reason he thought about Jenny. What would she do? He remembered watching her in quiet meditation while she was enduring yet another kidney-dialysis treatment. She didn't have the face of someone in pain or uncertainty. Her face was of someone totally at peace with who they were and confident about their place in the world. He remembered being drawn to that look—a look of strength and understanding, and an absence of fear.

Despite the brutality that was less than a half kilometer away, Sam leaned back against a fallen log, closed his eyes, and went inside. He was only gone for a minute, maybe less, but he knew the words that came to him were truly Jenny's.

All of us are on a hero's journey, brother. We just don't know it.
Some of us answer the call and some don't.
You know what to do. Now go do it.

*   *   *

It was almost midnight when Sam finished his recon of the Taliban hideout. One sentry guarded the barn while another circled the perimeter from a distance of about two hundred meters.

He waited silently in the forest, Gurkha kukri knife in his right hand, eyes glued to his prey, who was now just fifty meters away. There wasn't much of a breeze, and it was coming from the north, so there was no chance for the guard to pick up his scent.

Thirty meters away, Sam slowed his breathing, much as he did when he was on the mound: nice, calm, easy inhales through his nose; smooth, relaxing, cleansing exhales through his slightly open mouth. He had already planned his path and cleared off any dry leaves or twigs that might give him away.

Ten meters away, the sentry directed his Kalashnikov machine gun in Sam's direction, then swept it away. As soon as he passed, Sam made his move, his moccasins soundless on the forest floor. The sentry began to turn back, but Sam was too quick. His left hand gripped the back of the man's neck while his right placed the cold steel blade up against his throat. The guard jerked in surprise, the tip of the knife cutting him just above his Adam's apple.

Sam leaned in close and whispered in a cool yet commanding Pashto dialect, "Make one sound and I will kill you."

A shiver of fear shuddered up the man's spine as he very carefully offered up his weapon.

"Lay it on the ground."

The man did.

"Now, you lay facedown on the ground, and clasp your hands behind your back."

It took him only five minutes to remove the guard's jacket and Chitrali cap, tie him to a tree, and duct tape his mouth shut. He always kept a small roll of duct tape in his backpack. As an outfitter in Colorado, he had found it to be the savior of many potentially ruined hunting and fishing expeditions. Duct tape could repair a tent, a pole, a jacket, a raft, and in this case, keep a man quiet.

He put on the guard's jacket and cap, picked up his Kalashnikov, and then smiled down at his captive. "If I'm not killed, someone should be by to rescue you in a few hours."

Then he disappeared through the woods and tall grass, toward the soft glow of the Taliban campfire.

*   *   *

Sam stepped cautiously through the tall grass and stopped behind the hawthorn stand some fifty meters from the enemy campfire. Very slowly, he pushed aside a branch and scanned the area. A lone sentry stood with his back pressed against the wall of the barn, guarding whatever was inside. To the right were his teammates, still tied up to the tree. One was dead, body limp, a path of drying blood covering him from throat to feet. Frank Weber groaned and moved his head in a futile attempt to discourage the flies that buzzed around his wound.

Where were the other two men? Sam glanced at his watch. Midnight. They were probably in the barn sleeping, but how could he be sure? The two sentries had rotated every hour, one guarding the barn and the other checking the perimeter of the camp. It was time.

Sam looked up at the full moon. It was behind him. Good. The guard would only see the silhouette of a man as he approached. He clicked off the safety of his rifle and stepped onto the path, walking directly toward the campfire. Not five seconds later, the Taliban sentry spotted him.

"Usay!" he called out. "It's time to switch up."

Sam grunted an acknowledgment.

The guard laughed and turned toward the tree that held the American prisoners. "I've been busy chasing away birds who came to dine on our–" He said no more as the cold rifle barrel pressed against his neck.

"One move and you're dead," Sam growled in a hushed tone. "Now move to the barn."

The sentry took two steps before he collapsed on the ground, knocked cold by the butt of Sam's Kalashnikov.

*   *   *

"Carson?" Scott Thornton raised his tired head off his chest and strained to open one swollen eye. "Is that you?"

Sam looked back, raised an index finger to his lips, and moved on to the barn, rifle ready, his concentration centered only on the trouble that might be beyond the door. He remembered Jenny's words.

All of us are on a hero's journey, brother. We just don't know it.

Some of us answer the call and some don't.

You know what to do. Now go do it.

Inhaling a deep breath, he very slowly opened the door. The Taliban leader and his brother were sleeping in one corner. The rest of the barn looked empty. *This is it? No bombs or weapons? Just two men? What are they doing here? Is this a meeting place? Are more fighters on the way?*

He saw movement in the far corner, in a cage used for small livestock like goats or sheep. He squinted through the dim light and froze in horrified shock.

Dear God! There are children in that cage! What the hell is going on?

He stood in the middle of the barn, lips numb, finger trembling on the trigger of his weapon as he glanced back and forth from the Taliban men to the children. *Concentrate, Sam. Get your mind back in the game. Focus. Figure this out. Breathe.*

He motioned for the two children in the cage to stay quiet, then he crept over to the two Taliban men sleeping on the ground.

Time to answer the call.

He took another look around the room, raised his right foot, and slammed it down hard into the Taliban leader's ribs .

"Get up! Get up!" he screamed in Pashto. "You're under arrest!"

As the frightened men scrambled out from beneath their blankets, Sam thought of anything else he could make up that might keep them from fighting back, for the last thing he wanted to do was shoot anybody. "Army! Navy! Marines! Ute warriors have you surrounded! Get up! Out the door! Go! Go!"

His captives hurried outside, arms raised above their heads, as if expecting to find a mighty force of American troops waiting for them.

"On the ground! Hands to the backs of your heads!"

They complied, but they continued to search for the enemy.

Within seconds, Sam was at the tree that held his DiamondBar teammates, cutting the rope that tied them. The dead American slid into a pool of his own blood, and Weber and Thornton stumbled forward on weary legs. Sam caught Thornton, but Weber pushed past and kicked the Taliban leader in the head.

"Stop!" Sam yelled and turned his weapon on Weber. "They're our prisoners. And by order of the Geneva Convention, I demand you stand down!"

Weber turned slowly to face him, his eyes glassed over, his long, blood-drenched hair stuck to his swollen face. "Geneva Convention? Give me that rifle, ya goddamn pussy. You don't have the guts to shoot me."

"But I do." Thornton had picked up an abandoned Kalashnikov and was now pointing it at his DiamondBar teammate. "Carson risked his life to save us, Frank, and like he said, our guys have this place surrounded."

Sam winced. "Sorry—I made that part up."

Thornton gave him a dumbfounded look.

"My sat-phone's busted, so it's just us." Sam headed to the decaying wooden structure. "And the children inside the barn."

*   *   *

"Children?" Thornton's swollen eyes narrowed even more as he pointed his rifle at the Taliban leader. "What are children doing in there, Ghulam Habib?"

The Taliban leader stiffened but said nothing. He tightened his hands on the back of his head.

"Tell him!" Weber stormed over and kicked him hard in the ribs. "We know who you are, Habib. Pakistan Taliban crossing over to steal what's ours. Whose kids are in there?"

The leader lay still on the ground, his eyes staring down, refusing to answer.

Weber kicked him again. "Answer me!"

The man grimaced in pain and finally coughed out, "They're mine."

"No, they're not," Sam said from the open door of the barn. Standing next to him were two children who looked like they hadn't bathed in weeks: one boy, probably four or five, and one girl, no older than seven. "Their village was attacked by Habib's crew last week. The locals fought them off, but these two children were captured. They told me their names are Malala and Mateen Hazrat." He paused and looked directly at Thornton. "Hazrat . . . does that name mean anything to you?"

Thornton glanced at Weber and then back at Sam. "Hazrat rules the region where we're building our road."

Sam shook his head. "So the road to nowhere actually does have a destination. What are you guys getting out of it?"

Neither Weber or Thornton spoke, but Sam could tell by the looks on their faces it was about money. Always money. He glared at Weber, whose bloody head was absent one ear.

"Geez, Frank, what's wrong with you? You're trading parts of your body for pieces of paper and shiny metal discs." He walked over to the campfire, whose coals had dimmed to a soft orange glow. The pot of stew the guards had been cooking was still warm, and Sam ladled out two bowls for the Hazrat children. "I'll feed the kids before we escort them home–"

"The hell we are." Weber cut him off. "As soon as we get within a mile of wherever they live, we're as good as dead."

Sam ignored him and began to look through the DiamondBar and Taliban satchels that were near the fire. He came across Weber's sat-phone that Habib had confiscated earlier.

"How about this, Frank? I'll call the choppers to come get you and these prisoners." He pointed south. "There's another guard a half klick away tied to a tree. You can take complete credit for capturing a Taliban leader and his men. I'm sure it will get you another bonus from Dixon and maybe even a shoutout in the press."

It seemed as if Weber couldn't trust himself to speak. He stood motionless for a spell, then merely jerked his head in an affirmative nod.

"I'm glad we're in agreement," Sam said matter-of-factly, and then powered on the phone. "The rescue team should be able to pick you up within an hour. That should give me time to hit the trail and take the Hazrat children home."

CHAPTER FORTY-SEVEN

Bagram Air Base, Afghanistan

Dixon sat impatiently in the waiting room of Bagram Military Hospital as the doctors and nurses finished cleansing and stitching the wounds suffered by Frank Weber and Scott Thornton. Both had been rescued by Special Forces that morning, and along with the prisoners, had been helicoptered back to Bagram. Thornton was fine, but it would take a while for Weber to recover from the loss of his ear.

Finally, a nurse came down the hall and nodded to Dixon. "You may see them now, sir."

Dixon smiled politely, then headed to Weber and Thornton's room. He glanced back to make sure no one was watching and shoved the door open.

"What the hell's wrong with you guys?" Dixon growled in a hushed but furious tone. "I had to fly halfway around the world because my security team couldn't protect one damn road."

Both Weber and Thornton were still on IV fluids. They shook their heads but said nothing.

Dixon separated his index finger and thumb a fraction of an inch. "I'm this close to taking billions from that mountain, and you just let Carson walk away with my leverage?"

"They were children," Thornton mumbled. "Seven-year-old girl and five-year-old boy."

"I don't give a shit if they were newborns, Scott! They're my bargaining chips." Dixon shook his head in genuine disbelief. "Now, here's what we're gonna do. I'll pull a few strings to see if Bagram can get some drones up to find Carson and those kids. All you have to do is stay in the recon room and report to me what they find."

Weber knew better than to argue with Dixon. Twelve years of working for the man had told him that suggesting a different strategy than the one Drake had proposed could get a man fired. He was ruthless when he smelled money, and word was the mountain he wanted was filled to the snow line with incredible riches.

"They can't be more than a few miles from where Special Forces picked you up. That's damn rugged country they're traveling, and two malnourished little shits are only gonna slow him down," Dixon said.

*   *   *

"Hush, hush, whisper who dares. Malala and Mateen are saying their prayers . . ." Sam sang the last stanza of the Christopher Robin lullaby to the children as they drifted off to sleep on the soft pine needles of the forest floor. He was pretty sure they finally trusted him now, but these kids had been through hell and back the last week: ripped from their home, imprisoned in a cage, rescued by some stranger, only to see a dead man laying in his own blood and a one-eared man cursing at their savior.

He had pushed them only two miles. The children needed to be cleaned up, fed, and rested, so he set up camp near a cold mountain stream, and with a makeshift wooden spear, caught two trout for their afternoon and evening meals. His attempt at conversation on the hike had mostly failed, the still terrified five-year-old boy hiding behind his sister, clutching her hand as Sam peppered them with questions about family, pets, favorite foods, and games, all while trying to find out where they lived. He'd seen trust in the eyes of the seven-year-old girl before they had left the Taliban hideout when he had questioned Ghulam Habib about the whereabouts of Hazrat's village. Upon receiving his answer, Sam had glanced over at the little girl who shook her head. It was then he realized there was no way Habib would offer up information to an infidel scumbag like Sam. He would have to find their village himself . . . hopefully, with a little help from Malala Hazrat.

* * *

He slept restlessly that night, images of frightened eyes staring at him from inside cages haunting his dreams. Rising before dawn, he went down to the stream to collect watercress and chicory, and to spear another trout for breakfast. He nailed a brown on his second try, and as he turned around, he was mildly surprised to see Malala watching him.

"*Wezzey?*" She innocently said that she was hungry.

He gave a quick smile, took a bite of the chicory leaves, and offered her one. She put it in her mouth and wrinkled her nose.

"It's good for you, good for heart and stomach. I eat the leaves raw, but you have to boil the roots," Sam said.

She nodded and followed him back to the fire. Mateen was still sleeping, and Sam could tell that Malala had recently put her own blanket over her brother to keep him warm.

"You're a good sister."

She smiled up at him and reached for the trout.

"Do you"—he didn't know the word for *fillet* in her native tongue so he motioned with his hand—"know how to skin a fish?"

She gave a quick nod and held out her hand for his knife.

He slipped the big Gurkha kukri knife out of its sheath, and, holding the blade, offered her the handle. She took it, swept the blade behind the gill of the fish, cut off the head, then grabbed the tail and sliced forward in one quick move.

Yeah, she's done this before.

* * *

"Is any of this area familiar to you?" Sam asked as they began their second-day quest to find the Hazrat village.

Malala shook her head.

He figured. In a time of war, it was highly unlikely two young children would be allowed to travel very far from the protection of their community. Over the last five years, the Taliban had been expanding farther into the Kunar and Nuristan Provinces, and every hamlet throughout these rugged hills was in danger.

"Tell me about your village," he said.

She cocked her head to the side as if confused by the question.

"Is it by a river? Is it in the mountains? Is it in a valley or built on the side of a hill?"

She stared out across the water, motionless. Her innocent dark brown eyes seemed to be conflicted as they rested sightlessly on a leaf that was being carried downriver by the current.

"Not all Americans are bad, Malala. I can't take you and Mateen home if I don't know which way to go. Please trust me."

"It's in a valley," she said softly. "Big mountains to morning sun. Creek downhill from our village."

"That's good. How many homes in your village? Ten? Twenty? One hundred?"

"No, no, one hundred." She raised her hands and opened and closed them three times.

"Thirty?"

She nodded and took her brother's hand. That small gesture reminded Sam of an Afghan saying he had heard from one of the children at the Friends of Everyone Hotel.

"A real friend," he said, his eyes encouraging her, "is the one who takes the hand of his friend in times of distress and helplessness."

The little boy's head popped up. "My papa says that at mosque."

"What?" Sam asked in English, a bit surprised to hear Mateen speak. It was the first time the little boy had said anything since he had rescued them from the Taliban stockade. He moved quickly in front of the children and went to one knee. *"Poheezzem?"* He motioned with his hands that he wanted to know more. "Is there a mosque in your village?"

Malala nodded. "In our village square."

"Does it have only one spire?"

Again an affirmative nod.

Sam's face suddenly widened into a broad smile. "Is there a hole in the spire that needs to be fixed?"

Her face went ashen, as if drawn back to a terrible memory. "It was broken when American birds dropped bombs on our village."

He touched her arm and waited for her eyes to come back to his. He could see that she was pained by some horrible flashback. Finally, she lifted her chin and, with her lower lip trembling, said, "My mama was killed."

Sam let out a long breath and waited a beat before gently saying, "I'm very sorry for what you and Mateen have been through, but I know where you live now. I'm going to take you home."

* * *

"So you can help us out?" Dixon said to Captain Mitch Rinehart, head of Bagram reconnaissance and part of an elite unit referred to as Task Force ODIN: Observe, Detect, Identify, Neutralize. They were the team that used low and medium drone sensors and cameras with fixed-wing aircraft and Apache helicopters to view trouble on the ground. This information would travel via satellite or other networks to ground-based military commanders, who would then decipher where the enemy was . . . and decide when to attack.

"I'll do what I can, Mr. Dixon," Rinehart replied. "But our guys are up there to find insurgents who have been seen crossing over from Pakistan into the Nuristan Province. The bad guys are pretty fired up after we took out bin Laden. Hell, they killed Karzai's brother two weeks ago and then assassinated one of his top advisors this week. We've got a lot on our plate."

"I'm not asking you to direct your drones away from your military operation. I just want you to keep an eye out for my top scout. Carson is a very valuable asset and has been paramount to everyone's success."

"I will, sir," Rinehart said. "Our drones are already in that area because we have pictures of another band of insurgents moving southwest from Kamdesh toward the bridge that was recently destroyed."

"I know this sounds personal"—Dixon feigned compassion as he placed his right hand on his heart—"but Sam's like a son to me. If one of your drones picks up any activity in that region, please let us know."

The Captain nodded. "I want to save him too, sir. He made sure Captain Freeman's choppers held back just before they blew the bridge. Then he rescued your men from Ghulam Habib, a creep we've been after for a while." Rinehart paused to make sure Dixon heard his next message. "But to be honest, sir, Carson's a wild hare. When he made the decision to return those kids to a warlord like Hazrat, well, he may have signed his own death warrant."

* * *

It was the end of day two of their journey, and Sam pushed the Hazrat children all the way to the ridge that looked across the river to the now-destroyed Bridge to Somewhere. He made camp and speared two more trout. Malala filleted and grilled them, and, just as the sun disappeared beyond the western hills, the children pulled their blankets over their shoulders and fell asleep to the sounds of another Christopher Robin lullaby.

* * *

Sam woke the next morning well rested and happy. It was odd. After all he had been through the last few days, he figured his old self would have been anxious, even afraid. But as he looked at the sun that was now shining down on the Hindu Kush, he felt very thankful. They were alive, had found food, had good weather, and were probably only ten or twelve miles from the children's village.

I am stronger than I ever thought I was.

His mind drifted to his family: to a father killed in this foreign land, a mother taken from him at home, and a sister destroyed by disease.

Death does not end a relationship. Death does not end love. Everything the Power does, it does in a circle.

He heard the sounds of a child and immediately knew it was Malala. Soft footsteps on the forest floor, blanket dragging behind, he shifted over on the rock to give her a place to sit. She wrapped her thin wool cloth around her shoulders and leaned up against his shoulder.

It felt good to be trusted.

"Are you hungry?" he asked.

She shrugged her shoulders.

"My sister used to tell me that I should rise with the sun every day to pray. That God would hear me if I was truly present."

"What is her name?"

"Jenny." He smiled down at Malala. "She once told me that the mountains and rivers and lakes and meadows are my church . . . my mosque, my temple." He opened his arms to the nature that surrounded them. "I feel closest to God when I'm outside."

They sat quietly, watching the river below, a buzz of activity with fish and birds feeding on mayflies and midges, squirrels leaping from tree branch to tree branch along the shoreline in a delightful display of freedom.

Just then, an odd shadow swept across the mountain, so small Malala didn't seem to notice. But Sam, whose innate awareness was like a hawk's, conscious of every sight and sound and smell that was different from the natural world, did. He covered his eyes and squinted up to the sky. About two thousand feet above was a drone. Was it searching for them? Or searching for something else?

He rose, surveying the mountain from water to ridgeline. Something felt wrong, but he couldn't put his finger on it. What was it? His question was answered a moment later.

"Malala," he said calmly but firmly. "I want you to wake your brother and very quietly go behind the fallen tree where we made last night's fire."

She looked up, fear in her eyes. "Where are you going?"

"There's something I need to do before I take you home."

She grabbed his hand. "I'm scared."

He looked her directly in the eyes. "Do you trust me?"

She nodded.

"There are some men on the other side of the river who I need to check out."

The little girl's lower lip began to tremble.

"This is very important, Malala. If anything happens to me, I want you to go in the forest." He saw her despair and took hold of her hands. "I want you to repeat what I am going to tell you to do."

She swallowed hard but nodded.

"Go downriver until you see a yellow-taped fence line."

"Downriver . . . yellow fence line," she whimpered.

"That's where they repaired the road near where you live. Cross the river and climb the mountain."

"Cross river at yellow fence and climb mountain," she repeated.

"There's a path near the top. Turn right on the path, and it will lead you through a pass in the mountains to your home."

He paused to make sure she was listening. "Do you understand?"

She nodded again, blinking back tears.

"Good girl. You can do this. You are very brave. Now go."

* * *

Sam brought the monocular up to his right eye and scanned the ridgeline. *Shit.* At least twenty Taliban soldiers. He swept the scope down the side of the hill to the remains of the bridge. All that was left was twisted metal rods and broken wood torn from the frame, now lying haphazardly in a pile near the valley floor.

Three damaged road graders lay like old dinosaur bones nearby. Not much was left, but . . . his vision stopped at the back of one of the graders. Two five-gallon gas tanks.

He ran down his side of the valley slope to the water's edge, stripped down to his shorts, and entered the cold river. It only came up to his waist, but the current was strong, pushing him downstream a good fifteen meters before he reached the far side. He scrambled up the bank to the dirt road. Hiding behind a bush of wildflowers, he blended back into the landscape, crossed at a point where he knew the Taliban above couldn't see him, and ran to the road grader nearest the bridge.

The gas tanks were dented but still full. *Better to be lucky than good.* He disconnected them from the cab, carried them down to the woodpile at the base of the bridge, and poured the fuel all over the timber. Hurrying back to the grader, he opened the side tool box and searched for the flare gun and plastic hose he knew each vehicle carried. They were at the bottom. *Of course they are, underneath all this other crap, always at the bottom.*

He slid one end of the hose into the main gas tank of the grader, stretched the other end to the wood pile, and with all the force he could muster, sucked mightily at the hose. The gas shot through the tube smoothly, and he dropped the hose at the wood pile and ran to the edge of the slope that would lead back down to the river.

Taliban soldiers were now at the top of the ridge, approximately one hundred meters away, moving down into the trees. He glanced up at the sky.

C'mon, drone, come back around.

The enemy was now eighty meters away.

Where are you guys? You usually circle an area four or five times. C'mon.

Sixty meters away. He inhaled a deep breath and looked back at the other side of the river to where Malala and Mateen were hiding. They were still there.

Aw, hell with it, I can't wait any longer.

He clicked the safety off the flare gun, raised up, and pulled the trigger. A stream of yellow light shot forward, and he didn't remember much about the next few seconds.

* * *

The blast was more than he had planned for, white and blue and orange flames erupting from the woodpile, the heat from the explosion knocking him backward down the hill and into the river. It wasn't until he landed in the cold water that he came to and heard the next eardrum-splitting boom. The fire had made its way through the hose and into the gas tank of the grader.

Sam dove under the water as shards of metal, rock, and glass splashed around him. Every instinct made him want to come up for air, but instead, he swam low to the far side, crawled up the bank, grabbed his clothes, sprinted up the hill, and dove for cover. Gasping for breath, he rose up and took one last look.

The fire was raging, black smoke billowing high up to the sky, twisting toward a silver bird that had just cleared the eastern sierra. He exhaled a thankful smile. Finally, the drone had come back.

*   *   *

"Captain Rinehart! We got action at PRT Seven Two!" the unmanned-air-vehicle pilot shouted through his headset. "Big blast by the bridge, and pictures now coming in of insurgents opening fire on the blaze."

The captain hurried over to the monitor for a look. The fire was indeed big, and black ash was still pumping out of one of the road graders. But he had no idea who or what the Taliban was firing at. He turned to his lieutenant. "Get Gene on the line. Have him send those Black Hawks we have scouting for Dixon over to check it out. Tell them the enemy is attempting to take the bridge."

"Yes, sir. Do you think Mr. Dixon's man might have something to do with this? I mean, he's said to be near that area."

Rinehart chuckled lightly. "It wouldn't surprise me at all. That dude has a way of showing up at the wildest of times."

CHAPTER FORTY-EIGHT

Nuristan Province, Afghanistan

It had been twenty-two hours since Sam had set fire to the PRT bridge, and it had proven to be exactly the diversion they needed to escape. The fire had not only slowed the Taliban pursuit, but it drew US Forces for help. An hour after disappearing into the woods, Sam heard the grateful sound of Black Hawks passing overhead and later their guns blasting away at the enemy, driving the Taliban back up the hill in full retreat.

Now, downriver some four miles, Sam lifted Malala and Mateen up in his arms and waded into the cold mountain stream. A blast of whitewater made him teeter like a pine tree in a thunderstorm, giving but not breaking. He lowered his shoulder and pushed through the water, now waist-high, to the far side. He struggled up the muddy slope and collapsed on the ground to catch his breath. *Thank God it isn't winter,* he thought. Snow and ice and fierce mountain winds would have made this journey damn near impossible.

"This is the fence you wanted me to find." Malala pointed to the yellow tape that signified repair of the road was still not finished.

Sam smiled. They had indeed made it all the way to the PRT road that had been bombed six months before. Now, he was back here again. Staying underneath the cover of pines and poplar to avoid being spotted by US drones and helicopters, they had had little trouble since leaving the bridge.

There was no way that he was going to turn Malala and Mateen over to either American or Afghan forces, where they could be used as political pawns in some power game. These children needed to be back with their family, with the people and community who truly loved them.

What was it about this mountain that was drawing everyone's interest? The Afghan government, the PRT, and the Pakistan Taliban were all here now . . . and the owner of DiamondBar Security was likely the mastermind behind it all.

* * *

"Are we almost there?" Mateen asked as they hiked up the mountain.

"Almost," Sam answered for the fourth time.

"I saw a big bird."

"Mm hmm."

"Black wings."

"It's called a vulture," Sam explained. "Pretty common in these parts."

"It's ugly."

"Hush," Malala scolded her little brother.

But Sam was glad that Mateen was finally talking. And so much so, that he was being reprimanded nearly every two minutes by his sister.

"I don't have to hush," he grumbled.

"Yes, you do."

"No, I don't."

"Yes, you do."

Mateen stuck his tongue out at his sister. "You're not the boss of me." He then tripped over a fallen log, getting leaves all over his shirt.

"I'm your boss until we get home," Malala said crossly, but she still helped her brother up and brushed him off.

Sam grinned through it all, listening to the little boy chatter on about birds and trees and insects that he found in the woods. They were getting close. And the closer they got to the Hazrat village, the more Sam wondered how he would be received. He may look Nuristani, but he was an American. An infidel. The Satan of the West.

*   *   *

Thirty minutes later, they reached the top of the tree line and stepped onto a narrow dirt path that brought a bright smile from Malala.

"I've been here before!" she screeched. "This is where Papa brings our goats in the spring."

Sam nodded, his apprehension growing with each step. The rest of their journey would be invisible from the sky, covered by poplar, pine, and oak, along with the rugged mountains surrounding the Hazrats' small town, making it less likely a destination for the US military to be interested in . . . until now . . . until a certain PRT bridge not but twelve miles away had been destroyed by Taliban insurgents.

They walked east two miles, turned north through a narrow opening in the canyon, and passed by the gray stone cliff where Sam had done reconnaissance back in January. He remembered studying the village through his monocular, watching the men he had been tracking be greeted by their children. They were the ones who had detonated the IED on the PRT road, but he had not, or would not, call in the coordinates of this remote village to his team. He was now glad he had made that decision or who knows what would have happened to Malala and Mateen if he had disclosed that intel.

"I'm tired," Mateen blurted out and then reached up to Sam, who cheerfully lifted him up on his shoulders.

"You're a big baby." Malala scowled until Sam winked down at her. She took his hand, and the three of them continued on.

It was late in the afternoon when they came to the end of the tunnel of trees. Both children shrieked with joy at what they found on the other side.

There it was—only a hundred meters away—home.

On closer inspection, it appeared to be a vibrant town, built of strong stone huts, with plumes of smoke rising from chimneys as the women were likely preparing the evening meals.

"No turning back now," Sam said to himself. The words were no sooner out of his mouth when a swarm of yapping, barking dogs ran out to greet them.

A few seconds later, out stepped two men with hunting rifles pointed their way. One man slowly lowered his rifle and stared at them.

"Malala! Mateen!" he shouted. "Malala! Mateen!"

Within minutes, they were surrounded by villagers: women hugging and kissing the children, while men surrounded the stranger, rifles ready, waiting for the leader of the village to arrive.

And then he did, Abdul Hazrat himself, hurrying through the stonewall entrance. He stopped, blinking back tears, his mouth slightly open, as if in disbelief, his hands clasped together in front of his chest.

"Papa!" the children cried out and ran into their father's arms.

Sam just stood there, watching and waiting, knowing the importance of how he would be received. Hazrat was fortyish, bearded, of medium height, but his dark brown eyes showed a man of intelligence. He lifted both children in his arms and walked over.

"Who are you?" he demanded.

Sam swallowed hard and looked the village leader directly in the eyes. "Sam Cloud-Carson," he articulated in perfect English. "American."

Hazrat's eyes went wide, and his men started shouting, shoving Sam, pointing their rifles at him as if he were a dangerous animal that had wandered into their village.

Sam's expression didn't change. He just stood there stoically, the grip of the villagers anger drawing closer until Hazrat raised his hand for quiet.

Malala pulled sharply on her father's shirt.

"Not all Americans are bad, Papa," she said, quoting Sam from a conversation they'd had three days before. "He saved us from the bad men."

"It's true," said someone from behind the circle of men surrounding Sam. The crowd parted, and a one-armed teenage boy stepped forward. "This is the man who was attacked by his own people when he tried to help us."

Sam's eyes narrowed as he studied the boy and the man next to him. Yes. These were two of the Afghan hunters who had been arrested by US Forces eighteen months earlier on the other side of this mountain range.

"I'm sorry I couldn't stop them," Sam said in their native tongue.

"How did you know how to find our village?" Hazrat asked, his eyes still filled with disbelief.

"The day your men blew up the PRT road"—Sam pointed back up the canyon—"I tracked them to the pass and saw where they lived."

"But you didn't tell the American soldiers?"

Sam shook his head.

"Why not?"

"I was afraid of what they might do."

Hazrat didn't speak for a long time. His gaze fixed on Sam, his brow wrinkled as he debated what to do with an infidel in his village. Then, one side of his mouth curled slightly, he kissed his daughter's cheek, and he motioned for Sam to follow him.

*   *   *

"You are one crazy American," Hazrat said when Sam finished his story. "I don't know whether to admire you or recommend that you have psychological help."

Sam chuckled at that, for there were many times that he wondered the same thing. But he now believed that everything that had happened in his life had led him to this moment, this understanding, this opportunity to reunite a family. He had had many teachers: his family, friends, and enemies. Some had taught him how to live a good life; others, like Drake Dixon, had taught him how not to. But all had been his teachers.

"Where do you go now, my new American friend?"

He glanced quickly at Malala and Mateen, who were seated next to their father, and then back up at Hazrat. "I–I don't know. I haven't thought past today."

"That is very wise," said Hazrat. "For many in this world are consumed only by the past or seeking tomorrow. That is why they come for our mountain."

Both of Sam's brows drew together. "Why is everyone so interested in this mountain?"

"It is rich in emeralds, rubies, coal and iron, lithium, timber, and uranium."

"That's why there's a bounty on your head?"

"Only one hundred thousand US dollars." Hazrat grinned as he stroked his full beard. "I thought I would be worth more."

"How long have you known?"

"There are no secrets among the hill people, my friend. The mayor of Parun was offered the bounty two years ago from someone close to our Minister of Interior." Hazrat inclined his head slightly and smiled. "Unfortunately for Minister Almeida Zubair, he did not know that the mayor is my cousin."

Sam nodded. "That's why they extended the bounty to the Pakistan Taliban."

"Ghulam Habib raided our village two weeks ago. He killed one man and kidnapped my children."

"Do you know where the money came from?"

"I only know that his people hired the PRT crew who were building the road."

Dixon. He was behind everything.

"One of my people met with an American in Kabul last year," Hazrat continued. "He offered us money for our land."

"You don't know his name either?"

Hazrat shook his head. "There are rumors that he works for the same man who sold weapons to our government several years ago."

Rumors, of course. Nothing concrete that could be tied back to Dixon. That's the way Dixon worked. In subtleties, promises, shady deals, nothing written down, so as never to be directly linked back with doing something illegal. What a con artist. He had conned Sam's father to work for him, bribed someone inside the Afghan government to build his road, and had blackmailed Sam into scouting these hills to make sure no trouble would come to the PRT. All so that Dixon could steal another man's property.

"How will this end?" Sam asked.

"I don't know. The greed of man is very strong. Whether it is our government or yours, the Taliban or a construction company, they twist information to get what they want. Then they give it pretty names, like Responsibility to Protect or Operation Enduring Freedom, to make it sound kind and merciful."

"You are a follower of Islam?"

"It is the foundation of my life," Hazrat said passionately. "But I am not a fundamentalist. The very word Islam means submission, submission to God, not to man or some mullah. At the very core of Muhammad's teaching was honesty, generosity, virtuousness, fairness, and respect for others. Yet there are these so-called men of faith who hide behind Islam or Christianity or politics so they can steal our land."

Sam's face tightened a bit, but he remained quiet.

"They are like locusts, devouring everything in their path and then moving on to the next mountain or prairie or river." Hazrat looked out at his mountain for a brief moment, then back at Sam. "My country used to be very beautiful. Then came the Russians, the Taliban, the Americans, our own government to steal our land and push the hill people to the cities. But the cities didn't have enough power to feed and shelter them, so they cut down our beautiful forests to fuel their homes and cook their food, never thinking of replanting. Much of Afghanistan has become a desert."

"Do you have a contract with the government?" Sam asked. "Any written agreement with the Ministry of Mines that proves you own this land?"

"I have several," Hazrat said with a soft, defeated sigh. "But this is Afghanistan, where one does not let a piece of paper get in the way of what one desires."

Sam couldn't think and tried not to feel. The depth of the sadness seemed overwhelming. "There has to be another way," he whispered.

"There is always another way," Hazrat said, the corner of his mouth lifting slightly. "Perhaps you can find it."

Sam didn't speak for a long time, his gaze hovering somewhere between the village leader and his children, much like the space between two tracks, studying, searching for the next track that would tell him which way to go. Then his vision slowly returned to Hazrat.

"Do you have a pen and paper, sir?"

Before he could even turn to his daughter, Malala was already out the door, hurrying to her cottage to grant her hero's request.

* * *

Sam signed his name at the bottom of the final page, folded the letter in thirds, placed it in an envelope, and handed it to Hazrat. "This copy is for you. I made two more and will give them to people I trust."

The village leader read the instructions on the front of the envelope, and his brows drew together in both concern and curiosity. "I will honor your wishes, my friend. My only advice is that you be very cautious in what you are about to do."

"I'm always cautious." Sam winked at Mateen, who was still seated next to his father. "Didn't your son tell you about the little campfire I started for him?"

Hazrat laughed out loud. "He called it *big fire to the sky*." He nodded to the door. "Now, go clean up. My sister drew a hot bath and laid out clean clothes for you. Our village has prepared a grand meal for the return of Malala, Mateen, and their new brother."

* * *

It was indeed a grand meal, complete with spiced cashews, chickpeas, and pita toast, tender lamb kebab with cinnamon, and fresh naan. As Sam sipped on his third cup of tea, he watched Abdul hover over his children, the frequent small touches, a hand on a shoulder, a pinched cheek, a kiss to a forehead. It all made Sam feel good to be part of bringing this family together again. His own life had been one of loss and death, severed from his parents, sister, and his tribe. But being part of this village's celebration reminded him of home. The joy in the simple things, food, family, and friendship, was perfect nourishment for him.

* * *

"Yes, it was delicious." He laughed as he rubbed his belly to let them know he'd had enough. Another piece of fruit was shoved in front of his face, and he threw up his hands in defense. "No thank you, I really can't eat anymore." Then he clasped his hands together in prayer and bowed. "Blessings to all of you. Good night."

As he turned to leave, he felt a tug on his shirt. It was Malala. Tears ran down her cheeks as she looked up at him. He went to one knee and held her at arm's length.

"I will never forget you," he said with a bright smile. "You remind me of my sister. She was small but strong." He drew his open hand together into a fist. "She was brave. You are brave. I am going to give you a Ute name. I will now call you *One Who Cooks a Tasty Fish.*"

She giggled and then looked up at her father, who was smiling near the door.

"We have a saying in Afghanistan," Hazrat said proudly. "The first day you meet, you are friends. The next day you meet, you are brothers."

* * *

Sam left the next morning, loaded with water, food, and copies of Hazrat's mining documents. It was a familiar trail, up the canyon pass, across the backbone of the mountain, and down to the big stream that snaked its way to the broad Pech Valley.

It was a glorious August day, with no sight or sound of any human activity. The humble beauty of gray mountain against blue sky, the smell of pine, and rush of fast water comforted him. It was as if Mother Nature herself was healing him, awakening his heart to some age-old memory, reuniting him with his Creator and the world. It reminded him of another quote from Jenny's journal:

See only love and oneness in the Great Spirit.

Was it really that easy? Was it simply shifting the way he looked at the world? Would he have been frightened had he met Abdul Hazrat in another setting? In the city? In a war zone? He didn't know. He only knew he was happy right now. Happy that he had risen out of his depression; happy that he had not taken his own life; happy that he had served and saved others. For what would have happened to Malala and Mateen, and even Frank Weber and Scott Thornton, had he not intervened?

It was in that moment that he saw movement far off in the mountains, a flickering shadow against stone. Tan. Gray. Black. The Ghost of the Mountain. The majestic and mysterious snow leopard. Had it been following him all along? Was it the same leopard whose track he had seen earlier in the week? Could it be another of his spirit totems?

His own Ute tribe looked at the land and animals as being spiritually alive. Those elements had a power that moved the world and affected the lives and fates of human beings. Utes believed the mountain lion to be the wisest and bravest of all animals. The lion was a totem of a solitary hunter. One who loved to sit atop a rocky outcrop, watching over and protecting all of his domain. Had this leopard been watching over him because he, too, had been protecting this land? The snow-leopard totem was a symbol of resilience, agility, strength, and perseverance, all traits that Sam had needed to survive the last two years.

He stood absolutely still and stared up at the big cat, who held his gaze as if they were truly connecting, and then the leopard drifted off, disappearing into the rocks and trees and shadows of his mountain. For the second time in the last two weeks, it reminded him of his moments with Old Mel, the mule deer of Pargin Mountain. Perhaps both had appeared in his life so that he could learn from the past, as troubled as it might have been, and realize that all events, past, present, and yet to come, had been gently planned by one whose only purpose was for his good.

CHAPTER FORTY-NINE

Bagram Air Base, Afghanistan

Three days later

"He's back," Charlie Whitson said as he clicked off his phone and looked over at his boss. "He showed up at Camp Blessing, near Nangalam, one hour ago. Just randomly appeared out of nowhere and walked up to the guard station. They thought he might be some suicide bomber, so they made him lay on the ground and searched him."

"Did he have Hazrat's kids with him?" Dixon asked.

Whitson shook his head.

"Shit! They would have been good leverage."

Dixon stared at the map, his eyes following the road that the PRT had been building. *Somewhere in those hills was Hazrat's hideout. Carson had been there.*

He turned back to his operations chief. "When will he be here?"

"Tomlinson went to pick him up. Should be back at Bagram in a few hours."

"Why the hell is he calling Special Forces instead of us?"

Whitson shrugged his shoulders as if he didn't want to know.

But Dixon knew why. Carson had called the Army colonel because he didn't trust anyone at DiamondBar. Whitson admitted that his crew had been tough on the kid. Sam was too idealistic, believing that they could help Afghanistan. It was hopeless. The government, the citizens, the tribal dynamics were a complete mess. Only an autocrat willing to work with someone like Dixon could pull this third-world country into the twenty-first century.

So what if DiamondBar profited along the way? That was the prize any gambler claimed when they bet on chaos. He was just fortunate that his gamble was being paid by American taxpayers who voted in politicians who had approved of the billions to rebuild Afghanistan.

It was now time to cast the financial lure in front of Sam Carson and reel him in. This would be a big payday for the kid as well, as long as he was willing to give Dixon what he wanted—the whereabouts of Abdul Hazrat.

He stood up and headed to the door. "Let's go to Bagram and welcome our boy home."

* * *

The *whump, whump, whump* of the rotor blades reverberating off the Black Hawk cab made conversation difficult, but Sam was sure he heard Colonel Tomlinson say that there was trouble at the Friends of Everyone Hotel.

"What happened?" Sam shouted over the roar of the engine.

"Taliban is claiming responsibility," Tomlinson yelled back and then handed Sam a headset so they could communicate better. "They accused them of trying to convert Muslims."

"When?"

"Two days ago. Two explosive devices were fired over the wall."

"Was anyone hurt?"

"Six injured, but only two needed to go to the hospital."

Sam turned his face away, appalled that anyone could be so cruel that they would take their anger out on innocent children.

"A mother named Berezira took shrapnel to her back and head, and her five-year-old daughter had burns to her hands and left arm."

Images of an explosion and screams of terror and pain filled Sam's mind as he fought back tears of sadness.

"Afghanistan is an Islamic state by constitution, Sam, which means any expression of faith other than Islam is strictly prohibited."

"But they don't profess any faith. McCracken only allows them to practice kindness and service."

Tomlinson pointed to his head. "The sick mind sees what it wants to see . . . and believes what it wants to believe is true."

Sam sat back in his jump seat and stared at the town of Nangalam. He was no longer in the rugged beauty of the Hindu Kush. This was the Afghanistan the world knew, damaged homes, scorched land, and broken hearts. A place where the innocent would be hurt by the *believers*. And the more grotesque their dreams, the wilder and more powerful their attacks seemed to be. Then, in came men like Dixon, preying on the lawlessness and the vulnerable.

"Do you want to stop by the Friends Hotel?" Tomlinson asked.

Sam nodded, recovering himself. "Do you have a computer on board?"

Tomlinson raised a curious brow. "We do."

"I'd like to use it if you don't mind," Sam said with a determined look. "I need to figure some things out."

* * *

The front gate looked much the same, as did the interior defensive wall, but inside of that were remnants of war, of a burned-out building, black-and-gray ash blisters covering the bright purples, yellows, and pinks that had adorned the main house. There were a few red splotches of blood still on the wall and floor, eerie reminders of pain and fear.

The place was empty save for McCracken and his assistant, Hunoon, an Afghan woman who had lost her husband and son in a NATO bombing in 2006. They had been instructed to clean up the grounds and then turn the property over to the government.

McCracken saw Sam and Tomlinson and waved them over.

"Well, shootfire! We had a pretty good run!" McCracken called out as he pulled out the baseball gear from the dugout metal crate and stuffed it into a canvas bag. "Three years of peace before they found me out."

Sam was stunned by McCracken's upbeat attitude. Even Hunoon had a soft smile lighting her face.

"I'm very sorry to hear about Berezira and her daughter," Sam struggled to say. "How are they?"

"Much better, thank you. Doc expects a full recovery."

"What happened?"

"It was actually pretty innocent." McCracken sighed. "One of our volunteers made a tiny mistake a few weeks ago. She wore a cross necklace to the market, and rumors spread that we might be selling Jesus."

Sam took a deep breath, steeling himself for what was next.

"Poor girl was very sorry for her mistake and flew back to the States yesterday, but that's why I told everyone, no expression of religion. It's Afghanistan's land mine. We're only here to serve."

"We were fortunate to place the families very quickly," Hunoon cut in. "Some had relatives who took them in, but most needed our connections with Islamic Relief and Missionaries of Charity to find them food and shelter."

"Muslims and Christians actually working together?" Sam muttered.

"It happens more often than you'd think," McCracken said. "Islamic Relief was one of the few aid agencies to continue to work in Afghanistan during the military incursions, and Mother Teresa's charity has an orphanage for disabled children that also helps poor families."

Sam's eyes scanned the baseball field, and McCracken seemed to know what he was thinking. "Nahal's family was taken care of, Sam. Islamic Relief found them a place to live until, well, hopefully they're able to return to their mountain village."

"Do you really think they'll ever be able to go home?"

"I don't know with the Taliban coming in from Pakistan and causing problems near their village." He shook his head sadly. "Roads have been bombed, and villagers are living in fear. Many markets and local governments have closed, so in come the pirates, searching for booty. Whether it's the sex trade, poppy harvest, or timber and minerals, foreigners want their piece of Afghanistan's pie."

"Will you rebuild?"

McCracken shook his head. "The government shut us down. We've been kicked out of the country."

Sam's mouth dropped open in outrage. "For what? You didn't try to convert anybody!"

"Says who? The truth isn't important to fundamentalists, Sammy. This bombing was simply a warning. The next one won't be."

"If an Afghan converts to a faith outside of Islam," Hunoon explained, "that is considered treason, a betrayal to family, tribe, and country. At least half of Afghanistan's provinces are still ruled by the Taliban, so you must appease them or they will bring violence."

Sam pushed his hand through his hair in frustration. When would Afghanistan's misery ever end? This poor country had experienced brutality for centuries as both foreign and domestic power brokers twisted the truth so they could control trade routes, steal land, and build their empires.

"Where will you go?"

"Wherever I'm needed," McCracken said. "Apparently I have a git-'er-done reputation."

Hunoon walked over and slipped her arm through Whiplash's. "The day after they closed our hotel, we received emails from relief organizations around the world offering us work."

Sam stared at Whiplash, then back at Hunoon. "Us? What do you mean *us*? You're not being forced to leave too, are you, Hunoon?"

Her hand went to her face to hide a shy smile of embarrassment.

Whiplash pulled her closer. "I ain't goin' nowhere without the love of my life, dude. Hunoon and I are takin a sweet deal in Nicaragua. You're welcome to join us. The guy who owns the orphanage we'll be running also owns a slick casino and the town's baseball team."

Sam's eyes went wide. "You guys are dating?"

McCracken's index finger shot up to his lips. "Don't say that so loud! We might get another grenade tossed our way. But as soon as we set foot on Central American soil, I'm asking this beautiful lady to be my wife."

Sam's eyes went even wider as Whiplash, Hunoon, and Colonel Tomlinson laughed out loud.

"How the heck do you find anything in the wild, Sammy, when this track has been right under yer nose?" McCracken wisecracked. "I've been chasin' Hunoon around this ballyard since before you got here, and you never figured us out?"

"I . . . uh . . . no."

"That's because you have a good heart, dude. Always hovering around the children like a mother hen, bringing treats and sweets, making sure every child was happy. I think that was part of your healing, a way for you to escape from your own personal hell. And along the way you discovered that giving and receiving are one and the same. You helping our children helped *you* heal."

Sam let out a long breath and then eased himself down onto the dugout bench. It was true. This was his atonement. This was the decision Jenny had told him about the day she died.

You need to ask the Great Spirit anytime you need help, his sister had said. *Rely on that spirit to interpret everything that will take place in your life. Not just some things, but everything.*

He remembered Jenny looking out of the hospital window at the storm clouds building above the Rocky Mountains and then asking if he had heard of the famous Lakota medicine man Black Elk.

He'd said he had.

"Black Elk believes the power of the world is done in a circle," she had said. *"Look outside. The Earth is round, the sky is round, the stars are round. The wind in its greatest power whirls. Birds make their nests in circles, for theirs is the same religion as ours. Even the seasons form a great circle in their changing, and always come back to where they were. The life of a man is a circle from childhood to childhood, and so it is in everything where power moves."*

"What does all this mean?" he'd asked.

"It means even when I get rid of this physical body, I will still be with you . . . always. It's the cycle and power of giving and receiving, maintaining the circle of life. I will be with you always."

This was his choice now. This was his decision to accept himself as the Great Spirit had created him. And what was that choice except the uncertainty of what *he* truly was? It was the answer to two of the oldest questions of all time. What am I? And why am I here? Yet he had somehow known it all along, as if it were some ancient memory long forgotten.

To be alive and not know himself was to believe that he was really dead. For what was life but to be himself? His true self. Spirit. The circle of life. Wakan Tanka. It was time for him to truly be *Walks with the Wind*.

CHAPTER FIFTY

DiamondBar Headquarters, Afghanistan

Dixon stared at the secure phone in his DiamondBar barracks, his fury continuing to boil as he waited for a call about the whereabouts of his tracker. "Where the hell is he!" he shouted to no one in particular. "We've been to the colonel's office, the recon center, the air base, and no sign of Carson. Dammit, I can't go home until this shit is cleaned up."

Whitson shrugged his shoulders but didn't want to make eye contact with his boss. Dixon was a leader who didn't like to be questioned. Thin-skinned. Ego-centric. Those who challenged him were soon to be *former* employees.

"We've got to take control of this before it gets out of hand!" Dixon continued to rant. "I can't have the Defense Department or some oversight committee opening an investigation on why we started this project."

"That shouldn't happen, sir," Whitson said. "There are over twenty-five PRTs working in Afghanistan right now. Each one has countless projects going on, from road construction to building hospitals, to dealing with tribal, village, and religious politics, to mentoring the Afghan Army."

"That's why we don't need anyone snooping around, Charlie. I told Senator Richardson this road was needed to connect rural communities so the Afghan Army could do a better job of fighting the Taliban. We've got to keep that cover going until we get the rights to Hazrat's mountain." Dixon's gaze locked on each member of his DiamondBar team. "And you let the only person who knows where that scumbag's hiding walk away ."

* * *

An unexpected calm came over Sam when Colonel Tomlinson dropped him off at the DiamondBar barracks. It was a familiar feeling, the same he felt in the outdoors and on the pitcher's mound. Where others might fear being alone in the woods or anxious on the mound, he felt safe. Whether it was darkness or a hanging curve, a rattlesnake or screaming fans, a blizzard or base runners, coyotes howling or coaches shouting, he felt at home, comfortable, confident, and at peace. He trusted his mind, body, and spirit to do what needed to be done.

He walked up the lane and paused at the top step of the DiamondBar barracks. Then, much like he did before he delivered an important pitch, he inhaled a deep breath and pushed the door open.

"Hi, fellas," he said with a happy smile and headed for his sleeping quarters.

Dixon leaped out of his chair. "Where the hell have you been?"

"Out for a walk in the woods." He ran a hand through his long dirty hair. "Gonna shower and pack before I head to the airport."

Whitson moved over to block his path. "You're not going anywhere until you give the man answers."

Sam's mouth twisted into a grin, and he clapped his hands. "All right, why don't we start by talking about Billy Cutthredge and Rob Marcus? Two DiamondBar employees we haven't seen in a while."

All the color drained from Dixon's face.

Sam was conscious of everyone in the room. He registered Dixon's shock, but also the curiosity in his coworkers' eyes. *They don't know*, he thought. Of those present in the room, only he and Dixon knew that Cutthredge and Marcus were dead.

"How do you know Billy and Rob?" Whitson asked. "They left Afghanistan five years ago."

Sam eyed Dixon boldly. "Shall we talk about it in front of Charlie and the boys, Mr. Dixon? Or would you prefer some privacy to get this matter settled?"

Dixon glared back, as if trying to rally his old self-confidence in an effort to regain control of the situation. "This is between you and me. They don't need to be involved."

"Indeed." Sam gave a wry smile and motioned toward his sleeping quarters, "After you . . . sir."

* * *

"What the hell are you trying to pull?" Dixon barked as soon as Sam closed the door. "You want more money? Is that it?"

Sam didn't respond. He sat down on his bed and opened his large canvas travel bag.

"You have no idea who you're messing with, boy. My company has gone to great lengths to bring peace to this country. I'm not going to let some disgruntled employee screw up what we've done to help the good people of Afghanistan."

"Whatever," Sam said with a flip of his hand. "Tell me about Cutthredge and Marcus."

"They were loyal employees. Not subversives like you." Dixon crossed his arms over his chest, trying to calm his growing anger. "I did what I had to do to convince you that your skills were needed to protect our men and women over here."

"Drop the patriot bullshit. The only thing you care about is power and money. You used me to track for your road, so you and your snake inside the Afghan government could steal from this poor, oppressed country."

"But you were the one who murdered Cutthredge and Marcus. I still have the video to prove that you killed them in cold blood."

"And *you* covered it up," Sam said in a voice so low it sounded like a wolf warning a stalker to beware. "I'm ready to reveal everything to our intelligence community, to Congress, and to the press. I'll not only tell them what you covered up on Pargin Mountain, but what you're covering up here. While they may send me to prison, Congress will fine you millions and toss you in the clink for bribing a foreign government to kill one of its citizens so that you could steal his mountain."

"You don't have any proof!"

"How do you know?" Sam's dark eyes fixed on his prey. "How do you know what Abdul Hazrat told me? How do you know I don't know who your contact is inside the Afghan government? How do you know I don't have video and audio of those negotiations?"

He was taking a big chance because he actually wasn't sure if Almeida Zubair was Dixon's man inside the Afghan Interior Department, nor did he have any video or audio. But Dixon didn't know that, so he thought he'd take it a step further. "How about we call one of your bosses in DC and tell them you've been using US money to build your road to Hazrat's mountain?"

Dixon stood by the door, watching Sam with a look of absolute hatred, but said nothing.

Sam reached into his jacket and pulled out a copy of a document Hazrat had given him the day he left. "I also have proof you violated the 2009 Afghan Mining Regulations Act." He tossed the document at Dixon's feet. "You never placed a bid for a contract with the Ministry of Mines, and you never disclosed your plan to the Extractive Industries Transparency Initiative. I believe the Afghanistan Natural Resources Oversight Network will be very interested if I tell them about your plan to mine without a license."

"We . . . were in the process of doing that."

"When?" Sam asked. "After you had Hazrat killed?"

He paused to read Dixon's tell, and it was there, a slight twitch of fury near his right eye that told Sam he was ahead in the count.

He turned back to his work of folding clothes and packing his bag, but also to let Dixon think about what he had said rather than to continue to probe and have him explode in defense. Sam pulled out his entire sock and underwear drawer and dumped it into his canvas bag before returning his vision to Dixon.

"Consider today my last day of working for you. You're not exactly a man I can trust, so I wrote down all that I know and gave that information to three people I *can* trust." He paused and looked Dixon directly in the eyes. "If anything happens to me—if I'm killed or disabled by your goons—they'll release my findings to the press and Congress, and your bullshit career will be over." He shook his head sadly. "It's hard to believe that anyone would follow a con artist like you. You wrap yourself around our flag and call yourself a patriot while using truly honorable men—like my father—to do your bidding. And then you break a promise to a family when all they asked was could you help their little girl get a new kidney?"

The last part took every ounce of Sam's being not to rise up and punch Dixon in the face. The thought of Jenny reminded him of a message he had read in her journal the previous month. The date was March 11, 2007. Two days after their father had been killed in Afghanistan.

My heart aches today. I feel responsible for my papa's death.
I know he took the job with DiamondBar to get insurance for me.
Would he still be alive if I wasn't sick?
Would my mother have a husband if not for me?
Would my brother have a father?
These thoughts haunt me. I must now be even more determined, more focused, more vigilant to let these insane beliefs go.
Please help me, Great Spirit. Help me to forgive.
Forgiveness is the only way I can end this nightmare.
Please help me.

What an amazing spirit, Sam thought. If his sister had the strength to seek forgiveness in her darkest time, then he must too. Jenny had given him that message, knowing that he would need it sometime in his life. That time was now.

"Here are my demands," Sam said. "You're going to end construction on the PRT road and tell your friend in the Afghan Interior Department to leave Hazrat's mountain alone."

"I can't do that!" Dixon snapped.

Sam held up his hand. "I'm not finished. You also have to donate two hundred and fifty thousand dollars to Islamic Relief, two hundred and fifty more to Mother Teresa's Missionaries of Charity, and one hundred grand to the Southern Ute Cultural Center. I googled you. You can afford it."

"Who the hell do you think you are?"

"I'm the guy who will call CIA Director Theodore Johnson and Secretary of Defense Bill Clifford and tell them what you've been up to."

Sam knew Dixon was scared, and he wanted to keep the pressure on. "While I was googling you, I discovered that they're not fans of private military contractors. As a matter of fact, General Clifford was particularly critical of the way you handled the trouble near Mihtarlam in 2007. You remember, when my father was killed."

Dixon's eyes nervously darted about the room, and then returned to Sam. "There has to be a way—financially—where we can settle this. What you're asking could ruin me."

"You should have thought about that when you began this deception."

"I'll give you two million dollars to stay quiet."

Sam's face remained expressionless as he said, "I believe my grandfather once told you, Sam not for sale." He then pulled his phone out of his pocket and flipped it open. "I have General Clifford on speed dial if you want me to call him."

Dixon said nothing for a time, and Sam could tell that the Diamond-Bar owner was busy conjuring up all the ways he could escape from the mess that he had created rather than have any compassion for the people he had hurt. People were chattel to men like Dixon, only to be used for their personal gain and then tossed aside when the individual's talents no longer benefited them. Sam meant nothing to Dixon, nor did his father or sister or Cutthredge or Marcus or anyone. And that was the lonely castle that Dixon had built for himself, the one he self-created, self-maintained, and now self-defended, in need of nothing beyond his trophies.

He had no real connection to anyone, no true friends, only those who bowed down to him because he had money and power. That was Dixon's insane world. He couldn't be in his right mind. For who would trade their soul for simple profit?

Dixon's jaws slowly unclenched. He didn't look angry anymore. He looked distressed and confused, much like a batter walking back to the dugout after he had just struck out with the bases loaded.

"I'll agree to your demands on one condition," he said at last.

Sam cocked his head to the side.

"You can never talk about your time in Afghanistan." Dixon took a deep breath, as if trying to reclaim some semblance of control. "Because if you do, I won't take my vengeance out on you. I'll go after Hazrat and his family."

Sam rose up to his full six-foot-four height, his dark brown eyes locked on Dixon. "You leave them alone, and I'll stay quiet. You have my word." He then pointed to the door with a cold formality. "Now get the hell out of here. It's time I get to live the life you stole from me."

CHAPTER FIFTY-ONE

USA

August 2011

Sam was a bit surprised at the relative ease in which he had returned to the States. Colonel Tomlinson found him a jump seat on a military transport headed to Hickam Air Force Base in Hawaii. It was impossible to sleep, strapped in as he was to the nonreclining, cramped, iron chair, thoughts of *what will I do now* flashing through his mind. He could go home, but what then?

His most recent letter from Grandpa Douglas had revealed that he had finally sold SJ Outfitters and helped their hunting-and-fishing guides find work elsewhere. Grandpa had transferred much of the Carson property back to the tribe and moved closer to town. Jose and Teresa were married and living in the foothills east of Ignacio. His best friend had graduated from Mesa State and had taken a job with the tribal police, and Teresa was now a full-time registered nurse at the Durango Medical Center. What would Sam do?

Upon landing at Hickam, he cabbed it to the Honolulu Airport and purchased a one-way ticket to LAX. Bone-weary, he'd fallen asleep within fifteen minutes of taking off with Jenny's journal in his lap, open to a page about, what else?, baseball and spirit. It was her take on the unpredictability of the game: how a player could do everything right, but still lose; how someone could throw the perfect pitch or take the perfect swing and still fail. She wrote about appreciating *the quiet innings when time passed slowly and seemingly nothing happened as two boys played catch while the other seven watched an opponent futilely swing a wooden stick at the holy white orb.* Those were the last words he had read before drifting off to sleep.

He dreamed of Jenny. She was sitting in the dugout while he was pitching, chattering away to anyone who would listen about command over velocity, the advantages of strike one, and her disdain for the Player Empirical Comparison and Optimization Test Algorithm. Typical Jenny.

When he finished his inning and returned to the dugout, she turned into a hawk, flying above him, calling out, "Behold! All the wind shall come to you, for they are your relatives, past and future, ready to lift you up to the right here and right now." He stared up at her, wondering if the hawk was truly his sister. She saw his doubt and swept down, hovering directly in front of him, her eyes as bright as the sunset star. "This world is your test. Everything that has happened to you is your lesson. What have you learned, brother? What will you do with this new knowledge?"

He didn't know what to say, didn't know what she meant.

"A-hey! A-hey! A-hey!" she called out and then flew to his side so he could see past her. The baseball field was gone, replaced by the hills, valleys, and creeks of Pargin Mountain. Coming out of the clouds on painted horses were his mother and father, smiling brightly. His father was holding an arrow. His mother, a baseball.

"A-hey! A-hey! A-hey!" they all cried out, as if calling for greater spirit power.

"You know what to do, brother," Jenny said. "You know where to go."

"I'm going home," he whispered.

"No!" Jenny screeched. "You can only return to Pargin Mountain when you are ready to share your heart."

He didn't say a word, his confusion apparent.

"Freedom is given you to choose, brother. There are no chains or iron doors that hold you anymore. Now, go and do what you have been called to do."

He awakened suddenly to the jolt of wheels touching down on the LAX tarmac and turned, half dozing, to find a little girl no older than five staring at him.

"A-hey, a-hey, a-hey." She giggled, and her mother pulled her close, embarrassed by her daughter's exclamation.

"That's what he said, Mommy." She continued to giggle.

"I did?" Sam asked.

The mother gave an understanding nod. "You said it in your sleep several times. Once so loud the flight attendant thought you were calling her."

Now it was Sam's turn to be embarrassed. "I'm sorry. I usually don't talk in my sleep." He looked down at Jenny's journal and saw that the page had been turned. His eyes went wide as he read:

An arrow and a baseball can only be launched by taking them backward.

When life is dragging you back with challenges, it means it's going to fling you into something totally awesome. Don't quit, Sammy. Keep aiming.

Had he read this before the dream? No. Jenny's words had been about baseball. About her love of the game. These words were about the two objects his mother and father had been holding. But why? She'd told him he couldn't go home until he was ready to share his heart. What did all this mean?

*　　*　　*

When the plane stopped at the gate and passengers began to collect their things and file out, Sam winked at the little girl and said, *"A-hey."*

She giggled again and waved goodbye.

He followed them through the passenger-boarding bridge to the international terminal and stood alone, wondering what next to do. He had called Jose from both Afghanistan and Honolulu about picking him up from the Denver Airport, but now he wasn't quite sure. Was there something in his subconscious that had him only purchase a ticket to LAX and nowhere beyond? He sat down in a quiet area across from the big blue screen that listed all the flight departures and called his friend.

"What up, meat!" Jose's joyous voice came through loud and clear. "I'm ready to fire up the old Chevy and come get my bestest friend!"

He sighed. "I don't know if I'm supposed to come home yet, Jose."

"What the heck you talking about? Teresa and I can't wait to see you. We gotta surprise for you." There was a slight pause. "Ah, darn it, you know I'm no good with surprises. We're gonna have a baby."

"What? That's fantastic! How far along is Teresa?"

"Six months. If it's a girl, we're gonna name it after my grandma, Christina, and if it's a boy, we're gonna name it Dickhead, after you."

Sam couldn't help but laugh. "You're such an idiot. Congratulations. I just hope your baby has Teresa's brains and beauty."

"But my personality," Jose wisecracked. "You're only young once, but you can be immature forever."

Sam laughed again. Their conversation was like two old friends who had never been apart as they talked about baseball, old teammates, and hiking the San Juans.

"So what are you gonna do?" Jose finally brought the discussion back to the original subject. "As much as I wanna see you, Sammy, there's something in your voice that says you're not ready to come home yet."

He looked up at the flight monitor that listed every future flight alphabetically.

Anchorage . . . too cold.

"I had a dream on the flight. Jenny was in it."

Baltimore . . . too far east.

"What did she say?"

"She said something about this world being my test. That everything that's happened to me was a lesson."

Detroit . . . no mountains.

"That sounds like her."

"She said I couldn't return to Pargin Mountain until I was ready to share my heart."

Houston . . . too humid.

"What does that mean?"

"I don't know, but I like myself again. I'm over my depression."

London . . . too crowded.

"I'm happy to hear that, bro, because Teresa and I were worried about you for a long time, thought you might do something bad. But in your recent letters, we thought the old Sammy was back, that you were on a good path."

His mouth opened, but he didn't know what to say. What was his path? His grandfather had given him the name *Walks with the Wind* and told him to stay strong and be courageous on his journey. But what was his journey? Was it a destination or goal, or was it some insight Jenny had revealed in his dream? Insight? Instinct? Intuition?

Heck, a young bird didn't know where the wind came from or where it was going when it first took flight. It simply had faith that its wings and the wind would work together so that it could fly. It believed in some internal compass to guide it safely home.

It was then that he looked up at the flight screen and saw Managua, Nicaragua.

Whiplash McCracken is there. The Friends of Everyone Hotel. A new start. He looked uncertainly from the flight time to the clock on the wall. Was he willing to let go? A pitcher didn't know where the ball was going once it left his hand, and a tracker didn't always know where the track would lead him. He simply trusted. Jenny's words from moments before came back to him. *When life is dragging you back with challenges, it means it's going to fling you into something totally awesome. Don't quit, Sammy. Keep aiming.*

He raised up from his chair and almost shouted into the phone, "I know where I'm going, Jose!"

"Let's hear it."

"Nicaragua!"

"Nica-what?"

"Managua, Nicaragua. Gate one forty-one. The flight is leaving in less than an hour, so I'd better get moving."

"Wait a second, Sammy—what the heck are you gonna do in Nicaragua?"

"What I was born to do! I'm gonna play baseball."

THE END

Keep up with Steve Physioc

Get updates on Steve's latest books, events and special deals!

Subscribe to his newsletter at StevePhysioc.com.

Read more of Steve's work

The Walls of Lucca and *Above the Walls*

Don't miss Steve's historical fiction series: two award-winning tales of love, life and forgiveness in Italy during World War I and II.

Available on Amazon.

Follow Steve online

BookBub | GoodReads | Facebook | Twitter | Instagram

Acknowledgments

When I first attempted to write a novel at age 52, I knew I would need plenty of help. Then, to further add to that challenge, I was writing about something that I had no previous understanding of: growing grapes in Italy during WW1. I even had a friend ask me, "Who's going to read an Italian love story written by a baseball announcer?"

Fortunately, I had a mom and wife who encouraged me. They knew I had a passion to write and believed my books – *The Walls of Lucca* and its sequel, *Above the Walls* – were both interesting and inspiring. I was blessed that both books were well-received, but I was very aware that it took a team to write them, and it took the same team to help write *Walks with the Wind*.

For their thoughtful and expert reading, I am indebted to my beta readers, Mark Mendizza (writing sage), Paula Donoho (book lover), Seja Bajich (apostrophe queen), Sister Rosie Kolich (spiritual advisor), and Bob Sommer (writing coach).

For his honesty on my writing and style, helping me condense my content, and more, I turned to my dear friend Joel Goldman, who is a gifted writer himself with over 10 novels to his credit. I advise no young authors to test Joel's sarcasm and wit, for he has no equal. I am so lucky to have a true friend on my team. and I cherish our connection.

For all things military, I sought the advice of former Lt. Colonel Scott Fehnel. Scott spent more than 20 years on active duty in the Army as an engineer officer, serving in Bosnia and Iraq. He was awarded the Legion of Merit and Bronze Star and was decorated for valor in combat. I leaned on

Scott for counsel when writing about overseas operations, weapons, military tactics, and working with private security companies during a military conflict. He is a "get-it-done dude."

Thanks to Royals Hall of Fame pitcher Jeff Montgomery for reviewing my pitching scenes and also for his friendship as a teammate in broadcasting Royals games. Monty is the guy I always go to when evaluating a successful or struggling pitcher. As Monty told me once, "Radar guns don't get people out, quality pitches do."

I would not have been able to move forward with this story without the blessing of the Southern Ute community in Ignacio, Colorado. For that, I give special thanks to Hanley Frost, the former Sun Dance Chief and Southern Ute Cultural Education Coordinator. I wanted to make sure I was both accurate and respectful of the Ute culture with the way I wrote about Ute traditions, ceremonies, family connection, and the spiritual awakening of my protagonist, Sam Cloud-Carson. Hanley was very patient in answering my many questions, and his answers were both informative and inspiring. Here are a few of my favorite quotes from Hanley...

«I want our children to understand our history.»

«Don›t ever forget where you come from. Remember that you are Ute.»

«Our spiritual beliefs and our songs are what kept us going.»

«I want to let our people know that our traditions are a way to find yourself.»

«When you find your inner spirit, you will find peace.»

And perhaps my favorite..."I am very grateful you chose me to read your book." Thank you, Hanley. I am very grateful to have met you.

I am also indebted to five fantastic women who have been my guides on this writing journey.

To Kerri Holtzman, who is my marketing and writing guru. I trust her judgment completely, her decisions on when to release, where to advertise, how to promote, and who to trust. I don't burp unless Kerri tells me to. She's fantastic.

To Beth Kallman Werner, president of Author Connections, for putting together a dynamic custom marketing plan for my first two books and now putting together a publishing team for *Walks with the Wind*. If you're a new writer looking to boost your platform, look no further than Beth. She's both a pro and a friend.

To my sister Cathe, for her beautiful cover art for all of my books. I've always admired my sister's gift and love seeing her art come to life and capture the soul of my story. She is one amazing artist.

Speaking of understanding the soul of my story, there's no one better than Nicole Ayers of AyersEdits. Nicole has been my developmental editor for all three of my books, and I absolutely love working with her. Nicole understands style, character development, and storyline. I follow her custom editorial summary all the way down to the final comma as I make my revisions while constantly asking myself, "WNLTR?" (Would Nicole like this revision?) She's a true pro who not only cares about improving my story but also cares about me and my improvement as a writer. Within five minutes of reading her first summary years ago, I knew Nicole would make my books better.

Finally, I would never have started this writing adventure if it hadn't been for my best friend in the world, my wife, Stace. She was the inspiration for my protagonist, Isabella, in *The Walls of Lucca*. Both Stace and Bella are kind, loving, encouraging spirits who look for the good in everyone. Thank God, Stace found the good in me and has the patience in my daily requests of, "What do you think of this line?" or "Do you have time to read this scene?" or the frequent, "Is this too corny?"

I'm very blessed to have someone to share my life with who encourages me to write about things important to me...important to us. For years I wanted to write a novel that was inspired by *A Course in Miracles*, a spiritual self-study that teaches that the way to love and inner peace is through forgiveness. I wanted characters emblematic of that philosophy, people who despite all odds would be vigilant to choose love over fear, forgiveness over attack and light over darkness. I hope those qualities came out in the writing of this book, for we are all on a journey without distance to a goal that has never changed. As is written on a sign that hangs in the Southern Ute Cultural Center, "If the songs are not sung and the stories not told, our Mother Earth will die." We are all One.

About The Author

Steve Physioc has been telling stories for the past forty years. He has been a play-by-play announcer for football, baseball, and basketball for both college and the pros. Physioc is currently the radio-tv broadcaster for the Kansas City Royals and Fox College Basketball. He won an Emmy in 2013 for his excellent announcing. Steve and wife, Stace, have two children, Ryan and Kevin, and three grandchildren. They make their home in Stilwell, Kansas.

Made in the USA
Columbia, SC
22 September 2021